CHASING
SYLVIA
BEACH

CHASING SYLVIA BEACH

A NOVEL

CYNTHIA MORRIS

Original Impulse, Inc.
DENVER

Published in the United States of America by Original Impulse, Inc., P.O. Box 300044, Denver, CO 80203.
www.originalimpulse.com

"Daybreak," from *New Collected Poems* by Stephen Spender, © copyright 2004, reprinted with kind permission of the estate of Stephen Spender.

Library of Congress Cataloguing-in-Publication Data

Morris, Cynthia.

Chasing Sylvia Beach: a novel/Cynthia Morris.—1st edition

ISBN 978-0-975-9224-2-2

1. Young women—Writers—Paris—Sylvia Beach—Fiction.
2. Exposition Internationale, 1937—Paris—Pre–World War II.
3. Booksellers.
4. Time travel.
5. Paris—Fiction. I Title.

2012902367

Book design by *the*BookDesigners
The cover typography is LHF Stetson, designed by John Studden.
The interior typography is Miller Text, designed by Matthew Carter, Tobias Frere-Jones, and Cyrus Highsmith.

FIRST EDITION

Printed in the United States of America.
10 9 8 7 6 5 4 3 2 1

This novel is dedicated to
Sylvia Beach,
who believed in books and the
people who write them,
as do I.

1

SO MANY THINGS were out of place in the bookstore: the volume of Keats in the fiction section, the study of exotic butterflies tucked away in history instead of natural history, the stack of books slumped against the shelf, fated to lean for life. But the young woman in the back was the oddest. She slouched in a chair wedged between two bookshelves. Her face, pressed against the red velvet upholstery of the chair, had the tranquility of an innocent in deep sleep.

Nothing moved in the tiny shop. Famous authors held their gazes from photograph galleries on the wall. Tiny statues of General Washington and his staff guarded the front door, three men mounted, seven on foot, forever vigilant from the confines of their glass case. The books overran the room, piling up on tables and lining rickety shelves that covered every inch of wall space. Shakespeare oversaw it all, his wooden bust majestically dominating the mantelpiece.

The grandfather clock, carved of mahogany, began to chime the hour: seven o'clock. Underneath the sound, a click-click noise came from the back of the shop. A dog poked his nose around the curtain hanging in the back doorway, nudging it aside. He ambled toward the woman and sniffed her face. She stirred and batted at the breath that moved her light brown hair. The poodle leaned closer, daring a lick. She grinned sleepily and sat up, finally opening her eyes.

Her smile disappeared. She squinted as if trying to understand her surroundings. The bookstore bore the musty odor of all secondhand bookstores—paper, ink, dust, and fingerprints. Not a whiff of the orderliness of a chain bookstore. No computer for researching titles. The dog poked the woman's shoe with his nose and gave a short bark.

"Who are you?" she asked. "I'm Lily."

The black poodle beat his tail against the floor and when Lily stood, he rose with her. She patted his head.

"Where are we, pooch?"

The dog's tongue hung from his mouth and he appeared to be smirking. Lily couldn't match his enthusiasm. The hair on her neck tingled and she felt off, quite off.

"Thanks for nothing," she said, looking around for clues. Her voice was loud in the hushed atmosphere.

Clearly this was an antiquarian bookstore, all the books covered in cloth or old-fashioned dust jackets. The atmosphere mimicked many of the bookstores she loved—overflowing, disorganized, a rich jungle for a book lover to hack into. But there were no bright paperback covers. No self-help books promising a perfect life in five steps. A rack of antique mass-market paperbacks was propped near the door. Lily paused to marvel at their pristine condition. They had to be worth a fortune, she thought. Like new, first paperback editions, dating from when?

She approached the desk, surveying its contents. A standing rack of rubber stamps. A pile of papers. A large notebook, its corners edged in worn brown leather. She ran her fingers over a brass inkwell and pen, then picked up a rounded blotter stained with ink. How quaint, she thought. Some nostalgic bookseller must have set it all up so people could get a taste of the era while buying their old books. Clever.

Picking up a rubber stamp, she turned it over and drew in a sharp breath. There, alongside a line drawing of William Shakespeare, was the name of the bookshop: Shakespeare and Company, Paris.

2

LILY SCANNED THE room again. It was just like the pictures she'd seen of Sylvia Beach's famous bookshop in Paris. But how?

The dog became frisky, lowering his front legs along the floor and giving a few sharp yips. He darted toward Lily, jumping up on her and scratching her bare leg with his claws. She pushed him away and shook her head. Impossible. Someone had replicated the Paris bookstore perfectly and for some reason she was in it. She leaned forward to put the stamp back and caught sight of a paper calendar on the desk. Squinting, she tried to comprehend the date. No way, she thought. It couldn't be. As she stared numbly at the calendar, a woman's voice, deep and authoritative, came from the back of the shop, startling her.

"Teddy! What are you into now?"

The stamp fell from Lily's hand and clattered to the desk. The sound of footsteps descending stairs came from behind the half-closed curtain. Panicking, she turned to look for her purse, and some papers spilled to the floor. No purse anywhere! She caught sight of the capped sleeves of her jacket and realized that she wasn't wearing her own clothes. *What the . . . ?* The dog nosed the papers on the ground, growling playfully now.

"Teddy, what are you doing?" The voice was closer. The dog paused, looking toward the curtain at the back of the shop.

Gathering the mass of papers from the floor, Lily threw them back on the desk and rushed to the entrance. Teddy scampered alongside and gave a short, excited bark. "Shhh," she whispered, fumbling with the handle. She nudged the dog aside and opened the door. The bell at the top of the doorway rang. She stepped outside as the footsteps drew nearer and pulled the door closed behind her.

Lily froze. She turned and peered into the shop, her hand still on the antique brass knob. There stood a woman dressed in a white blouse and dark skirt, with brown wavy hair just above her shoulders. The scene framed itself in Lily's mind with startling clarity. The woman looked exactly like photos she had seen of Sylvia Beach. The dog, his nose pressed against the glass, wagged his tail as if he had adopted her. The knocker on the door, a brass head of Shakespeare. And her hand, her very own hand, holding onto a piece of the world that all too vividly resembled the past. A shiver raised the hairs on Lily's neck. It wasn't possible!

The woman peered through the glass and gestured as if wiping clean the window. "We're closing," she shouted. "We open tomorrow at nine thirty."

Lily swallowed. Could it be Sylvia Beach? She backed off the steps and bumped into a man rushing past. He turned and tipped his hat but didn't stop. A signet ring on his finger caught Lily's eye, the evening light glancing off the gold.

"Watch where you're going," Lily muttered more to herself than to the man. Her eyes followed him down the street passing other pedestrians.

It took a second before Lily realized that it wasn't just the shop that was old—everything was. The man, now at the end of the street in front of an old-fashioned pharmacy sign, the people, all dressed like the woman inside the bookshop . . . it was Paris, but an older Paris: the buildings dusted in dark soot, the street paved with cobblestones instead of asphalt, a young boy in a cap and shorts propelling himself down the street on a scooter, the smell of carbon in the air. She turned slowly and saw the woman who looked like Sylvia Beach turn the sign that said CLOSED. Lily looked up. There, in large letters on the wooden façade of the building, were the words "Shakespeare and Company."

Lily stumbled away and leaned against a giant doorway next to the shop. Pressing her face to the painted wood, she tried to get a grip. Just then, the bookshop door opened, the sound of the bell accompanied by the rattle of windowpanes. Sylvia—yes, it was certainly the Sylvia Beach she had seen in pictures—emerged with the dog. As Sylvia turned to lock the door, Teddy sniffed the air and wagged his tail. Trailing his leash, he jumped off the steps, headed straight toward Lily, and started barking. She shrank against the doorway, gesturing for the dog to be quiet, but he just kept yipping and dropped his forelegs to the sidewalk. Sylvia finished locking up.

"Teddy! Come back here, you dirty, bad boy!" she said, her stern voice tinged with a smile. Teddy stared at Lily, tongue out, before trotting back to his mistress. Sylvia grabbed the leash, tousled Teddy's head, then headed away from the shop.

What in the hell? Bewildered, Lily began to walk. *I've been reading about Sylvia Beach and now here she is. Right here. Right now. This is crazy. It can't be. It's just not possible.* She searched her memory for the last thing she remembered but her mind was too confused to find anything.

She reached the end of the street before she realized she'd been walking, mumbling, trying to understand. Catching sight of herself in a shop window, Lily stopped, stunned.

Her reflection revealed not Lily from 2010 but someone who appeared like a young woman from the 1930s. She wore a skirt that hung mid-calf, with a matching jacket, a neat white blouse buttoned to the top, and Mary Jane shoes. Lily glanced down, sure that she'd seen a mannequin in the window that looked like her. But no, touching the skirt, straightening the lapels of the jacket, feeling her feet snug in the shoes, this wasn't a mirage. She stared at her reflection, seeing only herself: the same wavy brown hair, a little disheveled, wide blue eyes, and an unmistakable look of terror on her face. Lily whirled around, searching for an answer. But the street was nearly empty, and she found no clues in the limestone buildings that loomed over her. A rush of dizziness overcame her. After a few seconds, she snapped to. *I've got to get a grip*, she told herself. *This can't be real.*

Wavering at the Place de l'Odéon, she wondered where to go. The theater dominated the small square, the French flag fluttering at the top. The rush of the urban evening eddied around her. Men in suits and fedoras zoomed past on bikes. Women strolled by, most of them wearing skirts like Lily's with blouses, jackets, and stylish hats that cupped their heads. People clustered at tiny tables at the sidewalk café at the corner. Timeless Paris, gritty and elegant, swirled past, indifferent to her plight. Lost in wonder, she tripped over the curb and nearly fell, as if the city was tilting.

Hands on knees, she smoothed her skirt, trying desperately to focus and think. She stared at her Mary Janes. Whose shoes were these? The black tips appeared scuffed, as if they'd been worn awhile. But by whom? She glanced around furtively. Two women brushed past, ignoring Lily completely. After a minute, the dizziness passed. "Holy mother-of-pearl," she mumbled. "I better keep moving."

She entered the stream of foot traffic and continued around the curved sidewalk. Moving through this Paris, an earlier version of the one she knew, felt surreal, like she was walking in a film set. Everything, not just the buildings, was old. The signs, the cars, and the clothing were all like pictures she had seen from the thirties. Trees guarded the street, their thin trunks encircled with wrought-iron collars. Lily paused to look at the pastries in a shop window. Croissants and giant tarts with spinach, ham, and cheese huddled on racks. Hunger gripped her stomach. Did she have any money? She had no purse, no notebook, nothing to write with . . . nothing. A wave of panic overtook her. She had no money, no phone, no way to buy anything or contact anyone. She forced herself to keep walking.

At rue de Vaugirard, she waited for the light and, in a daze, watched the traffic zoom by. Round black cars careened down the street on thin tires, passing the Luxembourg Palace as if in a race. A taxi came within inches of Lily, the driver sounding his horn. The braying honk startled her out of her stupor, and she jumped back from the curb.

Two men speaking French moved past Lily and into the crosswalk. Lily followed, her breath shallow, like when she returned to Colorado from sea level. Her world in Denver—her job at the bookstore, her father, her apartment, the familiar feeling of wondering when her life would really start—felt impossibly far away. And Shakespeare and Company? She'd been fascinated by the plucky American woman who had moved to Paris and opened a bookshop, and now here Lily was, around the corner from her shop. She had seen Sylvia Beach in person. How had this happened?

A memory surfaced: she was on an airplane headed for Paris. She tried to locate herself in a sequence of events after that but found nothing. Ahead of her, people flowed through the gateway of the garden. The Luxembourg Garden had been a refuge when she'd been a student in Paris. The quiet calm, the flowers and trees, all reminded her of her mother. Lily had passed hours in the garden with friends, strolling in the shade, lounging in the green chairs that dotted the pathways, watching French life unroll slowly in the oasis in the city. Now she joined the other pedestrians and entered the garden. Almost immediately, the familiar quiet soothed her.

Gravel crunching underfoot, she walked past the Luxembourg Palace and the Medici Fountain. The familiar wide paths, the neatly trimmed flowerbeds, and the tall plane trees all seemed so ... normal. Only people's clothing indicated that something was very odd. She found an empty chair near the fountain, dragging it along the gravel to position it closer to the edge. She sunk into it, grateful for the odd comfort and the chance to sit still and sort this out. She was supposed to be in Paris, the year 2010, attending a literary festival at the contemporary iteration of Shakespeare and Company. But now, somehow, she was in the past. Not impossible. Yet the feel of her wool jacket, the whisper of the papers falling to the floor in the bookstore, the sounds of the children playing near the fountain, the dog who acted like her new best friend . . . it was all very real.

Gripping the arms of the chair, she ticked off different possibilities. It had to be a joke. Or a movie, or a dream. Time travel? Ridiculous. The date she'd seen on the calendar in the bookstore was stamped in her mind: May 10, 1937. How could it be? Sweating, her mouth dry, she searched for something to grasp. Without her cell phone, she felt naked. She'd left it in Denver because she wouldn't have reception in France. Back home she'd be dialing someone right away. Now there was no one to call. The bookstore, Sylvia Beach, all the people going about their normal day—it all tripped through her mind like a film on fast-forward. But it wasn't a film. There was no doubt that the world around her was real. Valerie, her boss, would have an explanation for this. She was quick to assess situations and people.

It was eight hours earlier in Denver. Not even noon. The bookstore would be just warming up to the day, employees finishing their coffee, the buckling floors creaking under their steps. Would Lily ever walk the stacks there again? Would she ever see Valerie, her father, or Daniel again? She had a date with Daniel immediately following her return. But when would that be? Thinking of Denver only exacerbated her distress. Her mother would tell her to buck up. She sat up, determined to make sense of this madness.

She smoothed her hands over her skirt, made of light brown wool with pleats at the waist. It fell below her knees. The skirt fit her perfectly. Passing her hands over her waist, she found a rough piece of folded paper poking out of a pocket. It was money—a 100-franc note with the imprint of an altar in the middle: Banque de France. A handful of women and children leaned on an altar and gazed disdainfully out of the frame. She turned it over. On the other side another idyllic scene was depicted with a man in blacksmith garb, his hand on a hammer resting on an anvil, the woman carrying a cornucopia overflowing with vegetables. It was the very picture of French abundance and prosperity. Where had the money come from? Lily glanced around her. She almost expected a camera crew to be hiding behind the potted plants, watching her, recording her perplexity. But no one seemed to notice her until a thin man pulled up a chair next to her and sat down. "Bonjour, mademoiselle."

Lily tucked the money back in her pocket and mumbled bonjour. She wished he would go away. Who knew what would come out of her if she tried to speak French now. And small talk? Forget it.

"Quel beau soir," he said, tipping his fedora. She shook her head, waving a hand next to her ear. Her student year in Paris had given her near fluency in French, but time away had diluted her confidence. And because of her inexplicable situation, she didn't feel safe speaking to anyone. It was better to be invisible until she had a plan.

The man scooted his chair closer to hers and opened his newspaper. It reminded Lily of her French professor at the

Sorbonne warning her of *draguers*. Perhaps he was one of those sleazy men who preyed on young women lost in Paris. If she fixed her gaze on the little red flowers ruffling in the breeze, she could tune him out. The man didn't appear concerned with Lily; instead, he flipped the pages of his newspaper, quickly scanning the articles. Lily saw a headline that mentioned Hitler and an increase in immigration from Eastern Europe into France. Of course. The war was imminent. A few years away. But Hitler's actions were already causing ripples of fear across the continent. She closed her eyes. Think, she urged herself. Who had dressed her and given her the money? How had she traveled through time to arrive in Paris 1937 and not in her own time? Before getting on the plane to come to Paris, she'd been focused on getting ready for this trip that had been her father's idea. Did he know she was in the past?

With that thought, Lily opened her eyes. The questions weren't getting her any closer to understanding how she'd gotten here. It was getting dark—where was she going to spend the night? And what after that?

Without a plan, without a purse, without a clue, she felt terribly exposed. If she were home, she'd have a pen and her notebook and would be able to at least write down the questions to stop them from nagging her. But she had nothing—just 100 francs.

Children squealed nearby and their nannies scolded them. The rhythmic rustle of the pebbles on the path gave her something else to focus on. Soon the everyday sounds of the garden evoked a tiny sense of normalcy, and she rested her head against the back of the chair, closing her eyes once again.

Briefly, the wonder of her situation overrode her confusion. Sylvia Beach. Lily shook her head and grinned. *I've just seen Sylvia Beach.* She had pored over Sylvia's picture countless times, even spent two days at the Princeton University Library engrossed in Sylvia's archives, touching Sylvia's belongings. And now she was alive and at the helm of Shakespeare and Company bookstore and was not a person from the past. But how?

A sharp whistle brought her around. She opened her eyes, groggy. A man in a blue uniform with a small hat pulled over his forehead strolled by. "Fermeture!" he called, tooting his whistle again and nodding at her. People flowed toward the exit. The man with the newspaper was gone. Lily struggled up from the chair, sorry to leave its comfort. Where would she go now?

3

THREE WOMEN SAT in the back of a café in the 5th arrondissement, well away from the glances of passersby. A waiter approached their table, his tray laden with tea, coffee, and a pot of hot milk. They waited quietly while he served them. The youngest, Louise, a fortyish brunette, wore her hair in a wavy bob. She lit a cigarette and inhaled slowly. To her left, Adelaide, her older companion—graying hair, a simple dress with a cardigan—adjusted the reading glasses perched on her nose. The third, a striking black woman, stood out most of all. Erect and dignified, Diana wore a look of weary disdain, as if time were of no importance. She leaned in and focused on Louise.

"What made you think that was a good idea?" she asked.

Louise exhaled smoke. "Weren't we preparing for this? Wasn't she marked as a possibility?"

"She was. Yes. But I'm the one making decisions about new candidates, when and where they arrive. I choose their tests, not you."

Louise sipped her coffee. "I'm sorry. But you have to agree the time was ripe. She was already coming to Paris. Alone.

When would that happen again?"

"You really have some nerve. You've put our work in jeopardy."

"Don't exaggerate, Diana," Louise said.

"I'm not. You well know how little control we have once you arrive."

The older woman intruded, again adjusting her glasses. "She seems fine. Have faith in her lineage."

Diana ignored her and spoke to Louise. "Yes, well, you better hope that she can pull it off. Otherwise—"

"Otherwise what?" Louise stubbed out her cigarette.

"Otherwise we'll be looking to replace you as well."

No one spoke. Café life continued around them, the hiss of the milk steamer, the clatter of dishes and cutlery.

"Diana, I can't believe you're thinking that. How long have I served?"

"You've served long and well," Diana said. "But we can't have our members making important decisions on their own. We have too much to lose. And you know it."

Louise collected her cigarettes and rose to leave.

"Watch her, Louise. We need to let her integrate, see how she does. You can trail her, but don't let her see you. We've got Harold making sure she doesn't get into any trouble. "One more thing." Diana paused. "Her success is in your hands. Since you brought her, she's yours."

"Understood."

Louise left, and the two women sat in silence, the coffee growing cold between them.

4

THE COMFORT SHE'D experienced in the garden dissipated as Lily slipped into the bustle of the city. The sidewalks were crowded with students walking together in small groups. At the Place Edmond Rostand intersection, the café terrace overflowed with people enjoying conversations with friends. Catching sight of the Pantheon at the far end of rue Soufflot, Lily gasped. A memory rose from her student days at the Sorbonne. She had been packing and leaving in a hurry, unsure about whether she'd return. Lily blinked the memory away, along with tears that had gathered. This was her first time back to Paris since then.

She shook her head, trying to understand the collision of her Paris past with this, a familiar but strange Paris. Suddenly she was aware that she was standing dumbstruck in the middle of the sidewalk. A couple passed and the woman tsked. Lily hurried through the crosswalk and continued down the boulevard Saint-Michel.

Small shops lined the boulevard. She passed grocery stores and *tabacs*, shops that served the people who lived in the neighborhood, not tourists visiting from around the world. It was more like a village than a corner of a cosmopolitan city. And she was the beggar who had arrived in the village with nowhere to stay. She felt exposed and conspicuous on the busy boulevard.

Ducking down the first side street, she found herself on rue Monsieur le Prince. A few steps in and a quiet descended, allowing her to assess her situation calmly. First, she needed to find a place to sleep. Then something to eat. She had 100 francs—how much was that in 1937? And who had put it in her pocket? Where had the clothes she was wearing come from? *Stop asking questions,* she chided herself. *Think. What do you know?* The last thing she remembered was being on a plane, on her way to Paris, to attend a literary festival. Then—bam— awakening in Sylvia Beach's bookstore. Nothing made sense.

Finally, a coherent thought arose. Surely being in Sylvia's bookstore wasn't an accident. Lily liked to believe in serendipity, but this couldn't be a coincidence. She had to go back. She had to do what other Americans had done—throw herself on Sylvia's mercy and ask for help. The thought of actually speaking to Sylvia made Lily feel numb with fear. But she had no choice. She would go back to the bookstore and see if Sylvia could help her somehow, help her figure out how she had gotten here, why she was wearing clothes from the thirties, and what to do next.

Moving with purpose now, she soon arrived at the Carrefour de l'Odéon. A flutter of fear shadowed her. What would she say? As she approached the bookstore, a dim light warmed the window and gave her hope. But the shop was closed and nothing moved inside, not even the dog she'd met earlier. *Of course*, Lily thought. *She was closing when I left. I'm not thinking straight. I have to find somewhere to stay tonight.*

On the boulevard Saint-Germain, she crossed the street and entered rue de l'Ancienne Comédie. She paused at Le Procope, where she had dined once with her parents. Supposedly the oldest restaurant in Paris, it had served mediocre food that she hadn't cared for. Her dad loved it, relishing the history that seemed to sparkle from the chandeliers. Her mom was uncomfortable in such a fancy setting, dressed in her sensible khaki pants and black top and requesting ice for her soda.

A small group of people passed Lily, talking and laughing loudly, nudging her from the restaurant's blue façade. A few streets away, she recalled that she had a reservation during the literary festival at the nearby Hotel Saint André des Arts. Perhaps the hotel existed in 1937. Her parents had stayed there when they visited her. Maybe she could get a room there. Certainly the cheap lodging she'd had as a student wasn't available and besides, those tiny rooms required proof of student status and a long application process. She wandered in the narrow and angled streets of the neighborhood before she found the hotel.

With relief, she recognized the street even if it wasn't illuminated with bright and gaudy neon signs. Gone were the throngs of tourists she'd known to crowd this intersection. The corners of the streets were still dotted with cafés and restaurants, but the atmosphere of the neighborhood was somber compared to the bright, busy quartier she'd known. She hurried down the street looking for the hotel. Yes, it was there; in fact it was nearly the same as when her parents had stayed there. Only the door was different—the entrance was now in the middle of the windows and not to the side. Light filtered through the lace curtains. Lily sighed with relief. She was just minutes from a safe haven. She gathered her courage and went inside.

Lily found herself in a small reception area, facing a desk with a high counter. The half-timber walls and the exposed wooden beams darkening the staircase made the reception area feel cozy and inviting. A door to another room behind the desk was ajar, and Lily heard a newspaper rustling from inside. She tapped a bell on the counter. The sound of a chair scraping on the floor came from the room.

The hotel keeper, a woman with graying hair pulled back into a bun, walked out and stood behind the desk. She wore a sleeveless blue housedress that stretched tightly across her breasts. Sizing Lily up, she frowned and grunted, "Oui?"

Lily asked for a room in her most polite French. The woman peered around Lily. "You are alone?" she said.

Lily nodded yes. At this, the woman frowned and asked where her husband was. Lily's blouse dampened with sweat. Mustering her courage, she pressed on in hesitant French.

"I'm not married. I just want a room for the night."

The hotel keeper raised her eyebrow and shook her head. "I'm sorry, mademoiselle. This is a hotel of good reputation. It's not the kind of place to harbor an unaccompanied, unmarried woman." With that, she closed the ledger on the desk and gave a scooting nod, urging Lily to leave.

Lily wavered, wanting to get away from the woman but needing a room more. She had money. Just because she didn't have a husband didn't mean she was immoral. Pulling herself upright, she spoke in what she hoped was correct French.

"What do you take me for? I can pay!"

The woman gave a mean smirk. "I take you for a foreigner! And here, rules are rules whether you have money or not. Now, please, I ask you to leave." She made as if to come out from behind the counter.

Lily gathered her dignity. "You are without heart, madame," she said, and turned to leave.

"And you are rude, mademoiselle," the woman rebutted.

An insult that Lily's French classmates used came to her, and while opening the door, in a low voice, she said, "Vieille truie!"

"What!" the woman cried, her voice quivering with shock. But Lily kept going, propelled by the injustice of it. Before the door closed, the concierge shouted, "Don't let me see you again here!"

"That's right," Lily groused to herself. "You won't ever see me in your hotel again." She stormed away, lost in anger, not noticing that night had fully fallen and that there were few people on the dark street.

It wasn't until she reached the Place Saint André des Arts that she realized there were few women on the street. Lily paused, her anger replaced by a growing hunger. She stuck her finger into her pocket, touching the 100-franc note. Crepe shops and pizzerias didn't yet line rue Saint André des Arts. The shops she'd passed were closed and shuttered for the night.

A few couples strolled by. Men lingered, engrossed in conversation. Lily noticed a man smoking a cigarette near a kiosk with a poster for the upcoming Exposition Internationale. The image on the poster was dreamy, with "Paris" written in neon blue script. Lily studied it for a minute before realizing the man was watching her. He wore his brown fedora low on his forehead, making it hard to see his expression. Suddenly Lily felt like prey, stranded in the middle of the square with no sense of where to go next. She tried to orient herself but without a clear destination, no direction presented itself. Taking a left, she headed toward the Seine.

Reaching the river, she immediately breathed easier. The open space gave her a chance to think. She strolled along the wall, watching the water and weighing her options. She could find somewhere to sleep outside. People did it all the time. Henry Miller had slept outside when he first came to Paris. But as pleasant as the river was, she sensed it wasn't a good place to take shelter for the night. She turned down rue des Grands Augustins, passing a group of well-dressed people leaving Lapérouse. The smell of perfume, cigar smoke, and roasted meats wafted out of the restaurant. Her stomach cramped with hunger. She caught a glimpse of red velvet as the door closed and the group moved down the sidewalk, laughing. Lily wanted nothing more than to be inside, warm and fed.

The street, dark and quiet, didn't yield shelter. Lily passed what seemed like private offices, but no small park or alley presented itself. As she approached a side street, a man emerged. She quickened her pace, hoping she didn't appear as afraid as she was.

"Ey, ma jolie!"

Lily startled, though she pretended to have heard nothing.

She kept walking, looking straight ahead. But rapid footsteps made her turn around. It was the man from the square catching up and coming alongside her. He addressed her in accented French.

"Where are you going like that?"

Lily walked faster. She could see the end of the street shining with light. The man merged toward her, opening his arms wide and forcing her against the wall.

"Ah! Leave me alone or I'll scream," Lily said, stumbling over the French. The man pressed closer, and he gave a creepy leer. Razor stubble covered his chin. "Non!" Lily shouted, trying to push him away. A loud click sounded and then his hand was in front of her face, an open switchblade almost touching her nose.

"I advise you to not shout," he warned. Lily paled and pressed herself against the wall.

"Give me everything you've got, fast," he said. Lily fumbled in her jacket pocket but found nothing. "Allez!" the man shouted, pushing her shoulder.

Lily whimpered and remembered the slit pocket in her skirt. "Wait!" she cried. She pulled out the 100 francs and gave it to him. "That's all I have," she said. He grinned and pocketed the money, keeping his knife out and open.

"Now give me that ring." He nodded toward her hand. Lily hid it against her belly, covering it with her other hand.

"Mais non! It's my grandmother's!"

He poked at her with the knife. "Ah!" Lily cried, twisting away. The man folded the blade away with a click, shoving the knife into his pocket. He grabbed Lily's fist and tried to pull the ring off. When she struggled, he quickly pinned her with his forearm. He pried the ring from her finger, wedging Lily against the wall. He put his hand against her mouth and whispered in her ear.

"You think you're going to get away so easily? Not yet," he said. "We're going to have a nice moment here together." He reached to put the ring in his pocket, and as he did, Lily gathered all her strength and kneed him in the groin. He bent over in pain and Lily pushed him away. He fell, dropping the ring. On the ground, hands over his crotch he croaked, "Salope!"

"Jerk!" Lily cried. She grabbed her ring and dodged away.

At the end of the street, Lily slipped the ring on, muttering "Crap! Crap!" Scanning the neighborhood, she saw only steel-shuttered windows and shadowy doorsteps. A dim streetlamp didn't dispel the darkness. A pair of men emerged noisily from an alley, startling Lily. They headed in her direction and she darted toward the only lit shop front on the street. She had the door open and was inside before she realized that she wasn't likely to receive warmth here, either. It was the hotel where she had been so cruelly refused.

5

LILY SLAMMED THE door behind her and ducked down, hiding herself from the street. A voice called out: "Mais qu'est-ce qui se passe?"

It was a young man peering over the counter. Placing his book down, he emerged from behind the desk. Tall, with dark hair, he crouched next to Lily. She struggled to catch her breath. Glancing out the window, she glimpsed the man who had assaulted her passing by.

"Are you okay, mademoiselle?"

Lily huddled against the door, adrenaline flooding her limbs and making her whole body shake.

"Uh, non . . . oui." She couldn't look at him. She wasn't safe here, either. Any minute that woman would come out and tell her to leave.

"Are you English?"

She stole a peek at him. He smiled down at her, his hazel eyes friendly. It was the first kind look she'd received all day. Her mind fumbled with her French. Nothing sorted itself into clear sentences. The memory of the man, his smelly breath and the grip he'd had on her arm, made her cringe.

"Come sit down," the young man said in English, leading her to a chair near the reception desk. He walked over to the door, opened it, and peered out. Lily shrank away. The hotelier, though young, was a doubtful match for the mugger. He shut the door and said, "Don't be afraid. You're safe here."

Lily leaned into the chair. The hotelier slipped away and returned with a glass of water.

"Did someone hurt you?" he asked.

She sipped the water, unable to reply.

"Do you want me to telephone the police?"

"Non!" Lily almost shouted. The police could be worse. She touched her ring, flooded with relief that she had gotten it back.

"I can take you home if you like. You live close to here?"

Lily snuck a look at him. He nodded gently, so she dared the truth. "Je n'habite pas Paris," she said.

"Vous parlez francais!"

Lily nodded. "Je pourrais avoir une chambre ici?"

He straightened up and replied in English. "I am sorry, but we cannot rent room to single woman. It is the rule."

Lily couldn't believe it. It was as the woman had said— single women weren't worthy boarders. Lily began to cry. The enormity of the danger she'd just escaped and the realization that now she had no money overwhelmed her. She sobbed without control.

"Ah, non, don't cry, miss! I will find a solution." Again, the hotelier knelt next to her. He reached his hand out as if to touch her shoulder but she pulled away. He spoke earnestly.

"Ecoutez. I have an idea. Since I work here throughout the

night, it's possible that you can pass the night in my room. While I am here. What do you say?" He gave her an encouraging smile.

Lily nodded reluctantly, her sobs tapering off. She wasn't sure she wanted to stay in his room but she had no choice. He went behind the desk and returned with a large set of keys. After locking the front door, he gestured for her to follow him.

They went to a glass-paned door at the back of the reception area and entered a dark courtyard. Lily's legs weren't quite stable and a whimper escaped before she put her hand to her mouth. He used a key to open another door that squealed slightly. Putting his finger to his lips, he whispered, "Silencieuse!" He started into an unlit stairwell and Lily followed, touching the cold wall. The wooden stairs creaked as they made their way up. Lily lost count of the floors after three, the circular staircase making her dizzy.

Finally, they arrived at the top floor. They were in a small landing with only two doors. He unlocked one of them, hurried inside, and illuminated a lamp. The room was tiny, with a sloping ceiling. A small desk was heaped with messy piles of books and papers. He gathered a heap of rumpled clothes from the bed. Lily lingered near the door; the room wasn't big enough for both of them to move. She didn't see where he would put the clothes, but eventually, with a shameful look, he stuffed them under the bed. The room smelled dank, like dirty socks and dusty books. There was only one window: a skylight in the curved ceiling.

The young man turned from tidying up and said, "Voilà, you will be safe here."

"Merci."

He pried a key off the ring and put it on the desk near the door.

"Okay, I come back in the morning at eight o'clock?"

Lily nodded, standing near the bed. At the door, he paused.

"I am Paul," he said.

"Lily," she answered quietly.

With that, he left. Lily rushed to the door and turned the key in the lock, once, twice. The lock made a loud clicking noise, and for a moment, there was no sound in the hallway. Then she heard Paul's steps as he hurried back to his station.

Lily turned around once, then twice, surveying the room. It was a mess of books and clothes. She sat on the bed, and the events of the day surged up: the bookstore, the dog, Sylvia Beach, the mean woman at the desk downstairs, the mugging, and now this, the inexplicable kindness of a stranger.

"What the hell, what the hell, what the hell," Lily chanted, until the refrain dislodged something from her throat and she was crying uncontrollably. Falling back on the bed, she gripped the dingy pillow with one hand and sobbed. Her hand on the pillow was so known to her, in such a foreign environment. She touched her ring, studying its ornate gold setting cradling a fiery opal. So nearly lost to that creep! The ring was her talisman—of what she didn't know, but she wanted to believe in talismans and their power to protect. It wasn't but a minute before Lily slipped into sleep.

THE SOUND OF a door slamming in the stairwell made Lily start up from the pillow. Heart pounding, she strained to make out her surroundings. Dim morning light fell through the skylight, barely illuminating the shapes in the room. At the foot of the bed, a brown jacket draped the back of a chair. Heavy footsteps passed by the door and she froze. The person descended the stairs and Lily released her breath. What had happened the day before wasn't a dream. She was in the thirties, and she had no clue how or why or what to do.

She lay there unmoving for several minutes, scanning the ceiling as if hoping a directive would slide down the sloping wall. A few wisps of cloud drifted by the skylight, offering only a thread of normalcy. A plane, far and high, floated across the sky and Lily had a flash of her own flight, of chatting with the bob-haired woman seated next to her, and of trying not to cry. The image passed and Lily lay quietly on the bed, trying to remember if it was an actual memory or just a dream.

Finally, she sat up, still wearing the clothes she'd woken up in the day before. Her mouth was terribly dry and hunger snarled through her belly. She rose and took up the pitcher on the table but it was for washing, not drinking. Pouring some water into the basin, she splashed her face. Hands wet, cheeks dripping, she searched for a towel. Not seeing one, Lily ran her fingers through her hair, drying them on her curls. Catching sight of herself in the mirror, she groaned. Her eyelids were puffy from crying, and wrinkles creased her blouse in the wrong places.

She took up the jacket she'd shed the night before and wrestled herself into it. The wool jacket fit snugly. Lily noticed an interior pocket and tucked her fingers inside. Maybe there was more money. And there was something—a piece of paper. Pulling it out, she found a cream-colored card, slightly bigger than a business card, creased in half. Unfolding it, Lily's scalp and neck tingled. The card was from Shakespeare and Company, the drawing of Shakespeare and the shop's address on the left. In tidy handwriting, it said:

ERNEST HEMINGWAY and STEPHEN SPENDER who
are in Paris for a few days will read—Hemingway
from his unpublished novel, Spender some poems—at the
Shakespeare and Company bookshop on
Wednesday, May 12th, at 9 p.m.
Please let us know as soon as possible if a seat
is to be reserved for you.

Lily turned it over. The back was blank. A rush of emotions coursed through her. Delight—Hemingway and Spender, reading in a few days, and she held an invitation—how cool! Excitement—she could see Hemingway in person! Fear and confusion—how had she come to have this card? And how had she come to be in Paris in 1937?

She dropped the card and fell back on the bed. Something from Sylvia Beach's bookstore—in Sylvia's own handwriting, no doubt—giving her access to this very special reading. She was reaching to pick the card up when two knocks at the door startled her from her thoughts.

"It's me, Paul."

"Ah!" Lily squealed. She tucked the invitation in her pocket. After quickly checking her hair in the mirror, she unlocked the door. Paul held a wooden tray aloft, arranged with a bowl of milky coffee and a lumpy package wrapped in brown paper. Tucked under his arm was a paperback book.

"Did you pass a good night?"

"Uh, hi," Lily said. He came in and nudged aside a stack of books to set down the tray. The smell of coffee pierced through Lily. Paul pulled the chair out and gestured to the food.

"Go ahead. It's all for you."

She approached and took up the bowl. Sipping the coffee, she made a small groan of relief.

Paul smiled. "But you can sit down. I bought you croissants, too."

Lily sat down and opened the package. Two croissants nestled inside, butter darkening the paper. She pulled the end off one of the pastries and ate it. The buttery croissant melted in her mouth. She nearly moaned with the simple pleasure of eating. She devoured it and drank half the bowl of coffee before noticing that Paul had sat down on the bed and was watching her. He smiled, encouraging Lily to take the second croissant.

She ate more slowly, peeking at Paul. Calmed by the food, Lily noticed that he seemed to be in his twenties, too, and was cute in a studious kind of way, with brown hair waved up and back from his forehead. His kind, hazel eyes smiling, he questioned her, his English not quite perfect.

"Where do you come from? You are English?"

"No, American."

"Ah, l'Amérique," Paul said. "Where in America?"

"Denver." Lily replied. She hated these "where are you from?" conversations, and it was even worse now that she had something to hide.

"Denver, I do not know it. Do you have grates-ciel?"

"Gracielles? What's that?"

He raised his arm up above his head. "The big buildings in New York!"

"Oh, skyscrapers!" Lily responded. His enthusiasm for New York architecture made her laugh.

"It's good to see you smile," he said.

She blushed and glanced away, noticing croissant flakes scattered on her shirt. Brushing them away, she adjusted her jacket.

"You have skyscrapers in Denver?"

She liked the way he pronounced the word, drawing out the syllables in an attempted American accent.

"Sure." She shrugged. She didn't know what Denver was like in the thirties. She'd given all of her historical interest to Paris and Europe. Pointing to the book on his lap, she asked, "What are you reading?"

He held up a tattered white paperback. "*Le Coup de Lune.* It is a detective novel that takes place in Afrique." Paul handed it to Lily. She inspected the front and back covers, then opened to the frontispiece. She knew of Simenon—yet another Belgian the French would love to appropriate as their own hero—but she had never read any of his mysteries.

"I read detective novels some nights at work. It helps me to stay awake. But I'm meant to be studying this." He held up *Le Droit Civil*. "For my law studies." Paul brought his hand to his mouth to cover a yawn. "Désolé," he said.

"Oh, you're tired! I should go." She began to rise but Paul gestured for her to stay.

"Non! Yes, it's true, I'm tired. I worked all night and I have to go to class this afternoon." Paul lay back on the pillow. "I just go to close my eyes, who hurt a little. But you can stay here— that does not bother me."

He held his book across his chest and closed his eyes. Lily watched Paul settle in, envying him the simple comfort of fall- ing asleep in his own bed. He had a small mole just above his lip, and his dove-gray shirt, meticulously ironed, had come un- tucked from his pants. His chest rose and fell, moving the book like a small ship moored on his body. Lily was about to speak when she realized that he had already nodded off. His lips fell apart and a small poof of air escaped.

She relaxed for the first time since she'd awakened. The coffee and croissants had soothed her. Surveying the desk, she scanned the titles of Paul's books: *Philosophie du Droit, Code Civil, Thomas Hobbes et le Droit Naturel*. They all sounded awfully boring to Lily. She drifted into a reverie about the books she had on her desk at home: a couple of novels, a vol- ume of essays, a book about how to write. She lay her forearms, then her head, on Paul's desk, and let her eyes close. The gentle rhythm of Paul's breathing lulled her toward sleep. Images skittered across her mind's eye: a book closing, the inside of a tilting airplane, a card fluttering to the carpet.

The last scene jerked her upright. That card! she thought, pulling it from her pocket. Yes, it was clearly an invitation to the reading at the shop. This confirmed her instinct to go back to the bookstore.

But just as she decided to leave, Lily's thinking became confused. *I'm safe here*, she told herself. *If I leave, who knows if I will find shelter again. I don't want a replay of last night. And what if that man is searching for me?* A shudder passed through her body. But at the same time, she couldn't stay there doing nothing. She frowned, wishing Paul were awake to help her sort it out. The card from Shakespeare and Company couldn't have been in her pocket by chance. She must go back and talk to Sylvia Beach.

Lily inspected herself in the mirror. She looked a little better after eating, her blue eyes bright again now that she'd slept. She looked younger somehow, younger than twenty-three. She fixed her hair, pulling the waves over her ears. Adjusting the lapels of her jacket, she took a deep breath and convinced herself she was ready to face the city. She opened the door and slipped out. Before closing it completely, she snuck a peek at Paul. Seeing him dozing so peacefully made her smile. He had saved her. What would have happened without him? She sent him silent thanks and closed the door with a small click. Lily descended the stairs as noiselessly as possible, but they released a whine with every step. She cringed with each note, afraid of being caught.

When Lily reached the ground floor, two women were talking in the small courtyard. She pressed herself against the wall in the dark stairwell, not daring to peek to see if one of them was the woman from the day before. They chatted on and on. Finally, the women left and silence fell in the dim yard. Lily peered out to make sure no one was looking out their window onto the courtyard, then slipped through the porte cochere and onto the street.

The Paris morning swirled around her. Merchants stocked their stalls with fruits and vegetables from crates. Smartly dressed passersby hurried on their usual path to work. Children skipped on and off the sidewalk, swinging their briefcases and getting in the way of housewives carrying their shopping baskets to the market. The coal man made his rounds, delivering enormous bags of coal on his back.

Lily shook her head in amazement. Her life back in Denver existed far away from this morning bustle. She, Lily Heller, was here! In the middle of all this . . . this normal Paris morning. It was crazy. She expected people to gawk at her, but she was the one staring in disbelief at the street life passing by. She gathered her courage and slipped into foot traffic on rue Saint André des Arts. It was odd to enter the city carrying nothing, no purse, no backpack, no passport. The streets felt much friendlier during the day, the shutters tucked up and away, revealing windows displaying here a dried goods shop, there a cobbler with a shoe stretcher and a pair of spats arranged as if ready to dance out of the window. She slowly eased into what was familiar about the city: the narrow streets forming cozy warrens, the spacious boulevards promising access. From her days as a student at the

Sorbonne, she knew this neighborhood.

She made her way toward Shakespeare and Company, feeling the same anxiety that she had before landing her job in Denver. It had taken Lily weeks to work up the nerve to ask if they were hiring. Capitol Books had been like a closed world, one she could only hope to enter. But with pressure from her father to get a job, she had finally approached Valerie. There weren't any positions open, but Lily had persisted, taking refuge in the bookstore every day after dull temp jobs typing in downtown offices. Finally, Valerie had called her for an interview.

But in Paris, Lily wasn't looking for a job. She only knew she needed to be at Sylvia's bookshop—the first place where she opened her eyes to this nightmare. The card, inviting her to a reading. She would find answers there. What story would she use to explain herself? "Hello, I'm Lily Heller. I'm your biggest fan and I've come from the future"? Maybe she could pass herself off as another writer wandering through Europe, searching for the bohemian life. She shook her head, trying to still her impatient thoughts with an imagined scenario.

She would enter the shop, and its bookish chaos would welcome her like an old friend. Sylvia, perched at the desk, would greet her warmly. Lily would linger, savoring the familiar aroma of ink and paper, hoping to find the perfect book. It wouldn't be long before she and Sylvia would be chatting about literature. And then Sylvia would somehow come to her rescue.

Lily shook herself from her daydream. She had to deal with the reality of her situation.

She arrived at rue de l'Odéon. The hubbub from the boulevard slipped away. The street was quiet. She passed two women dressed in hats and jackets that nipped the back of their waists. They stood outside a French bookstore with a book-laden cart parked near the entrance. A deliveryman pulled his wooden cart along the gutter toward Lily, whistling and winking as he approached. She glanced away and nervously approached Shakespeare and Company. But there was a sign in the window announcing an unexpected closure for the day. "See the concierge" was scrawled at the bottom of the sign.

Lily didn't want to see the concierge; she wanted to meet Sylvia. But this gave her a chance to inspect the shop that she'd rushed away from yesterday. She stepped back to take it in. A wooden façade covered the blond stone of the building. The name was prominently painted in gold letters on the lintel above the window. A smaller sign hung in the door's window, announcing:

Shakespeare and Company, Famous Bookshop
and Lending Library.
The Latest in English and American Books and
All the Classics.

The front windows harbored displays for books and magazines. Lily frowned when she saw the hardbacks haphazardly strewn in the case, like a party of books that had collapsed at the end of the evening, exhausted from holding up their propriety. Thin racks held chapbooks and copies of *Transition* magazine. Hardcover books with old-fashioned dust jackets littered the front window display: *Finnegan's Wake* and copies of T.S. Eliot's works, including *Essays Ancient and Modern* and

Collected Poems, 1909–1935. The covers were maroon, blue, and deep green. Lily felt the urge to run her hands over the taut cloth and rescue the books from their heaps. The window displays at Capitol Books would never be in such disarray. Lily took pride in decorating the windows with carefully lettered signs and clever props.

Another handwritten sign caught her attention:

Friends of Shakespeare and Company:
Reading from the works of
Ernest Hemingway and Stephen Spender
By the authors
Wednesday, May 12th, 9:00 p.m.

A rush of excitement overcame Lily. She was invited to this reading. It was easier to imagine herself among the famous literati than to understand how she'd gotten here, with an invitation to this event.

Rereading the flier, Lily remembered a presentation she'd attended for one of her classes at the Sorbonne called "Meeting Hemingway." Each speaker had shared something of the life of the author in Paris: his political commitments before the war, his passions, his work. No one had mentioned how he had gone from wife to wife, an unapologetic womanizer. Lily had wanted to join the rest of the world in admiring this manly hero, but the way he treated women was wrong to her. Still, Lily would love to meet the man himself. She could corner him and call him out on his philandering ways. She'd figure him out, the real man, and then be able to find inspiration from his sparse and powerful prose. And maybe she'd discover that same vitality in her own writing—if she ever put her stories to paper.

Now, by some magic, here she was, facing this poster announcing the real Hemingway, live, in person, in Paris. The possibility of seeing him sparked a desire, a deep need to write her own stories. It was a feeling she hadn't had since her mother died. Tears welled up and she pressed her lips together.

A horn tooting startled Lily and she turned away from the window. A black taxi pulled up behind her, the driver waving with his cigarette. Lily shook her head and stepped away from the shop; the taxi wasn't for her. Sylvia appeared in the doorway, the dog following. She locked up and hurried to the cab. Pausing at the door, she shouted to the poodle, who was standing alertly, staring at Lily.

"Teddy! Come, quick!"

The dog shook himself and ran to Sylvia. They got into the taxi and it bounced down the street. Lily's only hope vanished around the corner. Dejected, she cried out, "What am I going to do? What am I going to do until tomorrow?"

Steps away at the bookstore next door, two women perused books displayed on the cart outside. The first woman glanced at Lily, who hovered nearby, worrying her hands. The woman spoke to her companion while assessing the books.

"You know, my dear, you took a huge risk preventing me from acting last night."

The other woman shrugged. "But I trusted her. I knew she could manage alone." She, too, peeked over at Lily, who appeared to be entranced by the storefront.

"Whatever. Now I'm eager to see more." Adelaide, peering

over her glasses, held a tome open, her finger tapping the title page. "Aha! Look, Louise. Balzac, 1840. Not a first, but still. This will surely please Diana."

Louise leaned over, and after studying the page declared, "Yes! Perfect. Diana will love this."

With that, they entered the bookstore.

7

DOWN THE STREET, Lily paused in front of a pharmacy and thumbed her ring. What to do? What to do? A horse pulling a wooden cart clopped past, the cart creaking under the weight of its load, the driver perched on a heap of coal draped with a burlap bag. All around her, Parisians blithely went about their business. The sounds of traffic grew louder as she approached the boulevard. Cars chugged in every direction, honking impatiently at slower drivers. Stationed in the intersection, a policeman waved his white baton in an attempt to civilize the drivers. Buses regularly released flocks of riders who quickly dispersed to the four corners of the square.

Lily stopped at the Carrefour de l'Odéon and envied the people sitting at a café. How comforting it would be to take a seat, order a coffee, sort things out. But she had no money. The realization struck her fully: she was penniless, homeless, with few options. She needed money to survive. A flush of panic raced through her, heating her arms, her neck, her face. Bracing herself, she spoke to herself sternly. *We're going to figure this out. I can do this.* Paul's face came to mind—her savior, the one person who'd been nice to her. Could she go back so soon? He was probably still asleep. And it wouldn't do to encounter the shrew who'd turned her away yesterday; who knew what would happen if that woman saw her again.

Pedestrians moved impatiently around her, nudging her toward the boulevard Saint-Germain. The city's noise was overbearing. A green and white city bus roared past, barely slowing to make a turn, honking a bike out of its way. A man wearing a cap clung to the railing at the back platform, swaying with the bus on the turn. Lily tried to think. Rubbing her ring calmed her. The oval opal, which flashed green and blue when the sun hit, never failed to catch people's attention. Lily gazed at it and suddenly realized that the ring could save her. It had to be worth something. She could pawn it! It had been her grandmother's, passed on to Lily's mom. Even though her mother had never worn the ring, Lily was attached to it. She didn't want to sell it, but she knew her mother would approve of her resourcefulness. She had no choice.

But where did one go to pawn jewelry in Paris? Maybe a jeweler or a pawnbroker like back home. And what would she say once she got there? Would she have to haggle to get a good price, as people did in America? In any case, she had a purpose: find somewhere to pawn her ring. She scanned the intersection. Where to begin her quest? She caught sight of the café on the other side of the street. *Why not ask those people on the terrace?*

After fighting her way through the snarled traffic, she hesitated on the curb, watching the people sitting on the café terrace. A dapper middle-aged man read the newspaper. A young couple giggled over coffee and croissants, and an old woman with a boa offered bits of brioche to the dog on her lap. The sight of a young blond man writing in a notebook made Lily yearn for her own seat where she could sip coffee and write. But she had to focus. She couldn't entertain literary fantasies now. Her survival was at stake. But none of the people seemed approachable, and she felt her familiar reluctance to bother people. Back in Denver, she'd rather figure it out herself before asking for help. Here, she had no choice. If she did this, she could be sitting at a café like a normal person. She took a deep breath and approached the man reading the paper.

"Excusez-moi," she said. "Connaissez-vous un . . ." She hesitated, realizing that she had no idea how to say pawnbroker in French. The man squinted up at her from his paper. Lily continued, ". . . avoir de l'argent avec ma banque?" Blushing, Lily realized she'd said "to have money with my bank." A bus pulled to a stop at the corner, grinding its gears. The man frowned, apparently unable to hear her.

"Je ne vous comprends pas, mademoiselle, avec ce bruit. Vous demandez quoi?"

Lily tried again, using the words people often used to beg for money on the Paris metro. They sounded polite.

"Excusez-moi. Je ne veux pas vous déranger. Mais, j'ai besoin d'aide. Je veux vendre ma . . ." Her plea for help was rolling along until she forgot the word for ring. A skirmish broke out at the intersection behind her, a courier with a bicycle gesticulating and shouting to the driver in the noisy truck. The man shook his head as if he didn't understand her. He frowned and spoke quickly. Lily didn't catch a word. She searched for help but there was no one except a waiter who lurked near the bar, flicking his rag against the brass railing.

"I just want to sell my ring!" she cried out, realizing as she said it how much she didn't want to sell the ring.

No one on the terrace looked at her now. The dog growled from the old woman's lap, and the waiter hurried out of the café, placing himself between his clientele and Lily.

"Veuillez arrêter d'importuner ma clientèle! On ne veut pas de mendicité ici. Partez!"

Her face flushed with embarrassment. She'd been scolded, taken for a beggar and asked to leave.

"Pardon," she began. But the waiter would hear none of it.

"Partez ou j'appelle la police!"

The police! She stumbled back, bumping into another table, mumbling apologies. Stepping around the corner, she faltered near a doorway, shaking with embarrassment and anger. "Argh!" Lily muttered. She wanted nothing more than to destroy the calm of the French, to shatter the stubborn propriety that held everyone in their proper place.

"Excuse me, miss. Miss?"

A tall man in a suit with a navy blue ascot leaned over Lily, a frown on his handsome face.

"You all right? I heard you asking for help." He spoke English with a British accent. It was the young man from the café, the one with the notebook.

"I'm okay," she shrugged.

"I witnessed your nasty encounter with the waiter. They can be quite intimidating, can't they?"

"I was trying to find out where I could pawn something.

For my aunt," she added. "But I think they took me for a beggar."
She shook her head.

"Well, stupid they are—you look nothing like a beggar!"

Lily blushed, pleased to finally have an ally.

"I need to find a pawn shop. That's all I wanted."

The man smiled at her. "Not to worry. I can help. A friend
recently needed some money for two months' unpaid rent. He
found out none too quickly that the Parisian nightlife isn't
quite free. So he was forced to pawn some cuff links and other
family trinkets, hoping that his father wouldn't find out," he
said, winking.

Lily was heartened by his kindness. She leaned toward him.
"Where is it?"

"Rue des Francs Bourgeois in the Marais. Do you know it?"

"Yes, I think so. I know the Marais." She knew the neighborhood but not rue des Francs Bourgeois. But she would find
her way.

"Crédit Municipal is near the Église Notre-Dame-des-
Blancs-Manteaux. You cannot miss it."

Lily smiled at his heavily accented French. To cover her
amusement, she repeated his directions.

"Rue des Francs Bourgeois."

"It's an honest place. Government operated, you know."
He winked.

Lily didn't know how to respond to the wink. She giggled nervously.

"Thanks, thanks very much," she said. She wished she
had something more intelligent to say but she couldn't muster
a word.

He bowed. "At your service. You are American, aren't you?"

"Of course!"

He smiled. "Well, my dear American, it would be my pleasure to see you again. Paris can be smaller than you think."

8

"EXCUSE ME, OFFICER, can you tell me where I can
find the Crédit Municipal?" Lily spoke in halting French to a
passing policeman. He responded, speaking quickly and gesturing up the street with his baton.

"Only a few steps from here, mademoiselle, continue up
this street, then look for it on your right. You cannot miss it. You
will see a big door with a sign saying Crédit Municipal," he said.

"Merci." Lily was fairly sure she understood what he'd said.

"It's what I'm here for, mademoiselle," he replied. He
adjusted his cap and continued on. Finally, someone had given
her a straight answer. She'd stopped two other people to ask
directions. The first guy had offered to accompany her, but his
smile had seemed more lecherous than kind. The second man
cheerfully told her to go to her aunt. Lily had nodded politely,
wondering if this was some sort of French humor. Was he a
pervert? She had asked him again for the directions to Crédit
Municipal, firmly pronouncing the name in case he had mis-
understood her, and he had reeled off a series of directions, not
mentioning the aunt this time.

Lily finally reached her destination. She hadn't realized how tense she had been until the relief of arrival flooded her body. The route had been harrowing. Twice she had gotten lost in a Paris she no longer recognized. The streets and alleys were busier and more derelict in 1937 than what she knew from her student days. She didn't feel safe, especially when she got lost the first time and had to pass through an alley where three decrepit-looking men lingered in the middle of the street, waving their cigarette stubs as they argued among themselves. They stared at her, and the short one made a comment that Lily didn't catch but that made the others laugh. Safely past them and on a main street once again, her fear quickly turned to anger. Who were they to make jokes about her! The anger made her careless, and after returning to the same corner three times, she had finally surrendered and asked for directions from the policeman.

But now she was okay and soon she'd have money. She stood before the imposing façade of classical architecture. The enormous doorway loomed above her. Carved into the limestone next to it was "Liberté, Egalité, Fraternité." One of the wooden doors was propped open, as if inviting Lily in. She peeked into the porte cochere, where nobles and bourgeois had once entered by horse-drawn carriage and were deposited in the honor court. A not-so-noble couple emerged from the courtyard, the woman dabbing her eyes with a handkerchief. Affixed to the wall near the door, notices in a glassed-in box announced upcoming auction dates in blocky art deco letters. Each auction specialized in a different category: Friday, jewelry was sold, the following Monday, small furniture.

Lily followed an elderly woman who entered as if she knew

her way. They passed through a wide covered hallway lined with limestone columns. The hall gave onto a large courtyard surrounded on all sides by a three-story building. Lily paused, gazing up at the windows, wondering what went on behind the imposing façade. The old woman didn't hesitate, disappearing into a door in the corner with a sign above it announcing PRÊTS SUR GAGES. Lily followed, not sure what the words meant but hoping that she was in the right place.

She found herself in a large room. It was dimly lit, as if the workers were using only half the lighting to conserve energy. A row of windows behind bars, like those of a bank, lined the back of the room. A short fat man entered and passed her to get in line. She moved in line behind him. Lily counted five people in front of her and four people at the counters. No one in the line spoke. Lily imagined that everyone wanted to abandon their precious items as quickly as possible. From all walks of life, they would never rub elbows with each other without this painful problem of money that had them all by the throat. Her own hunger dug into her stomach after her long walk.

To pass the time, she studied the others. In the front was a young man in a cap and ill-fitting clothing, behind him a man in his forties sporting a rather bourgeois hat, followed by a demi-mondaine of uncertain age, a blue boa draping her neck, over-done makeup, and cheap fragrance that reeked of desperation. Behind the demimondaine, the old woman Lily had followed clutched her handbag to her breast and pressed a handkerchief to her nose. Directly in front of Lily, the fat man ducked his head under his hat as if wanting to remain incognito. And Lily was one of these desperate strangers.

The minutes dragged on. The men behind the varnished wood counter worked slowly, indifferent to the impatiently waiting people. Two others, a man and a woman, joined the queue behind Lily. The young man went to Window 3. From his pocket he removed a small canvas bag and presented it to the man working the window. The woman in the boa moved to the next open window, to the great relief of the lady behind her, who removed the handkerchief from her face.

Suddenly a tall man dressed in an impeccable chauffeur's uniform and cap entered and approached one of the tellers, disregarding the customer at the counter. Everybody in line shifted, outraged at this audacity. The fat man muttered recriminations. Others voiced their disapproval.

"Who does he—"

"He thinks he has a blank check, that one."

"In line like everyone else!"

After listening to the quietly stated words of the chauffeur, the teller got up and disappeared behind a door. The chauffeur left, passing the queue without a glance. A few minutes later, a man no taller than Lily entered the waiting room by an interior door. He nervously adjusted his suit, nudging his round glasses up his nose, his gaunt face tight with anxiety. A hush of anticipation overtook the room. Time seemed suspended as everyone alternated glances between the waiting man tugging his goatee and the front door.

Finally the chauffeur reappeared, carrying a black briefcase. This time he paused at the entrance, cap in hand, holding the door open. A haughty, elegant woman swept through. From behind a black veil hanging from her hat, she glanced around the room, her eyes resting on Lily for a moment.

"Who does she think she is?" muttered the demimondaine.

The man with the goatee hurried to the newcomer, bowing.

"Madame la Comtesse, come in, please. You should have called! I would not have received you in this place," he said. "Please, come in." He escorted her into his office.

He pulled open the door, bowing his head and clinging to the door handle. The countess removed an embroidered handkerchief from her pocket and, holding it under her nose, floated past them all and into the room. The driver followed with the black briefcase, and the little man scurried behind, closing the door with a click. A hint of the comtesse's perfume briefly overtook the fetid air.

"Pfft!" exclaimed the demimondaine.

With that, the play was over and the waiting resumed. The sense of urgency, a desire to be done as soon as possible, reestablished itself on the queue. At last, Lily was at the front, practicing her script in her head, trying to find the correct French. She overheard snatches of conversation from the customers at the counter. Interpreting them, she became increasingly nervous.

"I have a certificate from a reputable jeweler in the Place Vendôme for this bracelet," proclaimed the man with the hat, who was at Window 4.

"Can you justify a direct debit?" That from Window 2.

"You must complete the identification form to pawn your watch and receive the money that we propose," from the teller at Window 3.

The old woman tucked a wad of banknotes into her bag,

and, pressing it to her bosom, rushed away, leaving the window open for Lily.

Lily hesitated. Certificate? Proof of residence? Identity card? She had none of that. She had nothing but the card from the bookshop and her ring. How could she justify a direct debit? What address could she give? Certainly not 1640 Emerson Street, Denver. The address of Paul's hotel? She didn't know it. She didn't even know where she would sleep tonight. A small whimper escaped Lily's pressed lips. Behind her, people grew impatient, the queue already full of new faces.

"Are you going or not?" The man behind her voiced his annoyance.

Lily approached the window, twisting her ring. A fiftyish man sat behind the counter, his hair plastered to one side with hair cream. He peered at Lily from behind his bifocals. He wore black sleeve protectors over his white shirt, like a bank teller.

"Bonjour," he said, as if it was a question.

"Bonjour. Je voudrais vous donner ma ..." She lost the word for ring again, and pulling it off her finger, held it up to show him.

"Your bague. Bon, put it here." He handed her a silver tray.

She placed the ring on the tray, the sound of metal ringing in her ears above the murmurs of conversation around her. She felt dizzy and swooned against the counter. The teller raised an eyebrow but Lily just nodded as if nothing were amiss. The teller pulled the tray through the grille. He jotted something on a piece of paper and tucked it under the ring.

"An expert will determine its value. Afterward I will make you an offer," he said, raising his head. Lily nodded, trying not to look worried. He carried the tray to a long table in the back where men inspected the treasures brought before them. A man examined the ring with a jeweler's loupe. He then weighed it on a small scale, and tapped the opal with a small metal hammer. He took his time inspecting the ornate gold band from every angle. These few minutes felt like forever to Lily, who had begun to sweat, seeing her ring in this man's hands. Finally, he wrote on the paper and gave it to the teller. The teller resumed his position. He nodded at Lily and placed the tray with the ring and slip of paper on the counter.

"I can offer you 2,550 francs, mademoiselle," he announced. "With the proper paperwork and your identity card."

Lily wasn't sure she heard him correctly, and the sum he mentioned rendered her speechless. She didn't know the value of 2,550 francs in 1937, but it seemed like a lot.

"Alors? Are you satisfied?" The man prodded a response from Lily.

"Oui," Lily whispered. He pulled a sheaf of forms out and dipped his pen in his ink bottle.

"Bon, I need your name and place of residence."

"Uh …" Lily wasn't able to get anything but that out.

"Oui, votre nom?"

"Lily. Lily Heller," she stammered.

"Lili Elaire?"

Lily could feel his patience dwindling. "No, Heller . . . H—E—L—L—E—R." She slowly spelled it out, pausing to make sure she was using the correct French letters. He wrote painstakingly while she watched.

"Adresse?"

"Uh, je n'ai pas," she said, her French disintegrating as her nerves grew.

"You are in a hotel perhaps?" he suggested, poking his glasses up his nose. A tone of suspicion had crept into his voice. Lily didn't know what to say. He pressed her.

"Well? At a hotel? At someone's home? You are a foreigner, you certainly have a passport."

Lily looked at him, her light blue eyes betraying her panic. She glanced at her ring, then back at the man, a foggy confusion overcoming her.

"Mademoiselle?" The man spoke gently. A long minute passed. "Mademoiselle?" pressed the employee.

No answer came to her. Her thoughts gunned through her head, increasing her anxiety. *I just want to pledge my ring— why this inquisition? Why these questions I have no answer for? What should I say?*

Other staff behind the counter took notice of the awkward silence. Someone in the line behind her emitted a loud "Bah, alors!" Heat flooded Lily's face. A glance confirmed that all eyes were on her. Employees, customers at the counter, customers in the queue watched her drama reveal itself. They whispered among themselves. She thought she caught the words "thief" and "police." She couldn't be interrogated. She had no answers. She just wanted to pawn her ring, that's all. And that *Mademoiselle? Mademoiselle?* kept repeating in her head. She felt stifled, trapped, her ring already out of her hands on the other side of the counter and no proof that it was hers. She had to leave. She had to get out of there. She couldn't deal with the police. In total panic, Lily stared at the cashier and he, too, was speechless, dropping the *Mademoiselle?*

A woman's voice, not one in the line behind her, said, "You'll be fine," and Lily snapped out of her stupor.

She darted her hand under the grille and snatched her ring from the tray. Turning, she ran past the stunned onlookers and fled into the courtyard, stopping only in the porte cochere to slip it back on her finger. She ran and ran, not knowing where she was going, pushing past pedestrians on the sidewalk. She finally stopped on a deserted side street and tucked against the wall.

Hidden in a doorway, hands on her face, Lily cried bitterly. She didn't know what to do, or where to go. She felt terribly alone in the world.

"Why? Why?" she cried. Her throat tightened and she tried to fight the tears back. Why, when just before leaving Denver, things were starting to get better. Her job, a potential columnist position, Daniel. The thought of him made her cry even harder.

9

SHE HAD MET Daniel on a sunny day right before her trip to France. Spring was working its usual magic, making everything buzz with vitality. Couples strolled up and down Colfax Avenue, not noticing Lily running back to work from the Japanese noodle restaurant, clutching her book instead of a lover. She arrived at Capitol Books, crowded with customers on their lunch break. Valerie called her over to look at some books a customer had brought in to sell. Lily popped a mint in her mouth and headed to the back room, relishing the thought of going through a stash of books. A CD was playing Van Morrison, and Lily hummed along.

A young man in a red baseball jacket waited, surrounded by several cardboard boxes. Lily skirted the mess and stepped behind the desk, where she assumed an air of authority. Beginning with the box closest to her, she began assessing the books. She glanced at the seller, who wore his blond hair closely cropped. He leafed through a copy of *The Urantia Book* with a look of disdain. Surely the baseball jacket was an ironic choice. He didn't appear to be the sporty type, and shuffling through his books confirmed it.

It took only a glance to see that this was a great buy. Great buys included lots of interesting books in excellent shape that didn't need to be checked against the stock list. His books included a range of religious texts, spanning Confucianism to Judaism and some of the more liberal Catholic scholars, like Emmett Fox and Teilhard de Chardin. Lily made a stack of the certain buys and the few she would need to research, sneaking peeks at him. There was always a story behind someone selling his books. She couldn't resist asking if he was going atheist.

He laughed at the question and a conversation struck up between them. They were engrossed in book talk when Valerie hurried in, coming behind the desk to retrieve a roll of cash register tape.

"Good buy?" She winked at Lily, who blushed. After giving the guy an approving look, Valerie returned to the front counter. Lily could have been mistaken, but she thought that he blushed now, too. She worked through his last boxes, mostly fiction, classics in trade paperback editions. She flipped through the pages—no underlining, no notes in the margins. Perfect. The rejects didn't even fill one box. He would be getting a lot of books in trade or a decent amount of cash.

"Why are you selling your books? Are you moving?"

He folded his arms across his chest and appraised her.

"Are you always this nosy? They're my books, if you're thinking I stole them."

Lily's blush crept down her neck. She apologized for prying and focused on the books.

"I'm just clearing my shelves to make room. I'm not moving."

She glanced up. He was smiling at her. Nearby a few shoppers lurked, perusing the shelves but really eavesdropping. In a shop this small, every conversation was public, and the introverted customers often eavesdropped. Lily knew this because she eavesdropped all the time herself. She pretended it was just the two of them and continued chatting while flipping through the books.

As she was finishing, a woman wearing a bike helmet came in to sell a handful of books from her backpack. The guy gathered up his empty boxes. No one did that. They just took their trade slips and left. And most people requested money, using their beloved books as a cash cow. Lily respected him for going for the book credit. It was twice as much as cash, after all, and who wouldn't want more books?

Lily finished the transaction reluctantly, stamping his trade slip with "Capitol Books" and handing it to him along with the box of rejects.

"Can I donate them? And . . . how about a drink sometime?"

Behind him, the cyclist made a small thumbs-up gesture. Lily couldn't believe her face could get hotter, but it did. "Sure," she said, trying to ignore the woman.

"'Sure' I can donate the books or 'sure' you'll have a drink with me?"

"Both." She didn't think she could blush any more, but the flush spread from her neck down her chest. They made plans and he left, leaving Lily completely unable to focus on the next seller's books.

They met after work at the seedy bar next door. Politicians hunched around tables while scruffy street people cashed in their change at the bar. A few tumbleweeds wearing plaid shirts and work boots played pool in the back. Lily saw these kind of men on Colfax all the time—just passing through the plains, stopping in Denver to hook up with other drifters before heading on. The jukebox near the empty cigarette machine blared classic rock, the kind that didn't offend any of the patrons. She would feel uncomfortable in the bar filled mostly with men if it weren't for Daniel next to her. After he'd brought beers to their table, he told her that he worked in a bar downtown. "It's nothing like this," he laughed, looking over at the two men in plaid arguing loudly over the pool table. "It's upscale." He used his fingers to mark the undertone quotes around the word. It wasn't long before they were discussing books.

"What are you reading now?" Daniel leaned toward her over the table.

Lily pulled a paperback copy of *The Autobiography of Alice B. Toklas* from her purse. Daniel scanned the back cover.

"I've never gotten into that whole Parisian expatriate myth."

Lily grew indignant. "What do you mean, 'myth'? These were real people, living real life, making real art. Writers!" She snatched the book back from him. He pushed his hand through his hair.

"I can tell you're into it." He smiled and Lily's anger melted away.

"I am. I've read a lot about that time period. I love France. I did, anyway."

"What changed that?"

Lily put the book back into her bag. Right about now she wanted a cigarette, but she'd quit and had vowed never to smoke again. Besides, smoking was forbidden in bars now. That made it easier. She sipped her beer.

"Hmm . . . I still love it. But maybe you're right. Maybe it is the myth of it. Did you know that Gertrude and Alice worked during World War I, making friends with American GIs and supplying them with food and goodies?"

She went on to recount the stories of the women's lives with the artists. Daniel seemed to take as much pleasure in hearing about the stories as she did from reading them. He encouraged more than just the surface, and Lily kept talking. Usually she was the listener, absorbing the rants and complaints of her bookish customers. As he went to the bar to get another round, she had a moment of doubt: was he really interested in what she was saying or was he just trying to please her? But when he came back with their beers, the way he looked into her eyes made her believe his sincerity.

They talked and drank for a few hours, exchanging favorite book titles and making lists of each other's recommendations. Lily was more buzzed than she had been in a long time. She'd never met someone like this at the bookstore, and it felt good to talk with someone her age about books she liked. At the end of the night, Daniel walked Lily to her bike parked in front of the bookstore. Cars whizzed by on Grant Street while she fumbled with the lock. She extracted the coil from the frame and stood, the bike in between them. Daniel watched her, his hands in his pockets.

"I had a good time tonight," he said.

"I did, too. Thanks for the beers." She held her helmet in one hand while shrugging on her backpack. A man crossing

Colfax stopped in the crosswalk, shouting and gesturing at a car that had ignored the pedestrian signal, cutting him off in the middle of the street.

"It's not too cool around here at night," Lily said.

"Yeah, you better get home before the real weirdos come out." They laughed. Lily's palms began to sweat. He took her number and they made plans to go out again.

"Okay, then," she said, moving to strap her helmet on. Daniel stepped closer, putting his hand on her arm. He leaned in and kissed her. She kissed him back and for a moment she forgot they were on the street. He tasted like beer and she liked that.

A man stepped out of the Newhouse Hotel next to the bookstore, pausing on the sidewalk to light a cigarette. He blew out his smoke and whistled. "Get a room!" he shouted. "Right here at the Newhouse!" He chortled. Lily and Daniel drew apart.

"Yeah. Right. Okay . . ." Lily stammered.

"Right, mm-hmm," said Daniel, and bent toward Lily for one more kiss. They kissed for another minute, then Lily drew away.

"We're going to attract a crowd this way. A very seedy crowd," she added. She pulled her helmet on and Daniel stepped back and watched her get on her bike.

"Ride safe," he said. She rang her bell and pedaled away, her legs wobbly. She zoomed home along the bike path on 16th Street, buoyed by Daniel and the potential for another date with him.

The next morning she relished the details of the date in her notebook with a cup of coffee from her French press and her cat, Mr. Petey, curling around her legs. Lily was playing out different

Daniel scenarios: he'd come into the bookstore that afternoon and they'd make another date; he'd make her wait several days and she'd have to call him, showing him that she was assertive; or their date was a fluke and she'd never see him again.

The phone rang, saving her from her fantasies. It was her father calling from his home in Chicago. After the usual Chicago/Denver weather report, he announced that he had a surprise. A wave of fear shook Lily out of her romantic stupor. He was probably going to tell her that he and his girlfriend, Monique, were getting married. Lily knew it was inevitable, but it was still too soon for her. Her father went on to give her the good news: he was gifting her with a trip to Paris. Lily was shocked. He explained.

"There's a literary festival next month at that bookstore Shakespeare and Company. Monique found out about it. I thought you'd like to go. You can get ideas for your writing. Get inspired. Have some fun." Suspicion replaced fear as Lily listened. Her father wasn't given to grand gestures and had never appeared interested in her passion for France. Maybe Monique was having a good influence after all. Maybe there was hope for a real relationship with her father.

"Wow, Dad, that's a pretty big present. Are you sure there isn't some guilt motive? You aren't about to drop some big news on me, are you?"

"No, of course not. I'm just worried about you. You're too young to be moping around a bookstore, spending all of your time reading. You've got to get out, live a little."

She thought of Daniel. She was getting out, finally. She was living a little.

"Like you?"

He ignored her snippy tone. He told her the details, offering to buy her plane ticket and reserve her a hotel room if she could pay the rest. "I'll get you there, then you'll be on your own to make friends at the festival," he said.

The thought of the festival both excited and scared Lily. She could attend lectures about literature and view films about authors. She'd sit in cafés with other writers, talking about books, crafting her own stories. It would be the push she needed to start writing. But too much was happening at once, and the thought of returning to Paris was daunting. That evening, drinking a glass of wine on Valerie's patio in northwest Denver, Lily told her friend about her date and then sprung the news about Paris.

"What are we supposed to do while you're frolicking around Paris with the literati?"

"I'll only be gone for nine days," Lily said. It had turned chilly, forcing Lily to pull her sweater on. "Let's go inside."

Valerie ignored her. "What about the columnist job you applied for?"

Lily slapped her forehead. "Ahh! I forgot about that. Do you think Susan will let me have the job even if I take time off to go to France?"

Valerie shrugged. "I don't know. Ask her. It's a great opportunity. I wouldn't blow it. It's your big chance to break into print."

"You're right. I'll ask her about it when I send in my sample columns. The one about you is great. You'll love it."

"I'd love to drop everything and run off to Paris," Valerie

said. She pulled a box of cigarettes out of her bag. "Don't kill me. I only do it when drinking." She lit up and pocketed the lighter.

"Thanks a lot. That helps, smoking in front of me." Lily helped herself to more wine and stood up with her glass. She stepped off the paved patio and away from the cigarette smoke. "Well, why don't you?" she asked.

"Why don't I what?"

"Drop everything and run off to Paris."

"Excuse me? Did you notice I'm running a bookstore here?"

Lily pulled her gaze away from the stars and looked at Valerie.

"Hello! I know you are running a bookstore. That doesn't mean you can't take a vacation every once in a while."

"I'd love to. I'd love to have the money to go somewhere. I'd love to be able to leave the store for a week. But I can't. Enjoy it while you're free, Lily." She stubbed her cigarette out. Lily sat back down.

"Why do people always complain about their circumstances, like they have no control over them? Everyone has the ability to change their lives." Even as Lily said it, she knew she was wrong. She'd seen enough people limping along Colfax Avenue to doubt that everyone was capable of positive change.

Val cleared her throat and spoke quietly. "Lily, I'm sorry to break it to you, but you're one of the complainers. I love having you at the bookstore and I know you want more. What about your writing? Susan gave you that chance to apply for that column on the paper. Don't blow it," she repeated.

Lily sipped her wine to wash away Val's feedback. She was a complainer? She thought she kept her bad attitude under cover. And what about Susan's offer? Maybe she could write. But now she was going to Paris, and the time before her departure flew by.

Lily accepted Valerie's offer of a ride to DIA, and at the last minute Daniel asked to come with them. When Valerie pulled up in her blue VW Beetle, Lily wasn't ready to leave him. In the car, Daniel sat in the back and reached forward to touch Lily's hand in the passenger seat. Valerie had looked over at her and smirked.

"Watch out for those charming French men," she warned. "And be careful with those almond croissants!" As Valerie recounted a story of eating too many pastries after a particularly rowdy night with friends, Lily watched the flat plains unroll. It was hard to imagine that she'd be in Paris soon, and she doubted she'd be up all night partying with friends.

They arrived late, prompting quick curbside good-byes. Lily promised Daniel she'd email him.

"What about me?" Valerie teased. Lily gave her a last hug, blew a kiss to Daniel, and pulled her suitcase into the airport. On her flight to New York, she wrote in her notebook everything she would do and see in Paris:

1) Eat an almond croissant for Valerie.
2) Visit Shakespeare and Company
   (original one, rue de l'Odéon).
3) Check out the Pompidou Center.
4) Go to the Père Lachaise cemetery.
5) Buy something for Daniel at a quayside *bouquiniste*.
6) Buy French notebooks.

7) Picnic by the Seine. . .

Flying east away from the sunset, Lily realized that lots of activities might keep her busy enough to forget her last time in Paris, when her college education had come crashing to a halt. The colors in the sky intensified, pink deepening to orange, then maroon. Lily shook her head, and tucking her pen in her notebook, picked up her book to read.

In the departure lounge at New York, awaiting the next flight, she telephoned her father and assured him everything was okay. Monique came on the line, wishing her a pleasant trip to Paris. Pleasant? Lily thought. Who said "pleasant" anymore? It irritated her, hearing Monique's voice when she simply wanted to talk to her father. She barely had a chance to say good-bye to him before the call came to board her flight to Paris.

Lily situated herself in her seat by the window, tucking her book in the seat pocket. As the seats filled with new passengers, she caught snatches of French phrases, and she experienced a little thrill—soon, she'd hear French all the time. She was ready to go, and best yet, no one had taken the seat next to her. She might be able to lie down and sleep a little.

Her wish dissolved when a sophisticated woman who appeared to be in her forties came down the aisle, squinting at the numbers above the seats. Her dark hair was carefully coiffed in a thirties style and her lipstick was bright red. She stopped at Lily's row and smiled. "Here I am."

Lily removed her notebook from the seat. So much for extra room, she thought. "Sorry," Lily said, putting the notebook on her lap.

"Not a problem," replied the woman, taking her seat. She held her leather satchel in her lap until the flight attendant told her to stow it.

When they reached cruising altitude, Lily unbuckled her seat belt and picked up her notebook. Because she'd stayed up late with Daniel the night before, she hadn't slept much. Now she was paying the price. She wasn't able to focus enough to write anything, so she put her journal away. Through the window, she watched the clouds scroll before her eyes, thinking, *Only six hours before I arrive in Paris*. She pulled the window cover over the window and shifted to lean against it. Sleep would be good, she thought.

Opening her eyes, Lily awoke confused. It took a second to remember that she was on the plane to Paris. She had no idea how long she'd napped. The woman next to her was reading a book, peering intently through a pair of glasses attached to a chain of ruby glass beads. Her hair was as neatly arranged as it had been when Lily first met her. In comparison, Lily felt unkempt. She tried to read her own book but couldn't focus. She began obsessing over Daniel, missing him, and spinning fantasies of their future life together. When she tired of that, she peeked over the woman's shoulder to see what she was reading. Poetry, laid out in neat short lines, marched down the page. Lily sniffed. She didn't have the patience for poetry. Stories led her somewhere, and poems usually tricked her into looking at her own life. She wanted to get into other people's lives. Lily was staring at the page, thinking about Sylvia Beach, when the woman spoke.

"It would be easier if I read it to you."

Lily shrugged out of her daze. "I'm sorry. How rude of me. I wasn't reading over your shoulder. I was just—"

"That's okay." The woman closed her book, carefully inserting a bookmark between the pages. Lily wished she hadn't disturbed her. "I'm Louise. And you are?"

"Lily Heller. Do you go to Paris often?"

"I do. It gets a little tiring after awhile." She sighed and brushed the front of her wool jacket. "How about you? Been to Paris much?"

"I lived there as a student for almost a year," Lily said. "Are you traveling for work?"

Louise said that she was, but didn't reveal anything else. Instead, she got Lily talking. Lily told her about the festival at Shakespeare and Company. She told her about her job at Capitol Books and the kinship she felt with Sylvia Beach. Louise knew of the bookseller, which excited Lily. During their in-flight meal, Lily asked about Louise's work.

"Oh, it's boring. I can't explain the details. No one understands and it's a big waste of time."

Lily tried not to feel offended that Louise thought she was too dumb to understand her job. Louise was about her mother's age, but Lily couldn't imagine her mother and Louise talking. Louise was too proper, too cosmopolitan. Lily pressed a sliver of butter into the hard roll, scattering crumbs everywhere. Then she confessed to Louise what she told customers at the bookstore.

"I want to be a writer someday."

"Do you?" Louise glanced at her sideways. "I see you doing something rather more exciting than that."

"What could be more exciting than being a writer? Making things up, telling stories. I love it. I read a lot."

"Mm-hmm. More exciting? Read less, live more. That's the key, dear Lily," Louise answered, tidying the debris from her meal. Lily's tray was littered with crumbs and the crumpled plastic bag that had held the utensils and salad dressing. The flight attendant came through, taking the trays and removing the garbage. Lily was jealous of the simplicity of the woman's work. She knew what she did and just did it. The bookstore was great for now, but what would Lily do in the future? Louise was right. She should be doing something more exciting.

"And what do your parents think about this trip?"

"Well, my father thinks it is a good idea because it was his. He bought me the plane ticket."

"And your mother?"

Lily's throat constricted. She tried to speak but her voice came out in a croak. Outside the window, the night sky seemed both far away and incredibly close.

"She's dead. The last time I was in Paris, she passed away and I had to come home early." The last word clutched in her throat and she had to focus very hard on the hem of her dress to not cry. After a minute, she spoke again.

"It's been over a year but it still gets me sometimes. And now, going back to Paris, to the scene of the . . . of the finding out, I'm scared."

Louise nodded. "That's understandable."

Lily blew her nose. Louise was friendly enough but aloof. She hadn't done any of the normal consoling gestures: the patting on the shoulder, the desperate lunge for the tissue to stop the flow of emotion, the platitudes about grief and loss that Lily had been forced to endure whenever she told anyone about her mother. The flight attendant passed by with coffee and water. Louise pulled out her bag and removed a small pouch.

"How about a nice tea? I've got one to help you relax," Louise offered. Lily nodded. Louise ordered two cups of hot water, and removed two tiny cloth bags. She prepared the tea and passed a cup to Lily, who sipped the fruity, sweet brew.

"You're tired, dear. Why don't you try to sleep a little before we arrive in Paris, hmm? How about if I share a poem with you?"

"I'm not a big fan of poetry," Lily confessed. "I prefer novels."

"Yes, poetry isn't so fashionable these days. Let's try anyway." She turned to the table of contents of her book, a small leather-bound tome. "Okay, here's just the thing. It's Stephen Spender."

Lily wriggled in her seat to get comfortable, draping her lap with the blanket and tilting back her seat. Louise began reading, her voice rising above the drone of the plane's engines.

At Dawn she lay with her profile at that angle
Which, when she sleeps, seems the carved face of an angel.

Lily turned toward the window, observing the clouds.

Her hair a harp, the hand of a breeze follows
And plays against the white cloud of the pillows.

Just like the poem, she thought, softening.

Then, in a flush of rose, she woke, and her eyes that opened
Swam in blue through her rose flesh that dawned.

On the white screen of the clouds, she imagined Daniel's face, smiling at her.

From her dew of lips, the drop of one word
Fell like the first of fountains: murmured

She blushed, remembering their last kiss.

'Darling', upon my ears the song of the first bird.
'My dream becomes my dream,' she said, 'come true.

A red light blinked on the wing of the plane, lighting the night and the clouds with a warm glow.

I waken from you to my dream of you.'
Oh, my own wakened dream then dared assume

Louise's voice and the thrumming engines lulled her, and she relaxed, her book slipping to the side.

The audacity of her sleep. Our dreams
Poured into each other's arms, like streams.

Her eyelids grew heavy, and leaning against the window, she drifted to sleep. And that was the last thing she remembered before waking up at Sylvia Beach's shop.

10

SOMEONE WAS TUGGING on Lily's skirt. She looked down to see a little girl. The child spoke French in a squeaky voice.

"Mademoiselle! Mademoiselle, why are you crying?"

Lily did not know how to respond. She wiped her tears, assessing the girl. She had long brown hair pinned with a metal barrette, and wore a blue short-sleeved jacket with tiny white buttons and a short checkered skirt. Her tiny legs ended in black polished shoes and white socks. Lily tried to smile.

"It's nothing. I'm just have a little trouble," she confessed.

"Did someone hurt you?" Now the girl appeared worried.

"No, don't worry, cherie," Lily said. She couldn't resist the girl's adorable voice, small and sweet, speaking French.

"You're lost, then?" the girl asked.

"No, not quite."

"I am! I'm lost," the girl cried, her eyes filling with tears.

Lily crouched to face the girl. "Where's your mother?"

"Je ne sais pas. I was with my maman and brother on the bus. Maman told me to sit in the back, next to an old lady. I watched the cars go by. Then I turned around and maman wasn't there. She had forgotten me!" Now it was the girl's turn to throw her hands to her face and burst into tears. Between sobs, she tried to continue her story.

"I . . . I got off the bus. I searched everywhere. No maman! I tried to find them and now—" She couldn't continue, breaking into louder sobs.

Lily didn't know what to do. She reached out and grasped the girl by the shoulders and looked into her eyes. Gently but firmly, she asked the girl to look at her. The little girl responded, her big brown eyes glistening with tears.

"What's your name?" Lily smiled to encourage her.

"Emilie," she replied, sniffling.

"Listen to me, Emilie. My name is Lily and I promise you one thing. I'll help you find your mommy right now. Please stop crying." When the girl's sobs abated, Lily pressed for more information. "Which direction did you come from?"

Emilie pointed to the end of the street. "That way!"

Lily held out her hand toward the girl. "Let's go find your maman!"

The girl sniffed, wiped her face with her forearm, and took Lily's hand, pressing it hard. Lily had no idea how to go about finding the girl's mother, but she had made a promise, and she would keep it.

Lily tried to get Emilie to retrace her steps. They came to the stop where the child had gotten off the bus. They waited for a bit, Lily prompting the girl to look around to see if she recognized her mother among the passersby. But Emilie did not recognize anyone and grew more upset from trying. Finally Lily decided to retrace the bus route, stop by stop. She optimistically felt sure that they were bound to come upon the girl's mother. Holding Emilie's tiny, damp hand, they walked a long time. After nearly an hour, still nothing and the child was growing tired. At a pedestrian crossing, waiting to cross, Emilie began to complain.

"I'm hungry!"

Lily looked at her, frowning. It was almost noon. She became aware of her own hunger pains.

"I know, but we'll find your mom soon."

She couldn't say anything more, afraid that any more promises would risk not coming true. They continued across the road. But Lily was worried. She would like to be able to buy something for the girl to eat. But she had no money. What could she do? It crushed her that Emilie viewed her as her savior, as exhausted, hungry, and as lost as she herself had been just the day before. She had to do something, but she didn't know what, so she kept walking, now nearly pulling Emilie behind her.

Around them, people went along their way, heading home to eat lunch in comfort. Several times, they passed open windows, the smell of a simmering meal wafting out. The feeling of hunger tortured her, and she thought she heard Emilie's stomach growl in between sniffles. Lily stopped on a small street empty of people. She squatted down and spoke to the girl.

"Listen, Emilie, you stay here and wait for me a few minutes." She gently guided the girl to an unoccupied stoop. "I'll be right back, but don't move. Understood?" The girl nodded, tucking her skirt under her and crouching on the stoop.

Lily rose and glanced around. She spied a housewife's straw

basket, overturned and drying on the stoop in an alley. No one was around. It was noon, the only noise the sound of cutlery engaged in the noon meal, accompanied by a song warbling from a window. A mangy brown cat crossed the street, jumped to a windowsill, and disappeared in the opening. Lily acted quickly, grabbing the basket. She paused to wave at Emilie to reassure her. Then she slipped into the adjacent street, stopping in front of a small grocery store. Through the window, she saw it was empty except for a small woman who guarded the cash register. Lily entered, the basket swinging on her arm. A bell jingling above the door announced her entrance. The woman turned, greeting Lily with a short "Bonjour."

"Bonjour," echoed Lily.

In the tiny shop, shelves of canned food, meticulously stored by category, towered toward the ceiling. Several bags of grain lined one wall, and fruit and vegetables were heaped in crates near the cash register. The woman watched Lily peruse the wares. Lily approached a crate of shiny red apples. She smiled at the shopkeeper, pretending to search for something. She pointed randomly to an object on the top shelf. In her best French accent, she asked to see it.

"The potato masher?" asked the shopkeeper.

"Oui," Lily said.

"Wait, I'll get the ladder." The woman turned and disappeared behind a door Lily hadn't seen before.

As soon as she was gone, Lily snatched an apple and dropped it into the basket. The woman reappeared, struggling with a short ladder. Lily gave her what she hoped was an innocent smile. The woman regarded her briefly, then situated the ladder against the shelf. She climbed up, reaching toward the potato masher.

Lily took advantage of those few seconds to scoop another apple into the basket, as if nothing had happened. The woman finally managed to grab the potato masher. She descended and proudly placed the gadget on the counter, breathing heavily from the effort. Lily approached to inspect it. Just then, a tinkle of chimes announced another shopper, a burly mustachioed man who rushed into the shop.

"Marguerite, I need a pound of beans for my wife," he ordered. Then he caught sight of the young woman and said, "Hello, mademoiselle," his gaze assessing Lily.

"Bonjour," she replied shyly, heart pounding, holding her basket against her.

The shopkeeper announced the price of the potato masher to Lily and then left to serve the man. Lily pretended to inspect the masher, lifting the sieve basket, turning the crank. The grocer filled a canvas bag, using a scoop to shovel the beans, weighing them on a scale, all the while chatting with the man. Heart pounding, Lily took the opportunity to say, always with her best French accent, "It's too expensive for me."

She left the shop, setting off the door chime. Around the corner, she put the apples into her jacket pockets, causing them to bulge. She returned the basket and found Emilie patiently waiting for her. They found a bench near a newsstand. Lily pulled the apples from her pockets, wiped one against her sleeve, and handed it to the girl.

"Here," she said. The girl thanked her shyly and took the apple. She munched the fruit, swinging her feet high off the ground. Lily took a bite of her apple, her saliva glands responding to the food. She was suddenly proud to take care of this girl like a little sister. They watched the pedestrians, content to eat in silence. After a few minutes, Emilie spoke.

"You talk funny." She peeked at Lily, the half-eaten apple clutched in her small hand. Lily smiled.

"Probably because I'm not from here. I come from far away, all the way across the ocean, in America," she replied.

"Where the Indians live?" said Emilie, inspecting Lily even closer now.

"Yes! There are cowboys and Indians," she replied.

Emilie, still crunching the apple, gazed at the street, swinging her feet even harder, as if satisfied with Lily's answer. Soon, apples finished, they resumed their route, hand in hand, continuing along the bus line.

After a while, Emilie cried out, "I live near here." She pointed to children playing in the middle of a small side street. They crossed and entered the alley. Suddenly, Emilie released Lily's hand and ran in the direction of two little girls playing hopscotch under the watch of their mothers, who chatted near an open door.

"Pierrette! Marie!" she cried, happily joining the girls.

Lily paused at the alley entrance, watching the reunion. One woman glanced at her and then Lily was jostled by a woman pushing past, pulling a little boy with her.

"Emilie!"

The girl turned and shrieked, "Maman!" Her mother knelt in front of Emilie and grasped her by the arms, inspecting her to see that she was okay. She clutched the girl against her chest, weeping.

"I was so scared! I looked everywhere, everywhere! I thought I had lost you forever!"

Emilie began to sob, and the little brother, taken by the emotion of the moment, joined them. Tears came to Lily's eyes, too. She waved one last time at Emilie and slipped around the corner.

On the other side of the main street, two elegantly dressed women observed the scene. The elder of the two peered over her glasses and said, "She did much better than I had hoped."

Her companion nodded, adding, "She has audacity. And she cares. Exactly what we wanted."

11

LILY ARRIVED AT the Place de la Sorbonne without having noticed the route. *I must be on autopilot,* she thought. As a student, she'd gathered with her friends right here, around the fountain. They'd laugh about how their teachers wore the same clothes every day, and compare notes about how much French each of them actually understood. Lily claimed to catch fifty percent of what her art teacher said, but her friends teased her, knowing that she took cat naps during the slide shows.

Drawn in by her memories and the calm buzz in the courtyard, Lily lingered. Students clustered on benches, holding leather satchels, smoking and chatting. The men all wore suits, the women dresses or skirts and jackets. The clothing made everyone more formal and serious than when Lily was a student. The women styled their hair above their shoulders, curled back from their faces. Lily, with her naturally curly hair, was relieved; she could almost fit in with the look of the day. She was inspecting her skirt and wondering again how she'd gotten the clothes when she heard a voice nearby repeating a name. It took her a minute to realize that she was being called. It was Paul, from the hotel, at her side.

"Lily!" He pronounced it "Lee-lee." "I thought I'd lost you! Why did you leave and not say good-bye?"

Lily shook her head. That had seemed so long ago. So much had happened since she'd slipped out of his room. She smiled up at him.

"Salut, Paul." Before she could say more, he touched her elbow lightly and leaned toward her. She drew back before she realized he was just going to kiss her cheeks in the French style. He frowned and released her arm. Lily blushed and scanned the courtyard.

"What are you doing?" When Lily shrugged, Paul glanced at his watch. "I go to class soon. Have you had lunch?"

Lily shook her head, so Paul led her to a bench in the inner courtyard. Another memory arose in Lily's mind, of sitting on one of these benches looking at her French language exam, all marked in red by the teacher.

Rummaging in his leather satchel, Paul pulled out a package wrapped in brown paper. "Do you want to share my sandwich?" He unwrapped the paper and revealed a baguette cut in two. She nodded and Paul handed her half.

"Merci," she said. The sandwich was delicious despite its simplicity, the butter creamy, the ham salty, the bread just the right crunchiness. She didn't eat meat at home but here, practically starving, she was grateful for whatever she got. They ate in silence for a few minutes before Paul spoke.

"What have you done today?" Paul asked.

She hadn't accomplished anything. But she recounted her visit to the bookstore, missing Sylvia, and trying to pawn her ring at the Crédit Municipal. She didn't have a chance to tell him about Emilie.

"Vraiment?" he asked. "You really went to ma tante?"

"My aunt? There it is again! What does that mean? Someone else said that to me and I thought he was a weirdo!"

Paul laughed and Lily joined him. "Weirdo? What's that?" he asked.

"Someone strange, bizarre, not normal," Lily said. She took a bite of her sandwich and realized those words applied to her and her situation.

"Well, to go to the Crédit Municipal, it's also expressed by saying, when you want to put something on the nail, like your ring, you are going to my aunt," Paul explained.

"The nail?" Lily was even more confused.

"Yes, put on the nail, that is to say, pledge your ring."

Lily laughed, remembering that she had invented an aunt when she told the man who had helped her why she had to sell her ring. Thank God she hadn't mentioned anything about nails.

"Where does the aunt part come from?"

"We owe the nickname of 'my aunt' to . . . some prince, a son of Louis-Philippe. To honor his gambling debts, he had to drop his watch at Mont-de-Pieté. Not daring to tell his mother, the Queen, who was surprised to see him without it, he used the excuse of having forgotten it at his aunt's."

"You French!" Lily exclaimed. "Everything goes back to some royal story." She sighed. "I wish it had been an aunt. I might have had better results." She told Paul that she hadn't been able to complete the transaction. "I have no papers, no address. I only have my ring. I was really hoping to get some money for it."

Paul sat up, looking at Lily more closely.

"Seriously? You have no papers? Nothing? Where's your passport?"

Lily stalled by taking another bite of her sandwich. She hadn't expected to see Paul so soon, so she hadn't crafted a story to tell him. Chewing slowly, she glanced around the courtyard, still crowded with students smoking, chatting, laughing. For a second the scene was both normal and very odd to Lily. Then she realized what it was: no one held a cell phone to his ear. No one stared into a little screen cradled in his palm. The difference was startling to Lily, but she couldn't tell Paul; he'd think she was crazy. She finished chewing and turned to him.

"I was mugged in the street. Right before I met you in your hotel. He . . . he took my purse. He was trying to get my ring but that's when I got away and found you."

"Oh!" Paul said. "You didn't tell me you'd been robbed! That's terrible!"

Lily nodded.

"Well, where are you staying?"

Lily shrugged. She set the last bite of her sandwich on the wrapper on the bench between them and looked at Paul. He gazed back, his look first a question, then a subtle understanding. It was like he knew not to ask any more questions.

"Bonjour, Paul!" A young woman simpering came up to them, clutching her briefcase to her side.

"Ah, bonjour, Clémence," Paul said.

They spoke in French, ignoring Lily, who couldn't take her eyes off the young woman. She wore a navy dress, belted and draped by a lightweight beige cashmere coat. Her hair hung neatly past her ears and her expression was bright and engaging. Clémence asked Paul something and he leaned over to rummage in his leather satchel at his feet. The woman turned to Lily and smiled the kind of smile that wasn't friendly, her lipsticked mouth pursed, her jaw tight. Her eyes said something else: get away from him. Lily was shocked by the animosity that the woman emanated toward her. But she fixed the woman with her gaze, refusing to be cowed.

"Voilà, Clémence," Paul said cheerfully, holding out a handful of scribbled paper, cutting the tension.

The young woman quickly turned back to Paul as if nothing had happened, flashing a different smile to him, revealing perfect white teeth. She took the sheets and tucked them in her briefcase. Then gesturing to leave, she said, "On y va, Paul?"

Paul shook his head. "Non, pas encore, mais j'arrive."

"D'accord, à tout de suite!"

She glared at Lily again before joining a group of friends heading into the building. Lily, her hands on her thighs, felt ill, disturbed by the woman's hostility. *What's her deal?* she wondered.

Paul rose, smiling. "Bon," he said. "I have to go to class. If you don't have anywhere to go, would you like to come with me? It starts in a few minutes. It's a lecture in the Descartes amphitheater. 'Humanism and Romanticism in the Nineteenth Century.'"

"Sounds boring," Lily couldn't help but say.

Paul laughed. "It's not, but if you get bored you can always leave. Or take a nap, though if you do, the professor will surely notice and may throw a book at you." Lily gasped and Paul laughed again. "He's been known to do that, you know!"

"Okay! I'll pay attention," Lily said. "It will help me practice my French," she added, thinking that by now her comprehension was less than fifty percent.

"Allons-y." Paul took her hand and the heat from his body traveled through Lily. She let herself be led by Paul toward the entrance of the building and into the hall packed with students.

Paul guided Lily through the hallways, weaving among clusters of students rushing to or from class, pausing several times while waiting for a group to move on. The crush of bodies and briefcases, the chaos of conversation, the heat of Paul's hand all warmed Lily, making her glad to be inside and among others. Nudging their way through the crowd, Lily was forced to drop Paul's hand, but she kept close as he navigated their way. Suddenly he stopped in front of a pair of massive wooden doors propped open. A pack of students blocked the entry and Paul sent Lily a reassuring look. "Here we are!" he said. They forged a path into the lecture hall. Lily followed Paul, saying "Pardon" when she bumped against someone.

Inside, rows of desks descended toward a platform. At the front of the room, a small blackboard hung below a fresco depicting people engaged in discussion. The room buzzed with quiet conversation and the creaking of wooden seats and benches as the rows filled with students. Lily followed Paul down the steps, pausing here and there, waiting awkwardly while he chatted with friends. A blond guy with a bright red handkerchief sprouting from his jacket pocket said something that made Paul laugh. He smiled and nodded at Lily as if including her, but Paul didn't introduce them. Finally they slipped into a row on the side and took seats. He spoke to a serious young man next to him, who listened to Paul while straightening his already straight pens and papers. Clémence was seated near the front. Scanning the room, she brightened, catching sight of Paul. *She's so pretty,* Lily noted, but just then Clémence spied Lily and scowled, erasing her beautiful expression. Lily scowled back, tossing her head as if to say, "What's wrong with you?"

Students settled in, pulling out notebooks, pens, and ink bottles and arranging them on the desks. Paul didn't pay attention to Clémence, busy getting his things out. Lily, glad to have a seat inside, observed the students fill the hall. Their boisterous chatting created a din that somehow comforted Lily. She settled into her seat and smiled at Paul, who returned it. For a moment, strangely, she felt like she belonged here, with Paul, in Paris.

A short, balding man entered at the front of room. He wore a goatee and a rumpled jacket, and to Lily, he resembled the art teacher she'd had at the Sorbonne. Placing his briefcase on the table near the podium, he began to unpack it. By the time he'd pulled out his notes and books, adjusted his glasses and cleared his throat, everyone had quieted down. He began speaking, and after a moment Lily relaxed, content to be in a safe place with nothing to do.

Two years earlier, almost to the day, in a similar room, she had struggled to pay attention to a lecture about the difference between Gothic and Roman archways. Passing notes with her friend Colleen and doodling in the margins of her notebook, her mind was occupied with her plans for after class, when suddenly she saw her roommate Janet rushing up the aisle, with a furrowed brow and somber expression.

"Your father called," Janet whispered when Lily reached the end of the row. Immediately Lily's stomach dropped. Her father never phoned. If calling was to be done, it was her mother who dialed. She rushed to grab her things and followed Janet out of the amphitheater.

Lily pressed Janet for information as they descended the steps into the metro. But Janet knew nothing other than her father wanted Lily to return his call immediately. They hurried to their apartment, where Lily fumbled through a hundred numbers on her calling card to dial home. A neighbor of her dad's, someone Lily hardly knew, answered and passed the phone to her father. His voice sounded strange, garbled. But finally he got the news out. That morning, her mother had collapsed in the garden. A man delivering mulch had found her and called 911, but she'd died before reaching the hospital. An aneurysm had taken her life.

Lily's throat tightened and she wiped away a tear, trying to focus on the professor at the front of the room. She wouldn't lose it, not here in front of Paul. Paul paused in the midst of his note taking. "Tout va bien?" he whispered. She tried to compose herself, whispering back, "Oui." But she wasn't okay, and the memory of her mother's death brought back her desperation about her situation.

The class droned on, but finally the professor finished his lecture and the students broke into conversation while packing their briefcases. Paul chatted with a few friends who had been seated in front of them, young men dressed like him, suits and ties and scuffed wing-tip shoes. The blond guy with the red handkerchief passed by and gave Lily an inquisitive look.

Clémence, trailed by a pair of friends, paused and whispered something to Paul. Lily hovered awkwardly at the end of the row, suddenly aware that she wasn't an anonymous stranger in a crowd but an interloper in an exclusive setting. They climbed the steps of the amphitheater. Students teemed around them, the hallway crowded and hot.

"On y va?" Paul said. He led Lily around the corner and they took a seat on a carved wooden bench. Lily leaned back, relieved to be out of the fray. Paul set his bag down and turned to her.

"Where will you desire to go now?" he asked.

Lily watched the people, like students of any era except for the formal clothing and carefully coiffed hair, move down the hall toward the entrance. She realized she had relaxed during the class and, until the memory of her mother resurfaced, had forgotten herself and her situation for a short time. Shrugging, she looked at Paul, then glanced away.

"You can stay in my room if you want. I work tonight and there's no problem to stay there. Except we must hide you from my mother, who wouldn't like it at all!" He grinned and a flush of heat passed through Lily.

"The woman at the hotel is your mother?" Lily found it hard to believe that sweet Paul was related to that old crank.

Paul laughed. "She's fierce, but I think I can protect you."

"I don't know how to thank you," she said.

"Bah!" Paul said. "It's settled." He glanced at his watch. "I have to go to the library to study. Come with me?" Lily nodded. Even if she had somewhere to go, she didn't want to leave Paul. She liked the simplicity of trailing him through his day. A glimmer of guilt pulsed through her. What about Daniel? She'd felt this way about him, too—comfortable, interested. But they'd only been on one date and she may never see him again. Her thoughts became more confusing and she tried to focus on Paul.

They made their way down rue St. Jacques and Lily asked him about his studies. He told her about his courses and that he would finish his law degree in June.

"And what then?" Lily asked. "What will you do when you're done with school?"

Paul shrugged. "I don't know. Perhaps I take sabbatical and travel, to see the world. But I have to think of my mother. I can't leave her alone to run the hotel. It's complicated," he sighed.

Lily wanted to know more, like where he wanted to travel and what he wanted to do while there. But they'd arrived at the library, an imposing limestone building that spanned an entire block. It wasn't like any library she'd seen at home. Across the street, the Pantheon dominated the square, its dome enormous. Once inside the building, they found themselves in a regal marbled entryway. Pillars supported an arched ceiling, and along the wall, imposing busts watched over the students hurrying in and out.

They ascended a short flight of stairs and Paul led Lily into a giant hall lined with wooden desks. Lily tried to stay calm but the library's beauty stunned her. She'd never come here as a student. She stopped at the entrance: the massive curved ceiling, the giant arched windows along both sides, the carvings in the arches, the oak desks with their lamps with green glass shades, the people hunched over, reading, writing, whispering quietly.

She followed Paul until he found two empty chairs together. He put his bag on the table to secure their desk.

"What's this place called?"

"Bibliotèque Saint-Genevieve," Paul whispered. "Come on. I need to find some books for my research."

Bookshelves lined the walls of the hall, and they went together in search of the books he wanted. The enormous room, the quiet, the smell of books—aging glue and linen and a slight whiff of vanilla—made Lily feel both at home and homesick for the bookstore in Denver. She shook off the homesickness and stayed close to Paul, who was studying the shelves, his forehead creased. She was grateful for his help. Without him, she'd still be wandering around on the street, and it felt much better inside the library.

He found what he was looking for, and Lily grabbed a book off the shelf, too, just to have something to look at. They returned to their seats, weaving their way between the aisles. Paul settled in and began to turn the pages of a large volume bound in burgundy leather. Lily opened her book. It was a scholarly critique of Icelandic sagas, in French. She closed it. Next to her sat a young woman dressed much like Lily in a wool skirt and blouse. Her jacket was draped over her chair and she leaned forward, elbows on the desk. Lily eyed her leather satchel, her stack of notebooks, her leather pencil case, zipper open to reveal a handful of pencils. The woman took notes, using a striking fountain pen with a gray-and-red-swirled barrel and gold nib.

After a while, Paul closed his books and pushed his chair back. Glancing at his watch, he told Lily, "I have to go to meet a professor. Can you meet me later, say, eight thirty?"

They agreed to meet at the Sorbonne. He packed his notebooks into his satchel and leaned down to buss her cheeks. This time she lifted her face toward his, accepting his kisses, feeling the slight rub of his stubble. Lily watched him walk away, his stride sure, his jacket slightly rumpled in the back. At the entrance, he turned and gave a little wave. She waved back and returned to her book. She felt his absence strongly and told herself that she would see him soon.

Paging through the book, she quickly became bored. She could read French but it was work, and she wished for a book in English that she could lose herself in. She rested her hands on top of the desk, settling her cheek on top of them. Lily told herself she'd rest for just a moment. It wasn't long before she dozed off, her mouth slightly open, the book pushed to the side.

Lily awoke to the sound of a chair scraping against the floor. For a moment she thought she was back on the plane. She sat up, blinked, and looked around. The woman next to her stood and walked away. Lily sleepily eyed her stack of books and the ink-stained leather pen pouch. The woman's pen was elegant, and Lily gazed at the beautiful handwriting on the woman's notes. She wished she had a project to work on, something to devote herself to. Or at least her own notebook and pen. When the woman returned, settling back into her seat, leaning over her book, and holding her hair away from her face, Lily leaned toward her.

"Excusez-moi," she whispered. The woman continued reading. Lily gently touched her arm. "Pardon," she said. The student sighed audibly and turned to Lily with a raised eyebrow. Lily spoke the sentence she'd been silently forming. "Où se trouvent les journaux?" She figured if she were stuck here, she might as well try to read about current events so she'd know what was happening. The woman shook her head as if she didn't understand. Lily made gestures of opening and reading a newspaper. Finally the woman laughed, but not kindly.

"Il n'y a pas de journaux ici," the woman said. "Cherchez dans un kiosque à journaux à l'extérieur pour ça." She resumed her studies with a shake of her head.

Of course, Lily thought. This was a scholarly library, not one with items that would be of use to the general public. A passing librarian broke the stillness in the room.

"Fermeture."

The few people still present began gathering their things and tugging the lamp chains to turn off the lights. The great hall grew dim and cozy. Lily wished she could stay there. The woman next to her went to return her books to a wooden cart near the stacks. Without thought, Lily reached out and plucked the pen from the student's open pen pouch. She stood and adjusted her jacket, picking up her book.

Lily hurried out of the library, disoriented and glad to be outside again. The last of the sun was slipping from the day, and only a few students remained outside. Lily was unsure of which direction to take, but after a moment, the crisp evening air refreshed her and she followed the gently sloping sidewalk toward the boulevard Saint-Michel, retracing the route she'd taken with Paul. Again, with nightfall, the difference between the Paris she knew and this Paris was marked. No gaggles of tourists, no women walking alone, no sense of fun and vacation and play. The memory of the attack was all too vivid, and Lily hurried to meet Paul.

Finally, she arrived at the Place de la Sorbonne.

"La voilà!" Paul exclaimed. He bent toward her, quickly brushing her cheeks with his. "I worried. I will go to look for you."

"I'm sorry. I fell asleep in the library, and it took me a while to find it." Lily already was warmer by his side.

"You told me you knew how to get here!"

"I did. It just took a little longer than expected."

"No matter. On y va?"

They fell into step, and walking through Paris with him was better than walking alone. Lily enjoyed feeling like she had a place to go and that she was safe with Paul. When they arrived at the hotel, he led her to the side door. Pausing at the doorway, he handed her a key ring with three large skeleton keys. "You remember how to get there? Up the stairs, last floor, second door at the left?"

Lily laughed. "I don't think I can get lost on the staircase, can I?"

Paul smiled. "You never know."

"It's hard to believe it was only this morning that I left here. It's been a long day."

"You must be tired."

"I am. Despite my nap." Lily ducked her head and looked at her sensible shoes. "Paul, thank you for doing this. You've been so kind, so helpful—"

"It's nothing, nothing at all. I'm happy to help."

"But I have nothing to offer you in return. I can't thank you enough."

"I don't want anything. Like I said, I am happy to help.

And," he smiled, "it's great for me to practice my English. You are helping me."

Lily wished they could talk more but she knew he had to get back to work. "Okay, then. See you tomorrow?"

"Yes. À demain," Paul said, making a little bow. Lily slipped around the corner and into the courtyard. She climbed the stairs, trying to avoid creaky steps.

She reached the room and stepped inside. Again that musty odor, of books and old socks and guy. Turning on the lamp on the desk, she slipped off her jacket, releasing her own stale odor. "Mon dieu!" she grumbled. "I need to bathe. And when's the last time I brushed my teeth?" A glance around the room confirmed that there was no bathroom or sink. She went to the dresser and caught sight of herself in the mirror. Her disheveled hair clearly hadn't seen a comb in days and her eyes, usually so bright, revealed how tired she was. Rubbing her hands on her face, she released a deep sigh. Looking good was the least of her worries, but she didn't want to be taken for a bag lady, either.

Grabbing the pitcher, Lily slipped into the hallway. There were two other doors in the hallway. One was closed, the other ajar. Sure enough, inside was a tiny bathroom with an open shower stall and a child-sized sink. She filled the pitcher and brought it back to the room, then removed her blouse. Pouring some of the water into the basin, she applied a small, rough cloth and a yellowed bar of soap to clean herself. She used her finger and some toothpaste from a crinkled tube for her teeth. A proper bath would have to wait, until when, she didn't know. In the mirror, her face was pale, her freckled skin even lighter than usual. Her thick hair was flat on one side and scrunched up on the other. She frowned, then tried to smooth the desperation from her expression. She squinted, trying to imagine herself as a woman in the 1930s. She couldn't think of a future beyond tomorrow morning, when she'd go back to the bookstore and RSVP with her invitation to the Hemingway reading. She didn't want to depend on Paul forever. The bigger question of how she got here and how she would get home loomed, but this question tipped her into overwhelm and she forced herself to stop thinking about it.

Instead, she dried off with a musty towel, put her blouse back on, and sat on the bed. From her jacket pocket she pulled out the pen. Heavy and solid in her hand, the gray and red barrel was smooth against her fingers. She pulled the cap off and poked the gold nib with her finger. A tiny drop of ink marked her skin. Scanning Paul's desk, she found a sheaf of blank pages tucked into a book and pulled a few out. Sitting at the desk, she tried the pen.

She wrote for a few minutes, pouring her troubles onto the page. It felt good to write, and she wanted to keep going, but after a few pages, the ink thinned and then stopped. She shook the pen but it was dry. Recapping it, she tucked it in her jacket. Not sure what to do with the pages she'd written, she folded them and slipped them in a book at the bottom of a stack on the floor. It wouldn't do for Paul to find what she'd written.

Fully clothed, she lay down on top of the bed and pulled the rough wool blanket over her. She was hungry, but was getting used to the lack of food. Just then, a knock came at the door. She froze.

"Lily, it's Paul."

At the door, Paul handed her a small basket with an apple, pear, a bit of bread and butter, and a hard-boiled egg.

"Here, some dinner," he said. "This is all I could find. I hope it's enough. I must go!"

With that, he closed the door and his steps faded away down the stairs. He had fled so quickly she hadn't even been able to thank him. She took the basket to the desk and enjoyed the simple meal like she'd never enjoyed a meal before. She couldn't believe her luck.

Even so, she couldn't go on like this for long. How to get money, and how to get home, she mused, eating the pear. Her mind spun through scenario after scenario, trying to figure out how she could have gotten here, what she had been doing before she arrived that might lead to some understanding of this incomprehensible situation. The more she thought about it, the more her stomach tightened. Maybe sleep would bring an answer. *That's it,* she decided, standing and dusting the bread-crumbs from her lap. *Tomorrow morning I will know what to do.* She snuggled into the bed, this time climbing under the covers. She turned off the desk lamp and fell asleep under the soft glow from the skylight.

12

A SOFT KNOCK woke her, accompanied by a muffled "Lily!" A wisp of a dream—a crowded bookstore, a man reading aloud, a woman glowering at her—slipped away. Opening her eyes, Lily recognized Paul's small room, her jacket hanging on the chair, the stacks of books and papers on the desk. She was irritated to be awakened from the dream. Again the soft knock, followed by a muted "Lily, bonjour!" When she opened the door, Paul held a small tray arranged with a bowl of milky coffee and half a baguette with a small pot of butter.

"Bonjour," he sang cheerfully. But Lily didn't mirror his cheer. She eyed the bed, knowing that Paul would be taking his turn. She wished for her own bedroom in Denver. But the coffee smelled good, so she sat at the desk. As he had done the day before, Paul took a seat on the bed and watched.

"I'm sorry it's not more," he said.

"Mmmm," she murmured, chewing on the baguette. Paul rubbed his hands together, then studied them, then rubbed again. Finally, he clasped them together and began pacing the small room. He stopped in front of Lily.

"Maybe I have an idea."

"Maybe?" Lily took a sip of her café au lait. "About what?"

"I could help you sell your ring."

Lily started forward, nearly spilling her coffee. Carefully, she set the bowl on the desk.

"Do you really know another place to sell my ring? Crédit Municipal was going to give me 2,250 francs."

Paul winced slightly. "I think I can get you more or less that."

"Really? Where?"

"Don't worry about where," he said. "You can trust me. I take the ring and give you the money later."

Lily glanced down at her ring. He'd been so kind, so self-less; he wouldn't steal from her or otherwise harm her. Still, the ring was her only asset, and she was loathe to part with it. But she realized that it was only worth something to her if she could get money for it. And she needed money; she couldn't rely on Paul forever.

"I just want to pawn it, not sell it. I want to be able to get it back when I can," she said.

Paul sat on the bed. Reaching his hand to cover hers, Paul reassured her that she could trust him. Looking into his eyes, she knew she had no choice. She agreed, slipping the ring off her finger and placing it in his palm. He squeezed her hand and suddenly Lily wished she could hand herself over to him, tell him everything, let him help her sort this mess out. But she couldn't; kind as Paul was, he would surely think she was crazy. She pulled her hand back quickly.

"How can I ever thank you?"

"How about to smile?" Paul said, encouraging her with

his own.

She managed a smile to cover her discomfort.

"Okay, then, it's settled. I can meet you later with the money. First I need to sleep, then I can meet you before my first class. Say, at midday? We will eat something."

They made plans to meet outside a café near the Sorbonne. Lily told him that she was going to Sylvia's bookstore to see about the reading. "She might be able to help me, too. She's known for that," Lily said.

"For what?"

"For helping Americans in distress." Lily shrugged. "I guess that's me."

Paul said that he knew the bookstore. Lily couldn't hide her surprise. He grinned.

"How do you think my English is so perfect?"

"So you know Sylvia?"

"I have talked to her. I would not say 'know,' but yes, I borrow books there. It's a good place to practice my English."

Lily wished she could stay and talk with him all day, but he had to sleep and she had to see Sylvia. Standing, she put her jacket on, feeling the weight of the pen in the pocket.

"Okay, then," she said.

"Okay," Paul echoed.

She laughed. His accent was cute, and the more time she spent with him, the cuter he became. She turned to the door.

"Don't let my mother see you leave," he cautioned, following her.

"No way! See you later. And thank you, Paul."

He stared at her and for a second Lily thought that he was

going to say something, that she had revealed herself to him. But he just leaned over to give a *bise*.

"À bientôt, Lily." Paul said, his voice close to her ear. She held very still and accepted his gentle kiss on her cheek. Turning, she left the room and quietly descended the stairs.

13

ON HER WAY to the bookstore, Lily barely noticed the route. Absorbed in thoughts about Sylvia Beach, she paused for the light at the boulevard Saint-Germain. She tried to remember all the questions she'd had about Sylvia that hadn't been answered by her research trip to Princeton.

Lily's father had deployed a number of tactics to help Lily heal from her mother's sudden death. For months he'd let her wallow in grief in their Chicago house, where she'd grown up. He'd encouraged her to finish her degree. He'd suggested places where she could work in Chicago, friends of his that could help her get a job. None of it appealed to Lily, until he mentioned that he was going to a conference in Princeton and would be there for several days. Would she like to come? Lily had read in a biography about Sylvia Beach that her archives— her personal papers, items from her bookstore, all the things that were left behind after her death—were in the university's collection. Sylvia was originally from Princeton and had been buried there. When Lily told her dad she wanted to accompany him to New Jersey, he seemed relieved to have finally offered something that she wanted.

At the Princeton library, Lily gave her driver's license to a man who guarded the entrance to the collections rooms, telling him she was there to see the papers of Sylvia Beach. He didn't express interest in her or her subject. Not the chatty type, Lily thought. Then she spied the portrait on the wall.

"That's Sylvia, isn't it?" she said. He nodded, perking up slightly.

"Yes, it is. Done by Émile Bécat. It came with all the other things we got from her estate. We've even got the sign from the bookshop." He pointed into the library.

Lily peered around him. The wooden sign hung as it would have at Shakespeare and Company, perpendicular to the wall. The beruffled Shakespeare was completely at home in the proper Princeton library, but for Lily it was stunning to see these artifacts in real life. She couldn't help but gawk when he led her into the research room, a round space filled with blond wood desks and high windows that gave the room a quiet, open feeling.

Sunlight coming through the windows warmed the space. Two women sat at their desks, surrounded by stacks of books and papers. At the head of the room sat a larger desk, and at it an imposing black woman dressed in African garb. She bowed her scarf-wrapped head at Lily but said nothing. Lily was glad that she'd accepted her father's invitation to come.

Lily scanned the collection catalogue the man had given her. Hundreds of boxes held the possibility of finding something secret about Sylvia, something she hadn't read in the biography. She began noting the numbers of boxes she wanted to look at.

Once she had her list, she paused. The room was starkly quiet. The sun warmed Lily's back. The two other scholars were lost in their research. The African woman sat at her table still as a statue. Lily couldn't tell if her eyes were closed or if she was reading something on the desk. The woman's hands were folded in front of her. She could be mistaken for someone in meditation.

Lily scraped her chair back from the table. She hated to disturb the woman, but she only had two days here and there was a lot of stuff to look at. She approached the desk, a rush of anticipation making her hand shake and her list rattle.

"Excuse me," she said. The woman opened her eyes. She had been sleeping, Lily thought. She smiled, enjoying that a proper librarian had been caught asleep on the job. But the woman's gaze was clear and steady. It wasn't the look of someone who had been napping on the job. Lily tried to keep her cheerful expression, but the woman's demeanor penetrated Lily's false politeness. "I'd like to see these boxes, please."

The woman took the paper. She lifted her glasses off her enormous chest and settled them on her nose. The red, black, and yellow beads of the eyeglasses chain swayed slightly as she assessed the list.

"Sylvia Beach, hmm?" She raised an eyebrow at Lily. She had an accent, her English tinged with what Lily thought might be French.

"Yes," Lily said. "Do you know of her?" Right as she said it, she thought, of course she knows of her! The collection is here, after all. The woman ignored the question. She set the paper down.

"Not many people come here after Sylvia Beach. Why are

you interested?"

Lily flushed. She both liked the sense of being interested in an obscure public figure and wished that Sylvia had more fame. "I read about Sylvia in a book."

"*Sylvia Beach and the Lost Generation*," the woman filled in.

"Yes! It was great. She's so inspiring," Lily gushed.

"And you're lost, trying to find something here in her papers."

Lily fidgeted. She didn't consider herself lost. "My dad is here for a conference and invited me to come along. I'd heard that Sylvia's papers were here, and I thought I'd check them out."

"I see," the woman said. She nodded as if she didn't believe anything Lily had said. "Go back to your desk and I'll have these boxes brought up to you."

Lily thanked her and returned to her desk like a good schoolgirl. The woman inserted Lily's requests into a fax machine. Every gesture was carefully executed. When she had faxed the sheet, the woman returned to her seat and watched Lily. She began making notes in a notebook. Lily squirmed. This woman was weird. Was Lily lost? She didn't think so, but the librarian seemed to.

Lily's leg bounced up and down. She couldn't wait to see what was in Sylvia's archives. The boxes had indicated that there were more than papers. Lily had ordered boxes of her personal items, too, things from her desk. Also correspondence, drafts of her memoir, and letters to friends.

After about ten minutes, a door in the back of the room opened and a young blond woman with cat's-eye glasses wheeled in a two-tiered library cart lined with navy blue cardboard boxes. Scanning the room, she saw Lily, the only person not yet engrossed in study. The woman wheeled the cart to the side of the room. Lily went over. The young librarian handed Lily her request sheet, each item ticked off.

"I've got the first dozen boxes here. I thought I would give you these first. This should give you plenty to work with for a few hours. Just let Diana know when you want the others." She smiled at Lily. "Sylvia Beach fan, huh? Me, too."

Lily nodded, eager to get to the materials. The librarian left and Lily scanned the list. Choosing the box of personal items first, she carried it to her desk. She lifted the cardboard lid and peered inside. Tears filled Lily's eyes. A silver cigarette case. A small metal rack for stamps. The rubber stamps that went with them, the rubber peeling away from the wood. The bottom of the box was littered with shards of broken rubber bands, the bits stiff and lined like desiccated inchworms. The cigarette case had Sylvia's initials carved into it.

Lily sat with the objects, holding each one, touching Sylvia across time. An urge to take something, to have a piece of Sylvia for herself, overcame her. The cigarette case. A Shakespeare and Company bookplate. A piece of Sylvia's manuscript. The thought was immediately followed by deep shame. That she would steal from Sylvia Beach was unthinkable.

A brush with a pedestrian snapped Lily back into the present, where she found herself across the street from the bookstore. The wooden sign that she'd seen at the library hung from a hook in front of the store, the paint still bright, Shakespeare's superior smirk intact. A woman sat at the desk inside. Her back was to Lily, but her hairstyle and the way she sat was familiar. She resembled Lily's mother. A chill passed through Lily as she recalled her mother seated on the wooden bench in her garden at dusk. Only now Lily understood the way her mother had always been so comfortable in her world, so in possession of herself. She sensed that same at-homeness in this woman.

Lily watched as the woman walked to a shelf, removed a book, and brought it back to the desk. It was Sylvia. She wore the same simple white blouse and brown skirt Lily had seen her wearing two days earlier. She appeared rather ordinary, not the uncomplaining heroine portrayed in her pictures. Her hair was combed in a sensible style, its brown waves cut to hang above her shoulders. She picked through a small stack of books, engrossed in her work. Lily steadied herself to enter Sylvia's world.

14

LILY PLUNGED IN, setting off the bell at the door. Teddy lay on the floor next to Sylvia's desk. He raised his head, sniffed the air, and rose to his feet. Sylvia acknowledged Lily with a nod and went back to her books. Teddy rushed to Lily and nudged her hand, his tail wagging. He yipped loudly and Sylvia said, "He's friendly, don't worry." Lily gave a nervous laugh and was suddenly too shy to say anything to Sylvia.

I'll hang out for a few minutes first, she decided, and headed for the bookshelf in the back. A young man lingered nearby at a bookshelf, craning his neck to look at titles up high. Lily approached the fiction section. On the shelves, Lily recognized some of the titles, but most were as unknown to her as if they were in a foreign-language bookstore, not just in one that existed seven decades prior to her own. She searched for familiar titles. There was Fitzgerald's *The Great Gatsby. Dead Souls* by Gogol. She was suddenly aware that the customers talking behind her were dead souls and that she was not yet a living soul. Or was she?

Several books jutted from the shelf. They were old-fashioned but not old. It was strange to see them like this—usually by the time they reached her, books like this were worn at the edges, sagging at the spine, the fabric of their covers worn down to the stiff cardboard underneath. These volumes, without dust jackets and splashy author photos, were in good shape. Lily's bookseller's impulse took over. She tidied the shelves, tucking and aligning the books so that the spines were flush.

The bell above the door chimed. As if by instinct, everyone in the shop glanced up to see the newcomer. It was the man who had given Lily directions to Crédit Municipal. She grabbed a book from the shelf and ducked her head, unsure why she was hiding from him.

"Greetings, Sylvia!"

"Stephen, at last! Oh, it's tremendous to see you." Sylvia and the man exchanged air kisses. Lily's eyes widened and she averted her face again. Her hero was Stephen Spender! Sylvia's voice was warm and charming. Hearing it was like a space had been filled in, like she was watching a film with the sound finally turned on. The man took a seat next to Sylvia's desk, leaning toward her. Lily paged through the book, then put it back, inching along at the *I*'s now. *Mr. Norris Changes Trains* by Christopher Isherwood. She plucked it from the shelf, turning her back to eavesdrop.

"Would you care to join me for lunch?" the man asked Sylvia.

Sylvia gave a short laugh. "You're joking! I'd love to but I've got my hands full with the reading tonight. Keeping track of who's coming, worrying that there won't be enough chairs." She threw up her hands in mock despair. "And with my assistant abandoning me—"

"Sylvia, I am beginning to wonder if you just like to worry."

Sylvia laughed, though Lily could tell he had struck a chord.

"Oh, Stephen, I don't like to worry, but I certainly am accustomed to it. I imagine that I have been worrying all my life."

"Maybe that's why your head hurts so badly, so often."

"Oh, giving me analysis now, are you, Dr. Freud?"

Now Spender laughed. "No, of course not. I just want my Sylvia to be happy."

"Oh, I'm happy enough."

Lily could tell she was lying, even to a friend. Maybe Spender wasn't a friend, but just another bookish acquaintance. Maybe all the people who knew Sylvia from the shop were merely surface friends. Still clutching the Isherwood book, Lily did what she always did when she picked up a novel: she turned to the last page. Most people judge a book by its first line, but Lily chose the last line instead as a barometer of whether she wanted to read the book or not. She'd arrived at the last page when the man's question to Sylvia caught her attention.

"What are you reading now?"

Sylvia told him she was reading the French translation of *Voyage d'une Parisienne à Lhassa* by Madame Daniel Neel. She described how Neel had followed her passion for Buddhism and her curiosity all the way to Tibet, where she had gained an audience with the Dalai Lama.

"Sounds intriguing," the man said. "I'll have to look into it when you are finished."

Lily enjoyed hearing Sylvia's voice, deep and gravelly from smoking. She relished her enthusiasm for a great story and for adventure. She could see how Sylvia could talk anyone into a book that she was excited about, just like Valerie. She looked down at the page and read the last line: "What have I done to deserve all this?"

Lily made an involuntary noise, a sort of gasp laugh. All this, she thought, breathing in the scent of paper and the promise of a story, and Sylvia Beach is right over there. A rush of incredulity overcame her and she couldn't stifle a giggle. Spender glanced over and to Lily's dismay, recognized her.

"Oh, hello there!" He smiled and made a slight bow toward Lily. She shut the novel quickly and tried to reshelve it.

"Hello there," she replied. Nodding at Sylvia, she fumbled along the shelf trying to replace the book. Sylvia frowned slightly.

"Did you find ma tante?" he asked.

Flustered, Lily spoke quickly. "Yes, I did, thank you very much. I did, I found it. After a long trek, I must say, but yes, indeed, my aunt all right! Right there. Yes." She trailed off, clutching the book, dampening its linen cover with her sweaty palms.

"Very good. Well then, you're in good hands here with Sylvia. Lovely to see you again." He nodded to Lily, and turning back to Sylvia, asked, "What time am I expected for the reading?"

Sylvia rose and came around the desk toward him. She was nearly a foot shorter than him, but together they made a lovely picture framed by bookshelves, a stack of books between them.

"Please come around for dinner at Adrienne's. Number 18, just down the street."

"Lovely, I'll see you later. It will be my pleasure to read at your shop."

"Ah, well, we're delighted. It will be splendid, you and Hemingway."

He put his hat on, made a deep bow to Sylvia, grabbed the strap holding his books, and left the shop. Lily buried her face in the Isherwood, marveling that she'd seen him twice in two days.

The young man who had been examining books as carefully as Lily now took a stack of them to Sylvia's desk. Sylvia pulled a card from the file box on the desk and noted the titles he was borrowing. They chatted in French while she completed the transaction. After he left, Sylvia rose and stretched, then lit a cigarette and asked Lily if she needed help finding a book.

"No, thank you." Lily replied, stuffing the book back. "Well, actually . . ." She pulled another from the shelf. *A Portrait of the Artist as a Young Man*. "I'd like to get this." She approached the desk. Lily never bought books on a whim. And Joyce? Overriding her doubt, she thrust the book toward Sylvia.

The bookseller scrutinized Lily. "Weren't you here the other day? Trying to get in at closing time?"

Lily gave an awkward laugh. "Yes, that was me. How much is this?" She watched while Sylvia wrote down the title in the ledger. A tiny leather notebook sat on the desk next to the stamp carousel.

"That's two francs. You know Stephen?"

Before Lily could answer, the dog emerged from the side of the desk and licked her knee. She reached down and patted his head.

"That's Teddy," said Sylvia.

"Hello, Teddy. Does he read?" Lily smiled at Sylvia, who politely smiled back.

Suddenly Teddy jumped up, his paws grabbing Lily around the waist. "Teddy!" Sylvia shouted. "You're a dirty, naughty dog." Rushing around the desk, she pushed him off of Lily. "I'm terribly sorry," Sylvia apologized.

"It's okay," Lily said.

"Teddy only bothers people he likes."

"Yes, well . . ." Suddenly Lily realized that she didn't have any money to buy the book.

"Do you have information about joining the library?" Lily asked.

Sylvia pulled a leaflet from a drawer and handed it to Lily. The Shakespeare and Company logo marked the cover. An arch framed Shakespeare's head. He held a pen and a piece of paper, like he was in the middle of writing a masterpiece. His small mouth and mustache was eerily like Hitler's.

"Okay . . . um, I left my purse at the hotel. Can I come back later to get this?"

"Certainly," Sylvia said. "And I promise the attack dog won't pounce on you again." Now she smiled for real, taking the book from Lily.

"No problem, honestly," Lily said, returning the smile. "Oh, I have this." She pulled the invitation out of her pocket.

Sylvia took the card and squinted at it, then at Lily. "What is your name?"

"Lily. Lily Heller."

Sylvia sat at the desk and pulled out a ledger. Lily spied a list and recognized it from the Princeton archive. It was the guest list for the Hemingway-Spender reading. She began to sweat.

Sylvia frowned and shook her head. "I'm sorry, Lily, I don't see your name on the list." She picked up the card and inspected it more carefully. "Where did you get this?"

Lily laughed nervously. "I, uh, ha! Now that's a story. I won't bore you with the details."

Sylvia frowned. "I made out all the invitations myself and, well, I don't mean to be rude, but you're not on the list. And I don't know you." She eyed Lily.

"I'd really like to be there," Lily said. "I'd do anything—do you need help? I can help! I'm really good at—"

Sylvia shook her head. "I'm sorry, but I don't need help. We've got everything in hand. And anyway, we're full up. Didn't you see the sign out front?" She gestured to the window. Lily turned and could see a handwritten scrawl on the reading's sign. Even backwards she got the meaning: sold out. Lily faced Sylvia again.

"I could help. I could set up the chairs, take them down after the reading. I work in a bookstore back home."

Sylvia harrumphed and Lily could see she'd gone too far. "Really, we're set, and we have actually overbooked, so even one more person would—"

"Please, I am very useful. At the bookstore where I work, we hold readings all the time. I help organize them and seat people." Lily stopped. It was hard to tell if she was bothering Sylvia or getting closer to accessing the reading. "Et je parle le français," she added.

"And with a good accent," Sylvia replied in French.

"I hate to be a bother, but it really is important that I be there."

"Why? So you can gawk at Hem?"

"Well, no, not exactly." She didn't know why, but the invitation in her pocket meant something. It was her only clue. "It's just . . . I've come a long way to be in Paris and I would really like to go to a live reading. I love books and . . . I want to be a writer." Lily could feel how silly her reasons must sound. She needed something better than that. "How can I convince you that I can help?"

Sylvia sighed and pushed the stack of papers to the side.

"I already have so much work. I cannot waste time showing you around." She pushed her hair back off her forehead. "Do you know how many assistants I've had? How many pretty girls who were useless when it came to shelving and organizing and taking notes and giving me my messages?"

Lily did know. She had read about the assistants that Sylvia had and how tough she was on them. Sylvia, though kind, was a stern boss. But Lily could handle some abuse for a few weeks. Much as she liked Paris, the last thing she wanted was to be there during the Occupation that was coming shortly. The images she'd seen—crowds of desperate people lined up to cash in their rations, Nazis marching Paris's street—were not ones she herself wanted to inhabit. If she stayed in Paris, she would have no rations. Without identification papers, she wouldn't be part of the system. Maybe she would be interned like Sylvia and hundreds of other foreign nationals living in Paris. Her stomach turned at this idea.

"I'm coming," she said.

Sylvia started back. "Oh? And what if we don't let you in?"

"You won't need to pay me. I can be a volunteer. I will come early and help you set up. You won't be sorry. Trust me, I can help."

"I'm not sure where you get the idea that I so desperately need your help," Sylvia replied. Her voice had lowered an octave and had a menace in it like a growling dog. "And I'm not sure I like your pushy ways. You're just another American, here to drink in cafés all day and pretend to write. Now, please buy something or leave. I have work to do. The reading is tonight and I'm expecting a full house."

How did Sylvia know that she had fantasies of writing in cafés? Still, Lily held her ground.

"I'm sorry," she said. "I didn't mean to offend you."

Sylvia didn't reply, but stood and straightened her worn jacket.

"Good-bye." Lily turned to leave. "Wait—"

Sylvia exhaled a deep sigh.

"What if I come early and I promise to only help and not get in the way?"

Sylvia gave the tiniest of smiles, nearly an incredulous smirk. "I cannot believe you. You have some nerve. What is your name again?"

"Lily. Lily Heller."

"I'm Sylvia Beach," she said.

"I know."

"Aha! I've seen your type. Arriving on a one-way ticket, dreaming of a hypothetical artist's life in Paris, and after few weeks, coming to me desperate for a job. But it's been years. No one comes around anymore. What are you doing in Paris anyway? Don't you know? All the Americans have gone home."

Lily shrugged. "I'm here to help someone out. They needed me and I couldn't say no."

"I don't want to know. Now go away before I get really angry and ban you from the shop altogether."

Lily couldn't tell if Sylvia was serious or not, but she'd tested her limits enough for the moment. She mumbled an inane thank-you but Sylvia had already returned to the affairs on her desk. Lily sprang from the bookstore, hopping off the front steps to the sidewalk. The reading was tonight, and she was going to be there. No matter what.

15

OUT OF SIGHT of Sylvia's windows, pretending to browse the cart of the antiquarian bookshop next door, Lily caught her breath. She shook as she replayed the contretemps in her head. A wave of shame moved through her. She picked up a book, *La Psychopathologie de la Vie Quotidienne*, and smirked. What about the psychopathology of noneveryday life? Meeting Sylvia Beach and being kicked out of the shop surely would merit years of analysis to make sure she wouldn't become crazy. This was funny until she realized she was standing in an era where women were hauled off to insane asylums with very little proof of insanity. She dropped the book, nudging her thoughts toward the positive.

She'd had a run-in with Sylvia Beach—not so great. But she'd been bold, insisting on attending the reading. Not bad, she thought. In Denver, she would never have had the nerve to do that. She replaced the book and headed down the street, a slight skip in her step. At the corner, she pulled the invitation from her pocket. Why did she feel the need to go to the reading so badly? This was a clue, but to what, she didn't know. But it was one of the few things she'd arrived in 1937 with, and it must mean something. It must mean she belonged at that reading. Her need to know what was happening to her overrode her concern about Sylvia. She straightened her jacket and stepped into the flow of people bustling along the boulevard Saint-Michel.

Soon she found herself inside the spiked fence ringing the Luxembourg Garden. Nannies trudged behind iron-wheeled buggies and chased after toddlers. A young couple huddled together on one chair, their intimate embrace like a Rodin sculpture. The gravel crunched under Lily's feet, a rhythm accompanying and quieting her thoughts. She took a seat on a bench near the *pétanque* court. Men crouched and tossed metal balls along the ground. The click of the balls striking one another, the sound of the men's conversation as they teased each other and disputed calls, all made for a pleasant background noise. Nearby, a patch of grass was tastefully bordered by a flowerbed, held back by a black ankle-height fence. She would have preferred to sit on the grass, but the most she could do was enjoy the green from afar, relishing the tiny patch of nature. Her mother would have laughed at the sign that forbade walking on the grass. She also would have been pointing out the flowers and telling Lily their names: teacup roses, elegant Queen Anne's lace and cheerful red geraniums.

She wanted to be like her mother, the kind of person who knew the names of living things and could grow plants, but she was more at home with paper and books, words and ideas. When Lily was a girl, she loved going with her mother to shop for school supplies. It was their special tradition. It was the one time of the year her mother really came through, the one thing they shared in common—Lily even marked the day on the calendar. Together they made lists of things Lily would need. They always bought more pencils and pens than would fit into her zippered pouch, but the extras came in handy when she left something behind on the bus or in the gym at school. After buying notebooks and other supplies, they'd have lunch at Farrell's in the mall. Lily would order the cheeseburger with fries and they would share a sundae, an annual indulgence.

Lily sighed. She didn't eat cheeseburgers anymore but she'd do anything to sit across from her sensible mother and ask advice about how to get into the reading. But she'd have to figure that out herself.

Refreshed by her rest, she exited across from the Café Rostand. Pedestrians pushed past Lily. Passing a clock-making shop, she glanced in the window to check the time. Each clock—the cuckoo, the bedside alarm, the compact travel clock—all told her she was late for her meeting with Paul. She hurried on.

At the café she found Paul waiting outside, reading his book. "Salut, Paul!"

He looked up. "Rebonjour, Lily! How was your morning?"

"Well," Lily said. "I've had a . . . an odd morning. I just met Sylvia Beach. It didn't go quite as planned."

"Ah bon? Don't worry about it; I have something to tell you. Let's have lunch?"

Lily agreed and they entered the café. It was crowded, the bar lined with men in suits arguing over tiny espresso cups, students filling most of the other tables. A clutter of newspapers was heaped at the end of the bar and the room was filled with smoke.

Paul turned to Lily, "How about the terrasse?" She nodded and they wove their way through the crowd of tables outside until they found a small one near the back. "I have something for you," Paul said.

Just then, the waiter whisked up tableside, nodding at them, then looked away. "Je vous écoute," he spoke to the air. Lily glanced at the menu and asked for a cheese sandwich. Paul placed his order, adding water for them both. He then reached into his jacket, pulled out a small manila envelope, and slid it across the table to Lily. She tucked her finger under the flap and peeked inside. A stack of francs, all for her.

"Oh, Paul! You were able to pawn the ring?"

He shrugged. "I wasn't able to get 2,250 francs," he said. "But that should be enough for you for a while."

"How much?"

"One thousand." He swallowed and smiled slightly.

"That's great! That's a ton of money. Isn't it?" Lily had no idea of the value of one thousand francs in 1937. She could get her own room, buy a new dress, a notebook. Almost as soon as these thoughts arose, she knew what her father would say: save your money. And she knew that was the better idea. Who knew how long she'd be there?

Paul laughed. "A lot of money, yes. It would take a long time to save that kind of money now. What will you do with it? Do you have a purse?"

Lily realized the envelope wouldn't fit in the small pockets of her jacket. "Oh, no," she said. "I can't take this now. I can't carry all this."

"Yes, it's not safe. Especially since you were already stolen."

Lily laughed. "I wasn't stolen, my money was. I was mugged."

"Mugged?" Paul tilted his head.

"Robbed in the street," Lily said. "By a mugger."

Paul repeated the word mugger, his French accent making the word sound charming. Lily laughed and Paul smiled with her.

"Bon, écoutes, you can take some money for today with you and I can hide the rest of this in my room for whenever you need it. Alors, where should I put it? I will hide it in my civil law book? Under my mattress? Hmm . . . in one of my stinking socks, peut-être?" Paul seemed to enjoy practicing his English vocabulary. Lily laughed.

"No! Not in your stinking socks, please!" She stopped laughing to consider it. She didn't want him poking around his books and finding her writing. "Okay, how about under your mattress?"

Paul agreed and gave her half the cash. Their sandwiches arrived, shot onto the table by the precise and hurried garçon. Lily opened her demi-baguette, revealing two slices of cheese surrounded by wide swathes of butter. Even this blandest of bland sandwich was appealing now. They chewed together in silence. Lily cast about for something to talk about, but what came to mind were subjects she didn't feel safe revealing to Paul. After a few minutes, Paul spoke quietly.

"Et un ange passe," Paul smiled.

"What's that?"

Paul appeared surprised that Lily didn't know this expression. "It's what we say when there's a moment of silence in a conversation. An angel passes by."

"You believe that? An angel just went by?" Lily didn't believe it, but she glanced up, her gaze falling on the balconies across the street, potted flowers cheering up the wrought-iron balconies. She smirked, but she liked the idea of angels nearby. "Look! There's one now!" She pointed at one balcony in particular, the window open, a lace curtain waving in the breeze.

Paul laughed. "It's not really something to believe, it's just an expression. To make you smile."

It worked; Lily couldn't help but smile. With Paul it was easy.

"You know, Lily, this morning, my mother was a bit intrigued by my strange new behavior," he continued.

"Uh-oh! She knows about us?"

"No, when I went downstairs with the breakfast tray this morning, she questioned me." Paul adopted a new voice. "'I see you take your breakfast upstairs now,'" he mimicked. Lily smiled and he continued. "'Normally you're down here with me, hmm? And why are you eating again, as if what you had upstairs went down a rabbit hole instead of in your stomach?'"

Paul paused in his imitation to explain to Lily that he had to eat his own breakfast, there in front of his mother.

"'Mais maman,' I told her, 'I am a growing boy, n'est-ce pas?'"

"And she believed that?" Lily chuckled.

"She didn't disagree. Just went back to sorting the mail." Paul smiled as if he enjoyed thwarting his mother.

"But you have to be careful! What would she do if she caught me there?"

Paul shrugged. "Oh, don't worry. She's just very involved with what I do. Too much! She wants to direct my whole life. She thinks she knows better than me what's best for me."

"Huh," Lily said, taking another bite of her sandwich.

"Yes, listen to this." Paul sat up straight, forgetting his own sandwich. "So she finishes with the mail and comes back to interrupt my breakfast. She starts in again with Claudine."

"Clémence?" Lily interjected.

"Non, Claudine! Dieu, the famous Claudine! She's the daughter of the antiques dealer down the street. We grew up together. Our whole lives, my mother and her mother, Marie, plan for me to marry Claudine. Mais non! It's not what I want."

"You don't like Claudine?"

"Non, I like her very much. But not like that. She's my friend. We went through school together before she went to study painting at L'Ecole des Beaux Arts. We don't see each other so much now, but my mother still has her in mind for marriage. Like I can't find my own wife!" Paul shook his head and resumed his imitation of his mother. 'Paul, you know, yesterday I ran into Marie and Claudine. Et mon dieu! Claudine is truly radiant. You should see her.' Paul smiled and winked. "Yes, maman,' I replied, drinking my coffee to avoid saying something regrettable. So she continues!

"'I invited them for coffee this afternoon. Claudine is impatient to see you again.' To which I immediately thought, Oh poor Claudine, she, too, got caught in this conspiracy of mothers!

"'Don't let me down, Paul! I count on you to be here at four o'clock.'" Paul shook his head like a dog as if to release the memory. "After that, she then insisted on telling me to dress well! As if I cannot dress myself like an adult!"

Lily laughed. Indeed, Paul was dressed like an adult, not wearing the short pants of a boy.

He looked at Lily, his eyes smiling warmly. "But I am a good son, I will be there."

Lily liked watching his lips move, subtly shifting shape when he spoke French. His face lit up with his narrative and the animation of imitating his mother. She enjoyed being with Paul and hearing his stories. And she appreciated his loyalty even as she could tell it bothered him to be so controlled by his mother.

Encouraged by her smile, he related how his mother loved to shame him with a photo of him as a baby. She never tired of showing it to her friends. There he was, posed naked on a red cushion, looking like a plump little pig. His mother loved, he recounted, to point out his pretty little cheeks. And his plump, rosy butt, her friends never failed to add.

"The horror!" Paul cried, and Lily laughed, repeating, "Quelle horreur!"

Paul continued. "Even Claudine had been shown this beautiful view of my backside. Merci, maman," he said.

"Oh, that's so bad!" Lily commiserated. But she liked the idea of baby Paul naked on a cushion, cute and vulnerable. Her mother had never shown any pictures of Lily to friends. In fact, her mother didn't have friends, only her garden. This thought sobered Lily. Paul noticed the frown on her face and spoke quickly.

"We take a coffee?"

Lily attempted a smile. "Yes, that would be great. I love your stories! I could listen all day."

"Oh, no, I will not bore you with stories any longer. But watch this." He got two coins out of his leather change purse and showed Lily a magic trick. With dexterity, Paul made the coins appear and disappear through his fingers. Lily leaned forward, trying to figure out how he did it.

"Tell me! How do you do that?"

Paul shook his head and wagged his finger. "Never reveal the secrets. I just learned this from one of our regular guests. Mr. Armant is a wine merchant and I'm sure he uses this trick to hypnotize his customers!"

"Are you trying to hypnotize me?" Lily smiled in a different way now.

"Mais non, just trying to make you smile. Le sourire te va bien," he said.

Lily thought he'd said the smile did her well, but didn't know how to respond. Paul changed the subject.

"And what about that meeting with Sylvia? What happened?"

Lily hesitated as the waiter approached, and Paul ordered coffee for both of them. Lily wasn't sure how much to tell him about Sylvia. But after he'd shared his stories, she felt safer revealing her own. She got the invitation out and showed Paul.

"I found this invitation to a reading at Shakespeare and Company tonight. And I really want to go. But when I showed it to Sylvia, she was suspicious. She refused me, said the reading was completely full."

Paul held the invitation, inspecting it closely.

"Where did you get this?"

The waiter zipped by, delivering their coffees. Lily took the chance to stir sugar into her cup. "Paul, if you don't mind, I prefer not to talk about that yet. Now it's your turn to trust me."

Paul nodded and set the invitation on the table. But Lily

could tell that her reticence only piqued his curiosity and it was politeness that stilled his questions.

"So you will come back to the hotel after the reading tonight?"

Lily sighed. Paul's hazel eyes were so friendly, his expression generous. She couldn't believe he was doing so much for her. She told him it was time to get her own room and stop invading his.

"Invade!" Paul snorted. "It's hardly an invasion, Lily. I like your company." He ducked his head, then spoke. "But where will you go? It's not just our hotel that won't accept a single woman with no luggage. It's not very, how should I say, correct."

Lily grimaced. She wasn't correct in any era. It infuriated her to not be able to move and do as she pleased in 1937. It was all well and good to have met Sylvia Beach and received money for her ring, but she needed to remember her real priority: figure out how she'd gotten here and how she was going to get home. First, she needed to buy a purse to carry the money, her pen, and whatever else she'd buy.

"Surely some hotel or rooming house will take me. Do you have any ideas?"

Paul shook his head. "There are student dormitories for single women, run by nuns, I think, but they're full until the summer session." He shrugged. "I can ask around. But you can stay chez moi until you find a room. It's not hurry. I have to go to class all day. You can come there again tonight, pas de problème."

Lily was about to refuse when she realized she had no reason to. She had nowhere else to go. She could try to find something today, but she might as well say yes now.

"Oh, Paul. You've done so much for me. How can I ever thank you?"

"Stop—you don't have to worry about that. I am your angel."

"I guess!"

"What will you do this afternoon?"

"I think I should join you and Claudine and maman for coffee!" Lily giggled and Paul joined her.

"Ah, oui, that would be some scene!" Paul giggled. "But seriously."

"I want to buy a notebook. I would like to do some writing."

"You are a writer!"

"No, I want to be a writer. So I must start somewhere, right?"

"Oh, I'd love to read your writing."

"Bah, non, Paul! It's not . . . it's just . . . just journaling, nothing for anyone else to read." She felt awkward talking about writing that hadn't even happened yet. Except for the pages she'd hidden in Paul's room. A flash of panic coursed through her; what if he found them? She'd have to retrieve them tonight. They parted at the entrance to the café, promising to see each other later after the reading. Paul insisted on coming to fetch her afterward, and while Lily wouldn't normally worry about walking alone, she acquiesced. Paul said he'd pop by the bookshop at eleven to get her. They made a plan B: if Lily couldn't get into the reading, she'd go right away to the hotel.

Outside the café, they said their good-byes. "Alors, à ce soir, Lily," Paul said, bending to buss Lily's cheeks. "A ce soir," Lily repeated, and watched him hurry down the street to his class. She felt his absence immediately and regretfully. It had been like this with Daniel—Daniel! A pang of guilt passed through her. They'd only had a few dates, so she wasn't officially cheating on him. But she wondered what he'd think if he saw her enjoying Paul's company so much.

In a private residence nearby, a woman stroked the cover of a leather-bound book. Her hands, encased in white archival gloves, moved with tenderness over the tome.

"We've got it," she murmured. "Safe."

Diana, seated in an upholstered chair, nodded. "One more book secured, many more to go," she sighed. She rose from her chair, took the book from the other woman, and placed it inside a glass bookcase with care, her movements measured and practiced. Then she locked the case, took the keys to her desk, and put them in the middle drawer. "Now," she said. "About this reading."

Adelaide pulled her gloves off and tossed them on a side table near the fireplace. "Yes. Louise and Harold will be there, with a few extras to draw attention away from them. We know that Werden will be there, watching everyone's last move."

"Will she be there?"

"She better be. We can only wait and see. That girl is our only hope."

Diana settled behind the desk and pulled out a ledger. Dipping a pen in an inkwell, she said, "What have we come to that an outsider is our only hope for one of our most coveted manuscripts?"

"We've come to this," Adelaide replied. "Who knows? She might be perfect. We need new blood. I don't think we can keep that dead weight Harold for much longer." Adelaide paused.

"And you know, the choice is not ours. We have to accept it. This mission is her own even if she doesn't know that."

"Well, good riddance, I say." Diana began writing in the ledger.

Adelaide moved toward the door. "I'll be off, then."

Diana continued to write, her hand lit by the glow of the desk lamp. The door to the library clicked shut.

16

AFTER LEAVING THE café, Lily wandered a bit, enjoying the spring afternoon. She felt buoyed by her lunch with Paul, like she was a normal woman in the thirties who'd savored a rendezvous. It also was reassuring to have money in her pocket. Now she needed a purse, and some new clothes would be nice.

Strolling down the street, Lily passed a French bookshop, a *tabac*, and a milliner. She paused briefly in front of the hats, delighting in the bell-shaped ones adorned with feathers and ribbons. At the end of the street she found a papeterie and peered into the window. The floor of the display was lined in blue velvet, crumpled at the edges and giving the impression of a jewel box. A wooden lap desk was adorned with a glass ink bottle in the shape of a tiny ship, the fountain pen astride the bow, tipping away from the bottle like a plank out to sea. Elsewhere, a wrought-iron stand displayed a collection of more ink bottles, arranged in rows like soldiers. Classic fountain pens nestled in velvet-lined boxes.

With delight, Lily took in the notebooks, larger and thinner than American versions, fanned out in a rainbow of colored covers: maroon, navy blue, burnt orange. Her hand reached toward them, already feeling the smooth paper on her fingers, but the glass of the window stopped her. She saw herself tucked into a cozy chair with the lap desk, the ink and its bottle, writing her stories. She trembled with anticipation.

She entered the shop with a rush of enthusiasm, accompanied by the ding of the bell above the door. It was everything she loved: wood and paper everywhere. The shop seemed formal, like a pharmacy. But instead of medicines, there were supplies for people who wrote with beautiful paper and ink. A tall, graying shopkeeper stood at the counter helping a stooped old man in a suit and hat who peered at an assortment of pens in the wooden display case. Lily inhaled, savoring the smell of paper, glue, and possibility. Everyone ignored her, so she plunged in, the wooden parquet floor squeaking under her steps. At the center of the shop reigned a wide wooden table, a spool of brown wrapping paper at one end accompanied by scissors, ribbon, pots of glue, and other miscellany. Lily gasped at the rack of elegant wrapping papers draped one over the other.

"Bonjour, mademoiselle," the shopkeeper greeted her. Lily nodded, trying to contain her excitement. She knew from experience that you had to slowly warm up to a French shopkeeper. If you were too friendly right away, you'd be disregarded as a disingenuous American.

She wandered around, taking in the ordered charm. Everything had its own shelf, bin, or rack. Here, a stack of green leather account ledgers, there the bin holding a few of the year's agendas, 1937 embossed on the red covers in blocky gold letters. Lily was delighted to feel so at ease. This had to be where Sylvia got her office supplies, she thought. Lily recognized the kind of notebooks she'd seen in the archives at Princeton. Everything resembled what one might see at a flea market on the outskirts of Paris, but new—not worn at the edges, not sepia-toned.

She approached a table arrayed with purses and pen pouches. Scanning the display, Lily realized she could buy a small satchel here, to hold her pen, her money, and . . . she could buy a notebook, too. She picked up a leather pouch and tested the zipper. She'd need more than one stolen pen to merit a pouch like this. Instead, she inspected the small satchels, falling in love with the buttoned and zippered compartments. She tried a soft brown leather bag, adjusting the strap with its slim buckle. It fit her, nestled against her hip. There was plenty of room inside for notebooks, books, plus slots for pens and pencils. A small price tag hung from a string attached to the strap. Five francs. That seemed incredibly cheap, and with a handful of francs in her pocket, she could afford it. Leaving the bag slung over her shoulder, Lily continued to explore the shop.

Lily paused in front of a shelf of notebooks near the back. Her heart jumped. There, in the corner, she discovered a stack of little black notebooks. Moleskine notebooks! Not wrapped in plastic like in her time. One was even propped open, revealing its squared graph pages held in place by the black elastic band. The notebooks looked dingier, less polished, but they were the same style notebook, the edges of the covers rounded, a fabric tassel tucked in the spine. She peeked at the shopkeeper, who was busy explaining the differences between pen styles to a young man. Picking up one of the elegant cahier notebooks, she stroked the cover, remembering her first fancy notebook.

Lily was entering high school when her mother abandoned
their school shopping ritual. One Saturday afternoon, Lily
approached her to go to the store. But her mother waved her off.
She said that she forgot to put the date on the calendar. She was
transplanting a near-dead rose bush.

"Go on your own, honey. Take your bike to the store."

"But Mom, I like going with you. How am I going to decide
between college rule and thick lines?" They laughed. Lily's writing was tight and neat, and each year she lobbied for college rule.

Her mother lifted the plant out of the ground, her gloved
hand cupping the dirty roots. "You'll manage, I'm sure. Go on,
now." She rose with difficulty and carried the plant across the
yard to a shady spot by the house. "I'm not sure this one's going
to survive," she muttered, kneeling before the hole and leaning
forward to gently position the bush. Lily got her bike from the
garage and wheeled it down the driveway, for once not ringing
her bell good-bye.

At the store, she spent a long time cruising the paper supply
aisle. She chose each item carefully, putting a well-coordinated
combination of spiral notebooks into her basket. Scrutinizing
the pens, she weighed the advantages of a pack of multiple colors versus a pack of all blue ink. She finally decided on a two-
pack of blue, slipping it discretely into her fanny pack. She rode
through the rest of her shopping trip on a wave of adrenaline,
buying the items in her cart and leaving the store with her stolen goods. Later, Lily stopped at another store. There, an exquisite notebook with Florentine end papers and creamy, unlined
pages tempted her. It was expensive—thirty dollars, something
she couldn't afford and that her mother wouldn't approve of. She

added it to her contraband, slipping it into her shopping bag without remorse. But despite its beauty, she never wrote in it.

That year she mastered shoplifting, prying packets of pens off their hooks in the drugstore, tucking them into her pants. She would walk the aisles, pausing at the magazine rack, the cardboard package pressing against her belly. In college, while in a creative writing course, she stole more fancy notebooks, hoarding a box of them in the closet: marbleized paper, recycled paper, hardback notebooks, even regular school notebooks. She rarely wrote more than a page or two in them. But Lily had stopped stealing altogether when she got a job at the bookstore and was on the other side of the counter.

Choosing a pocketbook-sized notebook, she drifted toward the shopkeeper. A display of pens and ink were arrayed regally behind him. He glanced up at Lily. Taking her pen out of her pocket, she showed it to the clerk, asking for ink cartridges. He inspected it, unscrewing the swirled gray and red barrel and pulling out the cartridge.

"This is a very nice pen. Does it work well for you?"

"I just got it. I haven't used it yet. I need ink." They spoke in French and Lily felt a sense of pride at how easily her French was flowing.

He turned to the rack and chose a bottle of black ink. "Voilà."

"S'il vous plâit, can you show me how to fill the pen?"

He jerked his chin down like he couldn't believe she didn't know how to refill her own pen. Lily focused on the man's hands as he dipped the pen into the inkwell and drew the ink into the cartridge. He explained how she shouldn't overfill it. He replaced the barrel and gently tapped the pen against a blotter on the counter. He made a few scribbles to get the ink flowing. When he passed the pen to Lily, she uncapped it and pressed the nib to the paper. She started to write her name. Instead she wrote "Sylvia." The ink burbled out and made a big blob at the end of the *a*. The man demonstrated how to write more slowly and evenly so the ink wouldn't surge out. It soothed Lily to be taught something. She paid for the satchel, ink, and notebook and left the shop, pleased to have had a successful encounter.

Late-afternoon sun greeted Lily outside the shop. She paused, breathing deeply. Cigarette smoke, a trace of perfume, the fresh air of spring: the familiar mélange of Paris. The shop had been a treasure chest, a far cry from the sterile, wide-aisled supermarkets of her childhood. She felt the urge, the need, to capture everything. Shaken from her malaise in Denver, she now had something to write about. But where to go? Hemingway liked to write in cafés. Maybe she could do as he did and find a café where she could write. Motivated and armed with the materials she needed, she set off to begin her own life as a writer.

17

LILY ARRIVED AT the end of the boulevard Saint-Michel. Her memory of the giant square included overcrowded souvenir shops and student bookstores, and buskers who drew crowds in front of the enormous wall fountain of Saint Michael. Now, men gathered near the bronze statues of the two dragons at the front of the basin. The fountain never failed to impress Lily, who was particularly fond of the red and green marble. But it didn't feel safe to linger; it had been only steps from here that she'd been attacked, and again Lily noticed that there weren't a lot of women hanging around; indeed, a glance revealed only men.

Lily searched for a café. She spied two: one on either side of the sprawling square. The café closest to the Seine was packed with people, both on the terrace and inside, as far as she could tell. Turning, she noticed another tucked away on rue Danton. The terrace was dotted with people enjoying the spring afternoon, their chairs all facing the square as if to watch a show. She chose that one, and pushing open the door was greeted by the warm hubbub of a bustling café. The entry faced the bar, which supported a cluster of men chatting and arguing with the patron. They punctuated their conversation with puffs of smoke from their smelly hand-rolled cigarettes. Manning the counter stood a mustachioed man in an apron. Cheaply framed photographs of sports stars decorated the back bar. The men spoke over each other, the barkeep nodding sagely and refilling their glasses of red wine from an unlabeled bottle. Lily smiled; it was a real neighborhood bar, not one that catered to tourists. Surely this was the kind of joint Hemingway would feel comfortable in.

Passing several couples occupying wooden tables, Lily took a seat near the window at the back of the room. She removed her satchel, draped her jacket on the chair, and got out her pen and her notebook. Enjoying a moment of rest, she gazed out the window at the traffic and people crossing the square. After several minutes, mesmerized by the movement, she returned her attention to the café, looking for inspiration to start her pen moving. The coatrack near the door supported two forlorn umbrellas. Deco glass sconces allowed only a weak light that barely illuminated the corners of the room. She stroked the blank first page in her notebook. It was odd; on one hand, she liked feeling that she was here and not really here, this role of observer so perfect for a writer. On the other, she was acutely aware that she did not belong. She focused on the open page of her notebook. Where to start? She entered the date, European style, at the top of the page. The waiter arrived to take her order, his silver tray propped on his fingers.

"La petite demoiselle désire quoi?"

"A café creme et un verre d'eau, s'il vous plaît."

He moved away, and lulled by the rhythms of the café, Lily let her pen glide over the paper. She was just getting going when a man entered and spoke loudly to the patron behind the bar in a bad French accent. The man shrugged off his coat and hung it at the row of hooks near the door. Was it Hemingway? He looked her way, tossing a newspaper on a table nearby. It wasn't. She quickly lowered her head, nervously smoothing the pages of her notebook. The waiter arrived with her coffee and water and Lily was grateful for the distraction. After a sip of the creamy coffee, she plunged in. Within minutes, she was in the flow, words spilling out of her pen. She wrote, trying to capture the details of everything that had happened. She wrote about the way the air felt in Paris, 1937: thick, dusty. She described the people, detailing Paul's expression when he showed her the magic trick—focused and excited. Finally, she paused when her hand cramped up. She'd filled three pages with her neat handwriting. Sipping her coffee, she glanced around. The man she'd mistaken for Hemingway had finished reading his paper and now sat with an empty glass and an empty expression. The sounds of the café—the espresso machine hissing, the clatter of cup against saucer, the rhythmic flow of French that she didn't understand without focusing on it, all swathed her in a contented state. Shaking out her hand, she continued writing.

No one ever heard of emissions control, so cars and buses burp black plumes as they start, stop, start, and stop again, moving with maddening modernity along the wide boulevards that are, for one little bonus, the same as you remember them.

Being in the past . . . your skin feels funny, like there's an extra layer between you and the world. If you've ever felt like an outcast, a misfit, an outsider, sideliner, nonbelonger, as a time traveler, you've got gut-gripping proof that we are all completely alone in life and sink or swim. Not being born in the current generation gives a constant sense of dislocation—and your mother not being born in that time makes assimilating or even understanding hopeless.

Imagine being inside a TV show, or a vaudeville act, or a movie fully committed to a well-rounded portrait of the past. Everything that's quaint, old-fashioned, nostalgia inducing is actually quite modern. Spiffy and shiny, even. Art nouveau is passé, an outré expression of rebellion overcome by the masculine lines and blocky conviction of art deco. The modern bursts forth in an eruption of shorter skirts, tighter waists, and hats of absurdity only the French could muster with a straight face.

She shook out her hand. When she had tried to write as a girl, she'd been self-conscious of the words on the page. Everything she penned could be seen by someone else—namely, her mother. It wasn't that she went through Lily's things, but Lily didn't feel she had enough privacy to reveal her thoughts. Now, for once the words came with no concern about who would read them. They had no purpose other than for her, right now, suddenly less lonely because of the pages she was filling.

People's skin is different, a pallor that could be city life or malnutrition; with the coming war, food for the masses is dwindling in quality and availability. Every day, every moment is like moving through a spell that's been cast. Sometimes it's not so bad to be clueless about the current events everyone is talking about. It's the dislocation, the dischronation that's disconcerting.

Will you ever see a computer or cell phone again? Will you ever relish the joyful lightness of plastic—plastic pens, compacts, timers, keyboards, bottles, cups? Will you ever feel the freedom of getting a to-go cup of hot coffee wrapped in its little cardboard sheath, and relish the ease of tossing it away? With a desperation heretofore unknown to you, you find yourself craving and loving those very things that you cared so little about.

Everything is heavy; and you, too, lost in a time you used to fantasize about, you, too, are heavy. The objects in this time are made of real substances—metal, glass, wood. The books are bigger, heavier, with sturdy bold type and soldierly spines.

Lily came up for air. The sounds of the café came back into focus: the clink of glasses, the steady rise and fall of friendly arguments among the men at the bar, the hiss of the seltzer bottle. The people at the tables around her had been replaced by different ones; she had no idea how long she'd sat there. A couple was now in the man's place, leaning together and talking urgently over their beers. She dove back in, letting the activity around her fade away.

It's a new level of self-censorship, monitoring everything you say for its appropriateness. You discover, for instance, that you pepper your speech with the word "like" as a way to like what, you are not sure. With the hyperawareness of your words, you put your verbal tic on a short leash and discover that pausing before talking makes you feel smarter.

It's not the inconvenience of all this so much as the floating, the surreal sense that you are not yourself nor anyone else, that you do not and will not ever belong here nor anywhere. It's seeing yourself go through the motions of life as if they mattered. Here you are buying writing supplies. It's seeing yourself lose your life, seeing it and feeling it—like that time your new ruby ring slipped off and sank into the lake just off the edge of the dock, and no matter how much you dove and dove and dove after it, gasping for air, grasping for what you lost so easily—that makes this so weird. Knowing that you were spoiled by your near-perfect life, the ease of it, and that you have become what you would not wish on anyone—a single woman without a family in the path of Hitler's onslaught.

And why here? Why now? If I can travel through time, I'd rather . . . I'd rather be here earlier, or . . . I'd rather go back and see my mom one more time. I didn't know when I left for France that I'd never see her again.

Lily's throat clenched and she blinked several times. The waiter moved among the tables, wiping them down, straightening them. A few people lingered over empty glasses. The clatter of dishes being washed came from behind the bar. She pressed her fingers over the words in her notebook, testing to see if the ink was dry. The waiter paused by her table.

"Autre chose, mademoiselle?" he inquired. Lily asked if they served food. He nodded, telling her they had a few sandwiches left. Lily craved a real meal, something warm and savory, but she ordered a cheese sandwich. It had been hours since her lunch with Paul and she didn't know when she'd eat next. When the sandwich arrived, a tough, chewy baguette with a slice of mild cheese and a slathering of butter, she ate it slowly, considering what she'd written. Back home, she never made time to sit down and write. Now, she had something to write about and she enjoyed the freedom of describing her experience without needing to lie or evade. When she finished the sandwich, she sat back, full and momentarily content. It felt good to write. She stretched, catching a sniff of her blouse. She hadn't changed her clothes. Whoa, she thought. It's time to freshen up. She asked for directions to Printemps, one of the large department stores near the Opéra, and made her way there.

The giant stained-glass dome at the top of the department store glittered in the weak Paris sunlight. The store commanded an entire city block. The few times Lily had tried to find clothes in Paris had been a failure. She knew the sizing system was different, but the clothes seemed to be made for tiny women. Yet women in the 1930s were more buxom, shaped more like her, wide hips and generous bosom.

She entered the giant revolving door and found herself in the accessories department. Gloves fanned brightly on tables and costume jewelry winked from wooden display boxes. The hat department took up a whole side of the floor. There were so many to choose from: felt hats lined with ribbons, sharply sculpted hats, straw hats pinned with bunches of fake flowers.

An atmosphere of refined elegance drifted through the store like a fine perfume. Lily passed the cosmetics department, dotted with vanity tables. She only needed a dress and a few pairs of underwear and she'd be fine until she got home. If she got home.

The clothes weren't arranged as they were in modern department stores. A few mannequins stood around with lots of room in between. It was like a bad party, no one talking, no one connecting. Lily hovered near a mannequin wearing a full-length peach gown.

"Je vous aide?" A thin woman with penciled eyebrows and bright red lips hovered nearby, as if she didn't want to get too close. Lily responded in French. It came out like someone walking up a set of old steps, hesitant and creaky.

"Yes, I'm looking for a comfortable dress."

"For what occasion?"

Lily smirked inside. As if she would have the opportunity for an "occasion." "For everyday wear," she said.

With thinly veiled scorn, the woman pointed a long fingernail toward the corner of the store where steps led to the basement. Lily headed that way, insecurity shadowing her. Surrounded by the elegance, class, and grace of the French, she felt like a farm girl with dung on her shoes. She gathered her imagination around her. Clad in her sparkling shoes, tiara, and flowing peach evening gown, she floated past the woman in the dress department, outshining her in every way.

By the time she got to the basement, her pretend confidence was working. She found clothes that suited the average woman, not someone who dressed frequently for the opera and government cocktail parties. Other women perused the items on the racks, holding up dresses to show their friends.

She paused to inspect a row of long flowing pants with wide bottoms. She held them up against her body. They were too long and a drab shade of gray.

"Je vous aide?"

Another saleswoman. Maybe she did need help. She had no idea what size she wore, how much clothes cost, or what the dressing room policy was.

"Oui. Je cherche une robe."

"Your size?"

"I don't know. I'm American, and we do size differently."

The saleswoman pulled out a cloth tape measure and held it against Lily's hips. It was strange to be touched, even lightly, even in such a professional manner. She stood very still, letting the birdlike pressure on her hip bones sink in. The woman took the tape away.

"I'd say you're a size three. Let's look."

She guided Lily toward a rack. The woman presented dress after dress, then led her to the dressing room. Finally, Lily left wearing a new navy blue dress with a scalloped collar, her old clothes in a shopping bag.

Lily couldn't help but stop in the lingerie department, which mimicked a pastry shop in its color and extravagance. Corsets, garters, and other appliquéd contraptions were layered on tables like almond wafer cookies. Fluffy piles of silk were as tempting as meringue. She hesitated at a table of peach silk panties fanned out, their lace edges rippling like waves. Her fingers stroked a pair, relishing the velvet ribbon. She glanced up and saw a woman she recognized slipping behind the curtain to the changing room. Lily frowned. Was it the woman from the plane? Lily couldn't be sure. It was more of a sense of recognition than actual identification. A saleswoman approached her, and Lily stepped away. She tried on a camisole and a slip. In the end, she bought a few pairs of panties, including a pair of the fancy peach ones.

On her way out, she passed the makeup counter. Even in the thirties, the beauty zone was intimidating. Lily knew nothing about potions and compacts and powders. She'd spent her teenage years under the florescent light of the library, not caring how she looked. She preferred to spend extra time in the morning reading or lying in bed rather than applying makeup. Now, as a grown woman, she was adrift among feminine accoutrements. Still, a lipstick might help her blend in. What was the French word for lipstick?

A salesgirl with a tight roll of curls flanking her cheeks noticed Lily. She strolled over. Her makeup was applied as if she were going onstage, heavy and dramatic. Her bright red lips mouthed something that Lily didn't understand. Lily stammered and blushed.

"J'ai besoin de..." Lily gestured around her lips as if applying lipstick.

"Rouge a levres," the woman filled in. "Suivez-moi."

She led Lily around the maze of counters and displays. At the lipstick tray, she eyed Lily, squinting and surveying her clothes. She inspected Lily's light coloring, her small mouth, the slight dimple in her left cheek. She seemed to be studying a painting or something she wanted to know the secret of. Lily's shoulders relaxed. The woman glanced back and forth between Lily and the palette.

"Voilà!" she exclaimed. She plucked one of the tubes out of the holder. The lipstick was a pinkish brown color, mashed in at the top. The woman dabbed her pinkie into it and approached Lily's face. Lily reared back slightly. People didn't use their fingers at cosmetics counters back home. She was disgusted at the thought of where the woman's fingers had been, what other women's lips she had touched that day. As the woman's finger came closer to her face, Lily surrendered and let her apply the makeup with small, sure dabs. The woman's perfume and minty breath floated over Lily and she relaxed. At home she looked forward to her quarterly haircuts just to feel the stylist's fingers working the shampoo through her hair, hosing the warm water over her head. She might need to get a haircut here, merely for the feel of someone's hands on her head.

When Lily was a girl, her mother liked to fix her hair. Lily would fall into a sort of trance, her thoughts melting away with the strokes of the brush on her head. She'd hated the way her hair tangled and her mother worked the knots out, but she'd give anything for a second of her mother's attention now.

Claire Heller, dressed in her gardening clothes, stood at Lily's shoulder. "Do you really need lipstick? Shouldn't you be saving your money for food? You never wore lipstick at home."

Lily shook the thought off, talking back in her mind. *I'm not at home, am I? I'm in France, and I'm older now, and I want a lipstick.*

The woman finished with the lipstick and stepped back. She squinted at Lily, nodding with satisfaction. Lily felt like a living canvas, there merely for the woman to ponder. The woman handed Lily a heavy art deco hand mirror lined in silver. Lily regarded her face, pursing her lips, kissing the air. Her mother's face looked back at her. With the lipstick, she was transformed, more mature. Lily's mother had given Lily her delicate features, though she'd kept her blond hair to herself. A wave of goose bumps passed down her spine.

"Ça vous va?"

She continued to stare into the mirror, pressing her new lips together before nodding. If her mother didn't care for lipstick, she knew both her mother and father would be proud of her resourcefulness.

For a year after her mother's death, Lily had lived in Chicago with her father. In an attempt to get away from the grief that haunted them both, Lily moved to Denver after several months, leaving her father to carve out a life with his new girlfriend, Monique. Her mother's garden fell into ruin, and when Lily came for her first visit she cried at the desiccated rose bushes and wilting lilac trees. The backyard was the same sad scenario, and when she saw the brown beds where flowers had once bloomed, she yelled, "Why don't you just sell the house?"

"I have," he said, glancing at Monique, who had accompanied him to the airport to pick Lily up. "That's why I wanted you to come. You'll have to clear out your room. You can have whatever you want from the house."

Lily slumped onto a chair at the kitchen table. She wanted the whole house, the way it was when she had left for France. With her mother in it, not some woman who wore artfully applied makeup and pastel sweater sets. She scanned the kitchen, seeing the scene as a soon-to-be extinct ecosystem. The appliances lined the back counter: coffee grinder, blender, food processor, toaster oven. She wondered how much her father used them. Monique wasn't the homey type. The house already felt different now that she knew it would be hosting another family's petty squabbles and dinner smells.

Lily expected her mother to emerge from the pantry with a stack of cans for dinner. She loved making casseroles, challenging herself to see how many cans she could use—green beans, diced tomatoes, chicken broth, and tuna—for a strange, quasi-

Italian casserole. During the months after her mother died, Lily had spent most of her time engrossed in cookbooks and recipes, cooking her way out of her grief.

Standing at the wine rack, choosing a bottle, her father spoke. "It's hard for me, too." "Would you like some wine?" He stabbed the corkscrew into the cork.

Lily took down two wine glasses and set them on the tiled counter between them.

"Lily, in case you didn't notice, *you're* not the one surrounded by the memories. You don't have to walk by her closet every day and know she'll never wear those stupid gardening clogs again." He poured the wine. "You haven't seen the garden slowly rot and thought…" He stopped, unable to finish the thought.

She handed his glass to him and they toasted. The cabernet was an attack, the first taste sharp and tough. She sat down at the kitchen table. Her dad joined her, bringing the bottle. His chair moved across the tile with the familiar squealing sound. They took tentative steps toward discussing their new lives without the house. He told her about a penthouse suite he had seen and liked. With his busy work schedule at the stock exchange, a condo would be easier to maintain. Lily wanted to ask if Monique was moving in with him, though she didn't want to think about her father as an eligible bachelor with new prospects. He could get a new wife but Lily couldn't get a new mother.

"I've got to start packing up your mother's belongings. I was hoping you could help. You might want to take some of her things."

Lily didn't want to go through her mother's things. It was an invasion of such a private person. Yet she didn't want Monique in there with her red fingernails.

"Of course," she said.

They ordered a feast from Thai Palace—spring rolls, jungle curry, pad Thai, extra spicy with prawns, and tofu plus mango rice for dessert. After dinner, Lily went upstairs to bed. At the top of the stairs she went into her parents' room. On the nightstand by her mother's side were a pair of reading glasses and a trashy paperback that surely wasn't her father's. So Monique was staying here. She stepped past the bed and into her mother's walk-in closet. Nothing had changed here, the rarely worn heels propped on the back shoe racks, the dresses sheathed in plastic from the dry cleaner's. The scent of her mother lingered. A garden scent—essence of rose paired with the crumbly smell of dirt, with a tickle of sharp fertilizer. The clothes she wore all the time—the chinos and jeans, the oversized plaid shirts—were at the front, ready to be released from the hangers, ready to head down to the backyard. Lily brushed a hand along the sleeves and suppressed an impulse to press her face against them.

She turned to a chest of drawers that had been there forever. She'd always wanted to know what her mother kept there. The top drawer held an assortment of accessories: a pair of gold square cuff links lying against each other, a collection of white jewelry boxes, a few small handkerchiefs embroidered at the edges. The kind of things she'd never seen on her mother or her father.

She pulled the drawer open further, rooting around the back. Behind the stack of hankies was tucked a blue velvet jewelry box. Inside, a ring nestled in the cleft—an opal sitting in a crowned gold setting. It fit her left ring finger perfectly. She spread her fingers and held her hand away from her, winging it back and forth. The colors in the ring pulsated with each movement—first pink, then green, then a shimmering blue. Lily had never seen this on her mother—ever.

Backing out of the closet slowly, she headed to her own room. The bed and dresser seemed smaller. The months she stayed here after her mother died had left no trace. But it was still her room. She searched for things she might want to bring back to Denver: the framed Renoir poster, the thick pink rug. The ugly dresser and too-small desk did not interest her. At the window, she looked out into the backyard.

Her mother used to joke that she wanted to be buried under the lilac bushes that formed a hedge around their backyard. She'd pull her Adirondack chair over to them in May and sit there, soaking up their scent and delicate petals. Lily watched from her bedroom window. Her mother's face would soften, finally, into something like love. Her eyes would close, as if she were listening to an exquisite piece of music from far away and deep inside her. Lily wanted to pull up next to her mother, to sit at her knees and rest her head on her leg. She contented herself with watching from the window.

Another time, she had lingered nearby while her mother crouched in the vegetable patch, arranging mulch around the leafy basil plants. With her folded legs splayed out to the side, she looked like a large insect. Lily sat nearby, under the oak tree with a book. She was reading a short story about a man who had a shoe fetish. She wanted to rename the character but didn't know what name to give him. All the ones she tried, Harvé, Pierre, Mack, didn't work.

"Mom, how did you give me my name?"

Her mother paused, her trowel dangling from her hand, staring into the tiny purple and white flowers on the basil leaves. "It was early spring and you were about to come," she said. "I didn't have a name for you. I was so desperate for my garden, for the green, that I'd lie awake at night going through the flowers in my mind. I would catalogue them and go over their ideal conditions, what they signified, and what time of the year they bloomed. It was a garden in my mind. I made up a contest—best flower. I gave categories, and went through all of them. Each one won a prize for something or other. And when I came to lily, it won the prize for most elegant flower, most noble." She paused, sitting back on the ground by the tomato cages. Lily realized how her mother got the mud flap impressions on her jeans.

"Suddenly it was clear—the name for you was Lily. It bloomed right there in front of me. Everything I wanted for you was contained in that name—elegance, class, beauty, fragility."

"Fragility? Why would you want that for your daughter?"

Her mother broke off a stem of basil. "So you'd always remember how precious life is." She sniffed the basil, her eyes closed, a look of ecstasy smoothing her face.

"Well, I don't think I'm any of those things." Lily felt anything but elegant in her tank top and running shorts. She felt like an oaf, clunky and clumsy. But she favored her mother's features: the reddish-blond hair, the round face, the small lips and chin. She was her mother now, or as close as she would get.

"Oh, but you are. You just don't know it. You'll see it someday, trust me."

Lily pulled herself away from the window and headed for a shower. It was easy to cry under the water, her sobs masked by the flow.

The next morning she and her father were in the closet, packing her mother's clothes into a big box. Every time she moved, she snuck a look at the ring.

"I see you found that," he said.

She held her hand out, admiring it. She liked to think her mother had some sense of femininity, that even if she didn't wear the ring, she at least had it.

"I love it. Would you mind if I take it?"

"Not at all. It was your grandmother's."

"Why didn't Mom wear it?"

"I don't know. Probably because of the gardening."

They continued folding the clothes without speaking much, Lily's mother in between every fold, every decision. Lily was sick at the thought of her mother's clothes being worn by some poor stranger who shopped at thrift stores. She struggled to not cry but tears blurred her vision. The ring kept catching her eye, filling her with its color.

"Did Mom get along with her mother?"

Her father knelt at the shoes.

"She was estranged from her family. They had an argument when Claire was in college and never really reconciled. She was a good woman, your grandmother, but a bit 'out there.' Always reading books. You get that from her."

Lily liked that she was wearing a book lover's ring. It belonged to her.

"Your mother loved you, you know."

"Dad. She loved her garden."

"Lily, don't."

Lily yanked a couple of flannel shirts off their hangers, rolled them up, and threw them in the box. She just wanted to be finished with the folding up of her mother's life.

"She loved you very much and she gave up her dream to have you."

"What dream?"

Her father stuck his hand into a black dress shoe. It was new; Lily had never seen her mother wearing it. He put the shoe and its twin in the box with the other shoes.

"She was a brilliant student at Princeton. She wanted to be a biologist, and I think she could have done it."

"But she married you instead and became a wife."

He flinched slightly and kept packing the shoes.

"So she gave up her dream for you, not for me," Lily continued.

"She gave it up for both of us."

Lily had reached the end of the rack. The wall that had been hidden behind the clothes held a wisp of cobwebs. Lily stared at it, hoping a pattern would appear and reveal something about her mother. She closed the lid on the box.

"Was she ever happy?"

"She was happy in her garden. She had that."

"Are you happy?"

He closed his box. The closet was now off balance, filled with his suits and dress shoes on one side, empty and haunted on the other side. They only had the dresser and the gardening shed to clear out, and that was it. So much for a life, Lily thought.

"I'm as happy as one can expect to be."

Lily dragged the box out of the closet. "Come on. I want more than that. That's just settling," she huffed.

"Well, are you happy?"

Lily thought about her job at the bookstore, her apartment, her cat. "No," she said.

18

LILY HAD STASHED the bag with her old clothes at Paul's. She'd slipped in without being seen by his mother, but she didn't feel comfortable lingering there in the daytime. Feeling fresh in her new dress, she made her way to the bookstore for the reading. She hurried through the dark city, fueled by nervous anticipation. She arrived early, too early. The shop wasn't open, though a light glowed dimly from inside. It wasn't cold but the air just after dusk didn't feel hospitable, either. Lily lurked in the shadow of a doorway across the street, adjusting her dress. She remembered her lipstick and applied it without a mirror. She could not be any more prepared to confront Sylvia Beach, to insist that she be allowed access to the reading. Dozens of arguments caromed in her mind. She stamped her feet against the chill, bouncing lightly like a boxer waiting to duck into the ring. Down at the theater end, Lily glimpsed a sudden movement. It had happened so fast she might not have seen anything at all.

But no, there it was, the form of a man outlined in the light that poured from a large doorway. One by one, others joined him, chatting and laughing. The group coalesced, the door slammed shut behind them, and they moved down the street. Their voices preceded them, one American loudly booming, "There, now, Syl, you don't really need me yammering away up there, do you?" This followed by a familiar British voice, "Oh, yes, she does, my friend." The group approached the bookshop and finally Lily could pick them out: Sylvia, even shorter than Lily had remembered, especially dwarfed by the man looming next to her: Ernest Hemingway. Then Adrienne Monnier, wearing her long blue dress and a patient smile. And finally, arms spread as if shepherding them all down the sidewalk, Lily's rescuer, Stephen Spender, wearing a look of bemused tolerance. They paused at the shop's entry. A cluster of people lingered on the sidewalk nearby, chatting and smoking. From across the street, Lily heard Hemingway. He tilted his head, his hat making a jaunty angle, and asked Sylvia, "Say, what have you got for hooch?"

Sylvia tsked and drew away from him. "I'm running a bookstore, not a bar. And surely you had enough Irish courage at dinner?" She smiled despite her stern tone. Lily slipped across the street and lingered near the others out front. From here she could better hear Sylvia's conversation. Hemingway peered inside the shop, then around the street. For a second Lily thought he paused when he caught her watching, but it was hard to tell where he was looking; the brim of his hat shaded his face. He focused on Sylvia.

"Say, I'll be back. Come get me when it's time?"

"Oh, you!" Sylvia mock-slapped his arm. But Hemingway slipped away, headed toward the boulevard. Sylvia turned to

Adrienne and spoke in French.

"I'm not going to be able to go get him. I knew this was a bad idea. He's going to need minding, isn't he?"

"Don't worry," Adrienne replied. "Tout ira bien." She ushered Sylvia into the shop, and Spender followed. Lily caught Sylvia's response to Adrienne. "I'm not so sure everything will be fine. I've never seen him this wrecked. What am I going to do to keep him calm?" The door shut behind them, the bell muffled.

Lily exhaled, unaware that she'd been holding her breath. She inched past two men and two women who were having an animated conversation in English. "Well, the Spanish didn't change him any," one of the men said. "Last night I saw him at Cloiserie, and he was nattering on about a fight with a Spanish nationalist sympathizer."

"That's our Hem," one of the women said. "Always the hero."

Lily loitered outside with the tiny crowd that grew with every minute. She'd missed her chance, she chided herself. She should have approached Sylvia before she went inside. Clutching the strap of her bag, she paced out of Sylvia's sight. After a few minutes, Sylvia opened the door, propping it with a doorstop shaped like a book. People tossed their cigarettes to the gutter and entered the shop. Lily reluctantly joined the queue that trickled from the door onto the sidewalk. From the back of the line, Lily could see Sylvia inside the entry, greeting people with *bises* and smiles. Adrienne moved about, turning on lights, straightening chairs. The line of people slowly advanced onto the steps, over the threshold, and into the shop. Lily fingered the ticket in her jacket pocket. What if Sylvia refused her?

Each step made her more nervous. She tried to distract herself by surreptitiously studying the couple in front of her. They were American, and nattily dressed. It took Lily a few minutes to realize that the man and woman were actually both women, but one was dressed in a man's suit and hat. Peering closer at the person under the top hat, Lily thought she recognized the mannish face with a prominent nose. The woman looked like Janet Flanner, *The New Yorker* correspondent who wrote a column called "Letter from Paris". Lily edged closer and tried to eavesdrop but Janet—if it was indeed her—was engaged in conversation with her friend, a younger woman with strawberry-colored hair and an easy laugh. Lily had read Flanner's missives from Paris; she'd introduced American readers to artists, writers, and notables in Paris, including Sylvia Beach. Her essays inspired Lily, who hoped to write about Paris life someday. This brush with literary fame distracted her enough to make the last few steps to Sylvia bearable. Lily watched while Sylvia greeted the women warmly, calling Janet's companion, Martha, and mentioning something about reporting on the civil war in Spain.

At last the women moved to their seats and Lily was face-to-face with Sylvia. Looking up from the clipboard, Sylvia recognized Lily and sighed.

"Hello," Lily said.

"You're back. You are an intrusive one, aren't you?" She peered around Lily, who sensed a crowd gathering behind her.

"I'm sorry, I just really want to be here. I'm dying to hear Hemingway read. I want to help, too. Can I some move chairs or something?"

"We already have the chairs set up. I don't think we need your help."

"Please!" Lily made a desperate attempt, suddenly grabbing Sylvia's arm. Sylvia recoiled and Lily whispered again, "Please!" Several people who had taken their seats stared at the spectacle.

Adrienne approached, her back to the audience. "Who is this girl?" she asked in French.

Sylvia shook Lily off and replied, "Just a crazy American."

"Come on!" Lily pulled herself upright. "Why be stubborn? I can help. I'll do whatever you need."

The foursome from outside had wandered in and chatted near the door. Sylvia glanced at them, then at Lily.

"No is no. Please, leave now. You're obstructing the entry and disturbing my guests." Sylvia turned her attention to the people behind Lily, welcoming them with a warm smile. Lily had no choice but to step back and out of the shop, shamed in the worst possible way—by her heroine, by not being on "the list."

Outside, she balled her fists and shook them at her sides. "Ack!" she cried out, startling a woman waiting to get in. There was still a group queuing on the sidewalk. A large green car glided up the street. It was a limousine. The driver stopped, got out, and opened the back door with a bow. An older woman with an aristocratic demeanor emerged, the netting on her hat subtly glittering, her spring jacket buttoned around her considerable bulk. With a slight nod to the driver, she approached the bookstore, and, passing the queue, entered. Whispered questions about her rippled through the crowd and Lily thought she heard the name "Rubenstein."

Lily couldn't imagine how they were all going to fit inside. Sylvia wasn't kidding when she said the reading was sold out.

But she wasn't going to be turned away. She had to get in. The ticket in her pocket wasn't there by chance. Lily joined the line again, crafting her next approach. When she was again facing Sylvia, she spoke quickly and quietly.

"Sylvia. Where's Hemingway? He's not even here and you're supposed to start in a few minutes." Sylvia regarded Lily with her bright blue eyes. Lily saw a flash of panic cross her face. She spoke up. "I'll go get him for you. You need to stay here; I can bring him back and the reading can start."

Sylvia sighed with exasperation. "I don't need you to—"

A crash came from behind the shop curtain, followed by a curse muttered loudly in French. Sylvia glanced toward the curtain, as did everyone in the nearly full room.

"Darn students, trying to come in the back way," Sylvia said. She turned back to Lily. "Fine! All right! Go. Get Hemingway. He's probably at the Danton. But don't think that guarantees you a spot at the reading. We're still full."

"Yes, ma'am," Lily said.

Sylvia repeated impatiently. "Go," she said.

"Thank you," Lily said. Sylvia waved her away and hurried to the back to investigate the crash.

19

OUTSIDE, LILY INHALED the crisp night air. She hadn't ma'amed anyone for years, if ever. But she liked the idea of being Sylvia's errand girl. She wondered how drunk Hemingway had managed to get before the reading. She made herself tipsy with a fantasy of befriending the great writer. She hurried to the corner, on a mission to get her friend Hem. He counted on her to help him with these kinds of events. After the reading, they'd go together with friends for drinks and she'd get him to reveal his editing secrets. He'd share his writing tips, encouraging her efforts. She'd blossom under his tutelage and become a famous writer in her own right.

At the door of the café, she saw him immediately, surrounded by a couple of admirers. He leaned on the bar, his foot propped on the railing near the floor. He wore a brown suit complete with vest. His cropped hair, ruddy cheeks, and smiling eyes drew Lily toward him. He drank beer from a mug and spoke to the man next to him. Lily hovered nearby, listening. He recounted a story in which he was helping a young Spanish couple whose mule had collapsed. The short man next to him laughed and leaned in to catch every word. Lily inched closer, drawn to the story, forgetting her mission. Hemingway finished with a loud clap signifying the death of the mule. The men laughed loudly. Hemingway waved toward the bartender and shouted, "Patron! La même chose!" Lily approached and stepped into his line of vision.

"Excuse me," she said.

Hem regarded her with interest. "Hello there," he said, sweetening his tone.

"Sylvia sent me to get you. The reading is in a few minutes."

He frowned. "Damn! I was trying to forget all about that."

The next round arrived. "What're you drinking?" He eyed Lily as he said this, taking in her face, her figure. She felt inspected, researched as if for a character in one of his stories.

"I'm not drinking anything, and neither should you. We have to go! Sylvia's waiting. And the audience who came to hear you."

"You had to mention that." He sipped from the fresh beer. The man with him chuckled and winked at Lily.

"I don't mean to be pushy, but Sylvia is counting on you. And she's counting on me to bring you to the shop."

He set the beer down. "Listen, dollface." He towered over her. His eyes were warm and friendly despite his tone. "Let me tell you one thing you gotta learn in life. A woman should never pry a man away from his drink."

Lily laughed. She wanted a drink, something fancy and French. She wanted to stay here all night with Hemingway, basking in his glow. But she had a job to do and it had to be past nine o'clock by now.

"Okay, tit for tat. Let me tell you one thing."

Now both men were looking at her.

"Perhaps you're accustomed to making women wait. But Sylvia Beach is not a woman to be kept waiting."

"Right you are!" He slammed his fist down, then finished his beer in one gulp. "It's nerves, that's all. No disrespect meant for Sylvia." He threw some coins on the counter. "Hasta la vista, Robert!" he yelled to his friend, who was right in front of him.

They left the café. Lily couldn't believe she was escorting Ernest Hemingway. He stepped into a *tabac* while Lily waited outside. She thought about *The Old Man and the Sea*. Here she was with the man who had written it, before he had written it. For some reason this bolstered her courage.

Hemingway burst out the door, holding a lighter to a cigarette. He moved like a ship steering through a storm—tilting first this way, then that way. Clutching his cigarette in one hand, he gripped his hat on his head as if protecting it against a gale wind. Lily scooted along behind him like a tugboat. He was talking, but she couldn't tell if he was speaking to her or to himself. She caught up to him, pacing herself so she was at his elbow.

"What did you say?" she asked.

"I said, I don't know why I agreed to do this."

"What's the big deal?"

He pulled up short and took a drag from his cigarette. They were a few doors away from the shop. A group of people lingered at the doorway, waiting to get in.

"'What's the big deal?' Have you ever read your stories to a group of snippety Parisian assholes?"

Lily laughed. She had never heard the word snippety. "No,

I haven't."

"Well, then, who are you to talk?" he said. She couldn't believe that Mr. Bravado, Mr. Ambulance Driver, Mr. Hunter of the Wilds was afraid to read in public.

"Oh, just suck it up," she told his back.

He glanced over his shoulder. "Suck what up?"

"Get over it," she replied. "Get over your big bad self."

He smiled. "You are one weird bird," he said.

"What are you reading from tonight?"

"The latest. *To Have and Have Not.*"

Lily didn't know it. But now that she'd met him, she wanted to read everything he wrote. And confront him about his womanizing.

They arrived at the shop. Sylvia hovered near the threshold.

"Hem!" she called. "Get in here!"

He tossed his cigarette aside and went in. Lily followed and Sylvia, with a slight shake of her head, let her pass. A chorus of voices filled the space, crowding out the books and shrinking the space in the shop. A buzz of anticipation circulated through the room and Lily caught her breath as she was pulled into the excitement. Several younger people sat on stools near the front. Spender calmly surveyed the scene from the front of the room. He saw Lily with Hemingway at the door and winked. She smiled back.

Lily lingered out of the way near the fiction section, watching the literati trickle in. Most of them were older than her. There were a lot of men speaking French, and Lily knew that if they wore name tags, she'd recognize some of France's most famous writers. Sylvia and Adrienne welcomed the last guests.

They laughed and chatted but Lily could tell that Sylvia was anxious by the way she gripped the clipboard to her chest like a breastplate. She scanned the crowd.

A man wearing a shabby white suit and thick glasses entered with a sad-looking woman. They greeted Sylvia coolly. She returned the man's hello and smiled warmly at his wife. As he made his way to his seat, Lily realized it was James Joyce. He appeared skinny and sickly, but carried himself like someone important. Taking a seat near the back, he removed a tiny book from his jacket pocket and proceeded to read, ignoring his wife. Spender reappeared and Sylvia pulled him aside, pointing to the readers' table. Hemingway moved along the side of the crowd toward Spender. The pitch of conversation rose with the heat. A bouquet of perfumes produced an almost visible cloud above the crowd, not quite masking the body odor. The women wore neat bobs and heavy makeup. Many were adorned with tiny swaths of fur, a bit of trim on a wrist, a bit wrapping a neck. The men all wore suits and held their hats in their laps.

A group near the back was especially exuberant. The woman in the middle threw her head back, laughing with the man next to her. She wore a burgundy velvet jacket trimmed in some kind of black fur with a jaunty matching cap. The brooch pinned to her jacket caught Lily's eye. Lily had the feeling she had seen that woman before. She looked like the woman on the plane, the one who had offered her tea and poetry. Was it? How could it be possible? Lily held still, trying to grasp it.

The heat in the room overcame Lily. She fell back, pushing over a rack of magazines with a loud clatter. Sylvia glared at her as Lily quickly righted the rack. The noise brought the rest of the chatter in the room to a halt as everybody looked at Lily. Heat rose up around Lily's neck like a ruff. The woman studied her a second longer than the rest of her friends, her eyes narrowing. A shiver of certainty passed through Lily. This woman recognized her. No doubt about it, she was the woman from the plane. The man next to her also inspected Lily. The thin mustache above his lips twitched when he smiled. He winked and gave a series of nods like they were agreeing on something together. Lily frowned. She averted her eyes, desperately trying to get the attention of the woman sitting next to him. She had to speak to her. She started forward, but Sylvia assumed her position in front of the room. Lily clenched her fists and held her ground.

"Welcome, friends," Sylvia began. Just as she spoke, two more people squeezed in, taking up positions near Lily. They removed their hats and she took them in: two handsome men, well dressed, one wearing a thin mustache, the other blond and tall. The tall man peered at Lily and gave a slight nod, which made her glance away nervously. She tried to pay attention to Sylvia, whose voice, though authoritative, did not carry over the audience. Lily could barely make out what she was saying. Spender and Hemingway had seated themselves at the table. Hemingway sweated visibly, his forehead damp. Spender maintained his calm. Both of the men had books in front of them, and Spender held a sheaf of papers. A bottle of whiskey stood on the table. From what she could gather, Hemingway would read first. Sylvia gave an introduction, mentioning the books he had published, his place on the frontier of the short story. As she spoke, Sylvia gazed at Hemingway with a soft expression and a sweet smile. She finished her introduction and the room broke into applause. Hemingway rose, offered a slight bow, and resumed his seat. Clearing his throat, he picked up a thin book and coughed. He began talking about writing and war and what it was like to write in a fascist country. Finally, he flipped through the pages and plunged in.

> I took a quick one out of the first bottle I saw open and I couldn't tell you yet what it was. The whole thing made me feel pretty bad. I slipped along behind the bar and out through the kitchen in back and all the way out. . . .

Lily tried to focus on his words, acutely aware of the man next to her. His height emphasized his formal posture. He held himself very alert during the reading as if tasting every word, digesting every sensation Hemingway described. She risked a peek. He was quite handsome, his sculpted face focused in a look of concentration. He glanced down at Lily and raised one of his shaggy eyebrows. Blushing, Lily glanced away. A woman in the middle of the row cupped her hand around her red-lipsticked mouth and called out, "Louder, please, sir." Hemingway looked up, startled that someone had interrupted him. He cleared his throat, pulled himself up in his chair, and continued. This time he spoke as he had in the bar, loud and strong.

The presence of Sylvia and the woman from the plane, the tall man standing so close to her, all made it difficult for Lily to pay attention. The exploits of a Florida smuggler and his gangster friends were distant and uninteresting. Joyce wore a look of studied boredom. The genius was bored. Of course, Lily thought. The other people in the audience appeared engrossed in Hemingway's words. The only sound in the room was his voice, now projected with an air of authority.

Lily's impatience overrode her ability to listen. It wouldn't be long before she could corner the woman from the plane and get answers to her questions: What was the woman doing here? How had she, Lily, gotten to this era? And above all, how was Lily to get home?

When Hemingway finished, the audience clapped and he gave a tidy bow, then reached for the whiskey bottle. Spender adjusted his ascot again, preparing for his turn. The audience took the opportunity to stretch as delicately as one could in suits and furs. Joyce rose with a jerky movement and scooted past the knees in his row. Without a glance at anyone, he left the shop and slipped into the night. How rude, Lily thought. A hurt look passed over Sylvia's face. Lily checked to see how the man beside her reacted. He scanned the room as if taking roll call of the guests. Sylvia squelched the murmurs of the audience to begin her introduction of Stephen Spender.

"Thank you very much, Ernest," she said. "Your reading was enjoyed by all, I am sure."

"Not Mr. Joyce," Hemingway replied. He tossed back the whiskey.

"Well, then. Perhaps you inspired him to rush home and write." The audience tittered. Sylvia continued with the introduction.

"Now I have the pleasure of welcoming a young talent. He is one of Britain's up-and-coming poets. He, like Mr. Hemingway, was also in Spain during these last months of the war, so we are very grateful to have him here tonight. Without further ado, I present to you Stephen Spender."

The audience clapped politely, gloved taps muffled among more assertive applause by the men. Spender cleared his throat and picked up a sheaf of papers. He had the most incredibly sculpted lips Lily had ever seen. His blue eyes shone as if glossed with tears.

"I have prepared a few poems for tonight," he began. His formal British accent contrasted sharply with Hemingway's casual American diction. He proceeded to read. Lily listened to see if she recognized the poem the woman had read to her on the plane, but none were familiar. She stared at the woman, letting the poet's voice lull her.

A wave of applause snapped Lily out of her daze. The handsome man next to her had removed a small notebook from his jacket and had taken notes during Spender's reading. That's odd, Lily thought. Who would take notes on poems? After Spender finished, the applause faded and the audience broke apart, standing and pushing chairs aside, calling to friends across the room, reaching into purses and pockets for cigarettes. Sylvia bustled around the table where Hemingway and Spender had been positioned for the reading. Placing trays on the table, Sylvia transformed it into a buffet for the reception. Lily peeked at the woman from the plane, who was chatting with the man next to her. Lily pressed her way through the crowd toward Sylvia. She reached the table just as the man who'd been taking notes greeted Sylvia. Lily lingered nearby, but couldn't hear what they were saying. The man appeared to be questioning Sylvia and though she remained polite, it didn't seem that Sylvia was giving him answers. Lily thought the man spoke with a German accent. After a moment of conversation, he left, glancing at Lily as he passed. Sylvia resumed her task of situating a tray of small glasses.

"Please, can I help?"

Sylvia sighed. "You again!"

Just then Spender, who'd been signing a book for a woman nearby, caught sight of Lily. "You again!" he cried, but his tone was far different than Sylvia's exasperated one. Lily brightened.

"Hello," she said. "I loved your reading."

Spender mock-bowed. "I'm glad it's over," he confessed.

Sylvia put her hand on his sleeve. "It wasn't so awful, was it? How do you two know each other?" She raised an eyebrow at Lily.

Lily threw a desperate look at Spender, but he just smiled. "Oh, mutual acquaintances, isn't that so . . ."

"Lily," she rushed to insert.

"Yes, of course, Lily. We've forgotten how we met. No matter." He smiled again but Sylvia didn't appear convinced. She nodded toward Lily.

"She insists upon helping me."

Spender shrugged. "Well, then, why not let her lend a hand? Why refuse help so graciously offered? You certainly can use it."

Sylvia threw up her hands. "Fine. Quick, then, fold up these chairs so there's room for the reception." Turning back to the table, she added, "But leave a few in place."

"Of course. Done." Lily said. To Spender, she whispered, "Thank you!"

Moving through the aisles, she folded the small wooden chairs and stacked them against the wall in the tiny alcove at the back of the shop. The room was dark, unused bookshelves towering in the small space. She made out a cot and small sink. But there was no time to dawdle, for now Sylvia was calling her to help serve the guests. In that way Lily became the unofficial, and unqualified, bartender. Sylvia was serving cheap white wine from unmarked bottles and small bowls of nuts. Clusters of French men lingered nearby, discussing the authors and their own publishing efforts.

Lily greeted and served Paris's literati, filling the tiny glasses and passing them out as fast as she could. She knew she was among some of the great modern writers but luckily did not recognize them by sight. If she knew exactly who they were, she might be too tongue-tied to even smile. Flushed with activity, she had just replenished the wine from a wooden crate in the back when she turned and found herself facing the woman from the plane.

"A glass of wine, please." The woman spoke as if she had never met Lily.

"Hello again," Lily replied. The woman cast a bored glance around the room.

"Don't I know you?" Lily pressed. "I mean . . ." She lowered her voice and leaned across the table, handing the woman her wine. "Didn't we sit next to each other on the plane?"

The woman pulled back, taking her wine to her lips before responding. The din of the crowd rose.

"I'm afraid I don't know what you mean." She made as if to move away.

"Wait!" Lily threw her arm out to stop her. "I need to talk to you."

But the woman slipped into the crowd, the little face of the fox on her stole the last thing Lily saw before she lost sight of her. "But, but—" Lily sputtered, trapped at the table, able only to watch the party from the sidelines.

A man came over for a drink. It was the woman's companion. Up close, he was familiar to Lily, but she wasn't sure how.

"Hello there," he smiled. He was tall and much older than she had thought. He had dark green eyes and a saucy expression.

"Allow me to introduce myself. I'm Harold Pindale."

He presented his hand. Lily took it and he flipped his wrist and hovered his lips over her hand. He leaned forward, giving her a faux seductive look. His mustache tickled her hand as he brought his lips to it and planted a firm but delicate kiss on her hand.

"I see you've found the only girl in Paris who doesn't know your tricks," a woman's voice interrupted. She had returned without Lily noticing. Lily tried to pull her hand away but Harold held on.

"Oh, no, my dear," he said. "This is a new friend. This is—"

"Lily." She yanked her hand away. "And you?" she asked, turning to the woman.

Her eyes, small like a cat's, narrowed. "Louise," she replied.

"Didn't we meet on the trip over?" Lily insisted.

"I don't think so. Harold, let's go."

They moved toward Hemingway, who was recounting a story to Janet Flanner and her companion. The young woman leaned close to Hemingway, and when they laughed together it was clear they'd already done a lot of laughing already. Spender spoke with a French man nearby clutching a book to his chest. The rest of the audience had left and only a few remained, saying good-byes to Sylvia at the door.

Confused by the brush-off, Lily considered following Louise. She was certain it was the woman from the plane, and she couldn't lose her only lead. Now, Louise and Spender were engrossed in conversation. Lily abandoned the drinks table and hovered near the group that formed around Sylvia. The woman who'd arrived in the limo mentioned wanting to do a reading of her own poetry at the shop. Sylvia nodded politely and caught Lily's eye.

Sylvia excused herself from the conversation. She grasped Lily's elbow and steered her away from the group. "Thank God," she muttered. Lily was pleased to be singled out. "Miss Rubenstein can be quite persistent."

Lily laughed. That was Helena Rubenstein? Lily shook herself. She couldn't get distracted by celebrities. Sylvia and Lily stopped by the front desk.

"Thank you for your help. I hate to say you were right, but I will. It was useful to have you here."

"But it's a pleasure to help you. It's easy," Lily said.

"I'd like to talk to you. I have an idea. How long will you be in Paris?"

Lily didn't know how to answer. "I'm here . . . indefinitely," she said.

Sylvia asked if Lily could come by the next day, mentioning a proposition. Lily couldn't believe it. Her usefulness had paid off. Sylvia wanted to offer her something—maybe a job. Lily nodded eagerly. They arranged to meet and Sylvia returned to her guests. Lily watched the bookseller hug a flushed Hemingway. Lily wanted to talk to the famous author, but she needed to stick with Louise. She searched the room, but Louise must have left while she was talking to Sylvia. She had lost her chance. Lily grabbed her bag from where she had tucked it behind the magazine racks and rushed out. Outside, most of the people from the reading had dispersed. Across the street, a woman entered a cab. When she turned her head toward the driver, Lily saw that it was Louise. She leaped forward, but the cab driver gunned away. Lily swore under her breath, distraught to have lost her. Shivering, she wondered if she should go back inside to help Sylvia break down the party. Just then, Paul stepped from the shadows across the street.

"Lily! There you are!"

She'd completely forgotten that Paul had planned to pick her up from the reading. A flush of relief passed through her. Paul looked so much younger than the people at the reading, and for all their erudition and savvy, she was more comfortable with him. They strolled back to the hotel and Lily recounted the highlights: fetching Hemingway, seeing Janet Flanner, and finally, having a meeting with Sylvia. He listened and seemed happy for her successes. At the hotel, they went through the now-familiar ritual. He handed her the keys and went back to the desk while she ascended to the room she now considered comforting.

20

THE NEXT MORNING, Lily hurried through an overcast Paris toward Shakespeare and Company. The façade, the door, and the scent of the shop were all becoming familiar. She hurried in, excited to see Sylvia. Inside the shop, a woman in a gold tweed jacket spoke with Sylvia near her desk. Holding a stack of books, Sylvia greeted Lily, asking her to wait. Teddy thrust his nose into Lily's hand and leaned against her leg, his paw pressing into Lily's foot. Smiling, she patted his side. This somehow helped her breathe easier.

The air in the shop retained a whiff of the night before, the reading leaving an invisible but perceptible mark. The tables replaced the chairs, and were once again piled high with books. A tiny vase of daffodils adorned Sylvia's desk. Lily browsed the displays and came upon a stack of James Joyce's *Ulysses*. She knew how important this book was for Sylvia. She had made a lot of sacrifices to publish it, pushing her business toward bankruptcy. Lily also remembered the paltry gratitude Joyce had shown Sylvia afterward. She opened to a random page but couldn't concentrate on the text.

Instead, she fantasized about a future at Sylvia's side. In this other reality, she managed to make her way through the entire book, and to her surprise, she not only understood it, she liked the modernist masterpiece. She and Sylvia had long discussions about the text, about the choices Joyce had made with language. Sylvia showed her some of the printer's proofs, where Joyce had blacked out certain lines and scribbled new ones in. Lily gleaned some ideas for her own stories and jotted them down in her notebook, the ink flowing magically over the page.

The women's conversation broke into Lily's daydream. Sylvia's customer reported that she and her husband were going back to New York.

"Our banker told us it would be best to leave Europe now, before things get worse," she continued. "With the strikes at Le Havre, we're afraid we won't be able to leave at all."

"Hmm," Sylvia said, writing down the woman's book titles in her ledger.

"Are *you* going to leave?"

Sylvia laughed. "And go where?"

"Back to the States. Back to your family."

Sylvia frowned and kept writing. Lily perused a copy of *Transatlantic*, its blocky, deco font and contemporary short stories emphasizing the era she had slipped into. The paper, rough and thick, was nothing like the glossy, sleek magazines back home. She thought about buying a copy. When she traveled, she always wanted something to take home. But would she ever go back home? She replaced the magazine and tuned back into the conversation.

"Constance, my world is here." Sylvia spread her arms to

encompass the shop. Lily ducked her head toward the magazine rack, not wanting to be caught eavesdropping. "I can't leave my life!"

"But how will you survive?"

Sylvia laughed. "I guess as I always have."

Constance intimated that Sylvia belonged back in the States with her family. But Sylvia shook that off.

"Paris is my home. I've been here for twenty years and honestly, Constance, I have nowhere else to go. When I die, I want to be buried here, near my friends."

Tears welled up in Lily's eyes. She'd been to Sylvia's grave, in Princeton, and had been sad that Sylvia hadn't been interred in her beloved Paris. Constance handed Sylvia some francs.

"You're a braver woman than I," Constance said. She gathered the books in a leather strap, pulled it tight, and paused at the door, giving Sylvia a last plaintive gaze. Teddy, from his spot on the rug by the desk, whined, his puffy tail beating against the floor. Lily wanted to assure Constance that Sylvia would be okay, that she would survive the war, that she would close down the shop herself in a few years, before the Nazis had a chance to. But she couldn't say anything. Part of her liked thinking that she had information others did not. Of course she had read some science fiction, and she knew about time travel and the noninterfering rules. But that was just fiction; maybe now that it had really happened to her, there were no rules. Maybe she could do what she wanted.

Standing in the middle of the shop, surrounded by books, Sylvia became a real person for Lily, with a real life and real challenges, and not just a story she had read about in the comfort of a book. Caveat lector, Lily thought. Beware of reading books that suck you in and spit you out in a whole other world. She imagined Sylvia moving through the war years, surviving by a thread, made old less by deprivations than by seeing her city overtaken by invaders. And Lily might be there to witness it all.

Constance left and Sylvia sat down, bending her head as if trying to get her bearings.

"Do you get that often?" Lily approached the desk.

"Get what?"

"People telling you to leave Paris."

"I do. There's the assumption that I am as rootless as the rest of the Americans who parade through here like it's a playground. But Paris is my home and really now, there is nowhere else I would want to live." She paused. "But thank you for coming. I'm sure you have other things to do in Paris."

"I don't consider Paris a playground. But I like it here, at the shop. I work in a bookstore back home, so this feels comfortable for me."

Sylvia pulled a cigarette out and held the pack toward Lily, who shook her head. Sylvia lit the cigarette, clicked the lighter shut, and tossed it on the desk.

"I would like to thank you for last night. You ended up proving quite useful."

"I was glad to be here, to be part of it."

"Well, I was a nervous Nellie. That's the last one of those I want to do." She blew smoke into an arabesque that twirled up toward the ceiling. Sylvia asked Lily how long she planned to be in Paris. Lily hedged and gave a vague answer. But Sylvia was tenaciously curious about why Lily was in Paris. Lily hesitated, then spoke without thinking.

"I'm here to help with my aunt's move. She lived in Paris and I'm helping her pack up to return to the States."

"What's her name? Maybe I know her."

Lily could feel the hole she was digging getting deeper and deeper. "Mary Stone. She lives in the 13th. You wouldn't know her. She's not—"

"Not what, not a reader?"

"No, not really. I'm the only one with the reading gene in my family," Lily said.

"Reading gene?" Sylvia laughed. "That's funny. I've never heard of the reading gene." She stubbed her cigarette.

Lily gripped the back of a chair near the desk. Behind a smile she urged herself to pay more attention to her speech.

"Well, if you're helping your aunt, you probably don't have much time for fun. Or anything else." Sylvia, too, wore a tight smile.

"Anything else?" Like what?"

"Have you read *Ulysses*?"

Lily shook her head at the non sequitur. She wished she could say, "Of course I've read it. Twice, in fact. I wrote my college thesis on it and it is being considered by a publisher." But she told the truth. "Not yet. I'm waiting until I am laid up in bed for months with nothing else to do."

"Well, don't wait. It's a masterpiece and will last long after those piddly paperbacks become rags."

Lily promised to read it and Sylvia grasped a stack of papers and struck the edge of them against the desk to neaten them. "Much as I'd like to chat about books, I have something else in mind for you."

Lily leaned forward. "Do you think you can spare some time to help me here? I need someone in the shop while I set up at the Expo this week. Do you think you can mind the books while I deal with that?"

Lily thought about the hours she had put in at Capitol Books and the trade shows she'd been to with Valerie. Hauling boxes of books, long hours in fluorescent-lit convention halls, eating tasteless food during brief breaks from the booth.

"I'm a fast learner. I'm good with people, too." Lily knew that everyone said that when they were desperate for a job. But to tell the truth, she was desperate, for the first time in her life. She needed to find Louise, she needed something to do in Paris other than wander around worrying. And who knew how long the money from the ring would hold out.

Sylvia sized her up with a dry regard. Teddy stretched out, his black nubby legs reaching in front of him, and Lily bent down to rub his belly. Teddy kept his eyes closed and rolled onto his back.

"Well, Teddy appears to trust you. I don't know how picky I can get," Sylvia said. "The Expo is slated to start next week. Though they've been putting it off for years. Terribly embarrassing for the French."

She went on to explain what she'd need from Lily: answering the phone, taking deliveries, preparing books for shipping, and being useful in the rare event that someone came in. It was true. The shop was nearly deserted. No one had come in since Constance had left.

Lily could scarcely believe that Sylvia was offering her a

job. To be a girl Friday, to work side by side with Sylvia, might make this whole weird experience worth it.

"I can't wait!" Lily burst out.

"Reserve your enthusiasm. You'll see, I'm very demanding and, honestly, I've sent many an assistant home in tears. And I can't pay you a lot," she said.

"That's okay," Lily said. "A little money is always better than none."

Sylvia invited Lily to put her bag behind the front desk, then gave her a tour of the shop. At Capitol Books, Valerie asked new employees to draw a map of the various sections in order to learn them better. Lily had made funny drawings next to each section: her philosophy section showed a group of stick figures with extra-large heads; her cooking section had a man jiggling a frying pan over a flaming burner; and her sports section showed a man crouching behind home plate while a barrage of sporting gear was thrown at him.

Sylvia escorted her around the shop. The photo gallery of writers on the walls—Walt Whitman, T.S. Eliot, and D.H. Lawrence—all seemed to welcome Lily. Teddy followed patiently, standing behind Sylvia as she explained the order of things. The books, arranged in alphabetical order, of course: essays, fiction, history. There weren't nearly as many categories as at Capitol Books. The books were mostly hardcover, and some didn't have dust jackets. No colorful paperbacks with catchy blurbs on the back. No remaindered books or oversized coffee-table books full of splashy pictures. Sylvia showed her a sideboard where she kept the first editions locked up. Lily could tell that Sylvia knew every title in the shop. She also saw the opportunity to sell the more expensive books if Sylvia didn't have to be the gatekeeper. She nodded when Sylvia showed her how she preferred the books to be shelved—pulled to the edge of the shelves in a neat line. She claimed to be fastidious, yet there were stacks of books on the floor by every section. At Lily's shop, the extra books were stored neatly in the basement, and replacements for sold books were brought up each morning.

"How do you keep track of which books are sold and which are loaned?" Lily asked.

"I write them down in the ledger at the front desk," Sylvia said. "I'll show you."

Lily chafed at the inefficiency of it. At Capitol Books they processed every sale through the computer database. That made it easy to track everything, and to even sell books online. Still, Sylvia was quite modern, selling and sending books to readers around the world. She showed Lily the back room, where a cot sat next to a vintage black typewriter on a metal cart. Sylvia passed the communal WC, a tiny closet with a Turkish toilet. A sheaf of newsprint hung from a chain affixed to the wall. A black cat that Sylvia introduced as Lucky lounged on a mossy cobblestone in the dim courtyard. Back inside, a wide, dark staircase led upstairs.

"That's where I stay," Sylvia gestured. She made no move to show Lily her private quarters.

Back in the shop, the two women sat together near the barely warm stove, working out the details of their arrangement. Lily would come in a few hours a day and help Sylvia with shipping, other errands, and minding the shop while Sylvia was at the Expo. After agreeing to return the following afternoon, Lily left and headed down the street, giddy with her luck. Strolling along, she felt the urge to write. She wanted to chronicle what she'd seen.

The clouds had drifted away, leaving a bright afternoon that lured Parisians outside. The Boulevard Raspail was particularly animated with pedestrians enjoying the spring day. Lily moved with the crowd, energized by her conversation with Sylvia. The terrace of La Rotonde was alive with people, conversation buzzing from all sides. Lily spied an empty table near a giant potted plant at the side. After settling in and ordering a coffee, Lily dove into her notebook, scribbling again and again. She worked on a piece about the Hemingway reading, wanting to document the details of the evening before she forgot them. A well of inspiration sprang free from deep inside her. She was charged up, as she had been in her high school journalism class. She had written a feature on the physics teacher who bungee jumped for kicks. Her journalism teacher nodded his approval, but Lily overheard him in the hallway telling another teacher that he hoped Lily didn't start snooping around other teachers' private lives. Lily scooted past, her head down. She began limiting her writing to the strict assignments, not wanting to expose anyone, not wanting to stand out. She got a B–, a grade that brought down her GPA along with her interest in journalism. She focused instead on history, becoming engrossed in the stories of people in the past, histories already written, decisions already made. What good was being able to write if you couldn't tell the truth?

She went back to her notebook.

And what about the beauty products aisle, where you spend a full two hours trying to discover yourself as a woman in the thirties? You're struck by the parsimony of it all, no fifty shampoos for all types of hair, colored, dry, flyaway, dandruffy. And deodorant? Forget it. Now you understand—it's the soap that does the job, sturdy lumps of lye. Where's the lavender French milled soap? No, it's serious here, no plastic push-up pumps of white chalk to swivel under your pits. No real hope of preventing a stink, because stink you do, your armpits a constant dank dampness signaling your distress in every situation. You swish feebly at the water basin, standing in your ivory slip, the water trickling down your side, the gesture of the raised arm, the view out the window past the heavy gray shutters, a collection of walls, buildings angled to keep you from a long view. If you hold this, hold this pose, hold it long enough, you can pause between time and not be that girl from the future or that ill-fitted girl from the past; you can become a model out of time, an essential part of a painting, girl at bath, trickling girl, girl outside herself.

For a second, you're perfect, until the trickle chills you and you grab the scratchy hand towel and scour your side dry. This is preferred to the shower/bath you tried to take down the hall, the communal bathing room ringed with the dirt of many men and few women—because what kind of woman, really, takes up residence in a hotel in 1937? You're a woman of dubious morals, and there are no concessions in the bathroom: no tiny unwrapped bars of soap or plush stacks of towels, no, not even a bath mat, just an enormous porcelain tub with a mallet of a shower head, heavy silver coils, large holes spitting out lukewarm water.

Lily didn't want to stop writing. She wanted to put black on white all this lunacy. Maybe she could make a story of it someday. She recorded everything, pulling in the sounds of the waiters calling out to each other, the clack of plates and clink of glasses, the faint whoosh of the espresso machine inside the café. When she relaxed her focus, only the din of voices, devoid of meaning, flowed around her. French sounded like a river, rushing and certain, always in a hurry to get somewhere important. Parisian conversation was heavy with emphasis, couples overriding each other's statements, voices rising, smacking against each other like water against rocks.

She breathed in the aroma of bread baking next door at the boulangerie, a hefty, yeasty smell. Hemingway could be around the corner, writing. Her pen flew and she hummed along with the rhythm of the ink on the page.

21

THE NEXT DAY, Sylvia put Lily to work at the shipping desk, showing her the labels, packing string, and paper. A stack of books sat nearby, ready to be packaged. Lily perched on the stool at the tiny table, feeling like a third grader prepared for an arts and crafts project. She picked up the first book, a heavy tome. Turning it over, she read the title on the spine—*Moby Dick*. She pulled a sheet of manila paper off the rack and wrapped the book. Writing out the label, she wondered about a person who would willingly read this monster of a book. She had never forgotten the shame of being caught cheating on the *Moby Dick* quiz in her honors class. It marred her grade and squelched her confidence.

As she wrapped the next book, she eavesdropped on Sylvia discussing printing fliers for the Exposition. Lily slipped back into her own memories, lulled into a daze by Sylvia's steady murmur. At Capitol Books, orders could be placed online. Lily communicated with people all around the world, finding the books they wanted and shipping them off. The store survived because of this service, where other secondhand bookstores had closed. The additional work from the Internet was almost more rewarding than the regular customers who frequented the store.

She unscrewed the cap on the glue pot, a squat bottle with a fancy blue label. The bristles of the brush, viscous with glue, were splayed in several directions. Oh, the joy of self-adhesive labels, self-adhesive stamps, and all the other little conveniences that made life easy. Sylvia again picked up the phone, her finger in the holes of the dial, circling again and again. Lily thought of caller ID, touch-tone phones, cell phones, and all the gadgets that saved time and money. Things moved much more slowly here and held their value. The postage scale seemed antique, as if Sylvia had been using it for decades. In Lily's era, if something stopped working, it was thrown out and replaced immediately. Here, you could spend a week's wages on a dinner in a restaurant. It was all so absurd, compared with the difficulties of the Depression and coming war. Lily wanted her easy life back home as much as she had wanted to inhabit Sylvia's Paris. Sighing, she set the book on the copper balance, adding a few small weights to the other side. Thinking about the conveniences of home wasn't helping, so she concentrated on calculating the postage. Sylvia was talking about the magazines she would feature in her booth at the Expo. She needed extra copies of *Life and Letters Today from England.* It didn't sound like things were going well; her brusque voice rose as the conversation went on, something about having to pay for extra shipping.

When she had wrapped the final book, Lily announced that she was done. Sylvia mumbled "Uh-huh" but did not turn around. She was bent over the desk, writing. Lily stood and stretched. After a few minutes, Sylvia spoke without looking up.

"You can go to the post office now. My bicycle is out back." Lily retrieved the bike from the courtyard. Lily looked around the shop for a basket or bag to carry the parcels in. Sylvia held up a leather strap.

"Surely you still use these in the States," Sylvia said.

Lily shrugged. "Mine isn't like that."

Sylvia harrumphed and showed her how to gather the books with a frayed leather strap, cinching the ends together and fastening the buckle. She gave a sharp tug and handed the bundle to Lily. At her desk, she pulled a metal lock box out of the bottom drawer, handed Lily a ten-franc note, and gave her directions to the post office near Les Halles. Then she walked Lily out to the front sidewalk where she helped strap the books to the bike's rack. The bike was a black one-speed, the kind that braked by reversing the pedals. Lily climbed on while Sylvia watched.

"You'll be okay?"

"I hope so," Lily said. They both laughed. Lily shifted the bike back and forth between her legs, the skirt of her dress draped over the bar. She pushed off and cruised down the sidewalk. Picking up speed, she dropped onto the street. She rang the bell, scaring a cat slinking along the gutter. After a few tours around the bumpy, small streets nearby, she felt confident enough to pedal toward the post office. There were more bikes than autos. The breeze caressed her face as she rode north, heading toward the Seine, trying to remember Sylvia's directions. She knew Les Halles was on the Right Bank, near Pompidou Center, which was built in the 1970s. Lily used a bike exclusively in Denver, a city that made cycling easy with its flat surfaces and quiet side streets. On her bookseller salary, owning a car wasn't an option. Riding in Paris on a simple errand, she felt the possibility that she could fit in here. Coasting along, she wondered what Paul was doing at that moment. If she were stuck here, would they do things like ride bikes together in the Bois de Boulogne? She had done nothing to find a place to stay. Hopefully she could crash again in his room tonight since he said he didn't mind.

She pedaled easily toward the Seine, feeling Paris's rhythm. People didn't hurry so much. When Lily moved at her twenty-first-century pace, it appeared she was operating in emergency mode. As she slowed down and integrated into this era, bits of home fell away. It was oddly difficult to remember what her father or Daniel looked like. Were they worried about her since she hadn't emailed as promised? With the immediacy of Paris around her, Denver was a lifetime away, one that may be lost to her.

Lily stopped with a group of people waiting for traffic before crossing onto the Pont Neuf, a lump in her throat. If she didn't find her way back to 2010, she would be here when Sylvia made history by shutting down the shop. She could help carry things upstairs, taking the portraits off the wall, holding the ladder while Sylvia removed the Shakespeare and Company sign from its post outside. She was used to carrying books, and could haul boxes to Sylvia's rooms to hide them from the Nazis. Warning Sylvia would be wrong, but she would be with her when things got bad. She would be a friend.

Traffic eased to a stop and Lily pushed away from the curb, moving slowly with the crowd over the bridge. It was a beautiful day, and the air seemed to wrap Lily in an invitation to stay. She was smiling, relaxing even, when she saw a familiar woman coming toward her. It was the woman from the reading—Louise, wearing a cloche hat and a smart cream-colored jacket with elaborate black trim. She moved with purpose, a clutch tucked under one arm. Lily's heart thumped; she stopped her bike, interrupting the flow of pedestrian traffic.

"Louise!" she called out. The woman continued on. "Please!" Lily shouted, causing several people to cast annoyed looks in her direction.

Louise turned and watched as Lily approached. She spoke calmly. "Finally, you made up your mind to come to me."

Lily was speechless. A confusion of thoughts tumbled in her head. "You're the woman from the plane! Are you the reason I'm here?"

"Let's discuss this calmly."

Louise led her past the statue of Henri IV to an empty bastion. She invited Lily to sit on the curved stone bench but Lily remained standing, her impatience seething inside her. She leaned her bike against the bridge's railing.

"So? Tell me. Who are you? Why am I here?"

Placidly, Louise observed a boat passing under the bridge. Turning to Lily, she smiled.

"Patience, my dear. This is all you need to know: we know all about you—Paul, your new job at Shakespeare and Company, Capitol Books, Claire, your hope to be a writer, and so on, and so on." With that, she extracted a cigarette case from her purse, opened it, and offered it to Lily.

Lily shook her head violently. This woman knew her

mother? She knew that Lily wanted to write? How?

"What? You've been spying on me? What do you want from me?"

Louise lit her cigarette and replaced her lighter and cigarette case. Exhaling, she spoke calmly.

"Listen carefully. You are exactly where we want you to be."

Lily guffawed. "Where you want me to be? I don't care what you want! I want to go back home. I want to go back to my life. I want to go back to 2010!"

"You have no choice, dear Lily Heller. Your only ticket back to your life will be acquired by following our instructions. You have no alternative."

Lily threw up her arms and shouted, demanding to know who Louise was. A mother crossing the bridge with her child pulled the girl away from Louise and Lily, muttering something in French. Lily didn't care what anyone thought—she needed answers.

"In such a rush to go back to your boredom." Louise tilted her head dismissively. "Well, you can't go home yet." Louise paused, eyeing Lily, who tightened her mouth in an effort to keep the tears back.

Even as Lily insisted, she also felt a pull away from her known, safe life. She realized she was demanding a thing she was no longer certain about—going back to Denver.

Louise flicked her cigarette into the river. "Go ahead and cry. But nothing will change this."

Lily stared out over the Seine, watching the white speck float down and away on the current. After a second of gazing at the water, she pulled back with a start and faced Louise.

"You mean you brought me here and I've been here, what—a week—without your help? Where were you when that guy mugged me? Where were you when I was trying to pawn my ring?" The thought that she might not have needed to sell her ring enraged Lily. Hot tears sprang to her eyes.

"Please, Lily, trust us. We were watching you the whole time."

"Trust you! You were watching me and never helped me. What is this? You kidnapped me and now you're blackmailing me to do—to do what? What do I have to do to get home?"

"You have no choice but to trust us. I understand that you're upset—"

"I don't want your understanding. I want answers. Go on! Say what you want from me. Maybe I will accept, maybe I will throw you into the Seine."

Louise smiled. "Well, you have put yourself in a perfect position to help us, and you don't want to blow it."

"What? What is it?"

"There's a very rare book that we need to get our hands on. And we know it is at this moment at Shakespeare and Company."

"A book? You only want a book? Just buy it!"

"It's more complicated than that. Only you can bring this book. And this book is your key, too. You will understand later."

Lily shook her head, trying to comprehend it. After a minute she asked about the book.

Louise leaned in and spoke quietly. "Its called *Yggdrasil: The Secret Power of Nordic Mythology.* We're very eager to make sure it doesn't fall into the wrong hands."

"Yig-dra-sil?"

"It's an English translation of an ancient Nordic book. But

it's useless to tell you more about it now."

"Wait—how do you spell that? What was the title again?"

Louise smirked and repeated the title that Lily tried to commit to memory. She had to write it down to remember it. She asked whose wrong hands they were saving the book from. Louise glanced at the pedestrians passing along the bridge and spoke in a whisper.

"Our German friends, of course. What's in that book could provide a significant advantage to Hitler during the next world war. We don't want that. We need you to get it for us."

"Why me? And how did I get here . . . in '37?"

But Louise shook her head. "Enough of your questions. You know all you need right now. Just get that book and you'll have your answers afterward."

"But . . ."

Louise rose. "No more chat. You have your instructions." With that, she moved away, heading across the bridge toward the Left Bank.

"Hey, wait! How am I supposed to contact you?"

But Louise just called over her shoulder. "We've got our eye on you. We'll contact you when the time comes."

Louise vanished among the other pedestrians. Lily grabbed her bike to follow, but a wave of people blocked her way. By the time she got her bike rolling, Louise was gone. A car honked and startled Lily. She pulled over. What was that title? *Gidril?* She couldn't remember. A flash of panic tore through her—her only salvation was a book whose title she couldn't recall. Things were becoming more and more bizarre. One minute she was an aimless bookseller, the next she was helping her heroine Sylvia in another era, and now, she was in charge of saving a very important book from evildoers. "German friends," Louise had said. Was she allied with the Nazis?

22

LILY WHEELED HER bike away, wishing Louise had given her answers. Instead she now had a task that she didn't feel capable of achieving. Steal a book from Sylvia Beach? Inconceivable, even for her. At the end of the bridge she mounted her bike and pedaled away.

Bumping along the cobbled street, Lily tried to recall Sylvia's directions. She pushed her bike along the quay, passing the *bouquinistes*. Distracted by the outdoor book market, she strolled slowly, attracted by the green boxes holding all kinds of books. She remembered an item on her list, buy a gift for Daniel at a *bouquiniste*. What would he think of all this? She wished he were here, someone smart to help her sort it out. But she was on her own. She gazed at the sepia postcards and the small cloth-bound books tucked in the wooden boxes. If she did buy Daniel something, would she ever be able to give it to him? She pushed that thought away. Eventually, the directions came back to her, at least part of them. The post office was on rue des Halles. She was to continue on rue de Pont Neuf until she arrived at the Place des Halles, then from there the directions had sounded simple enough. Lily mounted the bike and headed toward the post office.

At the Place des Halles, she found herself in a mass of controlled confusion. The square was packed with people and their wares; rickety wooden tables overloaded with vegetables, people pushing carts loaded with wooden crates. She dinged her bell to pass through, but was ignored. It was too crowded to continue by bike, so she parked with a group of others against a wall. She looked for a lock, but didn't find one, so she untied the books from the bike rack and turned back to the market.

A row of giant pavilions loomed over the street, and the cast-iron buildings imposed a regal order on the market. Lily moved among the vendors who lined the street outside the pavilions, finding it easier to navigate on foot. Men in long aprons and rolled-up shirtsleeves bustled around the market. Scraps of paper and debris skirted the dusty ground, moving under the breeze kicked up by market-goers. The aisles were lined with straw baskets, propping up sacks overflowing with potatoes. Rough wooden tables held bunches of onions, their stringy roots clumped with dirt. At a low table, a woman ladled something hot from a large soup pot and served a thin man. A worker with a ladder strapped to his chest passed Lily, and she stepped out of the way. The ladder, piled with boxes, spilled leaves of lettuce. It was like a circus act, only the man was not performing, but working. He bent forward from its weight as he moved his cargo through the market's aisles. Then someone jostled Lily from behind and she jumped back as a woman passed, pushing a wicker basket on a cart.

Suddenly, she was overwhelmed by it all—the crush of the

people, the smells, the banging of crates and boxes. She searched for something to lean against but she was surrounded by people moving about their business. Bending down, she put her hands on her knees, trying to regain her equilibrium. She breathed deeply to fend off panic. It was too crowded, too smelly, too close. This wasn't the Paris of her fantasies. Her mind returned to the conversation with Louise. What was that book? Why was she the only one who could get it? Why couldn't they just buy it? She cursed silently as she slipped inside an arched entry and into the covered pavilion. It was quieter inside, but still bustling with activity. To the left and right, vegetable stands overflowed with crates holding giant cauliflowers, heaps of carrots. Burlap sacks of onions and potatoes lined the edge of the rows. Past the vegetables, the smell hit her first—a stew of repellent odors that made her stomach roil. She was in the meat row. She hurried past a stall that sold horsemeat and at the end of the aisle, she turned and entered the colorful arena of fruits and vegetables.

Here it was easier to breathe, though the vegetables gave off their own odor. The grocery stores back home were sterile by contrast. She often went to the farmers' market, located in a big parking lot near the Cherry Creek Mall, but it was nothing like this. This was wild, loud, real, and raw. These working-class people bought and sold food for restaurants, not for chichi parties in downtown lofts. It was as if she had accidentally wandered into the docks in a busy, rugged port.

She passed into another row, where cheese makers sold their products. The smell here was more pungent than in the meat aisle, more pleasant but only slightly so. She inhaled the scent of tired feet and old leather. She paused at the goat cheese stall. The cheeses came in all shapes and sizes, tidy stacks and bricks, oozing rounds that puffed out like pillows she wanted to lay her teeth into. Square bricks, scored with indentations. A small man with a cap and a cigarette butt in his mouth winked at her.

"Bonjour, mademoiselle. Some cheese from my sweet goats?"

"No, I'm just admiring them, thank you."

She smiled and moved on, out of the building and into the light. The books were starting to weigh down her arms. She had to find the post office. The sky had become overcast while she was inside the market, threatening rain. Pausing at the edge of the fracas, she tried to recall the directions. The buildings loomed, impervious to Lily's search. Skirting the square, she finally found rue des Halles. A statue of a woman guarded the corner from her niche high above the street. The post office was right there, a cream-colored building flying the French flag from its pointed roof. Lily looked for a sign, and there it was: LA POSTE.

Inside, it took forever to find the right line, to stand in it, to fill out the forms, and then be directed to another line. While waiting, she read the painted signs and tried to memorize French names for customs, shipping, and insurance. Lily could see why Sylvia sent her. This was tedious. She couldn't imagine Sylvia waiting through all of this. The French bureaucracy was maddening.

Relieved of her duty, she stepped out into the day. Lily was hungry. She slipped back into the market. The vendors were closing down. Scraps piled up along the back of the stalls. Boys with giant brooms pushed debris. At the goat cheese vendor,

Lily ordered a small round of cheese. Further on, Lily surveyed the remaining offers from the baker: a few baguettes, a squat and seeded *pain de campagne*. She chose a demi-baguette. The baker enveloped it in a piece of thin paper, twisting the end to a sharp point.

Outside, she found a bench. Behind her, a pair of old men occupied their own bench, chatting under a cloud of cigarette smoke. Lily settled in, their heated conversation about the Front Populaire a backdrop to her lunch. The bread was crusty on the outside, soft on the inside, the cheese sharp and tangy. She munched, watching the market workers finish their day. What would these people do when the Germans commandeered the city? When food became scarce, surely they would be among the first affected. Lily stopped chewing. Could she do something to change what was coming? What could she do to stop Hitler, to eliminate the suffering of millions of people? She swallowed, doubting her ability to alter the course of history. Weren't time travelers forbidden to affect change? She finished the baguette, shaking her head. The fictional rules of time travel seemed silly now. She had no idea what forces had allowed these bizarre circumstances. All she knew was getting the book for Louise was her next best step.

Dark clouds gathered overhead. Lily brushed the sharp crumbs from her skirt and hurried toward where she'd parked the bike. But the bevy of bicycles only confused her. They all looked the same: solid, heavy, banged out of metal. She looked for Sylvia's book rack and didn't see it. A rivulet of fear trickled down her spine. Taking a deep breath, she tried to remember the shape of the seat, the color of the paint. Nothing came to her. She hovered for a long time, growing anxious. How could she face Sylvia having lost the bike? The first day on the job and she'd already messed up. She searched the crowd for a clue, for a kid who may have stolen it, any sign. Only rain came, spattering the pavement in large drops.

Desperate, she finally found it. At least it looked like Sylvia's, a rack on the back, the bell on the left side of the handlebars. But when she grasped the handlebars, she knew it wasn't Sylvia's. Lily glanced around. No one was watching her; people now rushed to avoid the imminent rain. Lily eased the bike away, her hands sweaty. She pushed it, heavier than Sylvia's, away from the others. Weaving around the men pushing wheelbarrows piled with empty crates, she tried to appear nonchalant. Lily was almost at the end of the block when a shout arose right behind her. "Ey, oh!" the man's voice pierced her back. Feigning calm, she turned, but when she saw the man bearing down on her, she let out a little scream.

He was short, his lip jerking as he shouted at Lily. She didn't understand what he said, but his gestures at the bike made it clear. He lunged to grab her arm, but she jerked away, releasing the bike. As the man reached for it, Lily ran, pushing people aside. For once she didn't care about being polite and not causing a scene. The clouds broke, sending rain pouring down, making the cobblestones slippery. She darted through the thinning crowd, the man's shouts following her. Another man tried to grab her but she slipped away, making a primal, piercing shriek. She was desperate, out of control, all the fear that had been lurking under the surface rising. The crowd gave way and she ducked down a side street. She didn't stop running until she reached the Seine. Pausing at the bridge, she leaned on the stone railing to catch her breath.

"Stupid, stupid, stupid," she muttered. The rain cascaded over her. She sobbed, her breath coming in sharp bursts. The danger she was in—and had put herself in even more by trying to steal—overcame her. Leaning on the stone of the bridge, she wailed, not caring who saw. No one knew her, no one cared about her, no one would ever even know if she was in jail to come rescue her. Perhaps she could just slip in, tumble into the rushing stream and let all of this go. Looking out over the bridge, she leaned toward the water. She wouldn't have to tell Sylvia anything, nor make her way out of this mess. She wouldn't have to deal with Louise and figure out what she was doing here and how to get home. She leaned further, leaning until the memory of Louise brought her back. Louise had mentioned her mother's name, Claire. How did she know her mother? Lily had to know. And if she fell into the Seine and didn't die, then she'd really be in trouble, explaining the inexplicable at the hospital. It would be better to tell Sylvia and risk being fired.

Sodden, Lily pushed away from the wall and headed toward the shop. Normally, she would offer to pay for the bike. She would put it on her credit card or ask her father to loan her the money. But she had no idea how much a bike cost, and how long her money would hold out. She wasn't expecting to be paid much for her work at the bookstore. Sylvia didn't have a lot of money. Despite her intellectualism, her books, and her friends, Sylvia was in the same position as the workers at the market: at the mercy of what was coming to Paris. But at least they had a position. Lily, on the other hand, was without status, without a home, without the means to work her way up. She might be forced to steal to survive. She had thought she was finished with stealing. The pen theft had happened without thought, but the bike was different. She wouldn't steal anymore. It was too risky. But what about the book that Louise wanted? Would she have to steal that, too? She pushed her wet hair off her forehead. She wished she could tell Paul. Louise hadn't forbade her to tell anyone, but how could Lily explain that she was time traveling when she didn't understand it herself?

Back at the bookstore, she plunged in, allowing no time to lose her nerve. Sylvia held the big black phone receiver against her ear and jotted notes, listening intently. Lily dawdled near the door, trying to not drip on the books. She silently rehearsed her apology speech. Finally, Sylvia hung up.

"I see you didn't take the umbrella." She went into the back room and returned a second later. She gave a small hand towel to Lily, who tried to sop the rain off her hair with the stiff air-dried towel. "You'll have to change out of those clothes," Sylvia said, lighting a cigarette.

"Never mind about that, Sylvia. I have some bad news."

Sylvia was back at her desk, reviewing the notes she'd just made. "Bad news, hmm? I'm used to it. Do tell."

"I've lost your bike. I mean, it was stolen . . . I think."

Sylvia looked at Lily, blowing out smoke. "You've misplaced my bike."

"Well, I put it with all the other bikes at Les Halles and when I came back from my errand, it was gone."

Sylvia threw up her hands. "I forgot to give you the lock. Zut! Still, Les Halles? What were you doing there?"

Lily shrugged. She couldn't say that she had to visit a site that no longer existed.

"Are you a foolish tourist or my assistant?"

Lily didn't have an answer, for she was neither, really. She melted onto the stool at the shipping desk. Her throat constricted and she felt the sobs coming back. She forced herself to speak, trying to squelch the tears.

"I'm sorry about your bike, so sorry. I . . . can I replace it? I mean, I can't afford to replace it. I . . ." Lily gripped the now-soggy towel. "I wish I could just charge it or get some cash from an ATM."

"Charge what? Cash from where? What are we going to do without a bike?" Sylvia shook her head.

Lily stood. "Can I work it off? I can work toward paying off a new bike." As soon as she said it, she felt a gripping in her stomach. She probably wouldn't be making enough money from Sylvia to live on, let alone buy a bicycle. Lily didn't know how much Sylvia was paying her. She'd been so excited to get the job, she hadn't asked. Tears welled up and spilled over.

"I'm sorry, Sylvia," she croaked.

Sylvia stubbed out her cigarette and waved her hand. "Please, stop apologizing, it will get us nowhere. And for goodness sake, stop crying."

The phone rang shrilly and Sylvia turned to answer it. After drying off, Lily set to shelving books. She was content to melt into the stacks, losing herself in the simple process of tucking books into order on shelves. The afternoon passed with few customers. At closing, Sylvia spoke while they pulled the book bin inside.

"You know, Gertrude mentioned recently that she had an extra bike. You could go round and ask her for it on my behalf. Maybe she'll take mercy on you, a poor young thing."

Lily nodded eagerly. "Of course, I'll do it. I'll try anything. You've been so kind to me and this is how I repay you. I'm appalled at my own lameness."

"Enough. Enough. You're not lame, you can walk just fine. Tomorrow before you come to the shop, go to Gertrude and Alice's. I'll send word that you'll be coming. Be polite but not too sweet. They can smell a swindler a mile away. They live at 27 rue de Fleurus. Do you know where that is?"

Lily did know. As a student, she had hovered in front of the security gate, trying to conjure up a sense of the literary salons that had happened inside. The wrought-iron entryway hadn't revealed much, but Lily enjoyed her fantasies nonetheless. Sylvia shooed her toward the door.

"Now, go home and change out of those wet clothes. It looks like the rain has stopped. You'll be safe out there now."

Outside, Lily avoided puddles on the sidewalk as she walked to the hotel, rehearsing possible scenarios with Gertrude Stein. Everything she had read about Stein made her out to be an intimidating ogre. But she had no choice; she couldn't let Sylvia down again.

23

THE NEXT MORNING, Lily skipped down the back stairs at the hotel, forgetting to be quiet. She had interrupted Paul the night before, getting ready for his graveyard shift. She wanted to tell him everything, but there wasn't time. After he left, Lily removed her wet clothes and hung them around the room to dry. She pulled the pages she had written from their hiding place in the book stack. Had he found them? She couldn't be sure. It might be safer to leave them in the room than to carry them with her, she decided. She replaced them, making sure the paper wasn't visible. Even though it was early, she slipped into the comfort of Paul's bed and promptly dozed off, waking in the morning after a night of uninterrupted sleep.

Now, nervous about meeting Gertrude Stein, she focused on what she would say instead of what she was doing. Rounding the last curve of the staircase, she jumped off the wooden stair and bumped into someone lurking in the courtyard. Startled, Lily said, "Pardonnez-moi," before realizing it was Paul's mother, blocking Lily's only exit. She pulled back as the woman spat out, "Vous!"

Lily squawked, then threw her hand to her mouth. The woman leaned toward her, a fierce look in her eye.

"What do you think you're doing?" she growled. Lily feigned ignorance.

"What?"

"You know what I mean."

Lily drew back, trying to inch toward the courtyard entrance. "No, I don't."

"I know you have eyes for my son."

Lily blushed despite herself. "Paul? Paul is very nice. He's been very nice to me."

The hotel keeper persisted. "Don't think I don't know everything that goes on in this hotel. I do. And I don't appreciate foreign tarts making my son a dishonest man."

Lily shook her head. "That's crazy. I'm not a tart." She didn't feel that her French was up to this conversation. No matter what she said, Paul's mother held all the cards. His mother insisted that the hotel wasn't "that kind" and that she didn't tolerate *conneries*.

Lily groaned with impatience. *Conneries*—tricks, games? She wished this were just a game. Where was Paul now to save her from his mother?

"You're mistaken. Paul is a friend, he's nothing but a friend."

"Don't try to fool me. You leave my son alone. He has places to go. He has a fiancée and a future, and not with you."

Lily recoiled. Paul had a fiancée? He didn't act like it. Still, there was a lot about Paul she didn't know. She shrugged. "I'm sorry. I'm not trying anything with your son."

"That's right you're not. You must leave the hotel at once. Like

I said the first time we met, I don't want to ever see you here again."

"But ..." Lily's heart skipped. She clutched her purse. She'd left her writing and her money in Paul's room.

"But what? Clear off now—point finale!"

Lily knew it was useless to argue. She walked away without another word. She could find Paul at his school and tell him what happened. Passing through the neighborhood, she barely saw the shopkeepers tending their sidewalk displays, gesturing and arguing with their neighbors. She leaned against a blackened building, tears forming. Where was she going to stay? Suddenly the familiar streets seemed menacing, the soot-dusted buildings looming against her. The people were all living utterly normal and probably boring lives, and she was in the middle of it with this incomprehensible dilemma. She tried to put the scene with the hotel keeper out of her mind. The last thing she needed before her meeting with Gertrude Stein was to be polluted with these negative thoughts.

At the Luxembourg Garden, Lily began to feel calmer. She skirted the fountain, heading toward the trees that surrounded a playground. Children ran and shouted in play, kicking up the gravel. Lily envied them their freedom from fear and worry. Past the tennis courts, she moved down the majestic and wide aisle that bisected the park. Before long she entered rue de Fleurus. If she were braver, she would be excited about going to see the famous author. But everything she had read about Gertrude Stein told her this was not a woman to suffer fools, and after leaving Sylvia's bike open to predators at Les Halles, Lily felt like a supreme fool.

She consoled herself with a fantasy. In her mind she stayed

for tea, spending the morning with Gertrude and Alice. They discussed writing, and Gertrude read a few lines from the essays Lily was working on. In the company of greatness, Lily felt witty and smart, and was invited back for salons any time she wanted.

At the majestic entry to Gertrude's apartment, she found no buzzer, no panel with names. The entry, two large gate-like doors with a stern bas-relief face at the top, didn't appear locked. She pushed the door open, surprised to gain access so easily. But she was only one step in before a door just inside the entry creaked open. A short woman in a brown housedress said, "Vous cherchez qui?"

"Mademoiselle Stein," Lily responded.

The concierge frowned. Stepping into the dim foyer, she indicated the courtyard at the back, telling Lily that Mademoiselle Stein's residence was on the left. Lily thanked her and passed into a small courtyard, open to the sky and filled with plants. She wondered who had the privilege of witnessing the famous people who passed through the entryway. Lily was aware of her every footstep tracing the route of countless others who had gathered their glory around Gertrude. She lingered in the courtyard, admiring the mini jungle of potted plants until the concierge's voice urged her on, "Par là!"

Lily scurried toward an entrance on the left and knocked. After several minutes, footsteps approached and the door was opened by a flushed woman wearing a flower-patterned apron. In Lily's best French, she explained that Sylvia Beach had sent her to talk to Miss Stein about a bicycle. The woman moved into the salon, gestured toward the sofa, and slipped out of the room. Lily gawked at the paintings clustered on the wall, works hung so closely together that it was difficult to see any one of them. There were many cubist works by Picasso. Suddenly, she noticed a pattern: almost all the art depicted Gertrude. She was studying a sketch when Gertrude spoke from the doorway.

"Everyone looks like that when they see my collection, a purely stupid look, a look of vapid unintelligence that even my dog has never mastered."

Lily turned and gave a curtsy. She'd never curtsied to anyone, but her body did an involuntary dip. Gertrude crossed the room and took a seat in a low-slung armchair. She wore flat leather sandals with socks. It comforted Lily that someone so powerful could get away with such a fashion faux pas.

"It's impressive, your collection."

"Interested in art?"

"No . . . yes—I mean, of course. I'm . . . I want to be a writer."

Gertrude eyed Lily and cleared her throat. "You've got some living to do first, I'm sure. Now what's this about a bike?"

Lily explained that Sylvia thought Gertrude had a bike she didn't want anymore. She tried to avoid admitting she'd been responsible for losing Sylvia's bike, but Gertrude pried it out of her. Lily confessed that this had happened to her before, back home.

"It's living, I mean, something to write about, these stolen bikes?" Lily offered. Gertrude grunted and shook her head. She hauled herself out of the chair and motioned for Lily to follow. They passed through the kitchen, a tiny room floored with uneven tiles, packed with cooking tools, and haunted by the smell of onions. The woman who had opened the door for Lily was plucking feathers from the pink skin of a dead bird on her lap. Beyond the kitchen was a door. Gertrude opened it, reached in, and clicked a light on.

"Down there, in the back," she said, pointing down the dim staircase. Lily hesitated before descending into the musty basement. At the bottom of the stairway, she shivered. She was in a dimly lit storage room stuffed with household items: lamps, a leaning end table with three legs, a collection of paintings stacked against each other. Lily nearly choked. What masterpieces might be lurking in the indignity of storage? The bike leaned against a birdcage that still harbored a few feathers.

"Wait," Gertrude said from the top of the stairs. She spoke to the cook, who called out, "Pierre!" Lily took the opportunity to peek at the paintings. She thought she recognized a Gauguin, but wasn't sure in the dim light. Moments later, she heard footsteps descending, and looked up to see a man wearing a cap and rough wool pants held up by a pair of suspenders.

"Attention," he said. Lily stepped back while he reached for the bike. "Vous pouvez remonter," he said, and after watching him scrape the bike against the birdcage, she scampered up the stairs. Back in the living room, Gertrude sat in her chair, pouring a cup of tea. She didn't offer Lily any.

"Thank you, Miss Stein. I know Sylvia really appreciates this, and so do I." This would likely be her only chance in Gertrude's world. "May I ask you a question about writing?"

She sighed. "Everybody does."

"What advice do you have for a writer just starting out?"

Gertrude's face deepened into a frown. "What do you write, anyway?"

"I'd like to write short stories. Or essays. And maybe a novel someday."

Gertrude seemed to soften and nearly smiled. "Read then. Read everything and then forget it all. You have to find your own voice. Don't go trying to imitate someone else's style. Just be yourself." With that, Gertrude settled back in her chair with her teacup. Lily couldn't believe that was the advice—that simple counsel was all that Gertrude had for her about writing.

"Thank you. Thank you, that helps."

"Pierre, put the bike in the courtyard, there. Sylvia can have it. And good riddance to it!"

"Thank you." Lily paused. Despite Gertrude's gruffness, she didn't want to leave. "Okay, well, I'll be going now." Gertrude appeared to have already dismissed Lily, and sat reading from a sheaf of papers. Lily slipped out the door and into the courtyard. The bike waited, its tires deflated and the frame out of alignment. But she wasn't about to reject it or Gertrude. With difficulty, Lily maneuvered the bike through the foyer and out the door. On the sidewalk, she noticed cobwebs draped in the spokes. Clutching the rubber handle grips, she paused to regain her breath. She repeated aloud what Gertrude had said so she wouldn't forget it. "Be yourself. Find your own voice."

It took almost an hour to wheel the heavy bike from Gertrude's to Sylvia's through the park. For the first half hour, she was energized and pleasantly astonished that she had encountered Gertrude Stein. She had gotten a bicycle and writing advice. Things were looking up. She replayed the scene with Gertrude, writing the story in her mind. She'd recount it in her notebook as soon as she had the chance.

When she arrived at the bookstore, it wasn't open yet. Sitting on the steps munching a *pain au chocolat,* she imagined going back to the hotel that night, but then remembered that she had been kicked out. At least she didn't have to sneak around, constantly worried about running into Paul's mother.

She mulled over possibilities of where she could stay. She didn't know how long her money would last. A hotel would cost a lot. She didn't even know where to start looking for a place. She could ask Paul for help, but when would she see him again? Going back to say good-bye meant she might encounter his mother again. The thought of never again seeing Paul brought up tears. But no. She knew where his classes were; she could try to find him at the Sorbonne to say good-bye and arrange to get her money back. But what about her writing?

She'd have to figure out a way to see Paul, and a way to get her pages back before he saw them.

The sound of the door being unbolted prompted Lily to her feet. She greeted Sylvia, who smiled slightly.

"You got the bike, I see."

"I did, and I met Gertrude. She gave me advice on writing."

"Of course," Sylvia replied. She eyed the bike. "No wonder she wanted to get rid of that. It's in a fine state. Well, we can take it to the repair shop and see what can be done. Bring it in."

Sylvia stepped aside as Lily wheeled the bike through the stillness of the shop and stored it in the courtyard where the other bike had been. Returning to the shop, she noticed the tiny back room. She hadn't paid much attention when Sylvia had shown it to her, but now the cot in the hallway could be a possible refuge. It sagged and the pillowcase was gray rather than white. Racks for magazines and stacks of boxes filled the space between the bathroom and the stairs. Perhaps she could stay here. Perhaps she wouldn't be homeless after all. She took a deep breath and pushed past the curtain and into the shop.

"Put the bin out, will you?" Sylvia gestured at a wooden box of books near the front door.

Lily knelt at the box. She had done this at Capitol Books. Part of the morning ritual involved wheeling out the cart of books that people still bought for a quarter outside the store. An old man came almost every day and stooped over the cart, fingering the pages, his hooked nose dripping in the cold. He'd hold the books close to his face and peer at the words. Lily would watch him from inside and wonder how much he could see. He'd shuffle in with a stack of five books, because if you bought four you got one free. The man would unfurl a crumpled dollar bill and fish a few coins out for tax. She witnessed his whole life in those gestures. He carted the books home, most likely a tiny apartment in Capitol Hill crammed with other people's unwanted books whose covers curled back on themselves. The smell of all that paper, the slight moldy scent that clung to the pages that had been sprinkled with rain, filled his home. His cat curled up in a musty chair and he inched his way around precarious stacks of books. He spent his entire day reading, eating Campbell's soup for dinner. He was Borderline Homeless Guy.

And now, so was Lily.

"Right, then," Sylvia prompted.

"Right," Lily echoed, snapping to. Picking up the heavy box, she nudged open the front door. Carefully, she tucked the loops on the box onto the hooks affixed to the wall. Back inside, Sylvia was at the desk, glasses perched on her nose, reading some papers. It was the perfect time to ask, but she didn't. Instead, Lily went about her tasks, rehearsing her request in her mind. She flipped the OPEN sign, pulled the stepladder out front, and hoisted the heavy Shakespeare and Company sign to its rung. She dragged the ladder back in.

"I need you to run this over to the library." Sylvia held a book out to Lily, who responded with a questioning look.

"The Maison des Amis des Livres. Across the street. And hurry back. I have some more books to package and ship today."

Lily crossed the street in the bright afternoon sun. She approached the French bookshop and paused to look in the windows. Small hardback volumes with gold trim were stacked in a spiral on green felt. The effect was very neat and proper, as a French bookstore should be. She pushed open the door. Her eyes slowly adjusted to the dark room. Bookcases lined the walls, and a few chairs held to the corners.

"Bonjour," came a voice from the back.

"Bonjour," Lily called out. She peered into the darkness. Adrienne sat behind a black lacquer desk. She was writing, her bosom pressed up against the desk. She was a large woman, even sitting down, with an incredibly delicate face. Lily approached Adrienne.

"You're Sylvia's new assistant?" Adrienne said in French.

"Yes," Lily said. "It's very kind of Sylvia to hire me."

"You were very helpful at the reading. We'll see what you're saying after a few weeks' work. It's not always easy chez Sylvia."

Lily put the book on the desk. "Here you go."

Adrienne pressed a piece of paper over her writing, blotting the thick ink. "Wait," she said. "I'll just give you this letter to take with you for when you go to the post."

As Adrienne folded the paper and tucked it into an envelope, Lily glanced around the tiny shop. It appeared more like someone's private study than a bookshop. All the books were French. Lily studied a shelf of poetry, recognizing the big names—Baudelaire, Lamartine, Rimbaud—but most of the volumes were a mystery to her. If she didn't find her way home, she'd be reading a lot more French. And German, too. The sound of a stamp pressed down on the desk brought her back to the room. She turned. Adrienne held out the envelope to her and returned to a small stack of books on the desk. She had already dismissed Lily, who lingered like a porter awaiting a tip. Adrienne glanced up without moving her head, her eyebrows neat lines across her brow.

"Okay, au revoir." Lily backed toward the door. Outside, she looked back. Adrienne had already returned to her books. Lily waved good-bye to the top of Adrienne's head.

As she made her way back across the street, Lily thought about the difference that seventy years of women's liberation had made. Gertrude, Sylvia, Adrienne were all so tough, but Lily had developed her own veneer from working on Colfax Avenue in Denver. Still, she wanted their approval. What would it take to be recognized by them? Sylvia and Adrienne respected writers—and women writers above all. If she failed with Louise's assignment, she might very well be stranded in Paris. How would she support herself? Perhaps she could sell articles to a newspaper back home, like Janet Flanner and Ernest Hemingway. She could start with simple observations, like the ones she'd been making in her notebook. Now that she had an in with Sylvia, maybe some of her contacts would help. Gertrude had given her advice. Maybe she could carve out a writer's life in Paris.

Back at Sylvia's, Lily shelved books. Sylvia greeted the few people who stopped in. Teddy welcomed everyone with a thumping tail and spent most of the day lying near the desk. A man cleaned the windows and Sylvia paid him five francs. Everyone who entered the shop was a friend and not a customer, and Lily witnessed very little money pass into Sylvia's hands. No wonder she had such a hard time doing business. Especially now, with so few Americans abroad.

"Who buys books these days?" she asked Sylvia.

Sylvia lit a cigarette and laughed wryly. "No one in Paris."

Lily was surprised to see her laughing. But perhaps she had long ago come to terms with the fact that her shop wasn't a viable business, but a charity case supported by friends. Lily imagined that it might be a relief for Sylvia to close the shop, not to have to run the business while searching for food and getting by under the surveillance of the Nazis.

"Yet you survive."

Sylvia blew smoke toward the ceiling. "Yet I survive. Thanks to the help I get. I'm glad you can lend a hand. Getting ready for this Exposition and running the shop is more than I can handle."

"It's my pleasure."

Sylvia asked her how long she planned to stay in Paris. This was Lily's chance to ask about the cot in the back. Lily hedged this question, as she had with Paul. She spoke of how she loved

Paris and said could stay here forever.

Sylvia squinted at Lily. "You aren't like those whooping Americans, here for a thrill. What would keep you here?"

"There's not a lot to take me back home," she said. "I don't really know what to do with myself there."

Sylvia smiled. "I understand that. That's what drove me here in the first place. My family doesn't understand."

"What did your family want for you?"

Sylvia stubbed out her cigarette. "They knew better than to want a good marriage for me. They knew I wasn't the sort to buckle under the regime of a man other than Father. Somehow they knew there was only one man for me: Father." For a few seconds, she was lost in thought as if imagining a life back in Princeton with her father. Then she brought herself back to Lily. "What about you?" Sylvia asked. "What does your family expect of you? A nice husband, of course."

"I studied writing in school," Lily said. "They think I should get a nice steady job at a newspaper. But news doesn't really interest me."

"What does?"

"Reading, and writing stories. Wandering around looking at things. I'm a bit of a dreamer, if the truth must be known."

"Then you are in perfect company at Shakespeare and Company. Dreamers abound there."

"Are you a dreamer?"

Sylvia narrowed her eyes and looked at Lily. Lily was beginning to recognize this look. It was probably not designed to intimidate whoever was under the gaze, but that's the effect it had on Lily.

"I was a dreamer. But the years have beaten it out of me. You'll see." She pointed at Lily. "Time withers dreams. You see all those old people sitting on benches in the Luxembourg Garden? They're replaying their early regrets, wishing they'd bought that bouquet of flowers, wishing they'd done something other than the correct and proper thing. Wishing."

"What do you wish you had done?"

"Hmm . . ." Sylvia seemed to contemplate Lily's question. "I can't say. I think I've done everything I wanted to."

"Surely there's something," Lily prompted. Sylvia lit another cigarette and held the pack toward Lily. She wanted one, but refused to get lured into the habit again. She said no and Sylvia exhaled smoke before continuing.

"Okay . . . I wish I had spoken up sooner to Mr. Joyce. Before things got so bad between us. There. I said it." She shook her head. "I don't know why I told you that."

Lily smiled. "I'm glad you did."

"Why, so you can run out and spread gossip around the town?"

"Of course not. Because now you have that off your chest. You can breathe easier."

Sylvia laughed, her chuckle turning into a cough. Lily waited until the spasm passed before asking another question.

"How have you survived all these years here by yourself in a foreign country?"

Sylvia's cigarette perched like a parrot at the end of her fingers. "First," she said, "I am not alone. I have Adrienne. And second, I don't feel like I'm in a foreign country. America feels more foreign to me now. I've grown quite accustomed to France and her ways. I think I've become more frog than American."

Nothing dampened Sylvia's determination. Maybe that's how she had survived so many years teetering on the edge of bankruptcy. It was so different from Lily's era, where if something didn't work out or wasn't comfortable—a marriage, a job—it could be swapped for a new one.

Lily asked if Sylvia ever wanted to return home, but Sylvia insisted that Paris was her home.

"I spent my childhood in the States," she said, "but from my adolescence forward I lived in Europe. My friends are here, my family comes to visit, and this is where I can live in peace in my small way and share what I love the most—good literature." She pronounced it "litrature," with a British accent.

Lily laughed. "Your bookshop is great. People sure love it, don't they?"

"Well, they used to, when there were people here with plenty of francs to spend. Now things just get worse and worse. Who knows what Hitler and Mussolini will be up to and what that will do to our little Odéonia."

The phone rang shrilly, ending their conversation. Sylvia chatted in French while Lily refreshed Teddy's water bowl. It was getting easier to connect with Sylvia. Here was her chance to ask about staying. The longer she waited, the tenser she became. She checked the grandfather clock. She hadn't made any progress toward finding the book Louise wanted. With Sylvia present, Lily didn't feel comfortable snooping around.

She wandered over to the window where the cat reclined alongside a stack of books. Two dead wasps cluttered the corners of the window box, and a thin layer of black cat hair carpeted the surface. Lily reached in and propped up a copy of Edith Wharton's *A Backward Glance* that had fallen over. She spread the pages so that the book would stay up. She could fix this display up in a jiffy. A dusting and a good clearing out of the cobwebs would make a big difference. She could place a copy of *Translation* in, alongside the T.S. Eliot books. Then people would know that Eliot was in *Translation* and buy a copy. The racks at the sides of the case were half empty; she could replace them with new books and literary journals. She glanced at Sylvia, who was still chatting. Lily pretended to straighten up the books on the table while keeping an eye out for the title Louise had mentioned. But nothing related to Norse mythology.

Sylvia hung up the phone and crushed out her cigarette. The ashtray was nearly full. *I'll have to empty that*, Lily told herself. Sylvia caught Lily staring and resumed her stern look.

"Sylvia?"

"Mmm?"

"I need to ask you a huge favor."

Sylvia frowned. "What now? You've lost the bike, now what? You want to take over the shop? Well, fine." She waved her hand as if dismissing something. "I should hand it over to a young whippersnapper like you."

"No, of course not!"

"Well, what is it, then?"

"It's ... I ... I need a place to stay. I can't stay at the hotel anymore."

"Why not? Run out of sous?"

"It's not that—though, yes, I can't really afford to stay there. It's ..." Lily wasn't sure how Sylvia would respond to the news that she was involved with someone on the hotel staff. It did seem awfully quick, even to her modern sensibilities. "It's the hotel keeper. She's kicking me out. I have to find another place to stay. Today."

"Today? You waited this long to tell me this?"

"Well, I didn't really have a chance until now. I'm sorry to ask. I hate to impose. But I promise I won't be a bother."

"Don't fret," she said. "You can stay on the cot in the back. There's no heat there, but the days are getting warmer so that might help. I'll warn you, though. Lucky will be very happy and will take it as an opportunity to use you as a hot water bottle."

The tension slid off Lily's back. She hadn't realized that she'd been scrunching her shoulders until she felt the release.

"Thank you, Sylvia! I didn't know where else to go."

"Your aunt can't take you in?"

Lily had forgotten her aunt lie. "She's, she . . . her apartment is a mess, what with packing up and all. I can't stay with her. Plus she's busy saying good-bye to her friends, so . . ." Lily trailed off, hoping this was a good enough explanation for Sylvia. Sylvia just stared at Lily, her forehead creasing in a frown. Finally, she spoke.

"The cot in the back room has sheltered many a writer, so why not you? Of course." She returned to her papers, still frowning.

"Thank you, Sylvia. You're the best."

Sylvia tsked. "Get to work, young lady. I'm feeling a head-ache coming on. Enough chatting."

24

LATER THAT AFTERNOON, Sylvia was at her desk going over an account ledger when she grimaced and let out a gasp.

"Are you okay?" Lily asked.

"It's just a migraine," Sylvia muttered. Her jaw was clenched and her eyes closed.

"I'm sorry to hear that. Can I help?"

"There's nothing to be done. Not that I haven't tried. Best to rest it out."

Silence settled between them while Sylvia kept her eyes closed. Lily wished she could take away her pain. After a few minutes, she spoke quietly.

"I've had migraines, too. They're horrible."

Sylvia leaned her head back like she was trying to catch rain on her face. Her expression was gray and tight, her mouth twisted into an ironic grimace like she was about to say something funny but was holding back. "Yes, well, I have them nearly every day. Life at the bookshop has given me a regular pain in the head."

Lily asked what remedies she had tried. Putting her head down on the desk, Sylvia replied, "Everything. Ampoules, black coffee, dark rooms, goat's milk, homeopathic treatments. Every remedy known to man. Nothing works. The only thing that ever got close was massage by an old doctor I saw. And the liver extract. That made me quite jouncy."

"I know of something that helps me. It might work for you."

"I doubt it."

"Well, can you try it at least?"

Sylvia raised her head an inch. She peered at Lily from under a wave of hair, her mouth pursed.

Lily sighed. "You're not very eager to get rid of this migraine, are you?"

Sylvia pushed off from the desk and sat back in her chair. "Fine. Try me."

"Okay. Lean back. Take your two thumbs, like this." Lily demonstrated, placing her thumbs at the bridge of her nose. Sylvia raised her hands and imitated the gesture. Lily instructed her to apply pressure. Sylvia closed her eyes. Lily had gotten migraines all the time when working at the bookstore. Maybe it had something to do with book dust or book customers. She guided Sylvia through the motions of rubbing her temples. Sylvia glanced up at Lily, her hands moving across her face. For a second she appeared hopeful, young almost.

"I can watch the shop if you need to lie down," Lily said.

"You can handle it?" Sylvia stood.

"Of course. And don't stop with the acupressure."

"The what?"

Lily gestured toward her head. "Pressing on your face."

Lily knew Sylvia soon wouldn't care if she could handle the customers or not. No one had come in during the last hour. Sylvia went upstairs, accompanied by the sound of creaking steps. Teddy stood at the curtain, glancing back at Lily as if unable to decide whether to stay or go. Finally, he nudged the curtain aside and ascended the stairs, click-clacking his way to his mistress.

Here was Lily's chance. She started at Sylvia's desk, crouching down to inspect the spines of the books stacked there. Nothing. Lily was about to peek in the largest drawer when the door chime rang. Looking up, she almost tipped over the ink bottle on the desk. Her heart beat faster at the thought of being caught in the act of snooping. A tall blond man who looked to be in his thirties walked toward her. She recognized him immediately. It was the man from the reading.

"Hello," he said, glancing around. "Is it possible to speak with Miss Beach?" He spoke in fluent French with a pronounced German accent. Lily stumbled over her French.

"No, she's not available. She's a bit unwell. Maybe if you return in an hour, she'll be available."

He frowned and glanced at his watch. Lily offered to help but he refused.

"Not necessary. I will return in an hour. Good-bye," he said, bowing slightly. At the door, he turned back around. "Hmm, perhaps you can help me with something else."

"Yes?"

"Do you have *The Autobiography of Alice B. Toklas* by Gertrude Stein? I would like to borrow it."

"Probably," she said, though she had no idea whether they

had the book or not.

Lily, scanning the shelves, wondered if it would be in fiction or biographies. She didn't know how to classify Gertrude's book, a collection of anecdotes about her circle of friends—Picasso, Matisse, Apollinaire, and many other great artists and writers. The style was rather plain but Lily loved being in the position of voyeur, looking through the keyhole at the sometimes-dissolute life of these artists seeking inspiration.

Within a few minutes she found the book and returned to the desk. The man watched her every move. He was attractive, his eyes a deep blue, his face sculpted, with an aquiline nose. He smiled and she blushed, hoping he hadn't read her thoughts.

"Is this the book you're looking for?"

The man approached the desk. "Yes, that's the one."

"I loved this book," Lily confessed. "Being part of their world, hearing about their lives driving an ambulance during the war, all the famous people they know ... it was fascinating." Lily stopped, embarrassed to have revealed such enthusiasm. The man just nodded, thumbing the pages. "Anything else?"

"That's it. Until I can speak with Sylvia."

"Your name?" Lily said, opening Sylvia's file box of library members.

"Heinrich. Heinrich Werden."

Lily flipped through the *W*'s until she found his card.

"Here it is. Werden." She silently read the addresses on the card:

Rathausstraße 15, Berlin
78 rue de Lille, German embassy, Paris

She wrote the title on his card, her mind racing. Was he a Nazi? That angelic face smiling at her now, was it hiding a future war criminal, a genocidal power monger? A shudder passed through Lily at the idea. She wondered why he was borrowing this book. Wasn't this the kind of work that would easily find itself on the long list of degenerate art banished from Germany by Nazi officials? Maybe this title had already been a victim of book burnings. Gertrude was Jewish and lesbian as well—two crimes in the eyes of the Nazis. Suddenly, she heard herself questioning him. "Why are you borrowing this book? Isn't this degenerate art, according to the Nazis?"

Heinrich pulled back as if surprised by Lily's random question. He stared at her for a moment, then grinned.

"Hmm! I do not see what is shocking about me reading this book. It's my job to be interested in everything that revolves around the arts and is also a great pleasure. Anyway, I do not know if this book is degenerate or not. I promise you'll be the first notified if this is the case." He paused and smiled. "And isn't it said that it's good to have your enemies close to you?"

"Enemies?" Lily retorted. "How can you have enemies in art? You either love or hate it, that's all. I'd say Hitler is the enemy of art!"

He raised a shaggy eyebrow. "You are a surprising young woman. Are you a communist sympathizer, being as virulent as you are?"

Taken aback, Lily stammered, "No, not at all. I just say what I think." She paused. "And Hitler will lead you to war!"

He slowly put his hand inside his jacket. Lily pulled back,

a crazy thought crossing her mind: *He's going to shoot me dead for that.*

"May I?" he said, taking out a metal cigarette case.

"Of course," she said mechanically, relieved.

He offered her one, but she refused. She watched him open the case and remove a cigarette with his nimble fingers, thin and long, perfectly manicured—a real pianist's fingers. While he lit the cigarette, she imagined those fingers on her skin. Shuddering, she immediately drove the thought from her mind. He released a puff of smoke and spoke calmly.

"It seems that you misunderstand completely the intentions of the Führer. He does not seek war. He would only like a relationship of peace and trust with our neighbors. He has said multiple times that he is an ardent pacifist."

Does he buy that? Lily wondered. Either he naively believes what he says or he really knows the purpose of Nazism and spreads its propaganda to quell suspicions. Lily brought up Spain, and Heinrich shrugged.

"To have peace, he must first show his muscles. With this, he gains respect in the eyes of others." Heinrich grew enthusiastic, waving the cigarette and speaking urgently. "Hitler has restored the German people's pride and self-confidence after years of chaos and despair. No one else could have done what he has accomplished."

Lily was incredulous. Couldn't he imagine that the chaos was not behind them but ahead? Could Heinrich imagine that his idol would bring unfathomable death not only to Europe but to his own precious Germany?

Heinrich chuckled to himself. "I do not know why I tell you

all this. Are you English?"

"No, American."

"American? Ah! We have many famous supporters over-seas. One day perhaps I will visit your country," he said, holding his cigarette aloft while expelling smoke.

Lily tucked his card back in the cardboard box. "I don't know if there are Nazi sympathizers in the States, but I do know one thing—"

Before she could finish her sentence, a noise on the back stairs interrupted her. Teddy emerged and rushed over to sniff Heinrich, waving his short tail with excitement. Sylvia appeared a moment later.

"What's this? A customer?"

Lily chimed in. "Mr. Werden came to see you."

"Bonjour, Miss Beach," the man said, tipping his head.

Sylvia nodded and smiled, brushing her hair back from her face.

"I learned from your assistant that you were ill. Are you better, Miss Beach?"

"It's nothing. Just an insignificant headache. To what do we owe this pleasure?"

Lily couldn't tell if Sylvia was sincere or not. She welcomed the man—the Nazi?—as she had welcomed any other customer.

"I'm here about the book I mentioned at the reading. I came to get it."

Sylvia shook her head slightly. "Ah, that book. It is very rare, you know. I am not certain I can bring myself to part with it."

Lily faded against a bookshelf, pretending to be busy neatening the books. What was so valuable to Sylvia that she resisted selling it?

"I'll give you a good price," the man said, stubbing out his cigarette in the ashtray on the desk.

Sylvia hesitated. Heinrich pulled a pen from his pocket, and wrote on a piece of paper on the desk. Then he handed it to Sylvia.

"I imagine you have some small financial worries at the moment. What I'm offering may help alleviate some suffering."

Reading the number on the paper, Sylvia pursed her lips. Finally, she spoke.

"You win. I cannot refuse this sum. This does not mean I'm happy to let go of this book."

Heinrich nodded, all gentleman. "I can understand that. I will take great care of it, I promise you."

Sylvia took a key from the drawer and went to the glass case. Opening the cabinet, she removed a book from the back shelf, then laid it gently on the desk. A large book, the binding appeared old but the gold embellishments on the cover shone. Heinrich leaned over it and smiled. He removed a checkbook from his pocket and wrote Sylvia a check. She quickly put it in the cash box in the drawer but not before checking the amount.

"Lily, can you prepare the book for Mr. Werden?" She held it out to Lily, who took the tome with both hands.

"Of course," said Lily.

Heinrich and Sylvia continued chatting. At the shipping desk, Lily turned the book to see the cover. She paled. In gold letters on the cover was the title: *Yggdrasil: The Secret Power of Nordic Mythology.* This was her ticket home, right here. And it was going to slip away, in the worst possible way, into the hands of a German who was likely a Nazi. She glanced at the others, but they were engrossed in conversation about Spender's poetry. Was this the Nazi who had demanded Sylvia's copy of *Finnegan's Wake*, the Nazi who had prompted the closure of the shop? What could she do? Take the book and run? But where to? She didn't even know how to contact Louise.

"Lily! Lily, are you asleep? Mr. Werden is waiting!"

Lily shook herself from her daze. "No, I'm not sleeping. I just . . . this is such a beautiful book, I couldn't help staring."

She quickly pulled a large piece of brown wrapping paper off the roll, tearing it with a loud shhhhoo! Carefully wrapping the book, surrounding it with string, she fought back tears. She couldn't let them see her like this. Swallowing, she passed her hand over the package, then turned to give it to Heinrich. He politely thanked her and Sylvia and left. Lily's only ticket home vanished, accompanied by the tinkling chime above the door. Heaviness settled on her.

"Lily, what is this Stein book doing on the desk?"

Lily came to. "Oh, no! He borrowed it," she cried.

She grabbed the book and ran to the door. She caught sight of Heinrich entering a limousine on the other side of the street. As she rushed to cross, a loud horn sounded, startling her backwards. A green behemoth of a vehicle shot past, sounding its horn again. In a flash, Lily Heller, born July 10, 1987, imagined being caught under the wheels of the Gare du Nord–Gentilly bus on May 17, 1937. Adrenaline coursed through her, making her tremble. She desperately wished to be somewhere, anywhere but here. But seeing the sedan ready to leave its parking place, Lily came to her senses and ran across the street, checking for traffic first. She tapped several times on the back window. It lowered.

"Miss Lily, what can I do for you?"

"You forgot your book on the degenerates!" She said, handing him Gertrude's book.

Heinrich laughed. "It's true. Where is my head? Thank you for your diligence, mademoiselle." The window started to rise. Then, he lowered it. "Miss Lily," he started.

"Heller!" she said.

"What?"

"My name is Lily Heller."

"Very well, Miss Heller. As I see that you are passionate about Germany, I'd be happy to guide you in the German pavilion of the Exposition Internationale to show you firsthand the revival of Germany."

Seeing her only ticket home on the seat next to him, she made her decision.

"Yes, of course. I would be delighted."

"Bon! I will be there in the afternoon on Monday, Tuesday, and Wednesday of next week. If you can come one of these days, it would be me who would be delighted."

Without thinking, Lily said, "Monday. I'll come Monday."

"Very well. Until Monday, Miss Heller."

She stepped back and he tapped the shoulder of the driver, saying, "Los gehts!" The car started and moved down the street. Lily paused before returning to the shop. What was she doing? She did not know. All she knew was that her only chance to get the book back was to become close with Heinrich. She crossed the street and was about to enter the shop when she heard her name. Looking up, she saw Paul hurrying toward her.

"Lily, I was so worried after hearing your argument with my mother this morning. Are you okay?"

She smiled, trying to look reassuring even as she shook from her encounter with the Nazi. "Yes, I'm fine. It's nothing."

"Who was that?"

Lily glanced down the street and saw the car slip into the place in front of the Odéon Theater.

"Just a customer."

Paul looked at her earnestly. Lily saw how young he was compared to Heinrich Werden. He apologized again for his mother but Lily brushed it off. Paul insisted, more for him than her, it seemed. Seeing him so frustrated made him even more charming to Lily. She smiled and touched his arm.

"Forget it, Paul. It's no big deal."

Paul gazed into her eyes. "Seriously, Lily, you can sleep in my room whenever you want when I'm at the reception. You will not have a problem with my mother. I set the record straight with her."

"Thank you, Paul, but really, I don't need to bother you anymore."

"But where will you sleep?"

"Sylvia graciously offered me accommodations. And I really don't want to create problems with your mother."

Just then, a toc-toc sound came from the bookstore. It was Sylvia, making signs for Lily to come back in.

"I have to go, Paul. Work's calling."

"Yes, I see!" He grinned. Lily took the door handle.

"Wait, Lily," Paul said. "I'm always there if you need me, you know?"

She smiled, wishing she didn't have to go in.

"Oh, Paul, you don't know how much that means to me." She stepped reluctantly into the shop but he called her name again. She turned.

"Do you want to visit the bird market with me on Sunday afternoon?"

She smiled. "I'd love to. But I have to go now, otherwise, Sylvia will kill me." With a little wave, she went into the bookstore. At the desk, Sylvia stood smiling over her cigarette.

"You have a French sweetheart now, Lily?"

"Oh, no, he's a friend . . . just a friend."

"The way you look at one another says something else, I think," Sylvia teased. Lily blushed, which made her boss smile. "Come! Joking aside, the day is not over yet. You still have some books to shelve, do you not?"

Lily hustled to work in order to forget the embarrassing moment. After a few minutes, she approached Sylvia, holding a stack of books in her arm.

"Sylvia, can I ask a favor?"

Sylvia placed her finger midway down a list of names in a notebook and glanced at Lily. "What is it now?"

"Can I have Monday afternoon off?"

"Monday? A date with the young man?" She smiled at Lily.

Lily wished it were as simple as a date with Paul. But it wasn't. It was her only chance out, the chance to see Heinrich again. She shook her head.

Sylvia returned to her list, making marks next to names and book titles. "Go ahead," she said. "There is never anyone on Monday anyway."

"Thanks!"

Lily plunged back into the shelves. While arranging the books in alphabetical order, she tried to imagine what strategy she would employ with the German to retrieve the book. But the image of Paul looking at her persisted.

25

SUNDAY AFTERNOON ARRIVED, beautifully
sunny. Lily felt a shiver of delight strolling the aisles of the
bird market with Paul beside her and the sunlight caressing
her face. Families milled about, everyone taking advantage of
the warm day. Children marveled at the aviaries, discovering
finches, canaries, parakeets, and other birds both common and
exotic. Bird owners passed Lily and Paul, new cages in hand.
A connoisseur and a merchant argued over the purchase of a
rare bird.

Lily was amused, seeing all this fuss over the featured crea-
tures. Never a fan of birds in cages, she preferred pets she could
touch and cuddle. Birds as ornaments or baubles in a house
seemed wrong to her. She liked to believe that they would be
happier in nature among their own kind. Still, they were pretty,
and she refused to let these thoughts dampen her afternoon
with Paul, which was going so well.

"Look how beautiful that is!" Lily pointed out a tiny cocka-
too with pink feathers and a red crest. The bird preened in its
cage as if enjoying the attention.

Paul smiled. But mostly he watched and seemed content that Lily was relaxed. A toddler in a frilly yellow dress held the hand of her father. She laughed and jumped with excitement, watching a parrot fluffing its white and yellow crest whenever someone approached too near the cage.

"As funny as she is cute," Lily said, enjoying the child's twinkling eyes.

They strolled through the aviaries near the quay. An old man passed, carrying a small cage containing a lark. Two women in the middle of the path offered their opinions to a third woman who displayed an ornate cage harboring a pristine white bird on its perch.

"Everything goes well at the bookstore?"

Lily nodded.

"Miss Beach is not the harpy she appears to be?"

Lily slapped him lightly on the shoulder.

"Paul! That's wicked! She is very endearing. It just takes time to know her."

"Oh, don't take offense, Lily. I'm just joking, and wondering if everything goes well?"

"Yes, absolutely. Sylvia is a character, but very nice."

"It's great that you like this job. Even if you are just twiddling your thumbs all day," he said mischievously.

This time he dodged Lily's slap. Thwarted, she tried to catch him.

"No, you will not get me this time!" Like a bullfighter, he darted away from Lily's charge and hid behind a lamppost.

"Wait until I catch you," she said playfully.

"In your dreams!"

Paul slipped out from behind the lamppost and hid behind a large woman who protested immediately.

"Jeune homme, s'il vous plâit!"

Lily faced the woman, trying to get around her to catch Paul. But he skirted the woman, going around and around while Lily gave chase.

"Stop, you kids! Have fun elsewhere!" The woman hid a smile under her protests.

"But madame, she wants to kill me!"

"She has good reason, I see. Because it will be me killing you if you do not stop now!" She grabbed at Paul's sleeve.

"That's right, hang on, madame," Paul said, then he cried "Help!" while pretending to struggle.

Lily pounced on him. "Gotcha!" Lily gave him the slap she'd been trying to deliver since the beginning.

"Ouch!" Paul pretended.

"Do what you can with him, young lady. A couple of slaps . . . or marriage. He'll be at your feet!" With that, she turned away, smiling.

"You are really goofy sometimes, Paul."

"No! I really liked seeing your eyes shine like a little girl's when you chased me. You were so fun."

Lily gave him another sharp slap on the shoulder. Paul rubbed it in a false pain.

"You're so violent! I cannot tell you anything."

"Yes, I am always ruthless with idiots!" Lily said, more amused than bothered.

"But I am not an idiot. Remember, I am your angel." He grinned and rubbed her arm in truce. "Let's go see the parrots."

He took Lily to the quay, where they found a pair of red and gold parrots that had caught the attention of a little boy. The child's gaze swung back and forth between the two birds, his mouth slightly open.

"You know, Paul, I still work hard in the bookstore."

"I know. I was just teasing."

Lily observed the birds. "Is it true that you're engaged?"

Paul gave her a surprised look. "Fiancé? No! I've never been and don't plan to be anytime soon. Where did you get that crazy idea?"

"From your mother. She threw that in my face the last time I ran into her."

"Oh, my mother, of course. She dreams this. Surely she was thinking of Claudine. But I've already explained that there will be nothing like that between us. We're just good friends."

They resumed their stroll among the market-goers.

"What can we do now, now that we've toured the bird market? It's almost four o'clock."

"You tell me, you're the Parisian."

"We can go strolling in the Jardin des Tuileries."

"Lead the way," she said, and they set off.

Nearby, two women inspected a parakeet in its cage.

"It's cute, isn't it, Adelaide?" said the one with the light blond hair.

"Yes, but I don't like the hooked beak. It nips too easily."

"Only if you're not paying attention." The woman cooed at the bird, then changed the subject. "So, do you understand why this Lily Heller was brought as a candidate?"

"No, not really," Adelaide replied. "I found this as unusual as you, Evelyn. The rules weren't followed, were they?"

"It's quite odd, especially from Louise, who's always on point about procedures."

"Not to mention she was silent on this choice."

Evelyn shrugged, squinting to inspect the bird. "She has her reasons and we cannot question her decision."

"Fine. But this is too strange, in any case." Adelaide turned to the bird tamer and asked how much the parakeet cost.

"Thirty-six francs with the cage, ma'am." He went back to reading his newspaper.

"Hmm! What do you think, Adelaide?"

"Whatever you like, Evelyn."

Evelyn smiled wryly. "So rarely is it about what we want, isn't it?"

Adelaide shrugged. "Maybe that's why Louise disobeyed." She gazed at the bird. "I'd like to disobey sometime. But I don't. I made my choice long ago."

Evelyn appeared not to have heard. The sun shone on the women, the caged birds, and the man sitting on a crate nearby selling bundles of cut lavender. The bird trilled a short song, sparking a smile on both women's faces.

"I'll take it," Evelyn announced to the seller.

In the Jardin des Tuileries, Paul and Lily sat in silence, enjoying the children playing with their boats on the pond. Paul asked her how she found herself in Paris. Lily didn't know how to answer. After all, she didn't know how she had found herself in Paris in 1937. Again, she was obligated to lie or at least expand on the lie she had told Sylvia. Gazing at the tiny boats sailing at the edge of the pond, she took a deep breath and began.

"It's a long story." She closed her eyes for a moment. "But basically, I came a few months ago to help my sick aunt at Versailles. She was really sick. A disease that doctors said was incurable. Then overnight, the damage worsened and she died suddenly." With that, Lily opened her eyes and saw a little boy nearly fall into the pond, saved only by his vigilant mother.

"Oh! I'm sorry to hear that," Paul said.

"If there was only that," she said. Paul's interruption was a hindrance to her fabrication. Perhaps one day she'd even write this story. She continued.

"Worse yet was the atmosphere at home. Horrible! Her husband wanted nothing to do with her. He had no use for her when she was sick and dying."

"What a con!"

"I tried to get him to give some attention to his wife. But he was cold, distant, the worst kind of alcoholic. He was always going out. I suspected that he was seeing other women." Lily thought she was perhaps going too far.

"So I tried to always be there with her and to be a comfort. I was there until her last breath."

"It's only natural," said Paul.

Lily was surprised to see how the story flowed out of her so easily, without even thinking too much.

"After my aunt's funeral, I had a violent argument with her husband. He dared to make a move on me. But forget it! I read him the riot act. And then I found myself outside with my suitcase and what little money I had in my pocket. He even chased me down the street! But I couldn't stay in the house with him anyway."

"I would like to put my hands on this man to give him a real correction. What a despicable scoundrel!"

Lily suppressed a giggle and kept going, even though she didn't know how to end it.

"So I took the first train to Paris. I thought I could get another train to Le Havre and take a boat to New York. But arriving in Paris, the night was falling. So I tried to find a room in a hotel, but it's not easy for a young woman to find a suitable room with the little money I had. I had to keep most of my money to pay for the train and the crossing."

"Especially since the hotels were full because of the Exposition Internationale," Paul inserted.

"Probably. So I was wandering in the night with my suitcase when I was attacked by a robber who threatened me with a knife. He stripped me of everything I had, including my suitcase and money." She took a serious tone.

"But this jerk wanted more. So I used all my strength, desperate to free myself from him and run as far as possible. Then I came upon your hotel, my only light, my only hope. And there you were, Paul. You were my savior. I can never thank you enough."

Lily was pleased to have finally come up with an explanation for Paul. She felt a twinge of guilt for having lied to him, the one person she could trust no matter what. But the truth was too bizarre, and she didn't know the whole truth anyway.

Paul looked sad. "I suspected there was something dramatic that you were hiding," he said. "But not that bad! I am sorry for everything that happened to you. That's awful!"

Lily shrugged. "That's life!"

"But why have you not caught your boat to the United States, Lily? You had money from the ring. You could use that to pay for the crossing."

"But no! The thought of leaving my ring behind makes me sick. I told you when I wanted to pawn it that I never planned to leave it for long. I'll get it back as soon as possible. And for that I have to earn money. So I am happy to work at Sylvia's until I have enough to get my ring back." On this matter, she was sincere. There was no way she'd go back without her mother's ring.

"Oui, oui, you told me."

Not wanting to be on the spot, Lily buttoned her jacket, pretending to be chilled.

"Are you cold?" he asked.

She nodded and they rose to head toward the garden's exit. On the other side of the bridge, at rue de Solferino, they decided to take the metro. On the way to the station Paul asked, "Lily, can I see you again tomorrow afternoon?"

She considered it. "Tomorrow? In the afternoon, I have to go to the Exposition. For work," she added quickly.

"Perhaps afterward?"

"Sure, but I don't know what time I'll be done there. I'll probably be there until five or six o'clock." She had no idea how long she'd be there, or even what she was going to do. Would she be able to get the book from Heinrich then? A creeping trepidation built inside her at the thought of having to cozy up to the Nazis. No, just one Nazi, she told herself. But Paul wouldn't be dissuaded.

"I can wait. I have nothing to do until eight o'clock. I can wait from five o'clock at the entry of the Trocadero, if that's okay."

"Okay, if you want." With this, Lily relaxed. Someone trustworthy would be waiting for her in case she got in trouble with Heinrich. "But I can't guarantee I'll be there at five precisely."

"I'll wait. I'm getting used to it." He winked at Lily and she laughed.

They paused at the boulevard Saint-Germain, hearing shouts from a crowd from nearby.

"Mais qu'est-ce qui se passe?" Paul said, breaking into French, a worried look on his face.

Dozens of men and women came from around the corner and ran past them. The sound of horse hooves hitting pavement and the shouts of the crowd increased. Uniformed guards on horseback appeared, followed by police on foot, who didn't hesitate to beat the people with batons. The majority of the police continued on the boulevard Saint-Germain, while three riders plowed toward Lily and Paul, followed by several officers on foot, ready to bludgeon anything that moved.

"Merde! It's a strike that has degenerated. We must get out of here!" Paul grabbed Lily's hand, pulling her away. They ran without clear direction. Protesting shouts from people being clubbed by the police grew fainter. A mounted guard crossed the street in pursuit of three people who were throwing stones at his horse.

"Lily, don't let go!" Out of breath, she clung to Paul's hand and ran with him. They fled along the walls to avoid the mounted police who moved along the middle of the street. Paul tried repeatedly to open doors they passed, with no success.

Finally, he found a gate open.

"In here, Lily!" They rushed inside, Paul immediately shutting the heavy door. They remained motionless, Lily's back against the wall, Paul against her, as if to protect her. Paul whispered, "Chuut!" The sound of hooves rushed past, accompanied by people running and screaming. On the other side of the door a policeman shouted orders. The noises slowly faded. Lily's heart beat wildly.

"You okay, Lily?"

She looked at him without responding. Watching his lips move so close to her, a warmth began to invade her body. She smiled nervously and he smiled back. And on impulse, she kissed him. Paul pulled back with a surprised look, and she kissed him again, as if trying to get all the emotion of the moment out of her. This time, he responded.

After a moment he paused, stroking her cheek, and Lily closed her eyes, feeling the warmth of his hand on her skin. He continued caressing her wavy hair and whispered, "How beautiful you are."

Lily opened her eyes to look at him before Paul's lips enveloped hers again. She put her arms around his neck and closed her eyes again—but suddenly the door opened, exposing them in the bright daylight. A man and a woman came in and stopped, as if surprised to see them entwined near the entrance.

The man cried out, "Mais qu'est ce que vous faites!"

Startled by this interruption, neither replied. Finally, their answer was to escape through the open door and flee, their laughter trailing behind them.

They held hands going up the now deserted street, kept

holding hands in the subway, and were still locked together as they approached Shakespeare and Company. They spoke little but looked at each other a lot. Lily spied Sylvia at her window upstairs. She turned back to Paul.

"I have to go in now." She opened the door but he stopped her. They kissed passionately, as if their lips couldn't bear to be parted. Lily pushed him back gently and gazed into his eyes. She stroked his face, inhaling his scent, a hint of sharpened pencil. She smiled, kissed him again.

"A demain, Paul," she said softly.

He stepped back, unable to stop smiling. "A demain, Lily." Lily shut the door and leaned against it, euphoria infusing her body.

26

LILY HURRIED THROUGH the corridors of the metro. It was a lovely Monday in May and she was going to meet the handsome Nazi at the Expo. But what was she going to do with these new feelings for Paul? She felt both confused and light-hearted. As the metro chugged toward Trocadero, she considered her situation. Here she was starting a love affair in 1937 when she should be focused on getting home. But why? What was waiting for her in Denver? Here, in Paris's dark past, she was experiencing what she'd always wanted: she was writing; she was working alongside Sylvia Beach, her cherished heroine; she had met and kissed a very charming French man; and she was finally involved in something bigger than her—even if she didn't know what it was about—and didn't that make life more interesting than any day she'd spent in Denver?

If she got the book today, what would she do? She couldn't bear to hurt Paul. He was so sweet and had been more than kind to her. His mother had been right. Paul was entitled to happiness, and who was Lily to spoil that? But at the same time, she knew that something had engaged in her yesterday in that dark passageway. Lily again felt Paul's lips on hers, smelled the scent of his skin, recalled the desire in his eyes. His words repeated in her mind: *Comme tu es belle, Lily. Comme tu es belle* . . . She was eager to see him again that afternoon.

Bright sunlight pulled her out of her thoughts. She found herself outside the entry of the Trocadero station. She followed a group leaving the metro and joined the line of people awaiting entry to the Exposition Internationale. She paid her six francs, and ticket in hand, she approached the parapet that provided an unobstructed view of the Eiffel Tower. This was the same spot where she had first seen the Eiffel Tower when she was visiting with her parents. Later, she had loitered here with her student friends. But while this vantage point still framed fountain water cannons dancing in the long rectangular pool, with the awe-inspiring Eiffel Tower in the background, everything else was different.

Along both sides of Trocadero Square, temporary buildings had been erected by participating nations, extending all the way to the base of the Eiffel Tower. The true story of what was developing in Europe was immediately apparent. Two pavilions framed the Eiffel Tower at the banks of the Seine. The German pavilion dominated all the others, even the one directly across from it, the Soviet pavilion. The hefty sculptures of the Soviet peasants, despite their determination, were no match for the emblematic German eagle spreading its wings to dominate everything in sight.

Visitors in their Sunday finest strolled the walkways, pausing to peek into other pavilions, but mostly heading straight to the German tower. A sick feeling pervaded Lily, knowing that these peoples' lives were about to be irrevocably changed. And she was the only person here who knew what was coming. She was about to enter the Nazi nest and had no idea what to expect. She turned away from the viewpoint and descended the stairs to join the crowds.

Walking toward her meeting with Heinrich, Lily decided she had no right to give Paul hope for something she couldn't follow through on. No way was she going to get stuck in Paris on the verge of war. She had to get this book. She couldn't fail. Her future was at stake, and perhaps taking this book away from the Nazis would save people in ways she couldn't know now. She was irritated that Louise hadn't told her more, but if she admitted it, she liked being part of something bigger than herself.

She didn't have any trouble locating the German pavilion. Large letters on the pedestal told her she was entering DEUTSCHLAND. A statue of two men and a woman, all naked and extremely buff, guarded the entry. She shook her head. What were they suggesting with this arrangement? They were backed by Nazi flags, swastikas fluttering on both sides of the looming tower. A shudder wracked her body and she was forced to lean against the pedestal, its stone warm and solid in the afternoon sun. Seeing the red of the Nazi flag in person was more powerful than all the black-and-white photos she'd seen. The bright fabric with its spidery symbol of doom snapped in the breeze. After a few minutes, the horror passed enough for her to continue on. She mounted the stairs with the other visitors and entered the devil's lair.

Inside the great hall, she was halted by the display of power. Hitler's megalomaniac grandeur loomed. Lily almost laughed at the blatant attempt to mimic the excesses of ancient Rome in modernist style of the thirties. Everything was of a grand scale: the giant paintings, the impossibly high ceilings, the vast entry hall, all letting the French know who dominated. Lily hurried to the information desk and addressed the woman there.

"Excusez-moi, madame. I have an appointment with Heinrich Werden. Can you tell me where to find him?"

"Herr Werden?" She pronounced his name with a German accent.

"Oui," Lily replied.

"I'll let him know you are here. Whom shall I announce?"

Lily gave her name, hoping it wouldn't end up on some register somewhere, embedded in the Nazi files.

"Please take a seat, Miss Heller." She pointed to a nearby bench, then left. Lily lost sight of her as she disappeared in the enormous showroom. Visitors paused in the entry to get their bearings, then descended the stairs into the temple to Nazi advances in science and technology. The woman returned and announced that Herr Werden was busy and would join her in a few minutes.

Lily thanked her and idly watched her return to her post. What would the woman be doing in a few years? Lily wondered. Guarding a concentration camp? A huge painting hanging over the red benches depicted an architect showing his blueprint to eager workers, a not-so-subtle allegory of Germany's empire building. Lily frowned.

"Miss Heller!"

She turned, and there was Heinrich, wearing a sharp suit, his hair carefully combed. He took her hand and smiled hello.

"I'm glad you're here. Since our last conversation, I've been eager to show you that your fears about Germany are not justified."

Lily knew she had to act like the queen of hypocrites. She smiled back.

"Of course I expect you will show me otherwise, Herr Werden."

He insisted she call him Heinrich.

"Then you may call me Lily, Heinrich." She forced another smile. He held out his arm and taking it, they began their tour. They paused at the entrance to the exhibit hall, where he bowed and waved Lily in. She started back with a small cry. It was impressive, a broad corridor flanked on both sides by glassed-in display cases. Above, deco chandeliers hung from both sides of the incredibly high ceiling, a lit panel that gave the impression of bringing the outdoors in to shine on the Nazi empire. At the far end of the grand hall, a short staircase led to a huge mosaic depicting, again, the eagle, spreading its reach wide.

"Tell me, how do you find our pavilion?" Heinrich asked.

"A little too pompous for my taste!" Lily burst out, then thought to herself, *Crap, why can't I keep my mouth shut?*

But Heinrich just laughed. "What I admire, Lily, is your frankness. It is true that I also found the building a bit bombastic. But that doesn't indicate evil, just a big vision, right? International expositions are a bit of a competition, a bit of flag waving, don't you think?"

Lily nodded, choosing to stay silent this time.

"The German pavilion has been admired by visitors since the opening of the Expo. That's what's important. You know, it's one of the great architects of the Third Reich, Albert Speer, who designed the pavilion."

He led her down the stairs to the enormous hall. They joined a crowd pausing to inspect the showcases insisting upon the renewal of science and technology in Nazi Germany. A large painting seemed to Lily a glorification of work, of family, and of the fatherland in the style of Stalinist propaganda posters. The only difference was that the painted figures met the Nazi's Aryan criteria.

This "art" interested Lily not at all. But she didn't reveal this to Heinrich. She smiled, asked questions, and adopted a look of perpetual amazement at what he was explicating. Heinrich glowed under her attention and continued the tour with relish. They passed more than an hour contemplating the greatness and splendor of Nazism. Lily looked for an opening to broach the subject of the book, but didn't find one. As they approached the end of the hall, she despaired at ever having a chance to bring it up. A silver Mercedes, with sleek, aerodynamic contours, attracted visitors, particularly male ones. To Lily, the car resembled a spaceship or a wing of an airplane, its sleek surface revealing no discernible moving parts. Lily drifted away and lingered in front of a display case holding what looked like complicated dental instruments. Just as she was about to bring up the book as a complete non sequitur, someone called out to Heinrich. A man with clipped dark hair and a military demeanor approached.

"Excuse me for a moment," Heinrich told Lily.

"Of course," she murmured, but the pair had already stepped away. Lily gazed at the high ceiling, a panel of lights that illuminated the room in what seemed like daylight. She tried to come up with a plan to get at the book, but grew distracted when she heard Heinrich's voice raised. The conversation had grown heated, and Lily caught the other man gesturing at her with a look of great displeasure. But Heinrich smiled and placed a hand on the man's arm. His friend shook it off and glowered at Lily. She shrank against one of the pillars of the hall. Finally, the men parted and Heinrich rejoined Lily, who grew more nervous the longer she stayed in the exhibit hall. The grand hall had become even more crowded and Lily had begun to perspire.

"Everything okay?" she asked, smiling nervously.

"But of course," Heinrich assured her. "That is my childhood friend Karl, who seems to think I need looking after. I know his family well, and he has plans for me to marry his sister."

"Oh," Lily said, startled. The thought of him having a normal family life at home in Germany was at odds with her image of him as a Nazi.

"No matter, nothing to concern yourself with. My dear Lily, how about if we go outside for a breath of fresh air. I imagine you're tired by this long visit."

"Lovely," she said, as if he had just suggested a stroll in the countryside.

"Allons-y, alors."

Together they made their way through the crowd toward the entrance. Heinrich complimented her along the way, expressing his delight at her company, claiming she had been the most charming and attentive visitor he'd ever received.

I'm a shoe-in for Hollywood, Lily thought, and with this,

she began to giggle. To her horror, found herself unable to stop. Heinrich peered at her with curiosity.

"But my dear Lily, what is so funny?"

Hearing that she had by dint of her attentiveness become "his dear Lily" renewed the giggles. Hand over her mouth, she tried to stop. But like laughter started in a solemn church, the forbidden emotion continued unabated. Between gasps, she got out, "I . . . don't . . . know . . . it's not . . ."

Heinrich joined in laughing, apparently delighted to see Lily in such a state.

"Aah! You are a constant surprise, my dear Lily. Perhaps if you rest you will feel better." He led her to a nearby bench and tried to get her to sit down. She apologized between jolts of laughter, wiping tears from her eyes with the handkerchief that Heinrich had offered her. Two old women, primly dressed in long skirts, noticed her outburst and frowned. Finally, Lily regained her composure.

"All better?" Heinrich asked with a condescending smile.

"Yes! Oh, I don't know what came over me. I must have been nervous."

"No matter! Nervous or not, I enjoy your laughter. It's refreshing, Lily."

He was holding her hand. While laughing, Lily hadn't noticed that Heinrich had taken the opportunity to touch her while giving her his handkerchief. She gave it back to him and kept her hand to herself. They mounted another set of stairs and emerged onto the roof of the pavilion. People strolled while others lounged on deck chairs under parasols. The more adventurous sat on the parapets. The cool breeze on her face calmed

Lily, and she wished Paul were at her side instead of Heinrich. Together, they leaned on the parapet, taking in the stunning view of the Exposition along the Seine and past the Eiffel Tower in the Champs de Mars. Beyond, the city of Paris sprawled in its magnificence. From here, the flow of people in the aisles of the Expo looked like ants. She was happy to avoid the crowds. Looking at the loop of the Seine, she breathed slowly, closing her eyes to better appreciate the feeling of expansiveness. Despite the oddness of her circumstances, she felt a thrill to be perched above Paris, her favorite city, like this. Next to her, Heinrich spoke gently.

"I like to take the air here when I work at the pavilion. Sometimes there are too many people down there. It becomes oppressive after a while."

"I understand completely," Lily said. "I felt it, too, that I really needed this breath of fresh air. Thank you for bringing me up here."

He smiled. "Would you like a refreshment?"

"Sure." The longer she stayed with him, the more she'd have a chance to mention the book.

Heinrich turned to a counter where a man in a waiter's uniform stood. They spoke in German. The man slipped away and came back with two chairs folded under his arms. Heinrich indicated a place in the shade near the pavilion's tower and the man set the chairs up quickly.

"Danke!" Heinrich told the man, who remained at attention. Heinrich invited Lily to sit down. She sank back in the canvas chair, relieved to sit after all that walking.

"Would you like something to drink, white wine, champagne, perhaps?"

"Water, please, I'm feeling a little dehydrated."

Heinrich gave her a puzzled look, but placed their order with the waiter.

"Is this the first time you've visited the Exposition?"

"Yes. I must say it's odd to come back to this place with all the Expo buildings here."

"You've been to Paris before?" Heinrich asked, squinting at her.

The drinks arrived. Lily's water was served in a tall, frosted glass. Heinrich took his glass of white wine. The interruption provided a screen for Lily, who sensed she'd said too much. Again, she was being forced to knit a new story. She didn't like lying, but truth be told, she enjoyed the thrill of improvising like this.

"Where were we?" Heinrich said after he sipped his wine. "You've been to Paris?"

"Yes. I came here with my parents as a girl. I love this city."

"I am like you. I love Paris, with her intense intellectual and artistic life. My first visit was two years ago when I had a yearlong post at our Embassy of Cultural Affairs. I find myself truly lucky. And what about you? Are you staying long in Paris or are you returning to the U.S. soon?"

Lily, glass in hand, sighed. "I don't know yet. It depends on some things I have to take care of." She took a sip of cool water. "But for now I'm happy to work for Miss Beach. She is a very interesting woman."

"It is true. Despite her flaws."

Lily started back slightly. She didn't like a stranger speaking about Sylvia's flaws. True, she was cranky and prone to migraines, but Lily sympathized with her.

"What do you mean 'her flaws'?"

"You know . . . her Sapphic ways."

Lily took a sip of her water to avoid saying something she'd really regret. This was not what she expected by "flaws."

"Why do you call that a flaw? Sylvia is free to make choices of her preferred sex, whether you like it or not."

"But I'm not against it. It's none of my business."

"That's right, it's not!" Lily said, flushing.

He smiled. "But there must be some difficulties inherent in this kind of choice."

"Like?"

"Like being rejected by society. She is lucky to live in Paris, to be independent and among the literary and artistic. That deviance is more accepted here."

"The 'deviance'? Being a lesbian is an anomaly in your opinion?"

"Of course she does not conform to each person's norms. But still, that reality can't be easy."

She took another sip of water, then spoke calmly.

"What reality? Homosexuality has always existed and always will. And I think that the sculptures out front aren't without some homosexual connotation. What's the deal with those two statues of naked men so close to each other, anyway?"

Heinrich burst into laughter at Lily's indignant question.

"My God, Lily, you're adorable when you respond with passion! But spare me a doubt. Are you of the same nature as Miss Beach?"

Lily was silent for a moment, unsure of his meaning. Suddenly it hit her: he was asking if she was a lesbian. Blood rushed to her face.

"Huh! And if I say yes, will you be done talking to me? You'll deny my existence?"

"No, not at all. I would just find it to be a pity," he said softly, looking her straight in the eye. Lily lowered her eyes, embarrassed by this look, no mystery this time about its meaning.

Finally, she spoke. "If it comforts you, I am not."

He appeared delighted to hear these words, his smile growing wider, his eyes glistening. Then he spoke.

"I understand that I might have upset you by what I said about Miss Beach. But know that I respect her very much." He paused, then continued. "Especially since she introduced me to such an intelligent and passionate young woman as you."

Lily blushed, for once speechless. Despite herself, Lily couldn't help but think he was even more handsome this close. Her whole body began to heat up, starting with her cheeks and traveling down to her neck, then lower. Then she remembered the reason for this relationship. She wanted to drive the conversation to the book, but her mind was distracted by what he'd just said. A sudden suspicion arose. Was he the Nazi who had provoked the closing of the bookshop, demanding Sylvia's copy of *Finnegan's Wake*? She stared at him, wondering how he could be so friendly with Sylvia and then so callous behind her back. He broke the silence.

"Lily, perhaps what I said disturbed you?"

"Yes, a little. I didn't expect that. I thought you were more . . . let's say rigid, constipated a bit."

Heinrich gave a short bark of laughter and she joined him.

"Constipated! I've never heard that one. You really are witty. A little too impulsive, perhaps. But even that's not so disagreeable." He squinted again as if inspecting her up close.

"You're joking?"

"Not at all. I am sincere. It's very refreshing to talk with you. Quite a change from the conversations with my colleagues."

Lily nearly cringed, not even wanting to imagine the Nazi conversations behind closed doors. She plunged in.

"Can I ask you what you will do with the book you just bought at Sylvia's?"

Heinrich's expression changed, and Lily feared she'd gone too far. He finished his wine, taking a moment before speaking.

"I cannot say much. But I didn't acquire it for me. I was following orders from the highest level of the state. I'm leaving this weekend to bring it to my superiors in Berlin."

Lily was jolted by this news. Her salvation was going thousands of miles into Nazi territory and probably to places inaccessible to the ordinary mortal. *I'm screwed if I can't get home,* she told herself. She briefly contemplated a life in Paris under the Occupation—at Heinrich's side, as a collaborator. She shivered.

"Cold?"

She shook her head.

"Why are you interested in this old book, Lily?"

Lily let her imagination guide her words.

"I'm interested in Norse mythology and the history of Scandinavia. The Edda, Thor, Loki, all those . . ." She reeled off these words quickly, things she'd picked up thumbing through a book on Norse mythology at the bookstore in Denver. She had soon become bored with it, preferring her fantasies of Paris life in the twenties. She continued her fabrication.

"And my family is of Swedish origin. This book seemed relevant to my interest in the myths and realities of my ancestors. As a German you can understand, right?" She paused to gaze into his eyes. "I would have liked to at least browse it for a moment, perhaps discover its secrets." She smiled coquettishly.

"I didn't know you were interested in such things, Lily. It's impressive to see the flame of interest in your eyes. I appreciate that." He leaned close in complicity.

Suddenly Karl was behind Heinrich, clapping his hand on his friend's shoulder. He spoke in German. Heinrich excused himself to Lily. After a few minutes of heated discussion with Karl, he returned.

"I'm sorry to leave, but duty calls. Enjoy the rest of your visit at the Expo. I hope I see you again soon." He kissed Lily's hand and bowed one last time, then left with Karl.

Lily followed them with her eyes, dismayed to have lost him so suddenly. Just when she felt she was getting closer to the book. She should have played up to him, poured on the honey. Was this really the time for her frankness? She reproached herself, then remembered Heinrich laughing at her when she defended homosexuality. Her anger shifted to him. How dare he laugh at her convictions? And soon he'd be on his way to Berlin with the book and she'd be stuck in 1937! Damn, damn, damn! Stranded among the happy Expo visitors, she felt desperately lost.

She raised her eyes toward the entrance of the patio and was surprised to see Heinrich coming back to her. Lily adopted a bright smile, ignoring Karl's dark look upon her. Lily's heart pounded as Heinrich approached. He bent toward her.

"Lily, I'll be quick. I'd like you to see the book, since you are so interested. The day after tomorrow, there's a reception at the embassy. Would you be my guest? If you'd like, I can let you glance at the book one last time."

Surprised by this proposal, she didn't even debate it with herself. She accepted immediately. "Yes, of course. I'd be happy to."

"Very good! I'll send the invitation around tomorrow. Until the ball, then," he finished, his face revealing his delight at Lily's acceptance. He hurried back to Karl and they slipped into the tower's stairwell.

Lily, shocked, slowly realized that she'd just gotten what she wanted. Sensing the book within reach, a wave of euphoria overcame her. Then she remembered Paul, who surely must be waiting outside for her. Lily rushed through the crowd, eager to escape the pavilion and meet Paul.

Out on the walkway, she rushed toward the metro entrance. Back on the square in front of the new Palais de Chaillot, she scanned the crowd for Paul's face. Nothing. She looked more carefully, making a slow panorama, right to left. Suddenly she felt a hand on her shoulder. She shrieked and jumped away. It was Paul, who bent to kiss her, murmuring, "Bon soir." She relaxed, happy to see him, and he took her hand.

"I accompany you home?"

"Oui," Lily responded. She felt completely different with Paul at her side. The touch of her hand against his felt good. She liked moving through Paris as a couple, even though she knew she should not let these sentiments root.

They boarded a train and found seats on a wooden bench across from an old woman. Paul still held Lily's hand. The old woman observed them, a tiny smile on her wrinkled face. At the next station she rose, looked at Paul and Lily, and announced, "Vous faîtes un beau couple tout les deux."

The woman disappeared into the crowd on the platform. Lily blushed, embarrassed, but Paul just giggled. Two ladies took the seats across from them. Lily gazed at them, thinking they looked familiar. The pale woman with very light hair caught Lily's gaze and smiled. Something about her look held Lily, and in her mind she heard the voice she'd heard at the Crédit Municipal, saying again, "You'll be fine." Lily shook her head and the woman broke her gaze, turning to her friend to whisper something. Lily couldn't see the other woman's face underneath her large hat.

She glanced down at Paul's hand on her thigh and squeezed it. Avoiding the eyes of the women across the way, Lily saw herself and Paul reflected in the dark screen of the metro window. She had to agree with the old woman's comment. They did make a handsome couple. But she couldn't keep this up. She would be leaving soon.

As the train slowed and pulled into another stop, Paul asked her if she had a good time at the Exposition.

"You can say that," she said.

"I have not been there yet," Paul said. "I would love to go with you. Would you accompany me one day?"

"Sure, why not? There's a lot more to see."

"Next Sunday is possible?"

Lily, who lived day by day since her arrival here, had no

idea where she'd be on Sunday. But she agreed anyway.

"Yes, maybe." She didn't want to talk in the subway. The women across from her were engrossed in quiet conversation, but Lily still sensed they had an eye on her.

"Let's change here," exclaimed Paul.

They got off when the train shuddered to a stop. Down the hallway toward another line, the flow of passengers moved in both directions, forcing Lily to release Paul's hand. Then she made sure to dodge the pedestrian traffic in the opposite direction of Paul, to avoid his hand. Yes, she loved the couple she had seen in the reflection. But she also remembered what she had decided at the Expo. She would not mess with Paul by allowing him to believe that anything could be possible between them. Even if every bit of her body and her senses told her otherwise, she would not. She put her hands in her jacket pockets even though it made walking awkward. And in the next train, she leaned against the window and kept her hands tucked away to avoid temptation.

"Ça va, Lily?"

"Ça va," she said. "I'm a little tired."

They said nothing more for the rest of the ride. Paul wore a hurt expression but gave her space. Lily cringed to think of the distance she was creating between them. A few steps from the bookstore Paul turned to Lily.

"I said something I should not?"

She shook her head.

"Then why are you so cold with me? What did I do?"

Lily dared not look at him, mumbling, "Nothing. I'm the problem."

"How is that?"

"Listen, Paul. You and me, it's impossible. We have no future together."

"You say one thing, Lily. Your kisses yesterday, even your eyes at the Expo, say the opposite. Why you do this?"

"Because I do not want to hurt you, Paul. There will be no affair between us. That's impossible. Because I'm going home soon."

Paul shook his head, his mouth open in surprise. Lily felt her heart sink.

"Paul, you're a nice guy, so helpful. I can never thank you enough for being there for me. You deserve to find happiness and I know you'll make the right woman very happy."

His eyes were red, as if he were going to cry. Lily glanced away. She couldn't look at him. Doing so put her at risk of giving in, just to allay his sadness. He rallied and questioned her again.

"Tell me the truth, Lily. There's another man in this, isn't there? You don't just become cold overnight for no reason. I want the truth! You met someone else, didn't you? That's why you went to the Exposition!"

"No, Paul. There is no other man, I swear!"

"I do not believe you, Lily. Not at all." He gave her one last, fierce look and then stormed off.

"Paul!"

She tried to grab him but he eluded her. Lily watched him disappear around the corner. She slipped into the building's entry and leaned against the closed door. Catching her breath in a jagged hiccup, she was suddenly in tears.

27

LILY PASSED A sleepless night on the thin cot in the back of the shop. Moonlight shining through the courtyard windows played on her bed. She couldn't avoid the light or her tortured thoughts about Paul. She felt terrible to have hurt him, leaving him with the impression that she cared naught for what had grown between them. Her sleep came fitfully, marked by dreams of Paul, and oddly, Daniel. In all of them Lily felt an uncomfortable urgency, leaving her unable to communicate clearly. Metro stations, airports, and giant spaces that looked like airplane hangars dominated her dreams and she awoke just before dawn, exhausted.

The dreadful feeling got worse the longer she lay there, so Lily rose and washed at the small basin. The smell of her blouse repelled her; she was loathe to put it back on, but she couldn't wear the nightdress Sylvia had thoughtfully loaned her. Shrugging on her jacket, she wondered what she would wear to the reception with Heinrich. Surely her skirt and jacket wouldn't do, and her dress, while nice, certainly wasn't a fancy dress. She doubted Sylvia would have an evening gown to loan her, too. Brushing her hair into a semblance of neatness, she flashed on Heinrich's friend's angry face. Why did she bother him so much? What had she gotten herself involved in?

She slipped out of the shop and waved at Lucky, who had fallen asleep in the shop window, displacing a stack of books. Lily followed her nose to a boulangerie at the corner, where she bought a *pain au chocolate*. She devoured it on the sidewalk, then ducked into the Café Danton for an espresso. Huddling over her notebook, fueled by the bitter coffee, she scribbled her thoughts, desperate to evacuate her guilt about her lies to Paul onto the page. Finally, she wound down, and after wandering the neighborhood, she returned to the shop, feeling only slightly better about it all. She wouldn't bother Sylvia with any of this; the bookseller had enough to worry about without dealing with a lovelorn assistant.

Sylvia was hunched at her desk when Lily came in. She raised her head from a stack of papers, her eyes droopy, with dark circles underneath them.

"Are you okay, Sylvia?"

"It's nothing," Sylvia said, attempting to put some order to the stack of papers she'd just been lying on.

"Come on, I can tell you're not well. You look terrible. Is it your migraines?"

Sylvia sighed. "Okay! I see I can't hide anything from you, Detective Lily. It is another migraine. But I can cope. I must deal with this now." She waved the papers in the air.

"But . . ." Lily pressed.

"I'm fine, Lily. Get to work now, please."

In the far corner of the bookstore, Lily tidied a stack of books on a table, occasionally sneaking glances at Sylvia, who sat at her desk, clearly struggling against her headache. When Lily came to the desk for another task, Sylvia, one hand on her temple, raised her head and smiled wanly.

"You're already done? Good!"

"Sylvia, your eyes are bloodshot and I can tell you're trying to stay upright. I can't stand to see you like this. Please take a rest. I insist."

Teddy lifted his head and stared at Lily as if surprised by her raised voice. Sylvia looked at her a moment, then sighed.

"You're right, nurse. I'm will rest for few minutes," she said, standing. Teddy followed, creaking up from his spot on the rug.

"Don't worry. I'll watch the shop. Take your time."

"I hope so, Lily. You are my assistant, aren't you?"

"Yes, of course."

"Good! Don't forget. You have some books to prepare for shipping."

Lily watched Sylvia shuffle toward the back room and disappear behind the curtain with Teddy behind her. The stairs creaked as Sylvia climbed to her apartment above.

At the shipping desk, a couple of books waited to be packed up. Lily set about making mailing labels. More people wrote and asked for books than came into the shop. She couldn't stop thinking about Paul, and Heinrich as well. In Denver, she hadn't been this attractive to men. Here, they seemed to relish her outspoken nature. At home, speaking up was normal and maybe not such a winning trait. Daniel came to mind. She imagined telling him all about this. Would he believe her? Would anyone?

Lily finished with the books and went back to Sylvia's desk. The stack of typed papers sat in disorder where Sylvia had left it. Lily had asked Sylvia once if she wanted to write, and Sylvia had scoffed. A couple of publishers were after her, she said, to write her memoirs, but she wasn't much of a writer.

"What about those poems and essays you translated?" Lily had asked.

"Translating isn't writing. I'm not crafting the words, only copying them into English. Or French, for that matter."

Lily commiserated. She couldn't imagine having the facility in two languages to leap from one to the other, carrying another writer's meaning. Sylvia shrugged it off. "It brings in money, so I do it. Which I doubt the memoir would."

Lily had read Sylvia's memoir, a book called *Shakespeare and Company*. Based on that, it was true that Sylvia was not a great writer. She recounted anecdotes of people she knew but didn't succeed in making them full stories. Lily suspected the publisher was interested because of Sylvia's celebrity acquaintances and because Sylvia was at the center of them all. Perhaps the publisher shared Lily's suspicion that behind every bookseller or person in the book industry was a closeted writer. She had to admit that was the case for herself, but not for Sylvia.

"I bet you could write great stories. Think of all the people you know, all of the great stories you have to tell."

"I'm more interested in reading great stories than in writing them. But I'm thinking about it. Maybe some literary criticism. If I ever get a break from the shop, I'd do it."

You'll get a break soon enough, Lily wanted to say. *Just hang in there a couple more years.* The mess of papers Lily held now appeared to be a promotional piece for the bookstore, pages filled with typed single-spaced lines that were heavily inked. Entire paragraphs were blackened out, as though the writer was at war with the content. Lily couldn't resist digging in. She shuffled through, reading quickly. Sylvia, if she was the author of the mess, was trying to write a piece called "The Successful Bookshop: A Manual of Practical Information." Lily immediately saw the problem, besides the fact that Sylvia's bookstore could not be called financially successful. The brochure was dry and stuffy, the ideas formulaic. There were so many misspelled words that Lily wondered if Sylvia was trying to be clever or just didn't know how to spell. She recalled a conversation she overheard when Sylvia had been on the phone with one of her friends, and it was like she was speaking a language other than French, but not quite English. Sylvia thrived on wordplay, but misspellings? Lily shook her head and pulled out her notebook. Picking up where Sylvia's best sentence left off, she started writing, drawing on the copywriting she'd done at the bookstore in Denver.

The afternoon's slow crawl sped up. A few customers wandered in and browsed. No one bought anything, but Lily checked out a few books for them from the library. In the meantime she continued to work on the brochure, crossing out entire paragraphs, scribbling new text.

When the grandfather clock struck five o'clock, Sylvia hadn't returned to the shop, so Lily decided to take a risk and type up her version of the brochure. She rolled the typewriter stand into the shop from the back room. Positioning it near Sylvia's desk, she admired the typewriter. Small, black, with the gold letters M.A.P. surrounded by gold embellishment at the top. The ribbons were exposed, the top part black, the bottom red. Her fingers caressed the white keys and she began typing her version of the brochure. The keys' metallic feel, and the way they resisted her fingers, was so different than the modern clacking of a plastic keyboard. She hadn't used a typewriter since she was a girl.

One evening, when Lily was twelve years old, she was in her room reading when her mother called her downstairs.

"Lily, we have something for you."

Lily had a whole list of summer reading and was then in the middle of *Jane Eyre*. She stretched and rolled over on the bed, noticing that the white eyelet coverlet had left tiny round circles imprinted on her thighs.

"What!" Her parents didn't give gifts unless it was her birthday or Christmas, and it wasn't time to go school supply shopping yet.

"Get down here!" She heard her mother and father laughing. She marked her place in the book with her tasseled Yosemite bookmark and slid off the bed. She dawdled down the steps.

In the kitchen, her parents stood at the table. They were drinking—her mother a glass of white wine and her father a gin and tonic. That explained the laughing. They huddled close together, hiding something on the table behind them.

"We've noticed you've been reading a lot this summer," her father started. "And we had an idea." He looked at Lily's mother, still clad in her grubby gardening smock. Smears of grass marked her knees. She smiled at Lily. It had been a long time since Lily saw her parents united like this on something.

"And—"

"And we took it as a sign of something budding in you."

"Mom! I'm not a plant! Come on!"

"Oh, Sedum," her mother crooned.

"Please don't start with that nickname again. I'm going back upstairs where civilization exists." Lily turned toward the stairs, but halfheartedly.

"Don't get hung up on words," her father said.

"Dad! Words are everything."

"That's why we got you this."

They parted, and on the pine kitchen table sat a baby blue typewriter. Lily stared at it. She couldn't believe it. Her parents had actually noticed she wanted to write. How did they know she preferred a vintage typewriter to a new computer? She ran her fingers over the plastic shell, looking for a way to open it. Her father showed her two white buttons on the front of the lid. She pressed them and the lid came up with a clucking sound. She pulled it off and set it aside. The typewriter was adorable, with white keys that bounced back when she hit them. The smooth platen was unmarked by letters.

A stack of paper sat next to the typewriter. She picked up a piece and rolled it in. She let her fingers dance over the keys, not worrying that the letters didn't form words. Her father coaxed her to type "the quick brown fox jumped over the lazy dog" to make sure none of the letters stuck. Lily couldn't believe it. Now she could type her papers for school. Now she could write down all those ideas for stories she had. It would be different than in her diary, which was too small and had narrow lines. Now what she wrote would be real, one step closer to a story. She clacked away on the keys while her parents smiled.

"Thank you! How did you know?"

"Oh, I saw the signs," her father said. "All those books you cart up to your room. Now take this upstairs and have fun with it."

Lily replaced the lid and, hugging the typewriter to her chest, made her way back upstairs. It wasn't too heavy, and when she got to her room she noticed that it had a white handle. She could carry it outside and to other rooms in the house if she wanted. She pushed aside a stack of books on her desk and squared the typewriter in the middle. She took the lid off and propped it against the side of the desk. Rolling a fresh piece of paper in, she took her seat. She sat for several minutes with her fingers poised over the keys, trying to remember one of her ideas for a story. The only thing that came to mind was the story she was reading. What was happening with Rochester? She couldn't stop reading now. She could write later. She flopped back down on the bed and picked up her book.

That summer Lily read the Brontë sisters, Nathaniel Hawthorne, and all of Edgar Allan Poe. The typewriter got a few runs but mostly sat covered, mocking her notion that she could be a writer. When school started, Lily used it for writing papers. Her teachers were impressed that her homework was so neat, but still, she wished she were writing stories. In language arts class she wrote a story that Miss Haring gave her an A for, but she felt it was just luck. Every time she tried to write, she didn't know what to do. Her ideas started out great, but after a few pages they fizzled out. By the end of the school year she had given up the idea of being a writer and stored the typewriter in the closet.

Now, clacking away at Sylvia's typewriter, Lily's thoughts

circled around Heinrich. She had to leave aside all the compliments he'd given her and focus on one thing: getting the book. He said he'd send an invitation to her, and now, each time someone passed the shop, she felt a twinge of anticipation. She paused in her typing. Maybe he was interested in her merely as a way to get closer to Sylvia. Despite her matronly ways, Sylvia could be an object of Nazi surveillance. She was the center of a group of international intellectuals. Her shop was, or had been, highly trafficked. A perfect place for dropping off information. A perfect place for sending information, with books, perhaps, in packages. A perfect center for the Résistance. Perhaps Sylvia had been part of the underground movement against the Nazis. Lily hadn't read anything about that in Sylvia's papers, but that's not the kind of thing you publicize. If she stayed, Lily would find out. Perhaps Lily would become part of the Résistance as well. And Paul, too. They'd be a heroic couple in the fight for France. They'd deliver secret messages at night by bicycle. She could help Sylvia convert the storage room upstairs to hide members of the Résistance or British pilots shot down in combat.

"What are you doing with my typewriter?"

Lily flinched. Sylvia didn't sound happy. The bookseller loomed over her, a frown wearing a pattern of wrinkles around her mouth.

"I ... I ... "

At Capitol Books, Valerie would have loved it if Lily had taken more initiative. She'd encouraged it. But maybe Lily had taken too much license here.

"That's my typewriter. How dare you get it out and apply your grimy fingers to it."

"Sylvia, I'm sorry. I was bored and saw the brochure you were working on. I thought you were having a hard time, so—"

"So you thought you'd meddle again." Sylvia ripped the paper from the platen and pulled her lighter out of her pocket. Lily thought she was going to flame her writing. Instead, Sylvia put a cigarette between her lips, lit it, and squinting through the smoke, read Lily's copy. Lily paced, as much to get away from the smoke as to work off the nervousness. She had almost finished reworking the paragraph about how events could help bring in new customers and encourage regulars to buy more books. She had itemized how sidelines—book paraphernalia, notebooks, magazines—can boost sales and attract a variety of readers into the store. Sylvia was already doing some of that, but with Lily's modern spin she hoped they sounded more appealing. Sylvia grunted occasionally, and Lily couldn't tell if they were noises of approval or disdain. By the time she reached the end, Sylvia was finished with her cigarette. She stubbed it out and put the paper down on the desk.

"You're better at writing than I am," she said. "I almost believe that these things could make a bookstore work." She sat down, her tweed skirt riding up on her knees. A trail of varicose veins worked its way up the side of Sylvia's calf. She seemed older than the fiftyish Lily knew her to be.

"I was trying to help, not hurt your feelings. Do you like it?"

A small smile appeared on Sylvia's lips. "I suppose I do. I suppose I do. Can you type it up properly so we can use it and send it to the printer?"

Lily asked what "properly" meant, and soon the women were working on the brochure together. Sylvia showed Lily how to get the margins straight, and Lily pointed out ways they could incorporate some of Sylvia's writing so it had her voice.

As they were working, a uniformed messenger came into the shop and held up an envelope in his gloved hand. "De livraison pour..."

Sylvia stood and held out her hand.

"... Lily Heller," he finished.

Sylvia looked startled, her hand still extended.

Lily blushed. "That's me," she said.

The messenger handed her a cream-colored envelope upon which her name was written in blue ink. Lily slid her finger under the flap and pulled out a heavy card. It was an invitation to a party at the German embassy. At the bottom, in the same blue ink, was a note: "I will fetch you at 7 o'clock tomorrow. Yours, Heinrich."

"Is that from your beau?"

Lily shook her head. "It's an invitation from Heinrich. He wants me to join him at an embassy party." At this, Sylvia raised an eyebrow.

"Have you a reply, mademoiselle?" the delivery boy asked.

"I'm not sure why you'd want to go," Sylvia said.

Turning to the messenger, Lily said, "Tell him thanks. I'll be ready."

The boy nodded. Sylvia roused herself from her surprise and pressed a coin into his hand. He bowed slightly and slipped out the door.

"What do you think you're getting into?"

"I don't know. What do you think I'm getting into?"

"Lily, it's none of my business, surely, but I am sure your

mother would appreciate me looking out for you. I'd be careful if I were you."

Lily swallowed. Here was Sylvia acting motherly. She wished she could tell her that it wasn't for Heinrich that she was going. If only she'd gotten the book before Heinrich had, she wouldn't have to do this. But she did.

"Thanks, Sylvia. But please don't worry about me. It will be okay." She knew it would be all right for Sylvia, but she wasn't sure about herself. She could only hope for the best.

They worked in an awkward silence until it was time to close the shop, when Sylvia gave Lily an appraising look.

"You're more helpful than I thought you'd be," she said.

"I'm glad," Lily said. "I want to help. I like to write, too."

"Yes, didn't you say something about being a writer?"

"Trying to be a writer. Trying."

"What do you mean, trying? You either do it or you don't."

"Yes ma'am," Lily said.

Sylvia asked what she wrote. Lily blanked. She hadn't really written anything, unless she counted her florid notebook entries. She wasn't sure whether to mention them or not.

"All my writing is back in the States. But I've been writing a lot in my notebook recently. Just some ideas."

"Well, show me something. I'd like to read something that wasn't an onslaught of persuasive writing."

Lily grinned. "Thanks, Sylvia. I will."

28

THE FOLLOWING DAY, Lily minded the shop. Sylvia had dashed to the Expo to oversee a delivery of magazines to her booth. Lily tried to avoid thinking about Heinrich and the book. Instead, she thought about the pages in her purse. She had written them out carefully, though her handwriting, big and loopy, was nowhere as neat as Sylvia's librarian script. Lily had penned a story about the Hemingway reading and she was eager to show it to Sylvia.

She hadn't slept well on the tiny cot, a draft invading from the courtyard. Sleep had been replaced by worry about the embassy party, how she'd get the book from Heinrich, what she'd wear, what would happen with Paul, what Sylvia would think. Finally around dawn Lily had drifted away, the weight of Lucky near her feet pulling her to sleep.

She neatened the shelves and made a mental list of books to read. She must at least try *Ulysses*. And Gertrude's *The Making of Americans*. With a jolt she realized how many books would be lost to her if she were stuck in 1937. She'd likely be dead before the nineties. That is, if she survived the war, which wasn't a given. Shaking off these thoughts, she stepped outside for air. Gazing at the wooden façade of the bookshop, Lily got the idea to tidy the window displays. They could use a good cleaning, she thought. She set to the project. When she had all of the books out of the window and stacked on chairs, she felt a moment of panic. What if Sylvia didn't like what she was doing? What if she disapproved of neat window displays? She didn't seem to welcome change but had come around to her brochure revisions. Teddy, who'd been tracking her every move, sniffed at a dead fly in the window.

She found a tiny whisk broom in the back closet and used a piece of cardboard to gather the cat hair and bug carcasses. She loved tidying up. At her bookstore back home, she had felt immense satisfaction using the hand-held vacuum cleaner to get rid of debris.

Once the window was empty, she began replacing things, rearranging the books in clever patterns, showing the spines, stacking them in ways that revealed the author photo, then the cover. She grabbed the red velvet pillow from the chair and placed it in a spot that wasn't visible from the front of the window. If the cat decided to sleep on it, perhaps her tail would peek out around the books and entice passersby into the shop.

While she worked, she ran different scenarios about how she'd get the book from Heinrich to Louise. Would he have the book at the embassy or would she have to go home with him to get to it? How far would she go to get a book she herself wasn't interested in? Finally, she popped outside to view the window, Teddy at her heels. It looked great, and standing in the Parisian afternoon, Lily wished Valerie were here to enjoy it with her.

Back inside, Lily sat at Sylvia's desk to rest. She missed Paul and hoped he would come visit. Not a single customer had come in since Sylvia left. Lily pulled open the desk drawer. A wooden tray held paper clips, loose stamps, erasers. Tugging the drawer out further, she spied something toward the back: a slim black notebook nestled on top of some envelopes. Lily lifted it out. She hadn't seen this in the library at Princeton. Printed on the inside cover was "Aid to the Bookshop 1935–." Sylvia's neat handwriting filled several pages. Two pages of names were listed under "Friends of Shakespeare and Company," along with the amount the donors had given. Natalie Barney, André Gide, and T.S. Eliot were among them, as well as many French names she didn't recognize. Pausing, she gazed out the window. She would meet these people if she was stuck in 1937 and had to stay at Shakespeare and Company. Lily had read about how Sylvia's friends had banded together to save the store. Friends of Shakespeare and Company paid a fee and then got into readings for free and had other privileges. She had told Valerie about it, hoping they could do something similar to keep Capitol Books going. Valerie dismissed the idea, saying she already relied on the goodwill of the customers without asking them for more money. She was as stubborn as Sylvia. Now, Lily could be part of all that Valerie had dismissed.

The clock chimed the hour. It had been almost two hours since Sylvia had gone to the Expo. Heinrich would be coming for her that evening and she had no idea what she was going to wear. If she spent her money on a dress, she would have to get the rest of her cash from Paul. Without knowing how much Sylvia was paying her, she preferred that he be her bank, keeping her money safe. Lily put the ledger away and pulled out her notebook and began writing. She picked up speed, listing the problems she was facing: what to wear tonight, how to stay safe while surrounded by Nazis, how she was going to get home, the impossibility of time travel. Suddenly the door flew open and Hemingway barged in, setting the bell to jangle loudly and bringing a waft of crisp spring air. His cheeks were flushed and the beginning of a double chin cushioned his collar. Still, he was quite handsome.

"Ahoy!" he shouted at Lily. She caught a whiff of alcohol on his greeting.

"Ahoy?" A nervous laugh escaped her. Lily closed her notebook and held it on her lap.

He rubbed his hands together, scanning the shop as if casting about for something to seize. He filled the space in front of the desk and Lily realized that she and Sylvia were tiny, appropriately so for the cramped room.

"Sylvia's not in. May I help you?"

"Read anything good lately?"

Since Lily had arrived, she hadn't read much and strangely, wasn't missing it. "Sadly, no," she said. "How about you?"

He caught sight of the notebook on her lap. "Say, what's that you've got there? You a writer?"

"I'm . . . you know, like, trying to write."

"What do you mean, 'like trying to write'? What a bunch of extra words! Let's hope you don't write that way. Let's have a look."

He held out his hand toward Lily. A surge of panic gripped her gut. She clutched the notebook tighter.

"Uh, no, thanks, that's okay."

He lunged forward and grabbed the notebook from her.

"Nice pad you got here. Not too nice, I hope. You don't need anything fancy to write well. Let's see . . ."

He opened the notebook. Lily leaped up. She came up to the middle of his chest. His small black mustache was only slighter longer than Hitler's. She gripped the side of the desk, stammering, unable to stop him. She grabbed the papers she had so carefully written for Sylvia.

"Here," she said. She pressed her writing into his hand, trying to grab the notebook. But he clung to the notebook, reading, engrossed. This was her big chance to get feedback from a real writer and all she wanted was to get her work away from him.

"Interesting," he said. He stroked his chin and kept reading, ignoring Lily's attempts to get it away from him. He could be reading any one of the vignettes she had written about her time here. The pages she'd written for Sylvia were more suitable for reading, less private. At one point he pulled back from the page and muttered, "Huh! You've got some issues with the run-on sentence. And your vocabulary—very creative. Hmmph," he said, continuing to read.

Lily paled. Her lips shook and she fought the urge to launch a defense of her writing. She knew she had none. She clutched the pages meant for Sylvia behind her back.

"Still, there's some interesting material here. You've got a vivid imagination." He peered at her over the notebook and she smiled like that was a compliment.

"Thank you." Lily nearly drooped with relief. He did like it . . . enough. She hoped he had not seen the most recent entry, where she had written about the deaths of those around them. She stepped closer. "Here, read this. You'll really like this. I wrote this out for Sylvia to see, but she hasn't had a chance to read it yet." Lily grabbed the notebook and switched it for the papers. Hemingway took one glance at the neatly written paragraphs, scanned the first one, and threw it back on the desk.

"Nah," he said, dismissing the work she had so carefully labored over. "The other stuff here," he pounded his finger onto the notebook that Lily gripped close to her chest, "this is workable."

Lily stumbled back and fell into the chair. Hemingway liked her journaling. Incredible. Later she would scan it all, rereading, guessing at what he could possibly have liked. She prayed he hadn't read anything too revealing, like the part about kissing Paul. Or the feisty conversations she invented with Sylvia on the page, where Lily gave her all kinds of advice she would never speak aloud. Or about traveling in time from 2010. She swallowed.

"Thank you. Thank you so much! It means a lot that you said that."

"Yeah, no problem, kid." Hemingway cleared his throat and rubbed his hands again. "Work on that. Work it till every word glows. Work it till you can't wring another drop out of the damn sentence, till you know it's right."

"Work it. Right . . . I'll do that."

"Okay, now. I've got to get some books. Need new material, new material."

Lily tried to think of recommendations but the author already hovered near the fiction section, pulling books off the shelves. He was hyper, revved up by booze or his own trajectory of fame or God knew what. Lily sat, stunned. Hemingway had liked her writing. She really was a writer. He brought a few books to the desk and Lily wrote them down.

"Borrowing or buying?"

"Buying. I'm terrible about returning the books. But I'll settle later with Sylvia."

He grabbed his books and left the shop. Despite his fame, despite his compliment about her writing, Lily was angry he hadn't paid. For as many friends who helped Sylvia, it seemed there were just as many who took advantage of her. She went to the door and watched him jauntily disappear down the street and around the corner. Looking the other way, she saw Sylvia coming. From afar, she appeared older than she was, walking slowly and with a slight stoop. Lily waited at the open door, excited to see Sylvia's expression when she saw the window display.

Sylvia approached, glancing up and catching sight of Lily. She smiled and gave a little wave. But when she saw the display, her face fell.

"What in God's name has gotten into you? What have you done to the window?"

Lily couldn't tell if Sylvia was really mad or just posturing. Still frowning, Sylvia entered, Lily trailing behind.

"Do you like it, Sylvia?"

"First the brochure, now this. Did I ask you to move things around? What . . . did you think I wasn't coming back?" Sylvia dropped her satchel and a parcel on the desk.

"I'm sorry. I should have asked first, right?"

Sylvia sighed. "I guess I should be accustomed to your impudence by now."

"I call it initiative. I think it looks great!" Lily gushed. "I got rid of all that cat hair and the dead bugs. The books are easier to see . . . and with the magazines arranged like that, people will know about them and come in to buy them." Lily glanced at the other displays she had hoped to reorganize. "I'm sorry if I overstepped—"

"You did, indeed. What moxie! I'd appreciate it if you keep to the tasks I assign to you." She went back outside the shop to appraise the display. Glancing back and forth between the two windows, the one Lily had arranged and the one she hadn't, her frown disappeared.

Lily went to the door. "Do you like it even a little bit? Are you really sore?"

Sylvia nearly smiled. "You . . . you . . . you bit of fluff. I can't help but like it a little bit. A little bit. Don't get any big ideas! I've been running this shop for eighteen years and I've done just fine without fancy window displays."

Lily tried to repress her pride. A couple passed by and the woman led the man over to the display, pointing at the magazines. They spoke in French, discussing the new literature that was crossing the Channel. Sylvia came back into the store.

"You can do the other one if you want," she muttered.

Lily grinned. "The same way? Should I do the second window in a different style?"

Sylvia waved her away. "Do whatever you want."

Lily went outside to inspect the other window and to assess the possibilities. She'd done it. She'd given Sylvia something. For the rest of the afternoon, she rearranged the other window. It was much easier than the first, now that she had Sylvia's blessing.

Lily put the final touches on the display. Now that her mark was on the front of the shop, she was more aware of people passing by. A woman paused at the windows. She wore a navy cloche hat and a tight-fitting jacket and skirt. Her waist was impossibly tiny. When she stepped into the shop, Lily noticed her tall heels, black leather with a strap across the instep. Sylvia, clad in her usual tweedy outfit, stood to greet her. The two women exchanged *bises* and hugged, a combination of French and Americans greetings.

"When did you have time to redo your windows? They look ritzy," the woman said.

"Carlotta, you know nothing would get me to crawl into those windows. It was my assistant, Lily, displaying her American moxie and doing something without me."

Carlotta glanced at Lily. "Well, it's a good thing she did. Take a look at the gawkers."

The women lingered near the pole in the middle of the room, peering out at the people on the sidewalk. A small crowd had gathered, two couples pointing at the displays and chatting. Lily could see it all: the shop's popularity swelled with the addition of a few modern marketing techniques; Sylvia earned enough to pay her bills and take all the vacations she needed; and sales soared—all because of the perky assistant who was willing to make some changes.

Sylvia gave Lily a look that Lily interpreted as "You'll get a raise for this." Lily still hadn't asked Sylvia about her wage details. She'd bring that up. After this coup, Sylvia would surely pay her more.

The foursome moved into the store and one of the women inquired about something in the window. Sylvia leaned in and with difficulty pulled out the Wharton book. Lily chatted with Carlotta, discovering that the two women were going to a concert the next night. Lily hoped to be invited but didn't say anything. She puttered around the back of the shop, getting ideas for new table displays until Sylvia finished with the customers, who ended up buying several books and a copy of *Transition*. Lily wished they had bought more, but Sylvia was humming after they left. Lily could tell that merely having people come in was a success for Sylvia.

Lily approached the desk, where Teddy lay gnawing a bone. "Sylvia?"

"Mmm." Sylvia didn't look up. She kept scribbling on the pad.

"I brought some of my writing for you." She placed the sheaf of papers on the desk. Sylvia didn't look up.

"How am I going to make this month's rent appear?"

Lily shriveled inside, wishing she could just suck the papers back up into her purse.

"I wish I could help. What can I do?"

Sylvia removed her glasses and tossed them onto the desk. She rubbed her eyes like she was trying to erase them, to press away everything she saw that she couldn't do anything about.

"Help me conjure up some customers." She put her glasses back on. "Nothing. You can't do anything to help."

Lily lost it.

"I already have helped! We already had more customers since I rearranged the window displays! No wonder you're in such a bad way—you don't let people help you. You could do a lot more if you collaborated, learned not to always be so damn stoic! Why can't you admit that you don't know what you're doing and are just hanging on because you're more stubborn than sensible? Why don't you go home, too, before it's too late?"

Sylvia sat back, a look of shock on her face. Teddy stood, abandoning his bone, staring up at Sylvia.

"How can you talk to me like that? You pipsqueak—after all I've done to help you?"

"That's right—play the martyr. You're so used to helping everyone else, you haven't even noticed how desperately you need help."

Lily stopped. She hadn't really said all that to Sylvia. She couldn't have, and yet the look on Sylvia's face assured her that, yes, she had spoken words she could never retract. Lily crept toward the back of the shop, but the tiny bookstore offered no escape. She heard Sylvia's chair scrape against the floor. Sylvia's cigarette lighter clicked and Lily smelled the smoke immediately.

"Come back here, you coward."

Lily inched along a bookcase and out into Sylvia's line of fire.

"Now you listen here." Sylvia jabbed her cigarette in Lily's direction. Both Teddy and Lily watched Sylvia.

"I'm here because I choose to be here. I'm no martyr. I might be a fool, yes, but I like my life here. I like the bookstore. I like this street, and I like my friends. I like Adrienne and I like Paris. What's back in the States for me anyway? Ha! A life in my family's shadow? It took an ocean between us for me to finally be able to breathe. Oh, I love them, of course, but try to have a life around them." She puffed on her cigarette and came closer to Lily, blowing the smoke toward the ceiling.

"And who do you think you are? Just because you rearranged some books and penned a few good lines doesn't give you the right to judge me. What makes you think you know anything about my life? I live under no one's scrutiny. My decisions are my own and I'll be damned if someone like you is going to come in here and pass judgment about me allowing help." She stabbed her cigarette into the glass ashtray on the desk. Her eyes were bulging—all traces of the old lady Lily had pitied earlier were gone.

"I'll tell you about help. I get help every damn month. Without help, I wouldn't be here. Without Bryher's monthly check, the shop would have closed years ago. Without Gide and his brilliant idea to have readings here and ask for donations from friends, I would have closed two years ago. Goddamn you, I do take help and don't you for a minute think it doesn't make me sick every time. I wish I could close up and go hide in my apartment, catch up on my reading, finally, instead of running this dying ship further aground. But I love it too much to admit defeat. And there is nothing else for me anyway."

She wound down and took her seat. For once, Lily didn't know what to say. After an uncomfortable silence, she apologized.

"I'm sorry, Sylvia. That was completely out of line. I had no right—"

"You and everyone else who comes in here think they know what is best for me. Do I look so feeble?" She slammed her fist on the desk. "Do I look so feeble?"

She did look feeble sometimes, but Lily wouldn't tell her that.

"Sylvia, I'm sorry. I didn't mean to upset you. And you're right, I don't know what is best for you."

Sylvia waved Lily's apology away. She lit another cigarette and paced the small rug in front of her desk. As she walked by, the rubber stamps shook in their rack. The piles of books and papers on the desk balanced precariously. Lily resisted going over and straightening them.

"Damn this headache. Damn this Expo—as if I didn't have enough to do just keeping this shop afloat."

The chime above the door sounded again and the women looked up. A young man in a uniform carried a large box into the shop. He doffed his hat and announced a delivery for Lily Heller. Sylvia gave an involuntary cry of surprise and Lily said, "C'est moi." The messenger set the box down on a table, right next to the sign that said DO NOT PLACE ANYTHING ON THE BOOKS! Sylvia pursed her lips while Lily signed for the package, and this time Lily gave the delivery boy a coin.

"What is it?" Sylvia asked.

"I don't know. Let's see." Lily placed the large box on the shipping desk. She untied the string and pulled off the cardboard lid. Inside, a dove-gray dress with pleats lay nestled in light blue tissue paper. Accompanying it was a pair of ivory gloves with a line of tiny seed pearl buttons running up the sleeve. She touched an adorable hat adorned with netting and tiny white beads. At the bottom of the box, in a cloth bag, Lily found a pair of heels. She grimaced when she saw the shoes, but the dress took her breath away. She pulled it out, and the dress cascaded down. Long and elegant, it was unlike anything Lily had ever worn. Poking around the box, she saw no name of the sender, no explanation. Heinrich must have sent it.

"Now where did that come from?" Sylvia wondered aloud. Lily held the dress against her body and smoothed her hand over the silk.

"It's just my size!" Lily couldn't believe it—she didn't even know her size in France, especially since she'd lost weight since being here. Sylvia sighed, while Lily for once was excited about clothes.

"Maybe I have a fairy godmother," she said.

"Hmmph. I could use a fairy godmother," Sylvia said. When Lily peeked at her from under the hat's netting, she saw that Sylvia was smiling.

"Is there a card?" Sylvia poked among the tissue paper. "Aha!" she said, holding up a small envelope. Lily grinned and snatched it from her. She tore open the tiny envelope, but her face fell when she read the card.

"Well?" Sylvia prompted.

"It says, 'We thought this would suit you tonight.' Who's 'we'?"

"Your guess is as good as mine. Heinrich wouldn't have sent this, would he?"

"Well, he would be the obvious one." Lily was suddenly aware that she was hiding most of the truth from Sylvia, and she didn't want her to ask more questions.

"You really are going with him to that party. Are you sure you want to mingle with those people?" Sylvia lit a cigarette while Lily pulled the shoes out. "You'd better put that on now. He'll be here to pick you up soon."

Lily put everything back in the box and rushed to the back room. How she wished for a hot shower to wash away the bookshop dust and the week's accumulation of city grit and sweat. But the best she could do was use the damp rag and the pitcher from the courtyard bathroom to wipe herself clean. Slipping on the dress, she found that it fit perfectly. She wasn't able to get the last part of the zipper up, so she left it while checking her hair in the mirror. Her cheeks were flushed. The dress revealed her bare shoulders and made her look most elegant. She hadn't gotten dressed up for a fancy occasion since her high school prom, which hadn't gone well. Lily had gotten ready in the bathroom that evening, and was curling her hair when her mother came in. Lily jumped, accidentally pulling the curling iron toward her head.

"Ouch! You made me burn myself!"

"I'm sorry, honey. You look so . . . all that makeup."

Lily inspected her face. She thought she looked good, grown up. "What!"

"Well, don't you think it's a little much?"

She had told her mother that her friend Sandy had done her makeup for her. "I like it," she said. "I think it looks good." She moved the curling iron to the left side of her head.

"I think you should take some of it off."

Lily slammed down the curling iron. "Oh, now you're giving advice." Her mother had spent so much time being an independent woman, and ruining her marriage, that Lily had gotten used to being more or less on her own. All the advice she got about female issues, sex, whatever, she got from her friends. "Well, let me tell you," she snapped at her mother.

"You're too late."

"If you just smudged off some of the blue," her mother persisted, "I think it would look great. Just a smidgen." She picked up a tissue. Her fingernails were broken and filled with dirt. Lily dodged her hand.

"Mom! Stop! You have no say." She pushed past her mother into her bedroom. Her dress hung from the closet door, a long lavender silk she'd borrowed from Sandy's older sister. It almost fit her. She sat on the bed and pushed her feet into a pair of pantyhose. Her mother sat next to her on the bed, watching Lily struggle with the hose.

"You have to roll them on one foot at a time."

"I know how to put hose on. Will you just leave and let me get ready? The big night of the year and finally you're giving advice? I told you it's too late."

Her mother stood, and for a moment Lily saw herself from her mother's perspective: her hair half curled, the pantyhose stuck at her knees, wearing enough makeup to cover two prostitutes. Lily went on struggling with the pantyhose, hoping her mother would just go away. She kept her head bent down so she wouldn't have to see her face. She had to hurry: Brad was picking her up soon.

Lily stared at herself in the mirror, watching her eyes well up. She hadn't thought about prom night for years. Now she saw that her mother had been trying to help, not interfere. Regret brought a lump to her throat. Lily wished her mother were here with her now. Her practical advice from her would certainly come in handy.

"I don't see what you want with Heinrich." Sylvia had

slipped into the back room while Lily wrestled into the shoes. They pinched her feet but looked adorable poking out from underneath the hem of the dress. She looked up at Sylvia, wanting badly to confess everything. She smiled brightly, turning slightly to show off the dress.

"Can you zip me up?"

Sylvia nodded. Grasping the zipper, she spoke to Lily's back. "Are you lovers?"

Lily was mortified. That Sylvia would assume she and Heinrich were intimate. That she'd said the word lovers. That Lily had indeed felt an attraction to Heinrich, especially when he laughed so easily. She felt the zipper reach its zenith.

"No! Of course not. Heinrich already has a girlfriend in Germany. I'm sure he just took pity on me, thinking I was too bookish." She turned and fanned the skirt out, posing for Sylvia.

"Still, I should know better than to wait up for you," Sylvia said. "You look lovely, as you should. The dress is perfect; whoever chose it has a sharp eye." Her expression softened. "Here," she said. She held out a silver lipstick tube. Lily gave a quizzical look.

"I didn't see any makeup in that soirée ensemble," Sylvia said. "This might come in handy."

"Merci," Lily said. "I . . . I wish I could explain why I'm going tonight. Maybe I just need a little excitement." She bent toward the speckled mirror and applied the lipstick, which seemed much too red to her. But Sylvia's look said otherwise. Lily even thought she saw her eyes glistening. She smiled and held her arms open, framing Lily.

"You look marvelous. Now, go, enjoy yourself."

Lily was pulling on her gloves when they heard the shop bell ring. Sylvia nodded and began to mount the stairs to her apartment. Lily slipped into the shop and found Heinrich near the door, dressed in a tuxedo, exuding charm with his smile.

"Bonsoir." He bowed slightly and Lily almost curtsied, then stopped herself.

"You look very nice," he said. "That dress suits you."

"Thank you," Lily said. She wasn't sure she was thanking him for the dress or the compliment. She felt uncomfortable asking if he had sent it, so she stayed quiet.

"Ready, then?" She nodded and waved good-bye to Sylvia, who leaned against the back bookcase, watching them leave the shop.

A black sedan was idling out front. Heinrich opened the door, gesturing Lily in with a smile. She was about to step in when she glimpsed someone coming toward the shop. It was Paul, and he caught sight of her just as she saw him. He was carrying a small bouquet of red flowers. The look of betrayal on his face turned Lily's stomach. She stared long enough to watch Paul turn his back with a shake of his head, the flowers falling to the ground.

Heinrich, seeing him, turned back to Lily, nodding her toward the back seat. "Please."

Lily refocused on Heinrich, producing a false smile. They got in the car and Lily tried to concentrate on Heinrich.

"You look stunning, Lily."

She tried to smile but the thought of Paul's expression made her feel like the worst liar. This traitorous feeling only grew as the sedan glided down the street toward Paul. Lily tried

to stare straight ahead but all she saw was the Nazi hood orna-
ment, and at the last minute, as the sedan glided past Paul, she
broke and dared one last peek. He strode toward the boulevard,
hands rammed into his pockets, the flowers cast aside.

29

LILY WATCHED THE Paris evening scroll past the sedan's window. She didn't like to admit it, but she enjoyed the comfort of the powerful car. At the same time, she wished Paul were beside her, not Heinrich.

"You're feeling well?" Heinrich interrupted the silence. Lily nodded. "Good. The embassy isn't far, a quarter of an hour away. If there is not too much traffic."

She smiled slightly and turned back to the window, watching Paris flow by.

"Are you nervous?"

"A little." Lily kept her gaze on the city.

"Do not worry. It will be a very ordinary night. Boring conversations, a buffet, and champagne," he said.

"I can tell you're thrilled," Lily said with a little laugh.

Heinrich joined her laughter. "That's why I'm glad you're my guest. You will hopefully help keep the evening lively."

"I'm sure I'll be out of place."

Heinrich made a ch-ch sound. "Really, don't worry. This will be a stuffy affair with officials, diplomats, men of the world and so on. Nothing frightening at all."

Lily smiled, trying to pretend that going to an event at the German embassy wasn't akin to entering the heart of the evil empire. She imagined the buzz there when the Germans occupied Paris. She prayed she wouldn't have to witness it. Smiling brightly and leaning toward Heinrich, she cooed, "Oh, thank you. I thought I would be surrounded by Germans speaking about Goethe and Schiller. It would have been a bit boring, I think."

Heinrich laughed. "You're so amusing! First the Norse mythology and now Goethe and Schiller, too? What else are you hiding in there?" He touched her hair gently and Lily resisted ducking away.

In truth, Lily had never read these authors. She was drawing on a vague recollection from her studies at the Sorbonne. At a party, a handsome German had literally stunned her with his passion for these authors. He went on and on for nearly an hour, especially excited about Goethe. Lily had remained immobile the whole time, feigning polite silence. Finally, a friend rescued her, facilitating her escape from death by boredom.

Lily now prayed that Heinrich wouldn't have any questions about these authors. Fortunately, the car slowed and turned into an honor court crowded with other cars. The Nazi flags floating above the portico of the *hôtel particulier* raised goose bumps on Lily's arms. She clasped her gloved hands in her lap, feeling restricted by the soft fabric.

"Here we are," Heinrich said.

Lily swallowed, trying to dampen the fear gathering in her belly. The limousine pulled up to the entry. Heinrich got out first, beating the porter to his duty. He reached for Lily, and steadying herself on his hand, she emerged from the car. No man in Denver had ever helped her so gallantly. At the foot of the grand staircase, two uniformed guards stood at attention. The usher bowed to Heinrich without a word. Heinrich asked a few questions in German and the usher showed him the list of guests. After a satisfied nod, Heinrich returned to Lily and escorted her up the stairs, her hand tucked onto his arm.

They found themselves in an enormous ornate ballroom, the crowd dressed in formal attire. The room buzzed with conversation. Lily said a silent thanks to whoever had sent her the dress. The din in the room was overwhelming to Lily. Most of the people there were older. She clung to Heinrich's arm, a smile pasted on her face.

"Allow me to introduce you to my friends," Heinrich said. He led Lily around, introducing her in French to his colleagues, tuxedoed men accompanied by women in floor-length evening gowns. He was completely at ease, introducing her by first name only. Lily felt like a trophy on his arm. But she reminded herself why she was there. She smiled and played the game in spite of a mean look from a woman wearing a decidedly un-modern dress. She caught an old man in a tailcoat regarding her with obvious interest. Lily tried to focus on Heinrich, staying close and quiet.

The waiters passed between the clusters of guests, bringing trays of canapés or white wine. Heinrich offered her something to eat but she shook her head, responding, "Non, merci." She couldn't imagine eating anything with her stomach so tense. She accepted a glass of wine, hoping it would give her courage. Scanning the room, she met the gaze of an older woman. The mutual recognition was instantaneous. It was the haughty countess she'd seen at the Crédit Municipal. The woman flushed and turned away immediately, continuing her conversation with the dapper man next to her. Finally, Lily found herself alone with Heinrich, away from the crowd for a moment. He smiled at her.

"You're not bored, I hope. You're very quiet."

"For once, I'm sure you're thinking," she teased. "I'm just observing. I don't think I've ever attended a party at an embassy before."

"Don't worry, Lily. Just enjoy yourself." He squeezed her arm and went about his mingling. He chatted about this and that, introducing her to his friends, whose names she instantly forgot. She smiled, again and again, with great conviction, and exchanged a few banalities with people who ventured to ask her questions. Heinrich was in his element, and seemed pleased to have her at his side, silent or not. He worked the room, cigarette in hand, always smiling smoothly. They danced, Heinrich holding her close and sharing gossipy tidbits, harmless barbs at his "friends." Lily pretended to share his interest. After a few dances, she squeezed his arm.

"Do you mind if we sit down somewhere away from the smoke? I'm starting to get a touch of a headache."

"But of course. Come."

He led her to a tiny alcove in the great hall, where they sat on a cushioned bench. He sat close and Lily felt slightly dizzy. She finally had his complete attention. Gripping her clutch, she brought the conversation around to books.

"Do you shop often at Sylvia's?" she asked.

"When I am in Paris I make it a point to visit the bookstore," he said. "I like knowing what Sylvia is up to."

"What do you mean?"

"She always has new books, new magazines. Sylvia always knows what is new and—more importantly—what is good in literature now. It was quite kind of her to sell me that book the other day. I know she treasured it."

"What's so important about the book?"

"You are most inquisitive, Lily," he said, and Lily wasn't sure if he was pleased or displeased by it. "I'll tell you: it is a very special book. It's an eighteenth-century English translation of Norse mythology. It was written by an unidentified monk in the eleventh century. It is the only one remaining."

"So it's very valuable for you?"

Heinrich chuckled. "Not so much as a collectible. But there are certain scholars who would very much like to study this work that is part of our heritage."

"How interesting. That makes it even more exciting to see it, then." She brightened with false enthusiasm.

Heinrich put his hand on Lily's and said, "Oh, yes! I promised you that you could see the book. Well, I always keep my promises." He stood and extended his arm. "Shall we?"

She nodded and leaned in, catching his woodsy scent. They left the hall and found the two guards still guarding the staircase. The guards moved apart and stood at attention with a Nazi salute. Heinrich led Lily between them without response and mounted the stairs.

In his office, he lit a stained-glass table lamp. Two of the

walls were lined with glassed-in bookshelves; the other held a
bank of French windows. Lily nervously pulled off her gloves,
and wished she could kick off the uncomfortable shoes. But
that would appear too familiar, so she left them on, watching
Heinrich carefully. Unlocking one of the bookcase doors, he
retrieved the book and placed it carefully on the desk. It was as
large as an encyclopedia but not nearly as thick. Lily admired
the cover and tentatively opened to the table of contents. It was
an illuminated manuscript, the letters lovingly written. She
tried to scan the contents to divine what might be so interesting
to the Nazis. But it was difficult to concentrate and decrypt the
old English with Heinrich looking over her shoulder, leaning
too close. After a few minutes, she pulled away from the book
and glanced at him. His eyes were glassy as he gazed at her.

"It's very beautiful," she said.

"As are you, dear Lily," he replied. He placed his hand on
her shoulder and leaned forward to kiss her. His lips were on
hers for several seconds before Lily drew away.

"Oh," she said. "No! I'm flattered, of course. But it's too
soon for me," she said. "Why don't we go back to the others. The
speeches must be starting."

Heinrich blushed slightly and murmured agreement. He
placed the book in a desk drawer and extinguished the lamp.
A light from outside illuminated his face, looking at Lily with
tenderness. She giggled nervously and he backed away, leading
her out of the room. She made idle conversation about the book
on the way back to the ballroom. The hallways were deserted
and Lily wanted to get Heinrich back to the others as quickly
as possible. They were nearly there when Lily stopped abruptly.

"Oops! I'm sorry, but I need to use the powder room. Where is it, please?"

"Oh. It's just here." Heinrich gestured to the door behind them.

"Thanks. Go ahead, I'll find you in a minute."

"I can wait. It's not a problem."

"But you're missing the speeches!"

"It's not too important; I can miss one or two of them."

Lily didn't know how to deflect his insistence. Finally, she spoke coyly.

"Thanks. It's embarrassing but . . . I wouldn't feel comfortable knowing someone is waiting for me behind the door."

He took her hand, shaking his head and smiling gently.

"Of course. Don't worry, I don't want to embarrass you. I will be downstairs."

"Thanks," Lily said, feigning shyness.

She walked slowly toward the restroom, listening to Heinrich's steps in the corridor, then going downstairs. Once inside, she looked in the mirror. Her face was flushed and her wide eyes revealed her terror. She gathered herself, tucking back a stray curl. At the door, her heart thumped as she peeked out to verify that the hallway was empty. Nobody. Just the echo of the reception below. She pulled off her shoes and ran to Heinrich's office, closing the door quietly.

She kept the lights off, slipped back into her shoes, and rushed to the desk. She jerked open the drawer, revealing the book. With a sigh of relief, she grabbed it. Certainly it wouldn't fit in her reticule. She had no way to conceal the book. She panicked—she had to get it out. But how? She scanned the room and spied a leather briefcase hanging on a hook in the corner. Grabbing it, she stuffed the book inside, then rushed to the window. Confirming that no one was in sight, she leaned over the railing and tossed the bag down. It landed behind a bush. She closed the window and glancing around spied her gloves on the desk. Grabbing them, she rushed out of the room, closing the door behind her.

Rounding the corner, she came upon the German from the Exposition, Heinrich's friend Karl. He seemed more aggressive in his full uniform. She froze, unable to speak.

"Guten nacht," he said coldly. He continued in French. "I hope you have a good reason for your presence here and not below with the others?"

Lily's legs shook under her gown. Her mind was suddenly empty. She stared at this man in his black Nazi uniform, his face steeled in righteous anger.

"Well?" he continued. "I am waiting! What are you doing here?" He spoke louder, as if Lily didn't understand him. His shouts snapped her out of her stupor.

She stammered, "I left my gloves in the office." She held them up. "Heinrich was showing me something and I forgot them there. Now I'm going . . ." She tried to move past him but he blocked her way, grabbing her arm and pulling her to him.

"Where are you going? You really think I believe that story?"

"Leave me alone!" she shouted in panic, trying to pull her arm back. But he merely held on more tightly.

"You will stay here while we sort this out. I will call the guard."

Lily shrank back. "Let go of me!" She tried to pull her arm back but Karl kept his grip. "Let me go!"

Suddenly Lily heard a shout come from behind the German.

They turned to see Heinrich at the bottom of the stairs, his expression angry. He shouted in German to Karl, who explained, pointing first at Lily and the door of Heinrich's office. Heinrich shook his head and sprinted up the stairs. He pulled Karl's hand off Lily and placed himself between them.

"Are you all right?" he asked Lily.

"No! This guard dog attacked me without reason," she said, nearly crying.

"What were you doing in his office?" Karl pushed at Heinrich's shoulder to continue his interrogation.

"I told you, I left my gloves there!" Lily shouted. "After the powder room I went to retrieve them. Who knew it would be such a drama!" She moved next to Heinrich and took his arm. Heinrich patted her shoulder as if to reassure her that it was okay.

"This situation is not normal, Heinrich," Karl insisted.

Heinrich responded firmly in German. Karl stiffened and looked away. With that, Heinrich escorted Lily down the stairs. She felt rather than saw Karl eyeing their backs angrily.

Lily began to breathe again on the way down, replacing her gloves. "I'm sorry, Heinrich. I didn't mean to make trouble for you."

"It's me who owes you the apology. I should not have left you alone upstairs. If I had informed the guards of your presence, nothing like that would have happened. Karl can be very protective of me. My apologies."

"I didn't mean to cause a problem between you. I just thought I could quickly get my gloves and not be a bother at all."

She smiled what she hoped was a wistful smile. He smiled back. "It's time for the buffet, then those speeches," he said. "Perhaps we can slip away before then."

They entered a room near the ballroom. Inside, liveried waiters served the guests from behind a laden buffet table. After choosing a few things from the buffet, they sat at a table with six other people. She tried to be as invisible as possible while eating, all the while thinking about the book in the shrubbery. The people at her table spoke German. She adopted a look of polite interest, pretending to demurely follow along. At one point, she caught Karl lurking near the door, staring at her with a threatening look. She was trying to conjure up an exit excuse when a man in uniform approached Heinrich and whispered in his ear. After a brief discussion, Heinrich turned to Lily.

"Again, my apologies. I have an urgent matter I must attend to. Would you like to stay and wait for me?"

Lily shook her head. "No, that's okay. I'm a bit tired, so I'll just go home now, if you don't mind."

"Of course not. I will call my driver."

"Oh, please, no, that's not necessary. I'll take a taxi." Lily stood and touched Heinrich's arm.

"I won't hear of it. My driver will take you."

Lily nodded. Heinrich motioned to a servant and spoke to him in German, gesturing to Lily. With a smile, he turned to her.

"It's all taken care of. My driver will pull the car up. Thank you for a lovely evening. I hope to see you soon, Lily." He bent to kiss her hand.

She blushed, grateful now for all the people around them.

They left the ballroom and Heinrich joined a pair of men in the foyer. They slipped into a side room and closed the door. Lily waited for a moment, then headed for the exit. Outside, night had fallen. Walking slowly, she pretended to admire the garden, making her way around the building. She spied the tree she'd seen from Heinrich's office and ducked toward the bushes. There, upside down, lay the briefcase with the book inside. She grabbed it, hugging it to her, then hurried around the corner of the *hôtel particulier*. Strolling calmly, briefcase against her chest, she arrived at the exit. Passing the guards manning the portico and a black car waiting for her, she broke into a cold sweat. She left the embassy grounds and hurried down the empty street.

After a few blocks, she released her breath just as she felt a hand on her arm. The briefcase fell to the ground with a thump. She cried out with surprise. It was Karl. He glanced at the briefcase, then back to Lily, a snarl on his face.

"Well, well! What do I see here?" He picked up the briefcase and shook it in Lily's face. He tugged her arm, pulling her back toward the embassy.

"Let me go!"

"No. You're coming back to the embassy, you little spy! You have some explanations to make, which I'm sure Heinrich will be happy to hear. Come!"

"Laissez-moi!" she cried, struggling against his grip.

"Enough!"

He forced her forward. Footsteps clattered behind them and Karl dropped his grip on her. Lily stumbled back, shocked to see Paul delivering a series of blows to Karl's face. Her attacker slumped to the ground. Karl's face dripped blood and he desperately tried to protect himself, crying out in German. The soldiers guarding the embassy rushed to the entrance and turned toward them. Lily tried to stop Paul.

"Paul! We have to go, now!"

Paul saw the men running toward them and grabbed Lily's hand to dash off.

"Wait!" She snatched up the briefcase, kicking at Karl's hand when he tried to grab it.

"Viens, Lily!" Paul pulled her away and they ran down the street. They crossed to a motorcycle parked on the sidewalk. The soldiers shouted in German but Paul jumped on the bike, urging Lily to get on the back. She kicked off her shoes and pulling her dress up with one hand straddled the seat. "Hurry!" she shouted, glancing back at the soldiers. Paul repeatedly kicked the starter, gunning the throttle. But the bike refused to start.

"Paul, Paul, Paul," Lily chanted under her breath, her heart thumping against the briefcase. The soldiers were almost upon them when he managed to start the engine, and the motorcycle lurched away with a bang, leaving the soldiers behind. One drew his weapon and aimed at their backs, but his comrade shouted, causing him to lower his Luger. Paul sharply took the corner and they sped away.

30

BEFORE LONG, LILY recognized the neighborhood, and minutes later Paul pulled to a stop in front of Shakespeare and Company. Lily climbed off, clutching the briefcase. Paul frowned when he saw it and gripped the handlebars of the motorcycle. To Lily, he was even more handsome astride the bike, wearing his stern look. She leaned toward him, kissing him gently, but when he didn't respond, Lily drew back. "Paul, thank you so much for saving me. I would have been toast back there if you hadn't come. How did you find me?"

He shrugged. "I was right—you are seeing someone else."

"No, it's not what you think! I'll explain everything." Lily kissed him again, reassuring him that she was interested in him, not Heinrich. After a second, Paul relaxed into her kiss. Lily moaned, relieved to be with him and away from the Nazis.

"Let's go to your room," she said softly, looking at him with a question in her eyes.

"Allons-y," he said, his expression now tender. She squeezed his arm and climbed back on the bike. He revved the motor, and as the bike took off, Lily looked back at the shop. Was that

Sylvia watching from the window? In a flash they were at the end of the street and turning onto the boulevard, leaving rue de l'Odéon behind.

It was late, and the streets glowed with the golden light from the streetlamps. Cars had replaced bicycles and well-dressed couples filled the café terraces. The moon shone brightly, making the top floors of the limestone buildings glow. Before long, Paul brought them back to the hotel, parking the motorcycle on the side street. He turned the motor off and Lily climbed off awkwardly. The sudden stillness and quiet emphasized the buzzing in her body. She wasn't sure if it was the motorcycle or nervousness. She hugged the briefcase to her, realizing she'd left her hat at the embassy along with her shoes. Her bare feet were cold against the cobblestones.

"Are you sure it's okay? Your mom might find me and you'll be in trouble."

Paul got off the bike and pulled it back to prop it up on its kickstand.

"I told you, I talked to her. Anyway, I am not afraid of my mother. Come here." With that, he drew her close and kissed her. This time, their bodies pressed together and Lily forgot her cold feet, focusing instead on Paul's warm lips and tongue. A few minutes later, when a group of young men passed by on rue Saint André des Arts, laughing and shouting, Lily and Paul broke apart. He gazed down at her, his hands on her waist. She liked his warm hands on her. Her face flushed and she was grateful for the dark night.

"You're shivering," Paul said. "Are you cold?"

"No . . . yes . . ." She was trembling. She bent her head

against Paul's shoulder, not wanting to break the comforting contact she'd felt on the ride over. He put his arm around her and led her into the courtyard and up the dark stairwell.

In his room, moonlight poured through the skylight. Lily relished the coziness, realizing that she missed being here. He closed the door and gently took the briefcase from Lily, placing it on his desk. She gave it a lingering glance. He hugged her close and she was happy to lose the barrier between them. He placed his hands on her bare shoulders, then ran them down her arms. His touch warmed her. Bending down, he murmured her name and brought his lips to hers. She pulled his shirt out of his pants and snaked her arms up his back. His skin felt hot and Lily instantly grew warmer. He leaned to kiss her neck, slowly unzipping her dress. It fell to the ground in a heap. He caressed her back, then followed his hands with his lips. Slowly, he tugged off her long gloves, one finger at a time. By the time they were off, Lily was no longer cold.

Paul fell back on the bed, pulling Lily on top of him. She leaned over, relishing his touch on her skin. Soon his pants and shirt were on the floor and for the first time since she'd arrived, Lily forgot everything: she forgot Louise, she forgot Heinrich, she forgot Sylvia. The only thing she focused on was one touch after another until everything, even the room, including the briefcase, fell away.

Lily didn't know how much time passed before they lay together, tired, their breathing in synch. Lily felt a surge of gratitude that Paul had helped her this whole time, but especially that he'd saved her from Karl. But it was more than gratitude, and she knew it. He held her close as the sweat on their skin dried in the cold air. Paul pulled a sheet over them and Lily snuggled against his side.

"Paul, you don't have to work tonight?"

He tucked her closer. "No, maman gives me a night off to catch up on my sleep." He traced her nose with his finger.

"How did you find me?" She peeked up at him.

He sighed. "When I saw you leaving with that Nazi, I was so angry. You were wearing that dress and I thought you were in love with him."

Lily giggled. Heinrich was handsome, but she certainly wasn't in love with him. Paul continued.

"I was bringing your money to you, and flowers to apologize for running off the other day. When I asked Sylvia where you had gone, she told me about the soirée at the German embassy. So I ran back to get my uncle's motorcycle and rushed there. I waited outside for hours, watching for you, wanting an explanation."

Lily squirmed at the thought of Paul and Sylvia discussing her whereabouts. She didn't want Sylvia to know why she'd gone to the embassy and wasn't sure she could tell Paul, either.

"Why were you there with him? I thought . . . well, after our day at the bird market, well, I thought perhaps . . ." He stared up at the skylight. His frown was lit by the moonlight. Lily kissed him several times on his cheek, then on his lips. After a few minutes, they drew apart.

"Paul, I'm not interested in him. I went because I had to."

Paul's expression darkened. "But why did you have to? What would you want with those people? Don't you know what they have done? Burning books! Passing laws against Jews and anyone who doesn't agree with them!"

He struggled to disentangle from her. Lily lay back on the rumpled sheets. He was right. They were doing terrible things, and he would be even more horrified when he heard what they did later. If he heard. Lily suspected Paul would go into the French army and might not come out. She swallowed hard, her throat clenching up against tears. But what could she tell him? She needed to get the book? Why and for whom? She wanted so badly to tell him everything, but she couldn't. She touched his back.

"I know," she said. "It's horrible. But trust me, it's not what you think. I'm not part of that."

"Then what?" Paul turned to look at her. "What are you part of? I don't understand you, Lily."

"I don't understand, either, Paul. I can only tell you that I am not in charge right now. I have obligations to others that I have to fulfill. Then I can go home. I needed to go to the embassy to make sure that happens."

"What do you have to do with the German embassy? Why did that Nazi attack you?"

Lily opened her mouth to speak, hoping a story would appear like the one about her sick aunt. But looking at Paul, who really wanted to know the truth, she had no words. She had no clever stories that only robbed her relationships of intimacy. Instead of an explanation, a sob escaped Lily. Suddenly she was crying, and Paul was shushing her. He lay down and pressed his body against hers. Her face against his neck, she mumbled, "I wish I could explain. Maybe later."

31

LILY HURRIED THROUGH the quartier, rushing past vendors taking down crates in front of their shops and street sweepers in baggy coveralls pushing debris along the curb with brooms. It was already afternoon. Barefoot and wearing a wrinkled evening gown and gloves, Lily felt a warmth in her belly from her night with Paul, which made her not care how she looked to others. Holding her dress up off her ankles, she skipped over puddles on the sidewalks, eager to get back to the shop and change clothes. She hoped Louise had somehow witnessed the events of last night and knew that Lily had the book in safekeeping. The book was safe in its briefcase under Paul's bed where she'd tucked it before leaving. It was safer there until she could make contact with Louise. She had no way to call Louise and could only count on her unannounced appearances.

Inside the shop, nothing stirred. Neither Sylvia nor the pets were there, even though it was past opening time and Sylvia liked to be punctual. Lily's hat and shoes from last night stood neatly on Sylvia's desk. Had Heinrich come back and taken Sylvia away? Lily's heart beat faster.

In her room, Lily slipped out of the dress, folding it into its box as she resumed her old outfit. She'd rinsed out the blouse and now it was dry and slightly fresher. While she was dressing, Teddy click-clacked down the stairs, greeting her with a bevy of licks. Rubbing his head, Lily crooned to him quietly.

She wandered around tidying things that didn't need tidying, wondering where Sylvia was and when Louise would contact her. She now felt like an easy target in Shakespeare and Company. Heinrich—or worse yet, Karl—would likely be coming to ask after the book any time now. Every passerby brought her to attention, fear coursing through her.

Footsteps crossed the room above her, causing the old ceiling to creak loudly. A palpable relief overcame her. Sylvia was upstairs after all and probably coming down now. Lily hovered near the desk, waiting for her. But after the steps crossed one way, then the other, the room above fell silent. Lily's relief faded, replaced by concern. Sylvia at least always came down to open the shop.

Lily pushed the heavy curtain aside to listen for other signs of life. She hadn't been up to Sylvia's rooms and didn't feel right going up now. But she had read about them at the Princeton library.

After two days of being cooped up in the research room, Lily paged through Sylvia's papers quickly. She was unable to squelch her disappointment that she hadn't discovered any secrets. She packed her things and rose to leave.

The woman at the front desk, who for the most part had been minding her own business, cast a disapproving look. Lily paused.

"We're not closing yet," the woman said.

"Yes, well, I'm leaving."

"You've got another forty-five minutes. You didn't come all this way to leave early. Now keep going."

Lily couldn't believe the librarian was telling her what to do.

"You never know what you'll find," the librarian said. Lily snorted. She hadn't found what she was looking for. Sure, she had been awestruck when she first touched Sylvia's things. But after a dozen or so boxes, she began to feel like a cheap voyeur. She wasn't a serious researcher like this librarian obviously was. Yet she listened to the older woman, pulling the last box off the cart next to her desk.

This box contained correspondence and items from the sixties. Lily found a letter, written in French, several pages long. The script was compact and sharply angled across the page. It took Lily several minutes to decipher the story. The letter was written by a friend of Sylvia's, the friend who had found her dead in her apartment. He detailed the scenario. He'd gone by to visit, and getting no response to his repeated knocks, had asked the concierge to open the door for him. Upstairs, in Sylvia's rooms, he found Sylvia, kneeling against the door to the bathroom. She wore her robe, and the bed remained neatly made. They weren't sure if she had died before going to bed or after arising. In any case, she died of natural causes and apparently with little suffering.

Lily sat absorbing the hush of the library. The librarian appeared to be reading. The image of Sylvia dying alone in her rooms moved into Lily's mind and rooted there. It was a disturbing image, one she tried to push away. She preferred instead the notion of Sylvia in the bookshop, among her friends and the books, alive and vibrant, enjoying her bookish life.

When the library closed, Lily left reluctantly, now regretting that she had only spent a couple of days with Sylvia's things. She said good-bye to the librarian, who gave her a strange smile and a nod. Lily made her way through campus and down Princeton's main street. She barely noticed the preppy shops with their jaunty mannequins, following the map the librarian had given her. She had arranged to meet her dad at a sushi restaurant and had one thing to do beforehand.

The cemetery was behind the main street, a few blocks down a tree-lined road. She entered and wove among the graves until she found the large ginkgo tree the librarian had told her about. There, sheltered by the tree, was Sylvia's grave. Lily lingered for several minutes, disturbed not by the grave but by the fact that Sylvia was buried in Princeton and not Paris. It felt like an insult to Sylvia. She had belonged in Paris during her life and belonged there in death, too.

She snapped a ginkgo leaf off the tree and knelt at the grave.

"Good-bye, Sylvia," she whispered. "Thanks for letting me go through your things."

The dimly lit staircase loomed above her. Lily took a deep breath and headed up. She kept to the wall, her hand sliding along the wooden railing, as her heart beat faster than her steps. What would she say to Sylvia? She hesitated at the top of the stairs, then decided to go back down but paused when she heard her name. There were three doors, all of them closed. She stepped onto the landing, nearly colliding with a coatrack.

The raincoat on the rack swung toward her as she brushed up against it. At the middle door, she whispered Sylvia's name. After a moment's silence, Sylvia called her in.

The dark room enveloped her immediately. A small cot jutted out from the wall between Lily and the windows. A tiny lamp on the nightstand illuminated a stack of books. She made out the shape of Sylvia on the bed, lying on top of a tiger skin fur. Lily approached tentatively. Beneath a compress, Sylvia's face was a grimace.

"Are you okay?" Lily asked.

Sylvia didn't move. "What do you think?"

"I'm sorry about coming up, but I wanted to see if you were all right. I was concerned that the shop wasn't open."

Sylvia removed the cloth and rolled onto her side. Lucky yawned widely but didn't shift from her spot at Sylvia's feet. Sylvia spoke with difficulty.

"The migraine has passed, leaving a normal debilitating headache in its wake. I wasn't able to muster it to come downstairs yet. We should be open—can you do it?"

"Teddy's down there. It's okay for a minute. I'm worried about you." Lily offered her some coffee, tea, or a snack, but Sylvia didn't want anything. Lily hovered near the foot of the bed, wishing she could open the heavy floor-to-ceiling curtains and bring in fresh air and light.

"I'm not the one to be worried about. It's you who are in trouble with our German friend."

Lily stiffened. "What do you mean?"

Sylvia eyed her shrewdly. "Late last night, I had a visitor. Pounding on the front door like he was trying to break it down.

It was your Heinrich."

"He's not my Heinrich."

Sylvia rearranged the bedclothes around her. "He was under the impression that you had the book I sold him. That you'd taken it from his office. He was quite upset."

Lily was speechless. If she told Sylvia about the book, she'd have to tell the whole truth. And she didn't know the whole truth.

"You have quite the guilty look. Did you indeed take his book?"

Lily shook her head, trying to stall, when she saw a trickle of blood coming from Sylvia's nose. She rushed to the bed.

"Sylvia, you're bleeding."

"Damn it. Get that handkerchief." She gestured toward the dresser. Lily found an old hanky, embroidered pink around the edges and slightly stained. She brought it to Sylvia and helped her sit up. As Sylvia pressed it to her nose, Lily half-sat, half-leaned against the bed and held her up. Sylvia tried to say something, but her voice was muffled by the handkerchief. Lily crooned, shhh, shhh, the way her mother had done when she was young and sick at home. They stayed like that for a few minutes, until Sylvia drew the hanky away from her face.

"Sorry about that."

"You don't have to apologize." Lily shifted toward the end of the bed. Sylvia closed her eyes.

"Happens every once in a while. When the headache wants more of me."

"It's more than the migraine, isn't it? You're not well."

Sylvia sighed. She reached for the glass of water on the table and took a slow sip.

"You're not going to tell me about the book, are you?"

Lily shook her head.

Sylvia sighed again. "Well, he seemed to believe me when I told him you would do nothing of the sort. But his friend was convinced you had something to do with it, and he wasn't so easily deterred."

"If you want, I can leave. I don't want to put you in trouble."

Sylvia waved her hand and grimaced.

Lily moved closer. "What's wrong? Are you sick?"

"The doctors can't find anything wrong. They say it's too much for me to run the shop, to live in a foreign country. Even my own damn doctor is telling me that."

"You might not want to admit this, but . . . maybe they're right." Lily was relieved that the conversation had shifted away from the Nazis.

"They're not. They're wrong." Sylvia almost growled. "I love this shop. I love this street, this city, and this country. If I weren't here I'd be dead at home in some stifling rectory. This is my choice. The headaches are my payment."

Back home, Valerie's sinuses had gotten so bad that she had to have surgery so she could breathe. The books, the dust, the dry air, the fruitlessness of running a business that wasn't successful exacted a cost on Sylvia that Lily hated to see.

"That's a pretty high cost, your health."

"It's not so bad. I just have these spells, but they don't last long. When I get a breath of fresh country air, I can do it. It's not being able to get away that exacerbates it."

"I wish I could help."

"Can you bring me more water?"

Sylvia gestured toward the stand with a water pitcher. Lily

took the glass, which was actually a jam jar, and refilled it.

"Everyone says they want to help. I just want people to come to the shop, to buy and borrow books. I want it to be like it was, when people still lived in Paris and read. Before the Depression. Before politics scared everyone away. It wasn't easy then, but at least it felt like I was doing something."

Lily sat in the chair by the bed and listened. Sylvia balled the hanky in her hand, then unrolled it, smoothed it out on the blanket, and balled it up again.

"Frankly, it is too much. I can't stand it, but on days like this, when I feel like this, I have to admit that it is too much. There. I've said it. Are you going to be like everyone else and try to talk some sense into me?"

Lily smiled gently. "No. I promise."

"Since I moved back here, it hasn't been easy. I didn't realize how much living with Adrienne made it all worth it. But when I left, I told her I'd never go back. I know she'd take me back, but I just can't do it."

Lily stayed quiet, hoping Sylvia would continue. She remained silent for a few minutes. Finally, Lily spoke up.

"It must be hard to be around her and have your relationship so different, so formal."

Sylvia closed her eyes, and Lily thought she saw a tear at the corner of her eye. Sylvia was quiet for so long that she thought she might have gone too far, or that Sylvia had fallen asleep. A wave of guilt overcame Lily. Here was Sylvia, sick, desperately trying to keep her shop open, and Lily had lied to her the whole time. Finally, Sylvia spoke without opening her eyes.

"It is hard. I hadn't admitted it, but it is what drives these migraines so far into my skull I think I'd rather be dead than go on. The shop, the lack of customers, without Adrienne at my side, it is that much harder." Her mouth clenched up. She shifted in the bed. "I can't believe I'm telling you all of this. I haven't spoken like this to anyone." She opened her eyes. "No one."

Lily got it. "I won't tell anyone."

Sylvia gave a wan smile. "I don't know how much of a secret it is. Everyone knows I moved in here last year. Everyone knew about Adrienne's affair with Gisele." She paused. "What they don't know is how badly it affected me. How much effort it takes to stifle the disappointment."

"I'm sorry, Sylvia. I can't imagine how painful that must be."

"Oh, well, I take it as I can and do what I can. My talking like this . . ." She peered at Lily.

"Don't worry. You sound like a woman who has been hurt and despite it has done very well. It's admirable."

"That's all well and good. But you really should be down in the shop. Can you please close shop for the day?"

"Are you sure there's nothing else I can do?"

"You need to figure out what you're going to do about Heinrich."

Lily jumped up. "Don't worry about that, Sylvia."

"Get downstairs and close before rapscallions rob us blind."

Lily hurried down the stairs. She had no idea what to do about Heinrich, but with the book she was one step closer to getting home. A note sat on the desk, on top of her writing. Louise wanted to meet her at a café in Montparnasse. She stuffed it in her bag and rushed through the closing tasks. She riffled through Sylvia's sign box, looking for the placard that announced an unexpected closure. Hanging it in the window, she went once more to the back curtain. She heard nothing from Sylvia's rooms. Locking the shop, she stepped into the quiet of the Paris late afternoon and headed across the street, clutching her purse.

At the Maison des Amis des Livres a small crowd filled the shop. Lily stopped on the doorstep. A man presided at the front of the room by Adrienne's desk. A cluster of men and women listened to him as he read in French from a book. Lily hovered at the door. She thought she heard poetry, but she couldn't make out the words. Adrienne leaned against the wall of books just inside the shop, engrossed in the reading, her chin propped in her hand, her other arm supporting the elbow. Her round face seemed soft, her attention focused on the reader. For a second Lily felt sympathy for her, for her life. She was another book woman, after all, like Sylvia, like herself. But if Sylvia could forgive Adrienne for her desertion, Lily couldn't. Sylvia had built a life here in Paris, but a large part of that life had been designed around Adrienne.

32

WHEN LILY ARRIVED at the café, there was no sign of Louise. Lily took a seat in the back room and ordered a glass of wine. The note hadn't specified a time, so Lily had no idea how long she'd be there. She pulled out her notebook and pen. Her wine arrived, but she kept writing. Now she needed to write daily, to clear her mind of all this drama, to bring herself back to herself.

"Look at the lovely scribbler," a voice interrupted her writing. It was Louise, as always smartly attired, today in a belted navy dress and a wide-brimmed hat.

"Louise! Would you like to sit down?"

Louise surveyed the people near Lily's table. "No. Let's walk. How about a stroll in the gardens?"

Lily gathered her things and joined Louise on the sidewalk. Louise smiled, her lipstick a perfectly applied red. Leaving the café, Lily glanced down the street.

"Aren't those Nazis going to be after us?"

"Don't worry about them right now," Louise asserted.

Right now? Lily thought. As if another time would be better

to worry about being found and taken for questioning or worse? Lily hurried after Louise, crossing the boulevard, turning on rue Brea. From there they moved onto rue Vavin, passing shops. The women entered the green calm of the Luxembourg Garden and walked in silence until Lily couldn't stand it.

"Are you going to tell me who you are?"

Louise slowed her steps, the gravel beneath her kicking up tiny dust clouds.

"Of course. In time. Where is the book?"

"I'm not telling anything until you give me information. Who are you and why did you bring me here?"

Louise nodded with surprised approval at Lily's strategy. She took a deep breath.

"Come, sit," she said, leading Lily to a bench under the trees. They sat and Louise fixed her gaze on Lily. With a start, Lily noticed that they had the same color blue eyes.

"What I tell you must go no further than this park. You can tell no one, or you won't get any help from me. Understand?"

Lily nodded.

"Every day rare and precious literary works disappear. Books, manuscripts, ephemera, some dating back centuries. Influential works—some that could change the course of history—alter the way we think and act. For us, it's inconceivable to bear the loss of these works. I'm a member of an organization that seeks to reclaim these items that might otherwise slip through the cracks."

"Slip through the cracks?"

"During times of upheaval, art and books and cultural artifacts tend to disappear or are destroyed. We're methodically going through history to retrieve them. And sometimes we intervene to keep powerful books out of the wrong hands."

"Wait. You time travel all the time?"

"I do, and you can, too."

"What do you mean? This isn't a fluke?"

"Not a fluke. I brought you here with me."

"I knew it! I knew it was you. But why me? And how?"

"Calm down. It was rather impulsive of me, but damn it, I'm desperate for impulsivity."

"So you just messed with my trip, brought me back here, and then refused to help me? What kind of crazy scheme is this?" She jumped up.

Passersby turned at the sound of Lily's raised voice. For once she didn't care if she brought attention to herself. The news about the organization and their literary mission had created an odd echo in her mind, like the information had generated too much space around her brain and she couldn't hold it all.

"Calm down. I'll tell you everything."

"That's right you will!" Lily remained standing while Louise explained.

"We're called the Athenaeum Neuf. We're doing rescue work. So far we've saved some very precious items."

"What precious items?"

Louise glanced around as if a concerned someone would overhear. But people passed by, engrossed in their own lives.

"Like Hemingway's missing suitcase."

"What!" Lily couldn't believe it. She remembered the story from the lecture about Hemingway's writing. He had asked his wife, Hadley, to bring some of his writing to him in Switzerland, so he could show an editor his work. Hadley dutifully packed all of his writing up, but when she got off the train briefly at the Gare du Nord, she left the suitcase on the rack. It was gone when she returned. No one knew its fate. Lily sat back down.

"Why haven't I heard about this? Why isn't this big news?"

"Why do you think? We're not doing this for publicity."

"What are you doing it for? Those manuscripts must be worth a fortune!"

Louise smiled, but there was no humor in her voice. "You needn't worry about that."

"Are you going to sell the contents of Hemingway's suitcase?"

Louise shook her head and said she wasn't allowed to reveal everything. Lily tried to imagine how the recovered Hemingway manuscripts would impact the literary world. People would fall over themselves trying to get those missing papers. The suitcase might even have contained a great novel. Lily briefly relished the thought of a new, undiscovered Hemingway book. But she couldn't get distracted. She still didn't trust Louise.

"I don't know. I don't like the idea of meddling."

"So all your other stealing isn't meddling? All that worthless stuff you take? You don't think that affects things? We're offering you a chance to finally do something worthy with your talent for spiriting things away."

Lily squirmed. So they knew about her stealing, too. What else did they know? She picked at the green paint peeling off the bench. After her attempt to snatch the bike at Les Halles, she had vowed to steal no more. Now stealing was presented as a noble endeavor, serving a higher cause. She turned to Louise.

"How did you bring me? How the hell do you move people

through time?"

"I can't explain that. And I wasn't supposed to bring you now. But we needed your help so I went ahead and did it."

"My help?" Lily laughed. Louise seemed so sophisticated. Lily didn't see how they thought she could contribute to their cause.

"We've been watching you. Ever since you came to Princeton, we've had our eye on you as a candidate. We needed you to get something for us. You were the perfect person for the job."

"What job? You knew I was at Princeton? You were there?"

"You'll understand in a minute. First let me explain."

Louise went on to tell Lily that they were in Paris now to collect books that were at risk of being confiscated or burned by the Nazis.

"That item at Sylvia's shop—you were the perfect person to retrieve it."

"It wasn't easy, you should know." Lily scraped out a line in the gravelly path with her toe.

"We do know." Sylvia smiled, and Lily remembered that they were watching her the whole time. Would they have interfered with Karl if Paul hadn't been there? What about when she first arrived, totally clueless, and was molested by the Seine— had they just sat by and observed? Lily hadn't noticed anyone else around. The thought that she hadn't been helped in those moments enraged her.

"And we know that you got the book. And we want it. It's just a matter of turning it in and then you can go home." She paused. "Unless you'd like to stay with us."

Lily stared at her in disbelief.

"Come, let's keep moving." She stood and drifted away. Lily followed.

"Wait! What do you mean 'stay with you'?"

"You got the book for us. Since you've succeeded so well with this first mission, there could be others."

Suddenly the scene in the park, the children playing, the old ladies chatting on benches seemed impossibly mundane to Lily.

"This is crazy! After all you've put me through, you expect me to join you willingly?"

"Aren't you dying of boredom? Wouldn't you love to have a purpose? Something other than chasing Sylvia Beach in your fantasies? With your inclination to theft, you're perfect. Almost."

Louise was trying to recruit her into something she had a hard time believing existed. But here she was, living proof, moving among people in the past. She shook her head.

"Almost?"

"You did very well in the incubation period, those first seven days. We were watching you to see how you'd acclimate. You did well, getting a place to stay, a job even. And friends."

"What friends?"

"Paul. Sylvia. Heinrich, even." With that, Louise shook her head in incredulity.

Lily shared her surprise that she'd done so well in such strange circumstances. Still, she knew it wasn't true that Sylvia Beach was her friend. Lily was just another person passing through Sylvia's world.

"In fact, you did so well that you failed. You connected too well. We have a few rules that, if broken, can compromise our work. One, don't affect change outside your mission. Two, don't connect. If you get close to people, it makes you vulnerable and weakens our link to you. You get attached and want to slip them information. We thought that with your lone wolf tendencies, your fantasies, that you'd be the perfect person. But you connected surprisingly well. You may be able to overcome that—that need to connect."

"That's nuts. We all need to connect. It's a basic human instinct."

Louise shook her head and glanced away. "Not all of us. Some of us prefer this lifestyle. It's easier this way. Less complicated, fewer relationships to deal with."

"That's sad. I'm not alone because I want to be."

"Oh, really?" She stared at Lily pointedly.

Lily's shoulders rose up. Then she recalled the feeling she'd had when she first left Paul's room. Her lightness, carrying nothing, expected by no one, open to anything. If they'd been watching her, she was never really alone. She loved books, and liked the idea of being able to recover old artifacts and artistic treasures. True, she liked her freedom in Denver, but it did get lonely. Sylvia's courage and her unwavering commitment to her life in Paris nudged Lily. If Sylvia could endure her declining shop and debilitating migraines, Lily could handle this. And she needed Louise.

"Why did you need *me* to do this? Why not you?"

"You're in with Sylvia. We were stunned at how well you integrated. First getting the job at the bookstore, then staying there. Well done, Lily. Clearly you have capabilities even we weren't aware of. And we need a new member."

Louise told Lily that her partner, Harold, was on the verge of defecting. No one left the group. But Harold wanted more adventure, the kind he thought he would find as a member of the Résistance.

"We work in teams. We need a new member. More precisely, I need a partner. And I choose you."

Lily shrugged sullenly. "You choose me? Why?" Louise remained silent despite Lily's demands for answers. Lily clenched her hands in frustration. Louise calmly laid her hand on Lily's fist and spoke.

"You'll need to trust me. But truly, I can assure you, I think you'll want to join us."

Lily pulled away. "If I join Athenaeum Neuf, what about my life in Denver? Would I be able to tell my friends and family about this?"

Louise shook her head. "This is the difficult part. Nobody would know. You can't tell anyone about us. It's a tight little group, as you can imagine, because we only have each other. But the compensation is quite compelling."

They walked across the park, Lily trying to understand everything Louise had told her. A silence ensued while they strolled like all the other people taking the fresh air in the park. They passed the playground and the puppet theater and entered into the English garden. The circular grass beds and leafy tree clusters soothed Lily. Still, one thing nagged her. "How do you travel through time?"

Louise smiled wanly. "I can't explain that to you. But this is what you need to know: we need nine people to hold the focus. When we're on a mission, the others are holding a net of concentration, a sort of focus for us, so we can stay in time. Without the whole group, things can get slightly tricky. Now, with Harold's imminent departure, we're left with a gap. If you say no—and I honestly don't know why you would—we will have to find a replacement tout de suite."

Lily found the "net of concentration" explanation vague. But she couldn't get caught up wondering about the time travel with this big decision in front of her. Louise's argument was starting to make an impression on her, like a piece of ripening fruit being bruised with an insistent thumb.

"You're asking me to abandon my family, my life? Even if I could do that, I can't imagine the pain that would bring to my father. Just disappear?"

"Don't tell me that's not something you've considered. Who doesn't dream of dropping everything and starting a new life?"

Lily thought about it. "At twenty-three, I feel like I *am* starting a new life."

"Yes, a new life with us." Louise's voice was warm with invitation and Lily studied her, surprised at this new sincerity. Maybe they really did want her.

"Are you ever going to tell me how I was on a plane next to you one minute and the next in Sylvia's shop?"

Louise sighed. "Trade secrets, my dear. I can't tell you that, but I can fill you in a bit more."

They strolled while Louise told her story. They passed by lovers, nannies with their children, men playing *péntanque*. Louise had been an Athenaeum Neuf member for twenty years, traveling back and forth in time, reclaiming books, notebooks, ephemera. Building their library. Lily listened and watched the people in the park, their lives tightly linked, needing each other, loving each other, fighting with each other. Her father and Monique, Valerie, even Daniel would miss her if she didn't come back. But they'd get over it. Like she'd gotten over her mother leaving. She swallowed and kicked at the gravel while they walked past the apiary.

"How did you get involved with this?"

Louise smiled. "I was young, like you. I studied without knowing what I wanted to be when I grew up. I had little sense of my prospects and was in the library researching graduate programs when Diana approached me. She invited me to coffee and as I followed her out of the library I caught a whiff of her perfume. The complex scent promised a glamorous life beyond what I had ever imagined for myself." Louise sighed. "I was taken in like a baby duck after its mother, and I haven't left Diana's entourage since. I was intrigued first by her, then with the mission of Athenaeum Neuf."

Louise continued on. Whenever she came to Paris, for that was her beat, she met people who were used to a turnstile kind of friendship. From them, she gathered information. Louise was more aloof than she needed to be, but intimacy was a sacrifice she was willing to make.

Lily tried it on, like a dress in a shop she wouldn't normally enter. Life as part of a secret time-travel group. It would be exciting to belong to something beyond herself. Her father was moving on with Monique anyway, and clearly wouldn't need her anymore. Her adventurous job would get her out from behind the pages of books and into the world. Was it the perfect solution to all of her problems?

The shouts of playing children punctuated Louise's speech, and as they paused near the big fountain in front of the Luxembourg Palace, they watched two children fight over a small boat. The girl gave a vicious tug, pulling the toy away from her companion, making him fall. He wailed and a young woman rose from her green chair and squatted next to him, drawing him into her for a hug.

"Why the name?" Lily asked.

"An athenaeum is a special library. Named after the goddess Athena." Louise smiled. "And neuf is French for 'new'—we like to think of ourselves as a new breed of library. It also means 'nine.' We always have nine team members."

"You're really not going to tell me how we travel through time?"

Louise shook her head. "I admire your persistence but I simply cannot give you that information. Listen. I'd like to present you to Diana." Louise clicked her lighter open and shut. "You've proven that you can span time and don't get too shaken about it," she said. "Just like me, my first time."

They paused at the balustrade overlooking the fountain and Louise described her first time travel to Lily. She had known she was going, was even excited about it, studying France in 1919, preparing the idioms and clothing of the day. But she had mis-arrived, showing up instead in 1916, with the war dragging on and people's mood bordering on panic. She stayed only for two weeks, working as a nurse in the field, picking up a valuable item that was in a mansion at the front. The mansion would be razed by German artillery, but Louise got it before the destruction. She had done such a good job, in fact, that she quickly rose up in the ranks. The steady increase of power suited Louise. She took lovers in distant times without repercussions, no ties to hold her down. She loved her independence, craved time alone, but now experienced a new restlessness.

"That's why I jumped rank and brought you with me. I needed to try something outside the program. And it worked. I did quite well with you. But if you can't help us, I'm afraid we'll both be in trouble."

"But I was alone! You weren't there when I arrived. You pretended to not know me!" Lily smacked the back of her hand against her palm. "I was scared. It wasn't like your first time. You knew what you were doing, and did it willingly. You—"

"I'm sorry. I wouldn't do it that way again. But I was watching you. Harold was with you that whole first day. You did so well, we realized the best thing would be to let you go it alone." Lily flashed on the man who had brushed past her outside the bookshop and the man at the Luxembourg Garden. Harold. Had he been nearby when she was mugged? When was he planning to intervene? Lily gripped the railing, unable to speak coherently. She wanted to scoop up a handful of gravel and throw it into Louise's face.

"God! Will I ever get to stop proving myself? What if I don't want to join? How do I get home?" Her jaw tightened as she tried to maintain some control.

"Calm down. You might like being with us. It's remarkably freeing, in some ways, after living a small life like you have."

Lily couldn't respond. Small life? How did one measure a life? The number of people you touched? The amount of books you read? The money you earned?

"Come, let's go," Louise said gently.

They strolled in silence until they reached the entrance of the park. Lily felt the same numbness she had when she heard the news about her mother, the same as when she moved all of her belongings out of her childhood home. She should be used to the disorder of a reordered world. Maybe she could be a time traveler. She turned toward Louise.

"I knew that secret organizations like this existed."

Louise laughed. "You're such a romantic. You're perfect for us."

"But what if I don't want to join? I like my life."

"Really? You're directionless. Ready for adventure." Louise arched an eyebrow as she said this and Lily felt unsure about what she wanted. She sighed.

"That doesn't mean I want to abandon my life."

"You need time to consider it. I've just downloaded quite a bit onto you."

The lingo of Lily's era soothed her. But she needed to know her options. "If I don't go with you, then what? Can you help me get home?"

Louise tilted her head. "I don't know why you'd want that meaningless life. How trivial. Don't you want to contribute to a worthy cause?"

Lily considered it. Louise pressed on. "When we get that book, we can help you go back. If that's really what you want. Now, where is the book? It can't be tucked in that little bag of yours. Nice touch, by the way."

I could end up in the heart of the Occupation. Lily felt anxious. *I could be subject to Hitler's whims.* The seriousness of her situation struck her. She couldn't believe Louise was casually commenting on her purse. Did she want to have anything to do with her? She had no choice. Lily thought of her mother, who shirked groups of any kind, preferring her own company and the subtle drama of the plant world, along with the quiet wisdom that came with it, to that of people.

The guard sounded his whistle announcing the closure of the park. They began to drift toward the exit along with the other Parisians enjoying the last sips of a perfect spring evening.

"You'll have to trust me, Lily. I know I haven't given you much reason for that. I don't know if I would trust me. But, alas, that's the kind of crapshoot you get when you leave home. All kinds of strange people come around. It's not the safe refuge of your novels. You don't have to join the Athenaeum, but we do need that book."

Lily didn't want to admit that she had the book safe at Paul's.

At the corner near the café, Louise paused. "Now, I'll leave you to consider our offer. But tell me, where did you leave the book? With that young Frenchman?"

At the mention of Paul, Lily blushed. Louise nodded. "As I suspected. Now go get it. I've got one thing to do, then I'll meet you at Paul's."

Lily turned to go. Louise placed her hand on Lily's sleeve.

"We're very proud of you, Lily."

Her mother had said that when Lily graduated from high school. But she had been too busy trying to get away from her mother's influence to pay attention. Tears sprung to Lily's eyes and she turned away from Louise.

33

LILY MADE HER way through Paris as if in a dream, passing people on their way home to ordinary lives and staid relationships. Home to their spouses, their children, their normal French existence. For once, Lily felt special, like an insider to something important. Hurrying to Paul's, Lily thought about what Louise had said. A small life? Did she choose a small life? Sylvia had a big life—a big circle of friends, a wide sphere of influence. The work she did was important.

Her mother, if Lily admitted it, had a small life. She was ensconced in the tight circle of her house, garden, and family, her influence small compared to Sylvia's. Lily felt a twinge of shame, then more shame for betraying her mother with that thought. Her mother had sacrificed her career for Lily. Walking past the Sorbonne and all of her old haunts, Lily let that worry slip away. Her mother didn't care about things like "big" or "small" lives. She cared about her garden, her home, and her family. Lily felt lighter.

Lily scampered up the familiar curved staircase to Paul's attic room. She'd miss it. The tiny room had become a refuge for her. And after last night, it now had a totally other feeling, one that made Lily tremble as she took the worn steps two at a time. Oh, Paul. Louise was right—she had connected too much. She found her heart catching, and it wasn't from the climb. The thought of leaving him was wrenching. She liked it here, with Sylvia. She liked Paul. No one else had treated her with such genuine affection. The men of her generation all wore the jaded affectation of their era. Paul's straightforward enthusiasm appealed to her. She wasn't sure she was making the right decision. If she joined the Athenaeum Neuf, would she be able to come back and see him? Could they be together, get married, survive the Occupation? And Sylvia? If Lily left, she might never see her again, never ask her all the questions she still had for her. But if she joined the group, maybe she could see Sylvia more.

At the top, Lily made to knock on Paul's door. But her hand remained suspended. What would she tell him? She shouldn't have given him false hope last night, but she had been carried away by the excitement. She rapped firmly and heard rustling inside. Paul opened the door and pulled her in. He wasn't dressed, the sheet wrapped around his waist, and he drew Lily to him and kissed her.

"Paul," she tried to speak against his lips.

"Shhhh," he replied, kissing her lips, her cheeks. "I missed you," he murmured against her neck.

She shuddered, his breath and touch sending heat through her body. "Me, too," she said.

Paul stripped her jacket off, and Lily considered resisting. She had to go. She didn't want to hurt him any more than necessary. But Paul's lips on her neck, his hands gripping her waist made resistance seem silly.

"I haven't stopped thinking of you," Paul said, looking into her eyes. His arms went around her, holding her tight. The sheet had fallen off and she felt him insistent against her. Lily's resistance dissolved. Before long, she surrendered her mind, her heart, and her body to Paul.

Even though he didn't know she'd come to say good-bye, a melancholy accompanied every caress and look. Their bodies merged and Lily felt a rush of love for Paul, her angel. Her head back on the pillow, her eyes closed, sadness overcame her. This was the last time she'd be with him. She pressed closer, her face against his shoulder, so he wouldn't see her cry.

Afterward, they lay entwined on Paul's bed. Clouds floated past the moon, framed by the skylight. Lily drowsed off. Images—not quite dreams—flickered in her mind. Bookcases in a library, Sylvia's bedroom, the light pooling on the bed. The pavement in Paris, bumpy and gray, her feet running, a hand grabbing her arm. With this image, she shuddered awake, startling Paul, who had also dozed off. Lily nestled her face in his side, not wanting to leave. She hugged him to her.

"Paul, I can't stay. I have to go."

He whispered no and squeezed her tighter, kissing the top of her head. "Come here instead."

"I'm serious, Paul.

"Okay, I'm listening." But he didn't release her. She pressed her nose against his chest and breathed in his scent, gathering her courage. Finally, she spoke.

"I'm leaving tonight."

"What do you mean by that?"

"I'm going home, Paul."

He pulled away with a frown.

"I'm finally going back. I won't see you again."

"You're going to the U.S. now, this late?" She nodded and sat up. Paul rose, too. "But I love you!"

"Oh, Paul, me too! I love you, too."

"Then why are you leaving?" He leaned away from her.

Regret over hurting him coursed through her. "I have to."

"Sure, you just come to Paris, have some French fun, and leave."

Lily couldn't tell whether he was teasing or not. She lifted her head and gazed into his hazel eyes, finding so much kindness and love reflected there. She spoke without thinking.

"You're not just a fling, Paul. I love you. And not just because you've been so helpful to me. Because you're a good, sweet person. And a lovely kisser."

She touched her lips to his, overcome with sadness and love at the same time. A tear crept out, and when she pulled back, Paul's eyes were moist, too.

"Why? Why do you have to go? Tell me!"

Lily couldn't stand to see him so upset and confused. She began scooting off the bed.

"I can't, it's too complicated. You wouldn't understand."

He grabbed her arm. "Mais non! Of course I would understand. I'm not an idiot. Tell me why. I love you and you just told me you love me. Why would you go?"

Lily wished she could explain everything. But she'd already intruded enough on his life. "I love you, but my life is not here."

"Look at me, Lily. Look at me. I love you. I want my life with you."

Lily rose, feeling heavy. Tears streamed down her cheeks.

"I can't, Paul. I can't. I need to go home." She dressed under Paul's watchful eye. Once she had her skirt and blouse on, he stood and placed his hand on her shoulders.

"Lily, please. Don't go like this."

She dared not look at him. "I'm so sorry, Paul." She picked up the briefcase, which felt as heavy as she did. Paul took her hand.

"What's that? A gift from him?"

"No, of course not. It's something . . . from my aunt. Something I needed to get for her."

"You don't trust me with the truth." Paul turned away, but not before Lily saw the betrayal on his face. Her heart ached for him. She put her hand on his shoulder, but he shrugged it off. Lily went to the door.

"Good-bye, Paul. Thank you for everything."

He stood. "Wait! Your money, for your ring."

"Keep it. It's okay," she said, the money being the least of her concerns now.

He didn't respond, and stifling a sob, Lily slipped from the room. Hugging the briefcase, she descended, circling further and further from Paul. She was two flights down when Paul came out into the hallway and shouted, "Go ahead, just disappear. I do not want to see you again! Go!"

Hurrying down the street crying, the book pressed against her chest, Lily felt awful. She was in this horrible mess by no fault of her own, and now she'd hurt the one person who had been unconditionally kind to her. She considered ducking into an alley to cry but knew she had to get back to Louise with the book. She was quickening her pace when she heard a shout behind her.

"Lily!" She turned and saw Paul running breathless toward her. She threw herself into his arms and wept. He kissed her cheeks, her forehead.

"Lily," he said softly. "You really have to go?"

She nodded against his chest.

"You will never return to France?

She shrugged. He smoothed away her tears, then kissed her.

"I love you, Lily," he said against her lips.

"I know."

He took her hand and placed something in her palm. It was her ring, the opal sparkling, the gold shiny. She looked into his eyes, glistening with tears.

"What? I thought you pawned this."

"I didn't." He smiled slightly.

"But where did you get the money?"

"I've been saving for years for my travels. It was that money I gave you for the ring."

"Paul! You shouldn't have done that."

"I wanted to see your smile. And now it's useless to discuss it. I have the money, or most of it, and you have your ring. Just take it." He took the ring and slipped it on her finger. Lily's tears flooded back and she desperately tried to brush them away when a horn tooted lightly behind them. A black Citroën stopped a few paces away. Lily heard her name being called.

"Lily, we must go now."

She turned and saw Louise holding the car door open for her. "I have to go, Paul."

"Wait," he said, reaching behind him. He pulled some papers from his back pocket. "I think these are yours."

Lily took the pages. It was her writing, the notes she'd first jotted when she stayed at Paul's that second night. She caught his eyes, searching to see if he knew. He smiled.

"You're very clever, Lily. Maybe someday I see you again."

"Lily!" Louise insisted.

Lily moved away, unsure whether he knew her secret. With a little wave, she was at the car door. He shouted her name again. She turned back. He was smiling gamely.

"Be happy, Lily."

She nodded, whispering, "You, too," and got into the car.

Louise was in the backseat, Harold at the wheel. "Go, Harold," Louise said urgently.

Lily turned to see Paul one last time. He was still there, watching. He stayed there until the car turned the corner and Lily lost sight of him.

Louise spoke. "I assume that's the book?"

Lily shoved the briefcase at her, glad to be rid of it.

"Take your stupid book," she cried. "I don't like what it's cost me."

Louise chuckled. "Ah, but you don't know what it's bought you."

Lily stared at her, puzzled. Harold said nothing, maneuvering the car through the quartier. Lily shrugged and turned away to watch the Paris night slide by.

The car made several turns, and she thought they passed

by the same café several times. Finally, Harold came to a stop.

"Here we are," Louise said. They got out, Louise carrying the briefcase, and Harold drove away. Louise led Lily into a porte cochere, then a wide passageway. Their footsteps were soft on the giant paving stones that lined the narrow path. Louise knocked on a wide wooden door. Nothing moved in the dim alley. Finally, Lily heard footsteps on the other side of the door. It opened, and a short woman with a kind face welcomed them. Louise hurried Lily inside and the door shut with a loud click.

They moved down a dim corridor lit only by a sconce on the wall emitting a steady orange glow. Louise whispered to Lily, "Don't touch anything. Don't pick up any books. They're not for reading. Don't ask Diana any questions. You'll learn everything you need to know when you join us."

She glanced back down the hall, as if she expected someone to be following them. Lily felt a shiver travel along her neck. They passed several closed doors before turning into a large room on the right. The smell that Lily had sensed in the hallway was stronger here: decades of books, a musty and familiar odor. Lily knew it from Capitol Books, but there it was like an infant smell and here the scent was that of an ancient, wise crone. Lily rubbed her arms.

The Princeton librarian stood in the middle of the room, as if expecting them. She wore her African garb again, a long dress crisscrossed with orange and green patterns, her head wrapped in a matching cloth. The woman made no sign of recognition when she saw Lily. Lily felt a weakness in her arms, a strange sensation of wanting to reach out and hug this woman. She'd seen her only briefly in Princeton and couldn't claim to know her at all, but the fact that someone she had seen from 2010 was here with her in 1937 undid a knot of tension in her stomach.

The woman moved to the desk and took a seat, resuming her posture from the Princeton library. Lily looked around: the room was appointed like a private library. Well-worn Persian rugs covered the paving stones in the center of the room. Dimly lit lamps dotted the periphery of the sitting space. A sideboard with a liquor cabinet stood near the door. All that was missing was a fire in the fireplace, but Lily immediately knew that no fires were ever burned in this space. The walls were lined with glassed-in shelves full of books. Locks gleamed on every case.

On the sofa two women sat, formally dressed and at attention. It took a few seconds before Lily recognized them from the metro. Had they been following her this whole time? It felt oddly comforting to know that they'd been watching over her.

"Have a seat." Diana gestured to a wingback chair. Lily sat and perched on the edge of the red cushion. "Would you like a drink?"

"No, thanks," Lily said. She felt jittery, her adrenaline pumping. It was hard to keep her legs from jiggling. Louise poured herself a thimbleful of amber liquor and squirted in some seltzer. The bottle made a loud phhhhhht noise. The woman behind the desk spoke.

"So you got the book?"

"I did," Lily replied. "What's the deal—Norse mythology? What's so vital about that book now?"

Diana leaned forward. "You may have heard of the Nazis' interest in the occult?"

Despite her interest in World War II in high school and college, Lily hadn't heard about this. She shook her head no.

"Some believe they are working with black magic. Hitler dreams of developing a miracle weapon that would allow him to win the war, all wars, using ancient sources like *Yggdrasil*. If we can remove that possibility, we're potentially saving a lot of people."

Lily found this hard to believe, that a book could have that much power. But she herself was proof that books could change everything. It was the book about Sylvia, after all, that had ultimately led her here.

"That's all well and good. But I want to go home." She tried to sound firm.

The woman tilted her head and nodded, like she found this very interesting. She crossed her arms.

"So you're in a hurry to resume your 'normal' life, are you?"

"Simple as my life is, I'd like to go back." Lily clasped her hands in her lap, feigning the good girl.

Louise joined in. "I'm not surprised. You prefer to have a small life than something . . . nobler. You adapted well but there's something, I don't know, timid about you."

"Timid? How can you say that! I did everything you asked. I got your book. I think you owe it to me to help me get home."

"Owe you? We could just leave you here, you know." She sipped her drink. "Then you'd really find out what you're made of. This has been a romp in the playground compared to what you would find in a few years."

"Louise, that's enough," Diana said.

Lily tried not to squirm. Would they really abandon her here?

"Despite Louise's misgivings about your ability to be detached, we invite you to join us," Diana said, and the women on the settee nodded agreement. Lily gazed at each of them, breathing in the scent of the books. It was what she'd always wanted. To be part of something. To be surrounded by strong women. To be a strong woman herself. But if she did, she'd be one of them. She'd be a person stealing from someone else. She wasn't convinced that the Athenaeum Neuf was serving such a noble purpose. They hadn't really explained what they were doing with the books. Finally, she spoke.

"Louise wouldn't tell me everything. But from what she said, I don't think this is for me. Spending my life as an invisible person, forbidden from making friends, from living a normal life—that seems sad." But as she spoke it, she was unsure. What was in Denver for her? Valerie, Daniel, the bookstore . . . a small life. She wanted to write, but was that enough? She wanted an interesting life. She wanted to be part of something, not reading about people who lived interesting lives.

"One more thing you might want to know," Diana said.

"What now?"

"There's another reason you may want to join us." She glanced at Louise, who took a sip of her drink. Diana continued. "It's part of your heritage."

Lily turned quickly. "What do you mean?"

"Have a seat, please," Diana insisted.

Lily sat and one of the women set a glass of water on the table next to her.

"Your mother, Claire, was a member of the Athenaeum Neuf. She made the choice you're trying to make now—going for a safe, normal existence."

Lily nearly choked. "What! My mother? Claire Heller?"

"Claire Abbott. She was about your age when she started. Claire pulled off several successful operations. Then something happened and she wanted out. Only Louise knows why."

Lily turned toward Louise, who merely sipped her drink and avoided Lily's gaze.

Lily rose and rushed toward Diana's desk.

"Tell me! Just tell me everything. I've had it with your secrets!"

Diana pursed her lips and took a deep sigh before speaking.

"Your mother and Louise were partners. On this same operation. But something happened, and Claire couldn't go through with it. She slipped back, leaving Louise in a dangerous situation. Now, Harold's pulling the same thing. Louise needs a partner, and she's convinced herself she wants you."

"Why me?"

"Because you remind me of her," Louise said softly. "You're just like her."

"I'm nothing like my mother! Are you kidding? She was a near recluse in her garden." Lily couldn't believe that her whole life she'd felt so different than her mother and now she was being chosen because of their similarities.

"She left Athenaeum Neuf for you. She wanted to have a child, and she got one. You."

"But she ignored me most of the time! She went and died on me, even!" Lily choked back tears, unable to believe that her mother was behind this whole thing. The last thing she wanted to think about was her mother.

"When you put her ring on, it alerted us. Wearing that ring means you're part of the group. It's what allowed Louise to track you and be on that plane coming over with you. Then you gave it to that nice French boy, but luckily by then we had you covered. You were easy to track."

Lily slumped back in the chair. She had been a puppet for these people—a player to get them what they wanted. Her mom had probably sat in this very room. And here was Lily making the same decision she'd made—to leave, and have a life of her own.

Diana rose and came around to Lily. She placed her hand on Lily's shoulder, and for a second, it felt incredibly comfortable. Then Diana spoke. "You belong with us. You know it."

Lily sat up and shrugged Diana off. "I'm sorry, but I can't join your group. Part of me wants to, but really, I want my own life. I think I can do something with it. I know I can."

Lily couldn't finish. She'd wanted so badly to get home but now sadness accompanied her determination to return home. Sylvia and her shop, and her mother with her garden . . . it was that kind of commitment that she wanted to express no matter where she was.

Diana sighed. "It's a shame. You could have done good work here. And now who knows what you'll do with your life?"

"Something different," Lily said.

Diana gave her a long look. "You do look exactly like your mother. She was a brave, good woman. You have the same determined look."

Lily didn't try to hold back her tears.

Diana shrugged. "Fine. If you're sure. Harold will take you

to the bookstore to say good-bye to Sylvia. Not a word of this to her."

Lily nodded reluctantly. She couldn't imagine Sylvia's reaction if she tried to explain this.

"Louise will come get you later. Be ready to go."

34

AT THE BOOKSTORE, Sylvia was on the phone. Lily waited, trying to absorb every detail about the shop: the smell of paper and linen and cigarettes and dog, the disorder of Sylvia's desk, the enveloping sense of all the books. When she hung up, Lily approached, unsure of how she'd say good-bye.

"Are you feeling better?"

"Better now that you've arrived just in time for closing."

"I'm sorry. It's been crazy. I . . ."

Sylvia started rifling through a stack of papers.

"I can't find the invoice for the books I shipped to Carlotta last week. Have you seen it?" Sylvia asked.

"I'm pretty sure I filed it with the others."

Sylvia shook her head. "Well, it's not here."

"Under *B* for Briggs?"

Sylvia let out an exasperated sigh. "No, it should be under *C* for Carlotta."

"Oh. I thought you alphabetized by last name."

"I do, but not for friends."

No wonder your shop is in the pits, Lily thought, and tears came to her eyes. She thought of all that Sylvia had put into this place. In 1941, she would box everything up and take it upstairs, hiding the shop from the Nazis. Lily wasn't sure what became of all those books.

"Aha! Here it is." Sylvia pulled out the invoice and shuffled it to the top of the pile. She peered at it over her glasses.

They passed a companionable half hour in silence, Sylvia going through papers and Lily trying to pretend she was present while sorting out everything she'd just heard. Did she really insist upon going home? Maybe joining the group was the best choice. She wished she could talk it over with Paul. She was no longer certain she'd been wise to not let him know what was happening with her. She was staring blankly at Teddy, lost in her thoughts, when the bell over the door rang. It was Louise.

"Hello, ladies." Sylvia took a few steps into the shop.

Lily rushed over. "So soon?" Lily said.

Louise nodded. "It's time."

"What? Just like that?" Lily glanced nervously at Sylvia.

"Hello, Louise," Sylvia said.

Lily began to speak, but Louise ignored her and greeted Sylvia.

"You're Lily's aunt?" Sylvia asked with suspicion.

"I am," she said, gazing at Lily fondly.

Lily stared back. Was she adept at fictionalizing, too? Of course she was; her whole life was steeped in trickery.

"Lily's mother, Claire, sent her to help me move," Louise said. "She's been remarkably helpful, and I've heard she's had fun helping you, too."

Sylvia smiled. "Lily's done quite a bit for our ragged shop."

"I'm sorry to take her away from you."

"But you're not leaving Paris forever, Louise. You'll be back, right?" Sylvia asked.

Lily was stunned. Did Sylvia know about the Athenaeum Neuf? Was that why she hadn't pressed Lily about Heinrich's claim that she'd stolen the book? If she joined the Athenaeum, she might be able to see Sylvia again. Lily felt her nose prickle and her throat constrict. She was sure Sylvia could see the emotion in her eyes, but she didn't mind. She tried to convey everything in that one look—how much Sylvia inspired her, how sad she was to leave her, how she wanted to assure Sylvia that she'd survive the war and retire in peace, how she'd refuse Heinrich her personal copy of *Finnegan's Wake,* and how she, Adrienne, and friends would quickly dismantle the entire bookstore and hide its contents away upstairs. If Lily wasn't mistaken, she saw a glimmer in Sylvia's eyes. Understanding? Tears? Lily would never know how Sylvia really felt, even after all this.

Louise broke the moment. "One never knows when one will be back in Paris."

"Good, then. Do visit when you're here." Sylvia smiled politely and Louise moved for the door.

"I need to say good-bye to Sylvia," Lily said.

"Of course," Louise nodded. "I'll wait outside. Good-bye, Sylvia." With that, she stepped outside.

"Well, that's nice," Sylvia said. "You can leave just like that. No warning." She paused to light a cigarette, her hands trembling. "I guess that's how you arrived—just showed up and barged in. Now you're just barging out." She straightened some books on the desk without looking at Lily. "Have a good trip home with your aunt."

"I'm sorry," Lily said. "I was really getting comfortable here. I'm so grateful to have had the chance to work here, with you."

"That's fine. They all leave at one point or another. Come and go, and I alone remain." It sounded like the refrain of a sad, sad poem.

"I'm sorry, Sylvia. I wish I could stay. I can always come back and see you." She heard how ridiculous that sounded. Certainly she would come back, but not for a long, long time, and not in this era. Not if she could help it.

"Well, you did turn out to be helpful, after all. Despite your spunky attitude."

Sylvia sat back down. Lily watched her shuffle papers. She would go on at the store as if Lily had not been there. Lily might have made a difference for Sylvia or not. She'd never know. Sylvia slapped her hand on a stack of paperback books.

"Oh, bother. I don't have money to pay you now."

"Don't worry about it, Sylvia."

"Hush." Sylvia pulled a thick book out from under a stack of other books. It was covered in a light blue dust jacket. She handed it to Lily. It was *Ulysses*, heavy in her hand.

"Sylvia, you can't do this. You can't give this to me. It's far too valuable. I mean, it will be." She blushed.

"Second edition. Not as valuable as the first, but it is signed."

Lily opened to the frontispiece. There, under the title, a scribble of two arcing *J*'s. She closed the book and rubbed her hand across the cover. It was pristine—no nicks, no bumps. The spine was intact, as was the dust jacket. This was worth a fortune. Rare first editions went for thousands of dollars. Even though this wasn't a first edition, it was bound to be a rare book, with Joyce's signature.

"Don't cut the pages. It will lose value if you do. I'm sure you need money like anyone, but I hope this is a better substitute. And you need to read it anyway."

Lily ran her fingers along the nubby edges of the pages. She flipped through the book, and the pages bowed out.

"Sylvia, I can't take this. I couldn't work a lifetime and have earned this."

"Well, it will have to do. I have to confess I've developed a soft spot for you. I don't know what it is about you, but I will miss you when you are gone."

"Merci." Lily couldn't believe it. Not only was Sylvia giving her a book that could fund a year off of work, she was admitting that she liked Lily. It made it even more difficult to leave, knowing that Sylvia was about to face Hitler's troops, an occupied city, internment in a camp outside Paris, and the demise of the shop. Should Lily warn her?

"Sylvia . . ."

Sylvia continued to paw through the mail on the desk. It was as if she was done with her flash of sentimentality and wanted to move on as quickly as possible.

"If I didn't have to leave, I wouldn't. I love it here and I even like working as your minion. But I have a feeling that you will be all right. No matter what, you'll be okay."

Sylvia glanced up at Lily. For a second Lily thought she saw a softening, a wave of relief washing over Sylvia, as if she actually believed what Lily had said. She smiled and returned to her cluttered desk with a muffled thanks. Lily took the book to the wrapping station and carefully centered it on the desk. She pulled a sheet of brown paper off of the rack and laid it on the shipping table. Valerie was going to flip. She wouldn't believe it. The book would be Lily's proof that she had time traveled. She didn't have to tell Louise about this. She finished wrapping the book and tucked the package into her bag.

"Well, then," Sylvia said.

"Good luck. Thanks for the book. It's awfully generous of you."

Sylvia waved her hand. "Good-bye, then. Bon voyage."

No embrace, no handshake. Sylvia held the door open and Lily stepped out into the evening shadows. Then Sylvia shut the door, pausing for just a second, and turned the sign to CLOSED. Teddy stood at her side, his tongue hanging out, his eyes focused on Lily.

Lily crossed the street to join Louise, whose cigarette punctuated the dusk with a red dot. Lily turned back for one last wave but Sylvia had already shut off the light. The shop was dark and Lily didn't see any movement inside. Her throat clenched up and she hurried away.

It was perhaps the last time she would see Sylvia alive. In this short week, Lily had only begun to understand the real Sylvia. Still, she knew more now than from her bookish pursuit. Lily knew that under Sylvia's tough demeanor was a beautiful, generous soul who gave more than she took. She knew that Sylvia's selflessness cost her more than she let on. Lost in her thoughts, Lily numbly accompanied Louise down the street.

At the carrefour, the squealing of brakes brought her to attention. Karl and Heinrich leaped from a car a few feet away. Karl wore a look that did not bode well. Heinrich, behind him, frowned. They started toward Lily but Louise grabbed her arm and shouted, "Come!"

Lily was tugged along, her feet stumbling as she ran to keep up with Louise. She heard the men's footsteps behind her. Louise darted into a side road, right in front of a car zooming toward them. It jerked to a stop and the driver shouted, "Get in!"

It was Harold. Louise leapt in the back and held the door open. Lily dove in, too. Louise shouted, "Go! Go! Go!" and Harold gunned it. The door slammed shut. Lily sat up to see Karl running alongside, trying desperately to grab the door. Harold accelerated, but Karl could not hold on. He fell and rolled on the pavement. Heinrich bent down to check on him. Harold took a sharp, fast turn onto the boulevard, and Lily thought that two tires lifted for a second before the car righted itself and zoomed away.

Louise turned worried eyes to her.

"You okay, Lily?"

"Are you kidding?" Lily gasped, unable to say more, her heart beating, panic flooding her body. She leaned back against the seat, trying to catch her breath and calm her shaking. The car turned quickly onto a side street, then another, and yet another. Then it slowed and cruised along the embankment.

"Well done! You're safe," Harold said, smiling at her in the rearview mirror. Lily couldn't help but smile back, a nervous, excited laugh bubbling up. They drove along the quay and soon Lily calmed down. Louise lit a cigarette and Lily asked the question that had been bothering her ever since their meeting at Diana's lair.

"Are you really my aunt or was that another of your ruses?"

Louise regarded Lily. "Can we call a truce? Can you forgive me for bringing you here? Can you honestly tell me it was so bad?"

"If you answer my question."

Louise bent her head slightly. Lily stared at her, taking in her dark hair, her profile. And she saw her mother, bent at her garden: the same jaw, the same nose. The same aloof demeanor. She fell back, incredulous. Louise avoided the question.

"Are you sure you don't want to join us? You are more capable than you think."

Lily watched the buildings as the car rolled along the river. She wasn't sure of anything. She didn't like how she'd been manipulated. But if she were part of the group, maybe she'd be in on the decisions. She considered her apartment in Denver. The thought of never seeing it, or Valerie, or Daniel, or her father, no longer provoked a reaction in her. If she were a member of the Athenaeum Neuf, she could perhaps see Sylvia and Paul again. It was certainly more interesting than her life in Denver. And an interesting life made for interesting writing. She couldn't deny she had written more since she'd been here than she ever had at home. And she could always quit when she wanted, like Harold did.

"I don't know, Louise. All I know is I don't want a small life. This might be a chance to do some good for books."

Louise tilted her head in surprise. "You're reconsidering?" She clapped her gloved hands in delight. Again, Lily was surprised to see Louise express such happiness over her. She nodded, wondering if she should take more time to make such a big decision. But she had gotten into this situation without any decision at all, and maybe this was the opportunity to live an interesting life befitting a writer even she couldn't dream up.

"I'll do it," she said.

Louise grinned, reaching out to squeeze Lily's arm. "I'm so pleased you've changed your mind. You'll love being part of our little group." She stubbed her cigarette out in the ashtray in the door, then opened her purse and handed Lily a card. In an elaborate script, Lily read Louise's name and phone number and almost cried out. The last name was Abbott, her mother's maiden name. Lily gaped at Louise.

"You really are my aunt."

Louise touched Lily's cheek with a gloved hand. "Maybe you will be able to trust me now. I'm so glad we'll have this time together."

Lily could only nod, unable to imagine any future scenarios. For once, the present was enough.

The car drove across the Pont Neuf, and Lily sighed. The open space offered by the river made her love Paris every time she saw it. The car turned left on rue de Rivoli and after a minute pulled up in front of the Palais Royal metro station. Louise stepped out and gestured for Lily to follow. They stood in front of the Guimard entry, its curved green arches providing a graceful entrance to the subway. The women paused and Lily took a second to savor the rush of Paris around her: the grumble of traffic on the boulevard, bikes zooming past gracefully, the scent of cigarettes and perfume. She closed her eyes to hold it in her mind forever.

"Come now, Lily, we need to go now."

"Go where?"

"We'll take the train to our next mission. Let's go."

Lily gulped. It was all happening so fast. She watched Louise descend the stairs to the metro. *I can just vanish if I want,* Lily reminded herself. *I've proven I can make my own way. I don't need the Athenaeum Neuf to live a big life.* She took one last look at Paris, 1937, then followed Louise. The further they penetrated the underground system, the fewer people they passed.

After walking in silence for several minutes, Louise finally turned into a deserted, dark tunnel. They descended a short flight of stairs. A train waited, the platform empty. At the open door of the nearest car, Louise gestured her in with a smile. Lily clutched her bag, *Ulysses* heavy inside. Her notebook was in there, too. She hoped to make some notes quickly while it was all still fresh. The women took seats in the empty car. The train started up with a lurch and slowly creaked away, its wheels squealing. Lily closed her eyes and whispered, "Good-bye, Sylvia."

fin

ACKNOWLEDGMENTS

Infinite gratitude to the brilliant people who cared about this novel and offered their help and support: David Hicks, Djellel Dida, Jody Berman, Valarie Abney, Gigia Kolouch, Carl Fuermann, Corinne Brown, Dorothy Williams, Niels Schonbeck, Heather Neher, Rosemary Carstens, Aevea, AJ Moses, Melanie Mulhall, Heather Stimmler-Hall, Cameron Kruger, John Talbot, Alyson Stanfield, Dan Blank, Charlie Gilkey, Rich Wagner, my Boulder book club. Thanks to all my writing friends who helped me write the best book I could.

Thank you to Ian Shimkoviak and Alan Hebel of *the*BookDesigners for making this a beautiful book.

Thank you to the Alliance Française de Denver for the cultural and artistic grant that allowed me to do research in Sylvia's archives. Thank you to the Princeton University Library Special Collections staff for your help. Thanks to La Muse writing retreat and my writing friends there.

Special thanks to Noel Riley Fitch, whose book *Sylvia Beach and the Lost Generation: Literary Paris in the Twenties and Thirties* introduced me to Sylvia Beach so many years ago.

Thank you to my parents and family who have always unconditionally supported my unconventional path.

Much thanks to my Original Impulse community, whose belief in this book and me made it happen.

BIBLIOGRAPHY

These were the main books I turned to for research on this
time and place.

Beach, Sylvia. *Shakespeare and Company.* New York:
Harcourt Brace and Company, 1959.

Benstock, Shari. *Women of the Left Bank.* Austin: University
of Texas Press, 1986.

Fitch, Noel Riley. *Sylvia Beach and the Lost Generation: A
History of Literary Paris in the Twenties and Thirties.* New
York and London: W. W. Norton & Company, 1983.

Flanner, Janet. *Paris Was Yesterday, 1925–1939.* New York
and London: Harcourt Brace Jovanovich, 1988.

Hemingway, Ernest. *A Moveable Feast.* New York: Bantam
Books, 1965.

MacDougall, Richard, translator. *The Very Rich Hours of
Adrienne Monnier.* Winnipeg, MB: Bison Books, 1996.

Weiss, Andrea. *Paris Was a Woman.* San Francisco:
Harper, 1995.

ABOUT THE AUTHOR

Cynthia Morris has been in love with Paris for as long as she can remember. Her literary heroine Sylvia Beach provided inspiration to dare a life of creative adventure. Cynthia is the author of *Create Your Writer's Life: A Guide to Writing with Joy and Ease*. She coaches writers and artists from Denver and visits France annually.

CPSIA information can be obtained at www.ICGtesting.com
Printed in the USA
LVOW07s1750091114

412761LV00001B/391/P